Michael Strogoff

or, The Courier of the Czar - Box Set - Modern English Translation - Illustrated

Michael Strogoff - Book I - Illustrated

Michael Strogoff - Book II - Illustrated

Juan José Piedra

QuantumDigitalPublishing.io

Contact us: Reviews@AuthorJuanJose.io

Book Design, Cover & Chapter Illustration Art and NFTs by: Juan Jose Piedra

Manuscript Editor: Dr. Jessie Keener - https://drjessie.life/

All Printable Downloads - https://qdls.io/msbxset-dnlds

Michael Strogoff Printable Art & NFT Collections: QuantumDrive.io/Michael Strogoff
Author WebSite: AuthorJuanJose.io

Author X.com: AuthorJuanJose

Book I - Old English - Author Jules Verne - First edition March 2025

ISBN 978-1-967405-00-8 (eBook) – ISBN 978-1-967405-01-5 (Paperback) – ISBN 978-1-967405-02-2 (Hardcover)

Book II - Old English - Author Jules Verne - First edition March 2025

ISBN 978-1-967405-03-9 (eBook) – ISBN 978-1-967405-04-6 (Paperback) – ISBN 978-1-967405-05-3 (Hardcover)

Book I - Modern English - Author Juan José Piedra - First edition April 2025

ISBN 978-1-967405-06-0 (eBook) – ISBN 978-1-967405-07-7 (Paperback) – ISBN 978-1-967405-08-4 (Hardcover)

Book II - Modern English - Author Juan José Piedra - First edition April 2025

ISBN 978-1-967405-09-1 (eBook) – ISBN 978-1-967405-10-7 (Paperback) – ISBN 978-1-967405-11-4 (Hardcover)

Box Set - Book I & II - Modern English - Author Juan José Piedra - First edition August 2025

ISBN 978-1-967405-22-0 (eBook) – ISBN 978-1-967405-23-7 (Paperback) – ISBN 978-1-967405-24-4 (Hardcover)

Presented with distinction by Quantum Arc Press, this Collector's Edition of* Jules Verne's *Michael Strogoff, or The Courier of the Czar unites both volumes of Verne's masterwork within a single, finely crafted set. Produced in celebration of the author's enduring legacy and the spirit of heroic adventure that defined his age, this edition preserves the grandeur of the original narrative while offering readers a timeless passage through courage, loyalty, and the unyielding heart of empire.

Bound for collectors and connoisseurs alike, this work stands as a tribute to the inexhaustible imagination of Jules Verne, and to those who, like Michael Strogoff himself, press ever onward through the storm.

Contents

About The Author

Michael Strogoff I & II

John Joseph Stone, Juan José Piedra

John Joseph Stone, writing under the pen name **Juan José Piedra**, is a **Science Fiction, Steampunk Science Fiction, and Historical Fiction** author and artist whose work seamlessly blends rich storytelling with visually captivating artwork.

His notable works include **illustrating the cover and chapter art** for *Michael Strogoff, or the Courier of the Czar* by **Jules Verne**. With **17 chapters in the first book and 15 in the second**, John's illustrations bring the adventurous world of 19th-century Russia to life. Additionally, he has created **full-color, high-resolution printable images**, available as **NFTs and free downloadable artwork**, along with meticulously designed **Asiatic Russian maps and illustrated scenes** from the novel.

Currently, **Juan José** is developing an **eight-part Steampunk Science Fiction novella series**, chronicling the **evolution of steampunk technology;** from the age of **steam, coal, and wood to high-tech advancements and space travel**. This ambitious project aims to **span the entire fictional history of steampunk innovation**, offering readers a deep, immersive journey through time and technology.

Inspiration & Background

John Joseph's writing is fueled by **extraordinary real-world experiences**. Having spent **over 40 years in the Secret Space Program** while serving in the **USMC Special Section Division**, he brings to life ideas and themes that stretch the boundaries of what most would believe possible; making science fiction the perfect medium to share his vision.

His experiences go beyond classified operations; John has **traveled and lived all over the world**, immersing himself in diverse cultures and perspectives. These global experiences have **broadened his understanding of life and humanity**, giving him a unique lens through which he crafts his stories; offering readers more than just fiction, but reflections on **our world, its possibilities, and its hidden truths**.

Attention to Detail & Creative Vision

A meticulous creator, John Joseph is deeply committed to **historical and technical accuracy** in his works, ensuring that every **story, illustration, and world-building element** is both immersive and authentic. His dedication to precision, combined with an artistic vision, results in stories that are **both intellectually rich and visually stunning**.

Personal Life & Creative Passions

John Joseph is **happily married** and currently resides in **Mérida, Mexico**, where he finds peace in cultivating a lush garden of **Taro, Avocado, and native Mexican trees**. His love for **creating visually compelling imagery** extends beyond writing; he designs **art pieces that inspire, tell stories, and stand as works of art in their own right**.

Connect & Explore More

X: https://x.com/AuthorJuanJose
Books: QuantumDigitalPublishing.io
NFTs, Illustrations and Printable Art: QuantumDrive.io
Contact: authorjuanjose@proton.me

Forward - Michael Strogoff

How Are These Books Unique?

1. Clear & Comfortable Reading: Designed for an enjoyable reading experience, this edition is formatted in 12pt EB Garamond font for excellent readability.

2. Expanded Glossary for Old English Editions: A comprehensive glossary is included at the back of the book to help readers easily understand historical terms and phrases.

3. Beautifully Illustrated: Both volumes feature high-resolution 300dpi illustrations, ensuring stunning print quality. Book I includes 17 chapter illustrations, while Book II has 15, totaling 32 unique images. Plus, enjoy a FREE downloadable version, perfect for printing or setting as wallpaper!

4. Modern English Edition – Coming Soon! We're currently working on a modernized version that updates the language to a smooth, reader-friendly 20th-century style, making this classic adventure even more accessible.

5. Exclusive NFT Collection – Coming Soon! We've also created a series of exclusive NFTs for Michael Strogoff, offering a unique way to collect and engage with this timeless story. Stay tuned!

Jules Verne's Michael Strogoff, or The Courier of the Czar is a thrilling adventure novel set against the vast and treacherous landscapes of

19th-century Russia. The story follows Michael Strogoff, a loyal courier entrusted by Czar Alexander II with a perilous mission: to deliver an urgent message to the governor of Irkutsk and warn him of an impending Tartar rebellion. With telegraph lines cut and enemy spies lurking at every turn, Michael must travel over 5,000 miles from Moscow to Siberia, crossing forests, rivers, and the formidable Ural Mountains while evading capture by treacherous forces. His duty demands unwavering courage and resilience, as failure could mean the fall of Irkutsk and disaster for the Russian Empire.

In Book 1, Jules Verne's Michael Strogoff, or The Courier of the Czar follows the fearless courier of Alexander II on a perilous mission across the vast, treacherous Russian Empire. Tasked with delivering a crucial message to the governor of Irkutsk, Strogoff braves Tatar invasions, the Siberian wilderness, and relentless foes while maintaining his disguise. Along the way, he encounters journalists, spies, and the cunning Ivan Ogareff, a traitor bent on bringing the empire to its knees. His journey is a test of endurance, loyalty, and sheer willpower.

In Book 2, the saga deepens as Strogoff faces greater trials after being captured and subjected to a brutal mock execution, leaving him presumed blinded. Against all odds, he pushes forward, relying on his instincts and unwavering patriotism to reach Irkutsk before Ogareff can unleash his treachery. As the Tatars tighten their grip, Strogoff's final confrontation with his nemesis becomes a defining moment for Russia's survival. Verne masterfully blends historical drama, adventure, and espionage in a gripping tale of duty and heroism at the heart of the empire.

SIA
Juan Jose Piedra
© 01/01/2025
QuantumDigitalPublishing.io
Michael Strogoff
or, The Courier of the Czar
Book I

Michael Strogoff - Book I - Illustrated

Juan José Piedra

QuantumDigitalPublishing.io

Prologue

Michael Strogoff I & II

From the frozen wastes of Siberia to the fortified cities along the Irtysh, whispers of rebellion rode upon the air, carried by merchants, Cossacks, and exiled men who knew too well the signs of coming strife. Across the vast and treacherous expanse of Asiatic Russia, where the Czar's grip stretched thin over steppe and mountain, the great empire trembled beneath the weight of an unseen enemy.

To the west, Saint Petersburg schemed in its gilded halls, while in Moscow, generals pored over maps marked with the ever-shifting borders of loyalty and betrayal. To the east, beyond the great rivers and dense forests, lay the frontier, a world where the authority of the Russian crown was measured not in decrees but in the speed of a courier's horse.

It was upon the Postmaster Roads that the empire lived and breathed. These arteries of communication, stretching thousands of versts through perilous terrain, were the veins of the Czar's will, binding the farthest reaches of his dominion. Across these routes, the couriers rode, men of iron endurance, bound by duty, carrying dispatches that could mean the difference between war and peace, between loyalty and rebellion.

And now, as the Tartar hordes gathered under the banners of an unseen leader, the fate of the empire depended more than ever on those men who rode alone into the storm.

In the city of Omsk, where the Siberian winds carried the scent of damp earth and the whisper of fate, one such man prepared for the road ahead. Michael Strogoff, a courier of the Tsar, stood at the threshold of history, unaware that he would soon become its author.

For the empire could not afford failure. The enemy moved in silence, striking in the darkness where no warning could be given. The couriers of Russia were all that stood between order and chaos, and of all those who rode, none would bear a burden greater than the one that now approached.

The dispatch was coming. The message that would change everything.

And when it did, Michael Strogoff would ride.

© 01/01/2025
QuantumDigitalPublishing.io
Michael Strogoff or, The Courier of the Czar
Book I - Chapter I

Chapter One

A FÊTE, A CELEBRATION AT THE NEW PALACE

With urgent news that demanded immediate attention, General Kissoff, his boots striking the marble floor and medals clanging, burst through the large, ornate wooden doors to bring this news to the Czar. As the aging general hurried through the palace corridors, his face reddened from the rushed pace of his journey.

"Your Majesty, we've received a new message."

"Where from?"

"From Tomsk?"

“Has anyone lost communication beyond there?”

"Yes, sire. Since yesterday."

"Send hourly updates to Tomsk, General. Keep me informed of any developments."

"As you command, sire," General Kissoff replied with a bow.

This exchange took place around 2 AM, while the grand celebration at the New Palace was reaching its pinnacle of magnificence.

Throughout the evening, the military bands of the Preobrajensky and Paulowsky regiments had filled the air with an endless stream of dance music, polkas, mazurkas, schottisches, and waltzes from their finest selections. The brass instruments gleamed under the crystal chandeliers as uniformed musicians performed with practiced precision. Countless pairs of dancers swept across the palace's grand ballrooms, their elaborate gowns and dress uniforms creating a swirling kaleidoscope of color against the marble floors. Only a short distance separated the elegant ballrooms from what locals called the "stone house," a weathered granite structure whose dark past contrasted with the radiant glow next door.

The court's grand-chamberlain received excellent support in carrying out his complex and sensitive responsibilities, his every command executed with swift precision by an army of attendants and servants. High-ranking officials, including grand-dukes with their military assistants and palace chamberlains, supervised the dance arrangements, scrutinizing every detail from the spacing between couples to the exact timing of each musical piece. The grand duchesses sparkled in their diamond jewelry, their tiaras and necklaces catching and scattering light like captured stars, while ladies-in-waiting displayed their finest attire, establishing the standard for wives of military and civilian officials in Moscow, the historic "city of white stone." When music signaled the start of the national dance at such gatherings, each step measured and dignified. The scene became magnificent as elaborate costumes, flowing lace-trimmed gowns, and medal-decorated uniforms moved through the ballroom in perfect synchronization, illuminated by countless chandeliers whose light multiplied in the many mirrors adorning the walls, creating an endless reflection of splendor that seemed to stretch into infinity.

In the New Palace, the grand saloon stood as the most magnificent of all chambers, providing an elegant backdrop for the parade of distinguished guests and ladies in resplendent attire. Above, the ornate ceiling's gilded details had mellowed with age, creating a subtle sparkle like distant stars.

Heavy damask curtains and door hangings cascaded in luxuriant folds, their embroidered patterns catching the light in a kaleidoscope of deep, shifting colors. Crystal sconces lined the walls between towering mirrors, their flames dancing and multiplying on the reflective surfaces. Floors, polished to a mirror sheen, displayed intricate geometric patterns crafted from rare woods, while marble columns rose from floor to ceiling, their fluted surfaces etched with delicate acanthus leaves and crowned with gilt Corinthian capitals. Even the air itself seemed charged with refinement, perfumed by the subtle fragrances of beeswax candles and exotic flowers arranged in towering porcelain vases.

Curved windows illuminated the grand halls like a blazing fire, cutting through the darkness that had enveloped the palace earlier. A striking contrast caught the eye of guests who weren't dancing, their faces bathed in golden warmth and deep shadow as they moved about the space. Those resting by the windows could make out the shadowy silhouettes of the old city's many towers, domes, and spires against the night sky, each architectural marvel etched in stark relief against the star-studded heavens. Below the ornate balconies, guards marched back and forth in silent vigil, their rifles resting on their shoulders while their spiked helmets gleamed like flames in the palace's radiance, brass buttons and medal ribbons catching every stray beam of light. The rhythmic footsteps of patrolling sentries echoed off the stones below, matching the steady tempo of the dancers above, creating an unconscious harmony between duty and revelry. Guards called out passwords between posts, their voices carrying through the cool night air, and trumpet notes pierced through the orchestra's music, signaling changes in the watch. Further below the front of the palace, dark shapes blocked the light streaming from the New Palace's windows, these were boats gliding down the river, whose waters, dimly lit by scattered lamps, lapped against the lowest terraces with a gentle, hypnotic rhythm that seemed to underscore the evening's grandeur.

General Kissoff addressed the host, celebrating the courtesy reserved for monarchs; the host wore a modest chasseur guard officer's uniform, its dark green fabric showing signs of regular wear. His understated attire didn't stem from pretense; rather, it reflected the natural preference of someone who prioritized function over fashion. His simple dress stood in sharp contrast to the lavish outfits surrounding him, as he moved among his entourage of Georgian, Cossack, and Circassian guards, a dazzling company adorned in the resplendent military dress of the Caucasus region.

The towering figure moved among the gathered crowds, his friendly manner and serene face masking an undercurrent of worry that ran deeper than the Neva's waters. He passed between groups with minimal conversation, offering only brief nods and polite smiles, indifferent to both the young guests' peals of laughter and the serious discussions of high-ranking officials and European diplomats stationed at the Russian court. A few of these shrewd political observers, skilled at reading faces through years of diplomatic service in the most demanding posts from Vienna to Constantinople, noticed signs of unease in their host's expression but couldn't pinpoint its cause. The slight tension around his eyes, the occasional distant look that crossed his features, these were subtle tells that spoke volumes to those trained to notice such things. None dared to ask him about it.

The commanding officer of the chasseurs was determined not to let his concerns dampen the celebrations, maintaining his composure with the same discipline that had served him throughout his military career. Given that he wielded authority over what amounted to an entire world's population, from the Baltic shores to the Pacific coast, the ball's cheerful atmosphere continued uninterrupted, a testament to both his self-control and the respect he commanded.

General Kissoff remained in place, awaiting permission to depart from the officer who had just received the Tomsk dispatch. But the latter maintained his silence. After studying the telegram, his expression grew even more troubled than before. He unconsciously reached for his sword hilt, then quickly shielded his eyes with his hand, as if the room's bright lights were overwhelming and he needed to focus his thoughts more clearly.

"Tell me," he said, pulling General Kissoff to a window for privacy, his boots making no sound on the polished parquet floor. The winter frost had traced delicate patterns on the windowpanes, offering them a natural screen from curious onlookers. "Have we received any word from the Grand Duke since yesterday?"

"Nothing at all, Your Majesty. I fear soon we won't be able to receive any messages across the Siberian border." Kissoff's voice was above a whisper, his weathered face betraying a deep concern that matched his superior's troubled demeanor. The sounds of the continuing celebration seemed to grow more distant as the weight of their conversation settled between them.

"What about the military units from Amoor and Irkutsk provinces, and those from the Trans-Balkan region? Were they instructed to advance toward Irkutsk?" The Czar's fingers drummed against the window frame as he spoke, his breath fogging the frosted glass.

"Yes, we transmitted those instructions in our final telegram before the communications lines beyond Lake Baikal were severed."

"And what's the status of our contact with Yeniseisk, Omsk, Semipolatinsk, and Tobolsk? Can we still communicate with these governments as we did before the uprising?"

"Our messages have made it through, and I can confirm the Tartar forces haven't moved past the Irtish and Obi rivers," the officer reported. "Though I fear this situation may change at any moment."

"What news of Ivan Ogareff, the traitor?" The Czar's voice hardened at the mention of the name, his reflection in the window growing tenser.

"Nothing yet," General Kissoff answered, clasping his hands behind his back. "Even our police chief can't determine if he's crossed our borders. He seems to have vanished like smoke in the wind."

"Send his description to all our telegraph stations still operating, Nijni-Novgorod, Perm, Ekaterenburg, Kasirnov, Tioumen, Ishim, Omsk, Tomsk, every single one. We do not want him slipping through our network undetected."

"It will be done at once, Your Majesty. I'll have our most trusted operators handle the transmissions."

"And remember, absolute secrecy about this matter. Not a whisper of this must reach beyond these walls."

The General gave a deferential bow of agreement and slipped into the crowd, departing such that no one noticed him leave, his polished boots making not the slightest sound on the marble floor.

Lost in contemplation, the officer stood motionless for several moments, his mind wrestling with the gravity of the situation and its potential consequences for the Empire. Then, composing himself with practiced discipline, he moved among the gathered clusters of people in the ballroom, his face once again showing its usual serenity after that brief moment of disquiet.

The incident that sparked this quick exchange wasn't as secret as General Kissoff and the chasseur officer might have believed. Despite restrictions on open discussion and the lack of official announcements, a select few high-ranking officials received varying degrees of accurate information about the developments beyond the border. At the New Palace reception, civilians without military uniforms or medals, were discussing something that was undisclosed and not even whispered among diplomatic circles. They seemed well-informed about the situation. They stood apart from the glittering crowd, their subdued attire a stark contrast to the ornate military dress and jeweled finery surrounding them. Their hushed conversation, punctuated by meaningful glances and subtle gestures, would have appeared innocuous to casual observers, yet their precise knowledge of classified details suggested connections to sources far more privileged than their modest appearance implied.

How had these two unremarkable individuals discovered what even many distinguished and powerful people suspected? Were they blessed with prophetic abilities that transcended ordinary human limitations? Did they possess some additional sense that let them peer beyond normal human perception, reaching into realms where secrets lay bare? Had they developed a special talent for uncovering hidden truths, honed through years of patient observation and careful analysis? Perhaps their constant immersion in gathering intelligence had altered how their minds worked, reshaping neural pathways until intuition became indistinguishable from fact. This explanation seemed hard to dismiss, especially given how naturally they moved through the corridors of power while remaining invisible to those who wielded it.

An Englishman and a Frenchman, both tall and lean, made up the pair. The Frenchman possessed the characteristic olive complexion of southern Provence, while the Englishman displayed the rosy cheeks typical of Lancashire nobility. The English-Norman moved with calculated precision, his demeanor cool and solemn, dispensing words and movements as if governed by clockwork. His French companion, however, was the embodiment of animation and vigor, conveying his thoughts through a symphony of facial expressions, hand gestures, and verbal flourishes. While the Frenchman expressed a single idea in twenty different ways, the Englishman seemed limited to one unchanging method, as if permanently etched into his mind. Their contrasting natures extended even to their attire, the Englishman favoring pressed wool suits in subdued grays and browns, while his Mediterranean counterpart embraced a wardrobe that spoke of careful attention to current continental fashions. Yet despite their apparent differences, or perhaps because of them, they moved through their work with an almost supernatural synchronicity, each man's qualities complementing the other's shortcomings.

The two men's stark differences would have been apparent to even a casual onlooker. Yet someone skilled in reading faces would have noted their most defining traits differently; the Frenchman lived through his eyes, while the Englishman existed through his ears.

Years of use honed the Frenchman's vision to remarkable precision. His eyes could process information as swiftly as those magicians who can identify a playing card from the briefest glimpse during a shuffle, or spot tiny marks others would miss. Indeed, his "visual memory" had reached an extraordinary level of development. He could reconstruct entire crime scenes from memory days later, sketching out the smallest details with uncanny accuracy, from the precise angle of an overturned chair to the subtle pattern of dust disturbed on a windowsill. This gift had proven invaluable countless times, allowing him to notice crucial discrepancies that others had overlooked in the heat of the investigation.

Unlike his companion, the Englishman seemed gifted in the art of listening. Once he heard someone's voice, it remained etched in his memory. He could identify it among countless others even after a decade or two. Though his ears lacked the mobility of animals with their flexible ear flaps, scientists acknowledge human ears have limited movement capabilities. One might observe, with some amusement, that this Englishman's ears appeared to pivot and adjust in all directions to capture sounds, a phenomenon only a trained naturalist might appreciate. He could discern the subtlest variations in tone and inflection, picking up on the microscopic tremors in a person's voice that might betray deception or distress. Even in a crowded room full of overlapping conversations, he possessed the remarkable ability to focus on a single voice and follow it with laser-like precision, filtering out all other ambient noise as if adjusting an invisible dial. This auditory prowess had proven especially valuable during witness interviews, where the slightest quaver or hesitation in testimony could point toward hidden truths.

These exceptional sensory abilities served both men well in their professions. The Englishman worked as a Daily Telegraph correspondent, while his French companion maintained an air of mystery about his journalistic affiliations. When questioned, he would jest about "corresponding with cousin Madeleine," a response that never failed to elicit knowing smiles from those who asked. Yet beneath this casual exterior, the Frenchman possessed remarkable wit and perception that manifested in unexpected ways. His casual chatter disguised his keen observation skills; he gathered intelligence through aimless, but calculated, meandering conversations. His apparent openness often masked a discretion that perhaps exceeded that of his British colleague, who tended toward more straightforward methods of information gathering. Both men attended the New Palace celebration on July 15th in their capacity as reporters, though their true purposes that evening may have run deeper than mere journalism.

These two individuals showed unwavering dedication to their life's work, pursuing every lead that emerged, no matter how unexpected. Nothing could frighten or deter them from achieving their goals, whether facing physical danger or social ostracism. They possessed the unshakeable composure and authentic courage typical of their profession, maintaining their poise even in the most challenging circumstances. Like passionate riders in a steeplechase racing for information, they bounded over hedges, forded rivers, and cleared fences with the fierce determination of thoroughbred horses willing to either win or perish in the attempt, their resolve never wavering even when the path ahead seemed treacherous.

The newspapers gave them unlimited financial resources, still recognized today as the most reliable, quickest, and most comprehensive way to gather information. Their expense accounts allowed them to travel first-class across continents, book rooms at premier hotels, and maintain the appearances expected of gentlemen in high society. It should also be noted that neither journalist, to their credit, ever spied or eavesdropped on invading personal privacy, but only pursued stories related to political or social issues. They maintained strict ethical standards even when competing papers might have stooped to less savory methods. They specialized in what we now call "major political and military journalism," focusing their considerable talents on matters of international significance rather than society gossip or local scandals.

As becomes clear when studying their work, they maintained distinct perspectives on events and their implications, each bringing his own unique analytical approach and interpretative style. While one might focus on the broader geopolitical ramifications, the other often delved into the nuanced cultural effects of major developments.

During a lavish celebration held within the opulent halls of the constructed palace, two journalists, unacquainted, encountered one another. Their respective newspapers had tasked the Frenchman, Alcide Jolivet, and to cover the event. Though their contrasting personalities and professional rivalry might have kept them apart, they chose instead to engage with one another. As fellow newsmen working the same territory, they recognized the practical benefits of cooperation. One might catch details the other missed, making their interaction helpful. Like hunters sharing the same grounds, they found it wise to exchange information and maintain open communication. Their initial wariness of each other gave way to a grudging respect, as each recognized in the other a dedication to journalistic excellence that transcended national loyalties. Despite representing competing publications, they discovered that collaboration often yielded richer, more nuanced coverage of complex events.

The anticipation was palpable that evening as both kept watchful eyes, sensing something significant was about to unfold in the crowded gathering. The air seemed charged with unspoken possibilities, and both men leaned forward in their seats.

"Even if it turns out to be nothing," Alcide Jolivet mused to himself, running a thoughtful finger along the rim of his untouched glass, "the possibility alone makes it worth investigating." His instincts, honed by years of chasing stories, had never led him astray.

With careful deliberation, the two journalists began testing the waters with one another, each weighing their words like merchants assessing valuable goods. The conversation started as they circled around their shared suspicions.

"I must say," Alcide Jolivet remarked with calculated cheerfulness, falling back on his French manner, gesturing at the assembled crowd, "this gathering is delightful!" His eyes, however, remained sharp and observant beneath his jovial exterior.

"I already sent a telegram saying 'splendid!'" Harry Blount replied with typical British composure, using that English word of praise. He adjusted his cravat around his neck with practiced precision, his expression neutral.

Despite his previous statements, Alcide Jolivet, leaning closer and lowering his voice to a confidential murmur, continued by saying that he felt obligated to inform his cousin about the matter.

"Your cousin?" Harry Blount cut in, his voice revealing his surprise, one eyebrow arching above his wire-rimmed spectacles.

"Indeed," Alcide Jolivet confirmed, adjusting the cuff of his well-tailored jacket with practiced nonchalance, "my cousin Madeleine. She's the one I correspond with, and she appreciates prompt and detailed updates. So I informed her that during the celebration, the sovereign appeared to have a shadow of concern across his face, like a cloud passing over the sun on an otherwise bright day."

"In my eyes, it was quite radiant," Harry Blount responded, attempting to mask his true thoughts on the matter, his fingers drumming an irregular pattern against his leather-bound notebook.

"And I assume you portrayed it as 'radiant' in your Daily Telegraph piece?" Jolivet pressed, a knowing glint in his eye.

"Precisely." Blount's clipped response carried the weight of unspoken reservations.

"Tell me, Mr. Blount, can you recall the events at Zakret in 1812?" Jolivet's tone shifted, taking on an air of scholarly inquiry.

"As clearly as if I'd witnessed them firsthand, sir," the English journalist replied, his shoulders stiffening almost imperceptibly at the historical reference.

Alcide Jolivet went on, leaning forward in his chair with the practiced air of a seasoned storyteller, "Emperor Alexander was attending a celebration held in his honor when news arrived that Napoleon and his advance forces had crossed the Niemen River. Yet the Emperor remained at the festivities, and despite receiving information that could lead to his empire's downfall, he maintained his composure with remarkable self-possession."

"Much like how our host stayed calm when General Kissoff reported the severing of telegraph lines between the frontier and Irkutsk's government," Blount observed, adjusting his cravat with deliberate precision.

"Are you aware of that?" Jolivet's eyes narrowed as he studied his colleague's face.

"Indeed I am!" Blount shot back, his chin lifting with concealed defensiveness.

"Well, I would know about it, as my telegram made it all the way to Udinsk," said Alcide Jolivet with a hint of pride, smoothing the front of his waistcoat as he savored this insignificant victory over his British counterpart.

"Mine only reached Krasnoiarsk," Harry Blount replied, sounding pleased with himself, though his fingers had resumed their nervous tapping against his notebook.

"Then you must also know about the orders sent to the Nikolaevsk troops?" Jolivet pressed, his voice dropping to just above a whisper, as if sharing a sensitive piece of intelligence.

"I do indeed. And I know that the Tobolsk government ordered their Cossacks to gather their forces," Blount declared with an air of professional satisfaction.

"Indeed, Mr. Blount, your statement is quite accurate."

"Just as the Daily Telegraph readers will know it," said M. Jolivet, his eyes glinting with competitive spirit.

"Well, considering everything happening..." Blount muttered, glancing around the crowded room.

"And all the talk going around..." Jolivet added, matching his colleague's conspiratorial tone.

"This should be quite the campaign to cover, Mr. Blount," he continued, drumming his fingers against his glass.

"And I intend to cover it, M. Jolivet!" Blount proclaimed.

"Then we might find ourselves in places far more dangerous than this ballroom floor," Jolivet observed, eyeing the polished parquet beneath their feet.

"More dangerous, true, but..." Blount began, taking an unsteady step backward.

"But with better footing," Alcide Jolivet quipped, reaching out to catch his companion who had lost his balance while stepping backward on the slick floor.

The two journalists parted ways with cordial nods, each satisfied that neither had gained an unfair advantage over the other, though both were already plotting their next moves in their perpetual game of journalistic one-upmanship.

The doors leading to the rooms next to the grand reception hall swung open with a dignified creak, revealing several massive tables set with exquisite china and golden tableware. For this occasion, they imported a magnificent, priceless centerpiece from London, which they placed on the center table reserved for royalty and diplomatic corps members. Surrounding this masterpiece of gold craftsmanship, illuminated by crystal chandeliers that cast dancing reflections across the room, were countless pieces of fine porcelain from the prestigious Sevres Shops, each plate and cup positioned with meticulous precision.

The dinner guests made their way to the dining halls of the New Palace, their shoes clicking against the marble floors as they moved in a choreographed dance of social hierarchy, each person knowing their designated place in the order of precedence. Ladies' silk gowns rustled and gentlemen's medals clinked as they filed through the doorways.

Just then, General Kissoff returned, his face flushed with urgency, and hurried over to the chasseur officer.

"Any news?" the officer demanded, as before, his fingers drumming against his sword hilt.

"Sire, the telegraph lines to Tomsk are now down. We've tried every connection through Kolyvan, but there's nothing but silence."

"Send a courier at once!" The command rang through the air with unmistakable authority.

The officer strode out into a spacious antechamber connected to the hall, his boots echoing against the parquet flooring. This oak-furnished study, nestled in a corner of the New Palace, featured several paintings adorning its walls, including works by the renowned Horace Vernet. The collection featured military scenes, their gilt frames catching the warm lamplight; someone had arranged maps and dispatches on a massive desk beneath them. The air carried the distinct scent of beeswax and leather that permeated all such official chambers.

The sentinel threw open a window with urgency, craving fresh air, and ventured onto a balcony to inhale the crisp atmosphere of a serene July evening. Below him, illuminated by moonlight, stretched a fortified compound featuring two cathedrals, three palaces, and an arsenal. Surrounding this stronghold lay three distinct districts: Kitai-Gorod, Beloi-Gorod, and Zemlianai-Gorod, representing European, Tartar, and Chinese quarters, each sprawling. Three hundred churches, with green cupolas crowned with gleaming silver crosses, along with towers, belfries, and minarets, punctuated the districts. A serpentine river meandered through the landscape, its waters catching and reflecting the moon's gentle glow, while the distant barking of dogs and muffled sounds of nighttime activity drifted up from the streets below.

This meandering waterway was the Moskowa; the grand city was Moscow; the fortified compound was the Kremlin; and the guard officer, who stood with crossed arms and furrowed brow, lost in contemplation as he listened to the distant sounds drifting from the New Palace across the ancient Muscovite city, was none other than the Czar himself. His imposing figure cast a long shadow across the balcony's stone floor as he gazed out over his capital, his military uniform adorned with medals that glinted in the moonlight, while a cool breeze stirred the epaulettes on his shoulders.

Juan Jose Piedra

Chapter Two

RUSSIANS AND TARTARS

News of grave developments beyond the Ural frontier had compelled the Czar to make an abrupt departure from the magnificent ball at the New Palace, where Moscow's elite, both civil and military, had gathered for a lavish celebration. Intelligence reports showed that a powerful uprising was brewing, one that threatened to tear the Siberian territories away from Russian control. The whispers among the gathered nobility spoke of tribal alliances forming in the east, and of foreign powers, stoking the flames of rebellion.

Siberia, also known as Asiatic Russia, is a vast territory spanning 1,790,208 square miles with a population of two million people. This enormous region stretches from the Ural Mountains in the west, which marks the boundary with European Russia, to the Pacific Ocean in the east. Its borders include Turkestan and the Chinese Empire to the south, while the Arctic Ocean forms its northern boundary from the Sea of Kara to the Bering Strait. The terrain varies from endless frozen tundra and dense taiga forests to rolling steppes and towering mountain ranges, making it as challenging to govern as it is to traverse. Its rich mineral deposits and fur-bearing animals have long made it a source of tremendous wealth for the Russian Empire, despite its harsh climate and sparse population.

Administrators divided the territory into several provinces and governments, including Tobolsk, Yeniseysk, Irkutsk, Omsk, and Yakutsk. It also encompasses two districts, Okhotsk and Kamtschatka, as well as two regions under Russian control: the land of the Kirghiz and that of the Tshouktshes. This expansive territory, extending over one hundred and ten degrees from west to east, serves as a destination for both criminal and political exiles under Russian authority, with many forced to work in the region's many mines and labor camps.

Administering this immense territory falls under two governor-generals, who act as the Czar's highest representatives. The more senior of these officials maintains his seat in Irkutsk, which serves as the distant capital of Eastern Siberia. Between the two Siberian regions flows the Tchouna River, marking their boundary. These governor-generals wield considerable autonomy because of the vast distances separating them from St. Petersburg, though they must still answer to the imperial bureaucracy through regular dispatches and reports detailing their governance of these far-flung lands.

The expansive plains, some fertile, remain untouched by railroad tracks. No iron rails connect to the valuable mines that make Siberia's underground wealth far exceed its surface riches. Travelers must rely on traditional means. In the warmer months, they use kibicks or telgas (horse-drawn carriages), while winter journeys require sleighs. These primitive transportation methods often mean journeys that would take days by rail instead stretch into weeks or months, testing both human and animal endurance against Siberia's harsh elements.

A solitary electric telegraph line, stretching over eight thousand miles with a single wire, provides the only connection between Siberia's eastern and western boundaries. After leaving the Ural, the line travels through many cities: Ekaterenburg, Kasirnov, Tioumen, Ishim, Omsk, Elamsk,

Kolyvan, Tomsk, Krasnoiarsk, Nijni-Udinsk, Irkutsk, Verkne-Nertschink, Strelink, Albazine, Blagowstenks, Radde, Orlomskaya, Alexandrowskoe, and Nikolaevsk. Sending a message from one end to the other costs six roubles and nineteen copecks per word. A branch line from Irkutsk to Kiatka on the Mongolian border forwards messages to Peking within two weeks at a rate of thirty copecks per word. This remarkable feat of engineering requires constant maintenance, with teams of workers stationed at intervals along its length to repair breaks caused by storms, frost, and falling trees or vandalism.

Someone severed the telegraph line running from Ekaterenburg to Nikolaevsk in two places, first past Tomsk, and again between Tomsk and Kolyvan. The damage appeared deliberate, with the copper wires cut and several support poles toppled.

This explained why, when General Kissoff delivered his second report, the Czar had commanded, "Send a courier at once!" His voice had carried the weight of urgency that only a ruler responsible for such vast territories could understand.

The Czar stood silently by the window for several moments, his reflection ghostlike against the palace glass as he contemplated the gravity of the situation. Then the door opened once more, and the chief of police appeared in the doorway, his brass buttons gleaming in the lamplight.

"Come in, General," the Czar said. "Tell me everything you know about Ivan Ogareff."

"He's dangerous, Your Majesty," the police chief responded, his weathered face betraying genuine concern.

"He held the rank of colonel, didn't he?"

"Yes, Your Majesty."

"Was he a capable officer?"

"Capable, but uncontrollable. His boundless ambition led him to pursue any means necessary. He became entangled in covert plots until His Highness, the Grand Duke, stripped him of his rank and banished him to Siberia." The police chief's fingers traced the edge of his uniform as he spoke of the disgraced officer's misdeeds.

"When did this occur?"

"Two years ago. After six months in exile, he returned to Russia, pardoned by Your Majesty's grace. He seemed repentant."

"Has he been back in Siberia since then?"

"Indeed, sire, though he returned of his own accord," the police chief responded, his voice dropping to a near whisper as he added, "There was an era, sire, when no one ever came back from Siberia. The frozen wastes claimed too many souls to count."

"As long as I draw breath, Siberia shall remain a place from which return is possible. Those who show genuine remorse deserve the chance for redemption."

The Czar could speak these words with genuine pride, for he had showed, through his acts of mercy, that Russian justice could be capable of forgiveness. His reforms, though debated, showed a judicious balance of compassion and justice.

The police chief remained silent at this remark, though his disapproval of such lenient policies was clear. He believed police should allow no one they had escorted across the Ural Mountains to return. These new governmental practices troubled him. The very notion that people could face punishment for non-political crimes without permanent exile seemed preposterous to him. Even more shocking was the fact that political prisoners were being permitted to come back from places like Tobolsk, Yakutsk, and Irkutsk. The police chief, who had grown accustomed to the unyielding imperial decrees that never granted pardons, found this fresh approach to governance incomprehensible. His weathered face, lined with decades of service enforcing the old ways, betrayed a mixture of confusion and quiet frustration. The reforms challenged everything he believed about justice and order in the empire. However, he held his tongue, awaiting further questions from the Czar, which soon followed.

"Has Ivan Ogareff made another trip back to Russia since his mysterious journey through Siberia?" the Czar inquired, his penetrating gaze fixed upon the chief's face.

"Yes, he has."

"And have our authorities lost track of him?"

"No, Your Majesty. In fact, a criminal becomes most threatening only after receiving your pardon," the chief replied, his weathered hands clasped behind his back.

Shadows fell across the Czar's noble features, darkening his expression. The police chief may have realized he'd spoken impolitely, despite his unwavering loyalty matching his stubborn convictions. The Czar, choosing to ignore these subtle criticisms of his decisions, pressed on with his questioning, each word measured and deliberate. "What was Ogareff's last known location?"

"Whereabouts was he last seen?" he demanded, leaning forward in his chair.

"Someone spotted him in Perm province, Your Majesty," the chief responded, his voice steady despite the tension in the room.

"Which specific town?"

"The city of Perm itself, sire. Along the banks of the Kama River."

"What were his activities there?"

"He seemed to live quietly, nothing aroused suspicion. He kept to himself, frequenting only a few local establishments."

"Was he being watched by our agents?" the Czar's fingers drummed on the armrest.

"No, Your Majesty," the chief admitted, a bead of sweat forming on his brow.

"When did he depart from Perm?"

"In March, as far as we know. The snow was thawing."

"His destination?"

"That remains unknown, Your Majesty. He vanished like morning mist."

"And his current location?"

"We've lost all trace of him, Your Majesty," the chief concluded, his voice heavy with the weight of this admission.

"In that case, I can tell you myself," the Czar declared, rising from his seat with a grim expression. "I've gotten secret messages that bypassed the police channels. Given what's happening at our borders, I have good reason to trust their accuracy."

"Your Majesty," the police chief exclaimed, his face blanching at the implications, "are you suggesting that Ivan Ogareff is involved in the Tartar uprising?"

Ivan Ogareff's path after departing Perm took him across the treacherous Ural mountains into Siberia. In the windswept Kirghiz steppes, he stirred up unrest among the wandering tribes, exploiting ancient grievances and promising riches from conquest. His journey then led him southward into free Turkestan, where through cunning manipulation and false promises, he convinced leaders in Bokhara, Khokhand, and Koondooz to commit their Tartar forces to invade Siberia. This brewing conflict has now erupted, like a powder keg ignited, severing all links between Eastern and Western Siberia. Also, Ogareff, driven by a consuming thirst for revenge that has festered for years, now seeks to end my brother's life.

The Czar was agitated as he spoke, walking back and forth across the room with rapid footsteps, his polished boots clicking against the marble floor. Though the police chief remained silent, his weathered face betraying nothing, his thoughts turned to earlier times when Russian emperors never granted pardons to exiles, times when plots like Ivan Ogareff's would have been impossible to execute. The very notion seemed to pain him. Moving closer to where the Czar had settled into an ornate armchair, its gilded arms gleaming in the lamplight, he inquired, 'Has Your Majesty issued the necessary orders to crush this uprising without delay?'"

"Indeed," replied the Czar, his fingers drumming on the chair's arm. "The most recent dispatch to Nijni-Udinsk has mobilized forces across multiple regions: the Yenisei, Irkutsk, and Yakutsk governments, plus the territories surrounding the Amoor and Lake Baikal. The entire eastern frontier is being fortified. Meanwhile, regiments from Perm and Nijni-Novgorod, along with frontier Cossacks, their horses already saddled and ready, are conducting rapid marches toward the Ural Mountains. However," he added with a grimace of frustration, "it will take several weeks before they can engage the Tartar forces in combat."

"Is your majesty's brother, the Grand Duke, isolated within Irkutsk's government, with no means of communication with Moscow?" asked the general, his brow furrowed with concern.

"Yes, that's correct," the Czar replied.

"But the recent dispatches must have informed him of your majesty's planned measures, and what help he can expect from the neighboring governments around Irkutsk?" the general persisted, leaning forward in his chair.

"The Czar is aware of that," he replied, his face darkening with worry, "but what remains unknown to him is that Ivan Ogareff isn't just a rebel, he's also a traitor and harbors deep personal hatred toward him. The Grand Duke handled Ogareff's initial fall from grace, but more crucially, he cannot recognize this man. Thus, Ogareff intends to enter Irkutsk under a false identity and pledge his services to the Grand Duke. After winning his trust, he'll wait until the Tartars surround Irkutsk before betraying both the city and my brother, whose death he seeks. I've discovered this through my confidential sources, reliable agents who've infiltrated Ogareff's inner circle. The Grand Duke remains unaware of these facts, but he must be informed before it's too late!"

"Your Majesty, we need a messenger who's both clever and brave, someone who can navigate the treacherous terrain and evade detection..."

"I'm expecting such a person any minute now," the Czar replied with quiet confidence.

"Let's hope they move quickly," the police chief continued, adjusting his collar. "If I may say so, Your Majesty, Siberia provides fertile ground for uprisings. The vast wilderness makes it difficult to maintain order."

"Are you suggesting, General, that the exiled prisoners might join forces with the insurgents?" the Czar demanded, his eyes narrowing.

"My deepest apologies, Your Majesty," the police chief muttered, realizing he had indeed revealed his own paranoid suspicions. His face reddened with embarrassment.

"I trust in their loyalty to our nation," the Czar declared, rising from his chair to emphasize his point.

"Siberia holds more than just political prisoners, Your Majesty," the police chief pointed out, trying to recover his position.

"Those criminals? General, they're all yours!" he declared with a dismissive wave of his hand. "I'll be the first to admit they're the worst humanity has to offer. They have no homeland to call their own. But this uprising, no, this rebellion, isn't directed at the emperor. Its target is Russia itself, the motherland these exiles still dream of returning to someday, and mark my words, they will return. Never would a true Russian join forces with a Tartar, not even for a moment, to undermine Muscovite power! The very suggestion is an insult to their honor!"

The Czar showed wisdom in placing his faith in the loyalty of those alienated by his policies. His tendency toward mercy, which guided his sense of justice when he could oversee matters, along with his softening of the harsh imperial decrees, suggested his judgment was sound. The emperor's instinct to temper justice with compassion had served him well in other delicate situations throughout his reign, earning him both respect and gratitude from those who might otherwise have turned against the crown. However, even without considering how this merciful approach might help quell the Tartar uprising, the situation remained concerning, as there was a significant risk that many Kirghiz people would throw their support behind the rebels. Their nomadic traditions and complex web of tribal alliances made them susceptible to the rebels' promises of autonomy and self-governance.

The greater, lesser, and middle hordes comprise the three distinct groups that organize the Kirghiz people, numbering around four hundred thousand (400,000) "tents" or two million individuals. Some tribes maintain independence, while others pledge allegiance to either Russian authority or the powerful Khans of Khiva, Khokhand, and Bokhara, who rule over Turkestan. The middle horde, being both the wealthiest and largest, controls vast territories between the Sara Sou, Irtish, and Upper Ishim rivers, as well as Lakes Saisang and Aksakal. The greater horde extends eastward from the middle horde's territory, reaching the Omsk and Tobolsk governments. Should the Kirghiz people revolt, it would mean an uprising in Asiatic Russia, with the likely consequence of Siberia breaking away east of the Yenisei River, destabilizing trade routes and diplomatic relations that had taken decades to establish.

The Kirghiz, inexperienced in formal warfare, excel more at nighttime raids and caravan robberies than traditional military engagements. According to M. Levchine's assessment, "a well-organized infantry formation or square could overcome a Kirghiz force ten times its size, while a single piece of artillery could inflict devastating casualties." Their military weakness stems from their nomadic lifestyle, which prioritizes mobility and quick strikes over sustained combat operations. Despite their tactical limitations, their intimate knowledge of the harsh terrain and ability to survive in extreme conditions make them formidable opponents in their native steppes, where conventional armies often struggle to maintain supply lines and cohesion.

While this observation may be accurate, it overlooks a crucial detail: such infantry formations must first traverse the vast distances to reach the insurgent territory, and someone must transport artillery pieces from Russian provincial arsenals, often located two or three thousand miles away. The journey is challenging since, apart from the primary route connecting Ekaterenburg to Irkutsk, the marshy steppes prove difficult to cross. This means Russian forces would require several weeks to engage the Tartar forces in their territory. During this extended march, supply wagons become mired in boggy ground, horses succumb to exhaustion, and soldiers battle both the elements and disease. The native insurgents, meanwhile, can monitor these slow-moving columns from the surrounding highlands, choosing the optimal moment to harass their flanks or cut off isolated units. Even when Russian forces arrive at their destination, they often find their opponents have long since dispersed into the wilderness, leaving behind little more than cold campfires and trampled grass.

Omsk serves as the military headquarters of Western Siberia, established to maintain control over the Kirghiz people. The boundaries, which the semi-independent nomads have crossed multiple times, were under threat, and evidence suggested that Omsk itself faced imminent danger. Multiple breaches likely occurred in the defensive network of military outposts, Cossack stations positioned between Omsk and Semipolatinsk. People worried that the "Grand Sultans," ruling the Kirghiz territories, might submit to, or be forced into, Tartar rule. The Tartars, sharing the Muslim faith with the Kirghiz, might unite two powerful forces: the resentment born from slavery and the religious conflict between Greek Orthodox Christianity and Islam. The Tartars of Turkestan had already been working to bring the Kirghiz hordes under their control, using both military force and diplomatic persuasion. Reports from merchants and travelers spoke of increased activity among the nomadic tribes, with large gatherings occurring on traditional meeting grounds and an unusual number of messengers moving between camps. Russian intelligence suggested that weapons and horses were being stockpiled, while tribal elders held frequent councils under the cover of darkness. The dire situation forced abandoning several frontier settlements, with their inhabitants seeking refuge behind Omsk's fortified walls.

The Tartars' ancestry comes from two distinct ethnic groups: Caucasians and Mongolians. Renowned orientalist Abel de Remusat identifies the Caucasian branch, which includes Turkish and Persian populations and many smaller Central Asian ethnic groups, as the ancestor of European peoples and the archetype of Western beauty. Three principal groups, nomadic steppe Mongols, the Manchu who would rule China, and the Tibetan mountain-dwellers, comprise the Mongolian lineage, distinguished by its unique physical traits.

Primarily Caucasian, the Tartars who threatened Russia's imperial ambitions during this period hailed from the vast expanse of Turkestan. A system known as Khanates divided this territory into several semi-autonomous states, each ruled by a Khan. The major khanats included Bokhara, with its ancient cities and trade routes, Khokhand, controlling the fertile Fergana Valley, and Koondooz, dominating the southern mountain passes. Among these, Bokhara emerged as the most formidable power, its military might and strategic location making it threatening to Russian interests. Russian forces had engaged in many bloody conflicts with Bokhara's successive rulers, who provided military support and sanctuary to Kirghiz rebels fighting against Russian dominion. This support was part of a calculated strategy to maintain a buffer zone between their territory and the expanding Russian Empire. The present ruler, Feofar-Khan, known for his tactical acumen and fierce independence, continued this long-standing policy of aggressive resistance to Russian encroachment.

The Khanate of Bokhara boasts a diverse and thriving population of two and a half million people, drawn from various ethnic groups, including Uzbeks, Tajiks, and Persian merchants. Its military might include sixty thousand soldiers during peacetime, which can triple during wartime, plus thirty thousand cavalry trained in the traditional mounted warfare tactics of the steppes. This wealthy region's resources span animal life, from prized Turkmen horses to fat-tailed sheep, plant varieties including cotton and fruits, and abundant mineral deposits of copper and precious stones. Its territory has grown through acquiring Balkh, Aukoi, and Meimaneh, and now encompasses nineteen major urban centers connected by well-traveled caravan routes.

The capital, Bokhara, stands as a magnificent city encircled by towers and walls extending over eight English miles, with many gates guarded day and night by the khan's most trusted warriors. Made famous by Avicenna and other tenth-century scholars, it serves as the intellectual heart of Muslim learning, with its countless madrasas and mosques drawing students from as far as India and Arabia, and stands among Central Asia's most renowned cities. Samarcand, another notable city, houses Tamerlane's tomb with its ribbed azure dome and the celebrated palace containing the blue stone, a crucial element in each new khan's coronation ceremony, believed to carry the blessing of ancient rulers. An impressive fortress, its massive walls rising from living rock and featuring sophisticated defensive works that have repelled countless would-be invaders, protects the city.

Karschi, with its three-layered defenses and towering watchtowers, sits in an oasis surrounded by treacherous marshlands teeming with tortoises, lizards, and venomous snakes, making it unconquerable. Is-chardjoui maintains its security through a substantial population of twenty thousand inhabitants, its streets bustling with armed merchants and skilled warriors. The khanate's natural defenses, including snow-capped mountains, treacherous passes, and vast windswept steppes that stretch to the horizon, make it a formidable state that would require significant Russian forces to overcome.

The ruthless and power-hungry Feofar, known for his piercing gaze and swift justice, now controlled this region of Tartary with an iron grip. He had formed blood-sworn alliances with other khans, those of Khokhand and Koondooz, savage and greedy warriors eager to join any cause that appealed to Tartar sensibilities and promised plunder. With growing support from Central Asian tribal leaders, who supplied him with horses and weaponry, he emerged as the rebellion's supreme commander, following the intricate schemes of Ivan Ogareff. This traitor, driven by both mad ambition and a rooted hatred born of past humiliations, had orchestrated an ambitious assault on Siberia, believing he could fracture the mighty Muscovite Empire at its eastern frontier.

Following Ogareff's masterful guidance, the Emir (the title claimed by Bokhara's khans since ancient times) had unleashed his vast armies across Russian borders with devastating efficiency. After invading Semipolatinsk province, he forced the outnumbered Cossacks to retreat in disarray, their defensive lines crumbling before his superior numbers. His relentless advance reached beyond Lake Balkhash, where he won over the nomadic Kirghiz people with promises of autonomy and shared spoils. His brutal campaign left a trail of unspeakable destruction in its wake, he plundered villages, devastated entire regions, conscripted those who yielded to his authority, and imprisoned or executed those who dared fight back. He moved from town to town, accompanied by his massive entourage of wives, concubines, slaves, and sycophantic courtiers, all the traditional trappings of Oriental power and wealth, displaying the brazen confidence and ruthless determination of a modern-day Genghis Khan, whose legendary conquests he sought to emulate.

His current location remained unknown, as did the size of his army's advance before Moscow learned of the uprising, and the positions to which Russian forces had withdrawn. All communications had ceased. Questions remained unanswered: Had Tartar scouts severed the wire between Kolyvan and Tomsk? Had the Emir reached Yeniseisk? Was Western Siberia in chaos? Had the uprising spread eastward? The electric current, the only messenger immune to winter's cold and summer's heat, capable of lightning-speed transmission, could no longer cross the steppes. Therefore, Ivan Ogareff's treachery prevented anyone from warning the Grand Duke in Irkutsk of the impending danger.

The only solution was to send a messenger in place of the disrupted telegraph line. Such a person would need considerable time to cover the vast distance of five thousand two hundred miles separating Moscow from Irkutsk. Getting past the rebel forces and invaders would demand extraordinary bravery and wit. Yet with sharp intelligence and unwavering determination, such feats were possible. The journey would require traversing treacherous mountain passes, crossing raging rivers, and enduring the harsh Siberian elements that had broken countless men before.

"But where can I find someone with such qualities?" the Czar pondered to himself, his fingers drumming on the ornate arm of his chair. The fate of his empire might well rest upon this single decision, and the clock was ticking against him. Every hour of delay gave the Emir's forces more time to merge their gains and push deeper into Russian territory.

Chapter Three

MICHAEL STROGOFF MEETS THE CZAR

The heavy door to the imperial cabinet swung open once more with a resonant creak of ancient hinges, and a herald in his crimson livery announced General Kissoff.

"What of the courier?" the Czar demanded, leaning forward in his ornate chair with contained anticipation, his fingers drumming against the polished armrest.

"He awaits outside, Your Majesty," General Kissoff responded with a slight bow, his decorated uniform catching the afternoon light streaming through the tall windows.

"Have you selected someone suitable for this task?"

"I stake my reputation on this man's abilities, sire. My word and honor stand behind this choice."

"Has he served within the Palace walls?"

"Indeed, he has, Your Majesty. For several years with distinction."

"You're familiar with him?"

"I know him, sire. He has proven himself repeatedly, completing challenging assignments with remarkable efficiency and discretion. His loyalty is beyond reproach."

"Has he worked beyond our borders?"

"As far as Siberia's depths, through the harshest winters and most treacherous conditions."

"From where does he hail?"

"He is Siberian-born, from Omsk. A loyal son of the frozen north."

"Does he possess the necessary traits, levelheadedness, wit, and valor?"

"Without question, Your Majesty. He embodies all these qualities and more. Where others might falter, he will persevere. His resolve is as solid as the Ural Mountains themselves."

"His age?"

"Thirty years, sire. Old enough for wisdom, young enough for vigor."

"And his physical condition? Is he robust and healthy?"

"Your Majesty, he's able to endure freezing temperatures, starvation, dehydration, and exhaustion to their absolute limits. I've witnessed him traverse hundred-mile stretches through blizzards that would kill lesser men."

"He must possess incredible strength."

"Indeed, he does, Your Majesty. He can wrestle a bear and climb sheer cliffs with nothing but his bare hands. His endurance is legendary among our couriers."

"What of his character?"

"He has the noblest spirit. Never once has he wavered from his duty or compromised his principles, even when faced with temptation or threat."

"Tell me his name."

"Michael Strogoff," the general replied with clear pride.

"Is he prepared to depart?"

"He's waiting for your commands in the antechamber, fully equipped and ready to move at a moment's notice."

"Send him in," commanded the Czar, leaning forward in his ornate chair.

The imperial library doors opened to admit Michael Strogoff, the courier. A tall and robust figure, with broad shoulders and a muscular chest, commanded attention, suggesting great strength. His facial features reflected his Caucasian heritage. His physique suggested a man was impossible to move against his will; when he planted his feet, they seemed to merge with the ground beneath them, as immovable as ancient oak roots. Upon removing his Muscovite cap, thick curls of dark hair cascaded over his expansive forehead like a warrior's crown. His complexion remained pale, showing color only when his heart quickened its pace, a trait common among those born to the northern reaches. Clear, direct blue eyes gazed out from his face with unwavering confidence, scanning the room with the practiced efficiency of one accustomed to assessing his surroundings. His furrowed brow hinted at a heroic spirit, what physiologists would call "the hero's cool courage", that rare quality that allows a man to think clearly even during danger. A well-proportioned nose with wide nostrils complemented his mouth, whose protruding lips revealed the generous and noble spirit within. His clean-shaven face bore the weathered marks of one who spent countless hours in the saddle, exposed to both bitter winds and scorching sun.

Michael had all the qualities of a man who takes action rather than lingers in hesitation. He moved with purpose, wasting no energy on needless gestures or idle chatter. When standing, he maintained the disciplined stillness of a soldier at attention, his spine straight as a ramrod, his shoulders squared with military precision. Yet when he moved, each step revealed a self-assured grace that reflected his sharp, agile mind, like a leopard padding through its territory.

His attire was that of a distinguished military officer, styled after a light cavalry dress uniform. He cut an impressive figure in his fur-trimmed brown jacket 20adorned with yellow braiding on the fabric, showing just enough wear to suggest regular use rather than mere ceremonial display. His form-fitting trousers, pressed to razor-sharp creases, tapered into gleaming cavalry boots, complete with spurs that clinked with each measured step. His chest bore the distinguished marks of service, a cross and several military decorations, their polished surfaces catching the light and speaking silently of battles fought and victories won in service to his country.

A member of the Czar's elite courier corps, Michael Strogoff held officer rank among these selected individuals, each handpicked for their exceptional abilities and unshakeable loyalty to the crown. His defining trait, clear in the way he walks, countenance, and entire bearing, which caught the Czar's attention, was his unwavering dedication to executing commands. This quality, which the renowned author Tourgueneff noted could "elevate one to the highest positions in the Muscovite empire," proved especially valuable in Russia, where absolute fidelity to duty often meant the difference between an empire's triumph and its collapse.

If anyone could successfully undertake the perilous journey from Moscow to Irkutsk through hostile territory, overcoming obstacles and facing many dangers, Michael Strogoff was that person. His reputation for completing impossible missions preceded him, and his fellow officers spoke in hushed tones of his remarkable ability to navigate treacherous situations with both cunning and honor. Years of service had honed his instincts to near perfection, making him as comfortable reading terrain as most men were reading books.

He possessed a major advantage that would help his plan succeed: his deep familiarity with both the region's geography and its various local languages. This knowledge came not only from his previous travels through the area but also from being a native Siberian himself, having learned to read the land's moods like most men read faces.

Peter Strogoff, who passed away a decade ago, made his home in Omsk, a town in the province bearing the same name. His widow, Marfa Strogoff, continues to live there, maintaining the family's modest but well-respected homestead. It was in this region, among the untamed steppes of Omsk and Tobolsk provinces, that the renowned hunter raised his son Michael to be resilient, teaching him the ways of survival that would later prove invaluable.

As a professional huntsman, Peter Strogoff braved all seasons. Whether in scorching summer heat or bitter winter cold, sometimes facing temperatures plunging to fifty degrees below zero, he roamed the ice-covered plains and navigated through birch, larch, and pine woodlands. He set traps, pursued small game with his rifle, and tackled larger prey with spear or knife, passing these ancestral skills to his son with the patience and precision that only a lifetime of experience could provide.

The most formidable of his quarry was the Siberian bear, a fierce creature rivaling the polar bear in size and known for its exceptional aggression during the harsh winter months. Throughout his career, Peter Strogoff had felled thirty-nine of these fearsome beasts, the fortieth becoming his ultimate conquest. According to Russian folklore, hunters fortunate enough to survive encounters with thirty-nine bears often meet their fate at the claws of the fortieth. a superstition whispered around campfires that proved prophetic for the elder Strogoff.

From an early age, Michael Strogoff showed exceptional courage and strength, inheriting his father's steadfast nerves and hunter's instincts. He began joining his father Peter on bear hunts when he was just eleven, serving as his father's spear-bearer while Peter carried only a knife, a testament to both the father's skill and his trust in his young son's reliability. At fourteen, Michael achieved a remarkable feat by single-handedly killing his first bear, using the very techniques his father had drilled into him since childhood. Even more impressive was the young boy's display of extraordinary physical prowess when he dragged the massive bear's hide several miles back to their home, a distance that would challenge even grown men, refusing all offers of help from passing woodsmen along the way.

The rigorous lifestyle shaped him into a resilient man, capable of enduring extreme conditions that would break others. He could withstand intense cold and heat, go without food for twenty-four hours, and stay awake for ten nights straight. Like the hardy Yakout people of the north, his constitution seemed forged from iron. When others would perish from exposure on the open steppe, he could craft shelter and survive, fashioning windbreaks from the sparsest materials and finding sustenance where others saw only barren ground.

His senses were sharp, rivaling those of the Delaware tribes of North America. He could navigate through white-out conditions when fog obscured all landmarks and even find his way during the extended darkness of polar nights. His father had passed down an intimate knowledge of nature's subtle signs, the shape of ice formations, positioning tree branches, distant mists on the horizon, faint sounds carried on the wind, far-off noises, and the movement of birds through heavy fog. These minute details formed a language he could read, a secret code written in nature's own hand that revealed itself to those patient enough to learn its ways. Even in the depths of winter, when the very air seemed frozen despite that, he could detect existing game or approaching weather changes by observing the subtle alterations in the surrounding environment.

The harsh winter conditions had tempered his body like a Damascus steel blade in Syrian waters, giving him, as General Kissoff noted, the strength of iron. Yet remarkable was his heart of gold, making him as noble in character as he was tough in the constitution. Those who knew him well often remarked that his resilience seemed supernatural, though he dismissed such claims with characteristic modesty.

Michael Strogoff's heart knew only one true love: his mother, Marfa. She remained in their family home in Omsk, situated along the Irtish river, where she had spent countless years with her husband, the old huntsman. Each time Michael departed, his heart grew heavy, though he vowed to visit whenever circumstances allowed, a promise he honored without fail. Despite the vast distances and treacherous conditions that often separated them, their bond remained unshakeable, strengthened by the shared memories of his childhood years spent learning the ways of survival in the unforgiving Siberian wilderness.

In his twentieth year, Michael earned a coveted position among the Russian Emperor's select group of imperial messengers. The youthful courier from Siberia showed his exceptional capabilities, showing remarkable physical prowess, sharp intellect, unwavering commitment, and strict adherence to duty. His first major accomplishment occurred while traversing the treacherous Caucasus territories, where he maneuvered through areas disrupted by Schamyl's insurgent forces, navigating perilous mountain passes and evading hostile patrols with an instinct that seemed almost supernatural. He later garnered additional recognition during a vital mission to Petropolowski in Kamtschatka, at the easternmost edge of Russia's Asian dominion, where he braved fierce storms and treacherous seas to deliver crucial diplomatic dispatches. Throughout his extensive journeys, Michael maintained exceptional poise, demonstrated sound judgment, and displayed unwavering courage, leading his commanders to advance him to higher positions. Because he was so reliable, people entrusted him with even the most sensitive messages; his fellow couriers spoke of his achievements with admiration and awe.

During his breaks from far-off assignments, he always made time to visit his elderly mother. His extensive work in the empire's southern regions had kept him away from old Marfa for an unprecedented three years, the longest separation they had ever endured. Though they exchanged letters when possible, the written word was a poor substitute for the warmth of her embrace and her home-cooked meals that reminded him of simpler days. He had been planning to use his upcoming leave to journey to Omsk within days when circumstances changed. As a result, Michael Strogoff stood before the Czar with no hunch of what his ruler might require of him.

The Czar stared at him in complete silence, while Michael remained as still as a statue, his military bearing perfect, his eyes focused straight ahead as protocol demanded.

Content with his examination, the Czar gestured for the police chief to take a seat and dictated a brief letter, his voice barely above a whisper to ensure absolute privacy.

After writing the letter, the Czar carefully reviewed it before signing with his characteristic flourish. Above his signature, he wrote "Byt po semou", written in Russian and translates to "Nothing to report here" or "All is quiet here" the traditional authoritative phrase used by Russian emperors since Peter the Great's time.

Someone put the letter in an envelope marked with the imperial seal and sealed it.

The Czar rose from behind his ornate desk and beckoned Michael Strogoff forward with a commanding gesture.

Michael took several measured steps across the plush carpet and halted with military precision, standing ramrod straight at attention, his shoulders squared and chin lifted, prepared to respond to whatever his emperor might ask.

The Czar's penetrating gaze, sharp and analytical, met Michael's eyes once more, studying him with imperial scrutiny. "Your name?" he demanded, his voice carrying the weight of absolute authority.

"Michael Strogoff, sire," came the clear, unwavering response.

"Your rank?"

"Captain in the Czar's courier corps, at your service."

"Are you familiar with Siberia?" The question carried particular emphasis.

"I am Siberian born, sire," Michael answered with quiet pride.

"From where?"

"Omsk, sire," he replied, naming the fortress city.

"Do you have family there?" The Czar's questioning grew more personal.

"Yes, sire," Michael responded, his voice softening.

"What family?"

"My elderly mother," he answered, a hint of warmth breaking through his professional demeanor.

The Emperor paused his interrogation, his fingers tightening around the sealed document. Then, gesturing with the letter, he said, "Michael Strogoff, I entrust you with this letter; deliver it only to the Grand Duke, no one else."

"I shall deliver it, your majesty," Strogoff replied with unwavering conviction.

"You'll find the Grand Duke in Irkutsk," the Czar continued, his eyes never leaving his courier's face.

"Then to Irkutsk I shall go," came the resolute response.

"You must cross through territories in rebellion, now overrun with Tartars who would steal this letter. They are ruthless, and their spies are everywhere."

"I shall cross through them," Strogoff answered, his jaw set with determination.

"Most importantly, guard yourself against Ivan Ogareff, the betrayer whom you might encounter during your journey. He knows our ways, our methods. He is as cunning as he is dangerous."

"I shall be on guard against him," declared Strogoff, his voice hardening at the mention of the traitor's name.

"Will your path take you through+

Omsk?" The Czar's tone grew gentler, almost paternal.

"Indeed, your majesty, that lies along my route," Strogoff answered, sensing the weight of what would follow.

"If you see your mother, you risk being recognized. You must not see her!" The command was absolute, though tinged with sympathy.

Michael Strogoff hesitated for a moment, the first crack in his steadfast demeanor showing at the mention of his mother.

"I will not see her," he said, his voice firm despite the pain showing in his eyes.

"Swear to me that nothing will make you reveal who you are or where you're going. Not torture, not threats, not even the pleading of those you hold dear."

"I swear it," Strogoff responded without hesitation, his right hand moving to his heart.

"Michael Strogoff," continued the Czar, handing the letter to the young courier with deliberate solemnity, "take this letter; the safety of all Siberia depends on it, and perhaps the life of my brother, the Grand Duke. Guard it with your very life."

Strogoff declared, "Someone will deliver this letter to His Highness the Grand Duke," securing the document within his uniform.

"Then you will get through, no matter what happens? No matter what obstacles you face?"

"I will get through, or they will kill me," he stated with unwavering conviction.

"I want you to live," the Czar insisted, placing a paternal hand on Strogoff's shoulder.

"I will live, and I will get through," answered Michael Strogoff, his eyes meeting his sovereigns with steadfast determination.

The Emperor nodded, appearing content with Strogoff's straightforward response, seeing in the young courier's bearing all the resolution he had hoped for.

"Proceed then, Michael Strogoff," he declared, drawing himself up to his full height, "go forth in service of God, Russia, my brother, and myself! Let nothing deter you from your sacred duty."

The messenger bowed to his ruler and departed, his footsteps echoing with purpose as he exited the New Palace moments later into the gathering dusk.

"You've selected well, General," the Emperor remarked, watching the door through which his chosen courier had disappeared. "Very well indeed."

"I believe so, Your Majesty," General Kissoff responded, clasping his hands behind his back with quiet confidence. "You can rest assured that Michael Strogoff will accomplish everything humanly possible. His record of service speaks for itself."

"Indeed, he is the epitome of capability," the Emperor affirmed, turning from the doorway to face his general. "There is something in his manner that inspires absolute trust, a quality most rare and valuable in these uncertain times."

Chapter Four

FROM MOSCOW TO NIJNI-NOVGOROD

The journey between Moscow and Irkutsk, which Michael Strogoff was about to undertake, covered a vast distance of three thousand four hundred miles. In the days before telegraph lines stretched from the Urals to Siberia's eastern border, courier services carried messages. The fastest riders could make the Moscow-to-Irkutsk trip in eighteen days, though this was rare. More typically, even with access to the best transportation options available to the Czar's messengers, the journey across Asiatic Russia took between four and five weeks, with many stops at posting stations to change horses and rest.

Michael Strogoff was someone who could withstand the harshest cold weather, having been born and raised in the severe climate of Siberia. He preferred to make his journeys in the depths of winter, as it allowed him to travel the entire route by sleigh. Winter travel offered distinct advantages, as the vast steppes became smooth under their blanket of snow, and rivers transformed into frozen highways of ice, perfect for swift and effortless sleigh travel. The bitter cold also kept bandits and marauders at bay, making the journey safer for those hardy enough to brave the elements. In these conditions, a skilled driver could cover fifty or sixty miles in a day, provided the weather remained clear, and the horses stayed strong.

The winter season brought its own perils, like thick, persistent fogs, bitter cold spells, and devastating blizzards powerful enough to bury and destroy entire caravans. The plains also teemed with thousands of ravenous wolves that roamed in massive packs, their haunting howls echoing across the frozen landscape. Yet Michael Strogoff would have preferred these natural dangers, as winter's harsh conditions would have confined the Tartar invaders to their urban strongholds, making troop movements impossible and his journey easier. The deep snows and frozen ground would have prevented their swift horses from covering any meaningful distance, halting their expansion. However, he had no choice in the timing or conditions, he had to accept whatever challenges lay ahead and begin his journey.

Michael Strogoff stood ready to face these daunting challenges head-on, his resolve as firm as the frozen earth beneath his feet. His years of experience traversing these routes had taught him that hesitation only bred doubt, and doubt could be fatal in such unforgiving terrain.

His first task was to avoid any appearance of being an imperial courier. In these rebellion-torn lands, where spies lurked at every corner, the slightest hint of his true identity could doom his mission. General Kissoff had provided him with ample funds to ease his journey. He deliberately withheld any official documents that would mark Strogoff as an imperial agent, such papers being the most valuable form of safe passage. Instead, the General gave him only a simple travel permit, a "podorojna."

The authorities issued the travel permit under the name Nicholas Korpanoff, identifying him as a merchant from Irkutsk. The document granted Korpanoff permission to travel with companions and included a special provision allowing him to leave Russia even if the Moscow government banned foreign nationals from departing the country. Strogoff had memorized every detail of his cover story, practicing the mannerisms and speech patterns of a seasoned merchant until they became second nature. He had worn clothes that showed signs of wear from long trading journeys, complete with subtle stains from marketplace haggling and the dust of caravan trails. Such attention to detail could mean the difference between life and death in territories where rebel sympathizers scrutinized every traveler with suspicion.

The podorojna granted authorization to use post-horses, though Michael Strogoff could only use it when certain it wouldn't raise questions about his mission, while in European territory. As a result, when crossing through rebellious Siberian provinces, he would have no special privileges at relay stations, neither in selecting preferred horses nor in requesting personal transportation. Michael Strogoff had to remember his cover identity: he was no longer a courier but an ordinary merchant named Nicholas Korpanoff, traveling between Moscow and Irkutsk, and thus subject to all the usual delays and difficulties of regular travel.

To move through undetected, quickly if possible, but at any pace necessary, these were his instructions. He understood that maintaining his merchant facade meant accepting the frustrations of waiting for fresh horses alongside common travelers, haggling over prices like any cost-conscious trader would, and showing neither impatience nor urgency when faced with the inevitable delays that plagued Siberian travel. Such restraint would prove challenging given the vital nature of his mission, but appearing too eager to proceed could draw unwanted attention from those who watched the roads.

Three decades earlier, when an important dignitary traveled, their entourage required two hundred Cossacks on horseback, two hundred infantry soldiers, twenty-five mounted Baskirs, three hundred camels, four hundred horses, twenty-five wagons, a pair of portable vessels, and two cannons. Such was the massive convoy needed for any Siberian expedition of significance, a small moving city that wound its way across the vast steppes like a great serpent, visible for miles around.

Michael Strogoff traveled light, with no military equipment or support, no artillery, cavalry, infantry, or pack animals. He would travel by whatever means were available: carriages or horses when possible, and on foot when necessary. This simplicity was both his greatest vulnerability and his strongest defense, allowing him to blend with the merchants and travelers who traversed these routes.

From Moscow to Russia's border, the first thousand miles would be fairly straightforward. The route was well-served by modern transportation, railways, postal coaches, steam-powered vessels, and horse relay stations were available to all travelers, including a courier serving the Czar. The infrastructure here represented the height of Russian civilization, a far cry from what lay ahead in the wilderness beyond.

On July 16th, Michael Strogoff arrived at the station in traditional Russian attire, having traded his uniform to catch the first train. He wore a close-fitting tunic, the characteristic peasant belt, loose trousers tucked into high boots, and carried a knapsack. Though unarmed in appearance, he had concealed a revolver beneath his belt and tucked a substantial knife away in his pocket; the blade, part cutlass and part yataghan, was of a type Siberian hunter used to gut bears while preserving their valuable pelts. He had adjusted his practiced stance and military bearing to mirror the casual slouch of a merchant or tradesman heading east, completing his transformation from imperial courier to common traveler.

At Russian railway stations, a diverse mix of people often congregates, creating bustling social hubs. These stations serve not just passengers embarking on journeys, but also friends and family who come to bid them farewell, merchants hawking their wares, and peasants seeking day labor. The lively atmosphere and varied crowd of characters, from noblemen in fine coats to bedraggled pilgrims clutching holy icons, make these stations feel like miniature public squares where news and gossip flow among the constant din of arrivals and departures.

Michael boarded a train bound for Nijni-Novgorod, where the railway line connecting Moscow and St. Petersburg ended, though it would later extend to Russia's border with the expanding network of iron rails. The trip covered less than three hundred miles through the heart of European Russia, with the journey taking ten hours to complete across the sprawling plains and scattered woodlands. Upon reaching Nijni-Novgorod, Michael Strogoff planned to continue his journey either by land or by taking a Volga riverboat, whichever would get him to the rugged peaks of the Ural Mountains fastest, knowing that speed was essential to his mission.

The vigilant Strogoff settled into his compartment corner, adopting the demeanor of a content businessman trying to pass time with slumber. But Strogoff maintained a watchful rest; one eye stayed alert, both ears attentive to his surroundings, prepared to spring into action at the first hint of danger or useful information.

Whispers of the Kirghiz uprising and Tartar incursion had circulated through the populace, carried along the railway like autumn leaves in the wind. His fellow passengers, thrust together by circumstance, discussed these developments, though with the characteristic restraint of Russians well aware that informants might be listening for any hint of seditious talk.

The journey included merchants heading to the renowned Nijni-Novgorod fair, along with many other passengers seeking fortune or fleeing troubles. This diverse group comprised Jews, Turks, Cossacks, Russians, Georgians, Kalmucks, and various others, their traditional garments and mannerisms, creating a vibrant tapestry of Imperial Russian society. Despite their different backgrounds, most of them communicated in the common Russian language, though breaking into their native tongues when emotion got the better of them. The rhythmic clicking of the rails provided a steady backbeat to their multilingual murmurings.

The merchants debated how the grave situation unfolding east of the Ural Mountains might affect them. Their primary worry centered on potential government restrictions, especially in provinces near the border, that could harm their commercial interests. They viewed the entire conflict purely through the lens of how it might damage their business ventures. Had a uniformed soldier been present, and uniforms commanded great respect in Russia, these merchants would have held their tongues. However, no one in Michael Strogoff's train compartment appeared to be military personnel, and the Czar's courier was careful not to reveal his true identity. He sat quietly and listened, his weathered hands folded calmly in his lap.

A man wearing an Astrakhan fur cap and a well-worn brown robe, marking him as Persian, spoke up, stroking his graying beard. "Word is that caravan tea prices are rising. The routes through Kashgar have become treacherous."

"Tea prices won't drop anytime soon," replied a grim-faced elderly Jewish merchant, adjusting the worn leather ledger on his knee. "The Western markets will snap up everything available at the Nijni-Novgorod fair. But Bokhara carpets, that's another story altogether. The warehouses in Moscow are already overflowing with last season's inventory."

"Do you source your merchandise from Bokhara?" asked the Persian merchant, adjusting his cap as a gust of wind swept through the gathering.

"No, we import from Samarcand, which carries even greater risks. It's practically impossible to rely on trade from those territories, there's unrest among the khans stretching from Khiva all the way to the Chinese frontier. Three of my caravans have already been delayed this season alone."

"Ah," the Persian responded with a knowing smile, stroking his beard, "I suppose if the carpets cannot arrive, we won't have to worry about settling the payments either."

"But think of the potential earnings, blessed Abraham!" the diminutive Jewish trader interjected, clutching his ledger tighter. "Surely that counts for something? The profits from a single successful shipment could offset a dozen losses!"

"You make a valid point," another merchant chimed in, his silk kaftan rustling as he leaned forward. "Though any goods coming through Central

Asia face significant market uncertainties, the same applies to the tallow and shawls from the eastern regions. We've all felt the sting of those risks."

"Hey, watch yourself, dear sir," called out the Russian journeyman with a teasing smile, his weathered face crinkling with amusement. "You'll end up soaking those fine shawls of yours if you let them get too close to the tallow."

The merchant, clearly irritated by the mockery, snapped back, his face flushing red beneath his turban, "You find that entertaining, do you?"

"Come now," the traveler continued, spreading his calloused hands in a placating gesture, "whether you pull at your hair or cover yourself in ashes, will it make any difference to what's happening? Only it would affect the stock market. Better to laugh than weep over matters beyond our control."

"It's quite obvious you're not in trade yourself," the diminutive Jewish merchant pointed out, adjusting the silver chain of his pocket watch with nervous fingers.

"Indeed not, esteemed child of Abraham!" he declared, puffing up his chest. "You won't find me dealing in any of those goods, not hops, goose down, honey, beeswax, hemp seeds, cured meats, caviar, timber, wool, decorative ribbons, hemp fiber, flax, leather, or fur pelts. Though I must say, the market for such items never ceases to fascinate."

"Do you purchase these items?" the Persian interjected, cutting off the traveler's enumeration, his dark eyes narrowing with suspicion.

"Sparingly, and for personal consumption," replied the other man with a knowing look, drumming his fingers against his knee. "A man must live, after all."

"He's quite the jester," the Jew remarked to the Persian, keeping his voice low and measured.

"Or perhaps an informant," the Persian whispered, leaning closer to his companion. "We should exercise discretion and limit our conversation. The authorities are especially vigilant these days. One never knows who might share our journey. These walls have ears, as they say."

Elsewhere in the train car, the discussion had shifted from business matters to concerns about the Tartar invasion and its troublesome effects. The air grew heavy with worried murmurs.

"They're going to take all the horses in Siberia," one traveler remarked, his weathered face etched with concern. "Moving between the regions of Central Asia will become challenging. The trade routes we've relied upon for generations may soon be lost to us."

"Have you heard if it's correct," the person next to him inquired, leaning in closer with furrowed brows, "that the middle horde Kirghiz has sided with the Tartars?"

"That's what they're saying," the traveler replied in hushed tones, nervously glancing around the compartment. "But in this country, who can claim to know what's really happening? The stories change with each passing village."

"Word has reached me about military forces massing near the border. The Don Cossacks have taken positions along the Volga River, preparing to confront the rebellious Kirghiz tribes. Their cavalry units have been mobilizing day and night, from what I understand."

"Should the Kirghiz move down the Irtish, travel to Irkutsk would become perilous," the other person noted, wiping perspiration from his forehead. "Also, my attempt to send a telegram to Krasnoiarsk yesterday failed. The operator couldn't even establish a connection. I fear it won't be long before Tartar forces cut off all contact with Eastern Siberia."

"Look here, my friend," the first man went on, his voice trembling with contained anxiety, "the merchants are right to worry about their business dealings. First, they'll take the horses, then the boats and wagons, every way of getting around, until no one in the entire empire will move an inch. We'll all be trapped like rats."

"I have a bad feeling the Nijni-Novgorod fair won't finish as successfully as it started," the other man replied with a worried shake of his head, drumming his fingers nervously on his knee. "But protecting Russia's borders must come first. Business concerns are secondary. God help us all if the empire's frontiers fall."

Throughout the train compartment, and indeed the other cars as well, passengers discussed the same topics, but with notable caution in their manner. While they spoke of actual events, they avoided speculating about Moscow's motives or passing judgment on the government's decisions. The tension was palpable as voices dropped to hushed tones whenever official matters arose.

A curious passenger seated in the front carriage drew particular attention to himself. This foreigner seemed determined to absorb every detail of the journey, peppering others with questions that were met with vague replies and uncomfortable shifting in seats. Much to his fellow travelers' annoyance, he kept his window lowered throughout the trip, frequently leaning out to study the passing landscape on the right side, letting in clouds of dust and soot from the locomotive. With meticulous attention, he jotted down in his already well-filled notebook details about each town they passed, asking about their names, geographic location, economic activities, population figures, and even mortality rates. His pen moved swiftly across the pages, recording every scrap of information he could glean from the reluctant responses of his fellow passengers, who exchanged knowing glances at his persistent inquiries.

The journalist Alcide Jolivet peppered people with trivial questions, hoping that amid the responses he might uncover a newsworthy detail "for his cousin," a phrase he repeated so often it had become something of a running joke among the other passengers. However, his persistent inquiries aroused suspicion, and those around him, believing him to be a spy, carefully avoided any discussion of current events in his presence, their conversations dropping to whispers whenever he approached.

Frustrated by his inability to gather any information about the Tartar incursion, he made a wry note in his journal: "Travelers of great discretion. Very close as to political matters." He underlined these words twice, then added with a touch of sarcasm, "One might think the fate of the empire hangs upon their silence." Closing his notebook with an audible snap, he turned his attention back to the dusty landscape rushing past his window.

Harry Blount and Alcide Jolivet, both journalists traveling on the same train to cover the war, were unaware of each other's presence since their morning departure from Moscow station. While Jolivet recorded his observations in his leather-bound notebook, drawing suspicious glances from fellow passengers who shifted in their seats, Blount took a different approach. His quiet, observant demeanor and minimal conversation helped him blend in with his compartment companions, offering only a polite nod or brief comment about the weather. Unlike Jolivet, whose constant scribbling marked him as an outsider, no one suspected Blount of being a spy, which proved helpful. His fellow travelers spoke freely around him, often revealing more than their usual cautiousness would permit, their voices carrying across the rhythmic clatter of wheels on rails. As a result, the Daily Telegraph correspondent gained valuable insights into how deeply recent events had affected Nijni-Novgorod's merchants, who spoke of empty warehouses and canceled shipments, and the growing threats to Central Asian trade routes, where caravans now traveled in heavily armed convoys, if they dared to travel at all.

"The surrounding passengers were on edge, their faces drawn and voices hushed. War was the only topic of conversation, and they discussed it with surprising openness, treating the conflict between the Volga and Vistula as if it were already underway," he documented in his journal, noting how even the wealthiest merchants spoke of abandoning their trading posts.

The Daily Telegraph's readership would be just as well-informed as Alcide Jolivet's "cousin." Harry Blount, however, positioned on the train's left side, only observed the rolling hills while ignoring the expansive plains on the right, his notebook balanced on his knee. With typical British self-assurance, he wrote, "The terrain between Moscow and Wladimir is mountainous," a description that would have amused any local familiar with the region's gentle topography.

The Kremlin leadership was preparing strict measures to prevent potential disturbances throughout Russia's heartland, dispatching additional troops to key cities and strengthening border patrols. While the uprising hadn't penetrated Siberia's borders, there were concerns about possible unrest spreading to the Volga regions, which lay dangerously close to Kirghiz territory. Military checkpoints had appeared at major crossroads, and telegraph operators reported increased surveillance of communications.

The authorities had yet to uncover any sign of Ivan Ogareff. No one knew if the traitor had joined forces with Feofar-Khan, seeking foreign help to satisfy his personal vendetta, or if he was trying to incite rebellion in Nijni-Novgorod. The city's great market attracted a diverse mix of Persians, Armenians, and Kalmucks at this time of year, and Ogareff might have planted agents among them to spark an uprising. Such schemes were possible in Russia, given the empire's vast complexity and the relative ease with which conspirators could disappear into its sprawling territories.

Indeed, this enormous nation, spanning 4,000,000 square miles, bore little resemblance to the more uniform states of Western Europe. Its territory, stretching across Europe and Asia, contained over seventy million people speaking thirty different languages, with dialects and sub-dialects multiplying that number several times over. While the Slavic peoples formed the majority, the empire encompassed Russians, Poles, Lithuanians, and Courlanders, each maintaining their distinct cultural traditions and social hierarchies. Beyond these were the Finns, Laplanders, and Estonians, along with many northern tribes whose names defied pronunciation by even the most learned scholars. The population also included Permiaks, Germans, Greeks, Tartars, various Caucasian peoples, as well as Mongol, Kalmuck, Samoid, Kamtschatkan, and Aleutian groups, each with their own customs, religious practices, and ancestral territories. Given such diversity, maintaining unity across this vast state was an immense challenge, one that required time and the careful governance of multiple generations of rulers, whose policies had to balance central authority with local autonomy to prevent the empire from fracturing under its own weight.

With relentless determination, Ivan Ogareff continued to evade capture, likely making his way toward the Tartar forces. At each railway stop, vigilant inspectors would board the train, examining every passenger under direct orders from police command to locate Ogareff. The authorities remained convinced that the betrayer was still within Russia's European territories. Any passenger who aroused suspicion found themselves detained at local police stations for questioning, while the train continued its journey without delay, the fate of those left behind of little concern to their fellow travelers.

Arguing with the Russian police is futile, as they operate with complete arbitrariness and military discipline, being organized as a military force. Their unquestioning obedience is not surprising, given that they answer to a monarch whose official title alone shows his vast authority, a ruler who commands an empire stretching from Poland to Siberia, from the Arctic to Armenia, whose symbol is a double-headed eagle grasping the scepter and globe of absolute power, whose crest bears the emblems of ancient kingdoms, and whose authority is ordained as Emperor and Autocrat of All the Russias. Such extensive dominion and claims to power translate into an enforcement arm that brooks no opposition. The police carried out their duties with mechanical efficiency, their faces stern and impassive as they moved through the carriages. Their dark uniforms and gleaming badges served as constant reminders of state authority, while their practiced movements spoke of years spent perfecting the art of intimidation. Those passengers wise enough to travel with impeccable documentation found the inspections merely inconvenient; those less fortunate discovered how swiftly suspicion could turn to detention.

Michael Strogoff had his documentation in perfect order, which meant he could travel with no interference from law enforcement. His papers bore all the necessary stamps and seals, each carefully maintained and protected within a leather folder that showed signs of frequent use but meticulous care.

When they reached Wladimir station, the train paused long enough for the Daily Telegraph's reporter to both observe and contemplate this historic Russian capital, forming a thorough impression of the city. The ancient churches with their distinctive onion domes pierced the sky, while the weathered stone walls of the Kremlin spoke of centuries of turbulent history.

As the train halted at Wladimir station, new passengers boarded, including a young woman who stepped into Michael Strogoff's compartment. Finding an empty seat across from the courier, she settled in, placing beside her a simple red leather traveling bag that appeared to be her only possession. The bag, though well-worn at the corners, was of good quality leather and bore no identifying marks or tags. She sat with her eyes lowered, avoiding any contact with her chance companions, and readied herself for the hours of travel still ahead. Her dark traveling dress, modest but well-tailored, suggested someone accustomed to moving in respectable circles, though her demeanor spoke of someone wishing to pass unnoticed.

Michael Strogoff found himself studying his new traveling companion with keen interest. He politely offered to switch seats with her, because he noticed she was facing away from the engine and thought she would be more comfortable in his seat. She declined his offer with a graceful nod.

The teenager appeared to be in her mid-teens, perhaps sixteen or seventeen. Her striking features embodied the classic Slavic beauty, with a hint of severity that promised to mature into true elegance rather than simple attractiveness. Light golden hair flowed from beneath the kerchief covering her head, the fine strands catching the late afternoon sunlight filtering through the compartment window. Her brown eyes radiated gentleness and warmth, while her straight nose connected to pale, slender cheeks through delicate, responsive nostrils. Despite her perfectly shaped lips, she seemed to have forgotten how to smile long ago. The overall impression was of youth touched too early by life's harsher realities, though her inherent grace remained undiminished.

The traveler stood tall and graceful, her posture clear despite the loose, flowing dress +

draping her form. Though still in her youth, her prominent forehead and sharp features suggested maturity beyond her years, in the depth of her moral conviction, a quality that caught Michael Strogoff's keen eye. Life had left its mark on this young woman; past hardships had shaped her, and her future path seemed uncertain. Yet she possessed an unmistakable resilience, facing life's challenges with unwavering determination. Her strength of character showed itself in both quick decisive action and steady perseverance, maintaining a composure that would impress even the most steadfast men in times of crisis. Her hands, though delicate, bore slight calluses that hinted at a life of practical necessity rather than idle comfort, and the way she carried herself spoke of someone accustomed to shouldering responsibility alone. Even the modest simplicity of her traveling attire seemed a conscious choice rather than mere circumstance, reflecting an inner dignity that transcended outward appearances.

The first impression she made was striking. Her distinctive features attracted Michael Strogoff, a man of powerful character. While avoiding any uncomfortable staring, he studied his fellow passenger with genuine curiosity. The young woman's attire was modest, yet suited to travel. Though clearly not without means, as was clear at a glance, her clothing showed meticulous care and thoughtful selection. She carried all her belongings in a single well-worn leather bag which, because of the cramped space, rested on her knees, its brass buckles dulled from years of faithful service.

An elegant dark pelisse, its neckline adorned with a pressed blue ribbon despite the rigors of travel, comprised the woman's attire. Beneath it, she wore layered dark garments, a short skirt over a longer robe that extended to her ankles, both pieces cut from sturdy wool that would withstand the harsh demands of long-distance journeying. Sturdy leather half-boots protected her petite feet with thick soles, suggesting preparation for extensive travel, their careful polish at odds with the obvious miles they had already covered. The practical ensemble spoke of someone who understood the balance between maintaining appearances and facing the realities of life on the road.

Something about her clothing style struck Michael Strogoff as distinctly Livonian. The subtle details of her ensemble, from the precise cut of her wool garments to the particular way she wore her layers, led him to conclude she likely hailed from the Baltic provinces, where such practical yet refined fashion was common among the merchant class.

Where was this solitary young woman headed, traveling by herself at a time in life when most would consider paternal guidance or brotherly guardianship essential? Was she perhaps arriving from somewhere in Western Russia after a lengthy voyage across the empire's vast expanses? Could Nijni-Novgorod be her final destination, or did her journey extend past the empire's eastern borders into territories less hospitable to lone travelers? Would she find familiar faces, family members or acquaintances, waiting with open arms when her train arrived? Or was it more likely that she would be just as alone in the bustling city as she was in this train car? The latter seemed more likely, given her composed but isolated demeanor.

Her solitary lifestyle was clear in her every movement and gesture, each one practiced and precise. As she boarded the carriage and settled in for the trip, she moved with a self-contained efficiency that spoke of long practice navigating unfamiliar spaces alone. She did not disturb her fellow passengers, taking great care to minimize her presence and avoid causing any inconvenience, her movements almost ghost-like in their consideration. Everything about her behavior revealed someone who had grown used to standing alone, relying on her own resources and judgment, having learned the delicate art of existing in public spaces without drawing undue attention to herself.

In the carriage, Michael Strogoff watched the young woman, though he maintained his distance and made no attempt to speak with her. There was only one moment when he intervened, her fellow passenger, a merchant who had earlier made those tactless comments about tallow and shawls, had dozed off and his heavy head was lolling close to her, swaying back and forth between his shoulders like a mounted pendulum. Strogoff gave him a firm shake awake and conveyed that he needed to sit upright.

The trader, ill-mannered, muttered complaints about "nosy people sticking their noses where they don't belong," and shifted uncomfortably in his seat. But when Michael Strogoff fixed him with a severe look, one that carried all the authority of a man accustomed to being obeyed, the drowsy man shifted to lean the other way, sparing the young passenger from his unwelcome presence.

In a fleeting glance, the passenger caught Strogoff's eye, expressing gratitude, before resuming her composure. A subtle exchange, lasting only a heartbeat, revealed much about her reserved nature.

The train lurched violently as it navigated a sharp bend of twelve miles before reaching Nijni-Novgorod. The jarring impact sent it climbing up an embankment's slope, wheels screeching against the iron rails as they fought for purchase. This incident revealed to Strogoff the true nature of the young woman's character, a revelation that would later prove significant.

The erupting chaos inside the train cars tossed the frightened passengers around. Shouts and clamor filled the air while confusion spread through every compartment, luggage tumbling from overhead racks and tea cups shattering on the wooden floors. The commotion suggested a severe incident had occurred, with some passengers crying out about derailment or worse. Before the train could even come to a halt, doors flew open as terrified travelers rushed to escape their carriages, fearing the worst, their faces masks of panic in the afternoon light.

A sudden thought of the young girl crossed Michael Strogoff's mind amid the pandemonium. As the other passengers in her compartment rushed out in panic, screaming and pushing, nearly trampling one another in their haste to reach the exits, she stayed in her seat, composed nevertheless, hands folded in her lap. Only a hint of paleness betrayed any emotion on her face, and her eyes remained steady, focused on some distant point through the window as if the surrounding chaos was a minor inconvenience.

She made no move to leave, and neither did Michael Strogoff.

They both remained motionless, like two islands of calm in a sea of panic and confusion.

"What remarkable composure," Michael Strogoff mused to himself, finding himself oddly impressed by the young woman's steadfast demeanor in the face of apparent danger.

The frightening incident turned out to be harmless. The luggage car's coupling had broken, which caused the initial jolt and brought the train to a halt. Had this not happened, the train would have plunged off the elevated track into marshy ground below. Though the accident delayed them for an hour while workers cleared the track and secured the wayward car, the train continued on its way, the rhythmic clacking of wheels on rails resuming their familiar cadence. They pulled into Nijni-Novgorod station at 8:30 in the evening, the platform lights casting long shadows across the worn wooden boards.

The police inspectors, stern-faced men in dark uniforms, positioned themselves at the carriage doors before any passengers could disembark, checking each person with methodical precision. Their presence created a bottleneck as the inspectors forced weary travelers to submit to their scrutiny.

When Michael Strogoff presented his podorojna papers under the name Nicholas Korpanoff, they quickly waved him through, not even glancing at the official documents bearing the imperial seal. The other passengers sharing his compartment, who were traveling to Nijni-Novgorod, also passed inspection without issue since none of them raised any suspicions in the watchful eyes of the authorities.

Instead of a passport, which had become obsolete in Russia, the young woman presented an unusual document, a permit bearing a distinctive private seal that shimmered in the lamplight. The inspector studied it carefully, turning the paper this way and that, before looking up to scrutinize her appearance against the description provided. His weathered face betraying nothing.

"Your origin is Riga?" he inquired.

"Indeed," she confirmed with quiet confidence.

"Your destination, Irkutsk?" he continued, making a small notation in his ledger.

"Correct," she replied, standing straight under his examination.

"Which path will you take?" His pen hovered above the page.

"Through Perm," she stated without hesitation, her fingers unconsciously adjusting the hem of her traveling coat.

"Excellent!" the inspector declared, closing his ledger with a sharp snap. "Be sure to have your permit stamped at the Nijni-Novgorod police station before continuing your journey."

The young girl nodded her head in agreement.

As Michael Strogoff listened to this exchange, he felt both astonished and concerned, his weathered brow furrowing beneath the brim of his cap. This young girl was traveling alone to distant Siberia at such a dangerous time? The usual hazards of the journey were now compounded by the risks of an invaded land during rebellion. Bandits and deserters prowled the roads while entire villages lay abandoned. How would she make it? What fate awaited her in those vast, unforgiving territories where even armed men feared to venture alone?

Once the inspection concluded, they unlatched the carriage doors with a metallic clang that echoed through the compartment. However, before

Michael Strogoff could make his way to her, perhaps to offer help or guidance, the young Livonian woman had already slipped into the bustling crowd that filled the railway station's platforms, her slender figure weaving between merchants, travelers, and porters. She became the first passenger to exit and vanishing from sight, leaving behind only questions in Strogoff's troubled mind.

© 01/01/2025
QuantumDigitalPublishing.io
Book I - Chapter V

Chapter Five

THE TWO ANNOUNCEMENTS

Situated where the Volga and Oka rivers meet, NIJNI-NOVGOROD (also known as Lower Novgorod) serves as the principal city of its namesake district. At this point, Michael Strogoff had no choice but to abandon his railway journey, as the tracks extended no further. From here onward, his travel would become increasingly slow and dangerous, forcing him to rely on more traditional means of transportation through the vast Russian terrain.

The city of Nijni-Novgorod, though home to around thirty-five thousand (35,000), residents, swelled to over three hundred thousand (300,000), people during its renowned three-week fair. This massive influx of traders and visitors increased the city's population by ten times its normal size, transforming the quiet streets into bustling thoroughfares filled with merchants, performers, and travelers from across Europe and Asia. Before 1817, these commercial gatherings had taken place in Makariew, but thereafter Nijni-Novgorod became the fair's permanent home, its strategic location at merging two major rivers, making it an ideal center for trade and commerce. The city's architecture reflected this dual nature, with its ancient kremlin overlooking the modern commercial districts that had sprung up to accommodate the fair's enormous activity.

Despite the lateness of Michael Strogoff's departure, both sections of Nijni-Novgorod remained bustling with activity. The city, divided by the Volga River into two distinct parts, featured an upper town perched atop a precipitous cliff, where a Russian fortress known as a "Kreml" stood guard, its ancient stone walls a testament to centuries of history and conflict.

Michael Strogoff struggled to locate suitable accommodations in the area. Though not in an immediate rush since he planned to travel by steamboat, he still needed to secure lodging. Before settling that matter, however, he confirmed the steamer's departure time. Upon visiting the office of the steamship company operating between Nijni-Novgorod and Perm, he received unwelcome news. The next boat wouldn't depart until noon the following day. A seventeen-hour delay frustrated someone on such a time-sensitive journey. Yet he remained composed, knowing that no alternative transport could match the steamer's speed to either Perm or Kasan. He reasoned it would be prudent to wait, as the steamboat's speed would help make up for lost time, even considering the crowds of merchants and travelers, who would compete for passage along the same route.

Wandering the streets of Nijni-Novgorod, Michael Strogoff searched for lodging, though finding a place to sleep wasn't his primary concern. His growling stomach drove him. Had he not been famished, he would have continued roaming the city streets until dawn. Fortune smiled upon him at the City of Constantinople inn, where he discovered both food and shelter. The establishment's proprietor, a stout man with ruddy cheeks, showed him to a modest room which, despite its sparse furnishings, featured a Virgin Mary icon and several saints' images adorned in yellow gauze frames. The flickering light of an oil lamp cast dancing shadows across their solemn faces.

Laid out before him was a feast: a goose stuffed with tangy filling floating in rich cream, accompanied by hearty barley bread and fresh curds. Steam rose from the browned bird. A sweet mixture of powdered sugar and cinnamon sat nearby, along with a pitcher of kwass beer, Russia's traditional fermented beverage, its distinctive aroma filling the air. He ate, savoring each bite with the appreciation of a hungry traveler, unlike his table companion, a devout member of the Raskalnik sect of Old Believers, who, bound by strict religious abstinence, wouldn't touch the potatoes served to him and drank his tea without sugar. The man's weathered face remained stern as he sipped his plain beverage.

After completing his evening meal, Michael Strogoff opted not to return to his quarters, choosing instead to wander through the streets of Nizhny Novgorod. Though daylight still illuminated the sky with streaks of amber and purple, the townspeople were heading home, their shadows lengthening as they hurried along. The wooden shutters creaked shut one by one, leaving the thoroughfares deserted until all inhabitants had retreated to their homes, save for a few stray dogs skulking in the gathering darkness.

What prevented Michael Strogoff from retiring to his bed, which would have been the sensible choice after such an extensive train journey across the Russian countryside? Was his mind occupied with thoughts of the young Livonian lady who had shared his travels, her quiet dignity and self-possession making a lasting impression? Indeed, having no other pressing matters, she occupied his thoughts, though he tried to dismiss such distractions. Was he concerned she might face harassment in this bustling metropolis, where merchants and travelers from all corners of the empire mingled? Such worries weren't unfounded, and he had good cause for concern, given the rough characters he'd observed in the taverns and marketplaces. Did he harbor hopes of encountering her again, perhaps to offer his guardianship through the city's winding streets? No, such a meeting seemed improbable in the sprawling town. And as for protection, what authority did he possess, being another traveler himself?

Whispering in solitude, he reflected on his isolation among the nomadic peoples surrounding him. Yet his own perils seemed insignificant when measured against what awaited her. The vast expanse of Siberia and the distant city of Irkutsk loomed ahead. While he faced these dangers for his homeland and his Emperor, her motives remained a mystery. What drove her? Who had granted her permission to cross these contested borders? Beyond lay territories in open rebellion, with Tartar raiders swarming across the steppes, burning villages and slaughtering those who resisted their advance.

Michael Strogoff gathered his thoughts, his hand unconsciously tightening on the leather strap of his travel pack as his mind wrestled with these troubling questions. The wind whistled through the tall grass around him, carrying with it the faint scent of wood-smoke from distant camps.

"Surely," he reasoned, "she must have planned this journey before the invasion began. Yet perhaps she remains unaware of current events. No, that's impossible. Nadia was present when the merchants discussed the Siberian unrest and showed no sign of surprise. She didn't even ask questions. She must have known what was happening and still proceeded. Poor girl! Her reasons for traveling must be compelling! But despite her clear courage, her physical strength will fail her. Even setting aside the dangers and obstacles, such a grueling journey will prove too much for her endurance. The harsh terrain and unforgiving climate would test even the hardiest traveler. She'll never make it as far as Irkutsk!"

Lost in thought, Michael Strogoff meandered through the streets, confident in his ability to find his way back, thanks to his thorough knowledge of the town. The evening shadows lengthened around him as he walked, and the sounds of merchants closing their shops for the day echoed off the weathered buildings.

After roaming for about an hour, he found rest on a bench beside a spacious wooden house, one of many surrounding an expansive clearing. The worn planks of the bench creaked beneath him as he sat, and the sweet scent of pine from the freshly cut lumber stacked nearby filled his nostrils. He had settled in when he felt the sudden weight of someone's hand press on his shoulder, the grip strong and purposeful.

"What do you think you're doing there?" barked a burly man who had materialized behind him, his shadow falling across the bench like a dark curtain.

"Taking a rest," Michael Strogoff said, keeping his voice steady despite the unexpected confrontation.

"Planning to spend the entire night on that bench, are you?" The man's gravelly voice carried an unmistakable note of suspicion.

"Perhaps I am," Michael Strogoff shot back, his tone sharper than befitted the humble merchant he was pretending to be. He regretted the slip in his crafted demeanor.

"Step into the light where I can get a look at you," the man commanded, shifting his weight forward with the practiced stance of someone used to confrontation.

Michael Strogoff, mindful that caution was paramount, recoiled. "That won't be necessary," he replied, taking ten measured steps backward, his boots scraping against the packed earth.

As Michael studied the stranger, he noted the man's nomadic appearance, the kind associated with wandering fair folk whose presence often made others uncomfortable. The man's clothes were well worn but maintained, speaking of a life lived on the move. Peering through the growing darkness, Michael spotted what confirmed his suspicions: a sizeable wagon-home parked near the small house, its wooden sides weathered by countless miles of travel, the sort of mobile dwelling favored by the Roma travelers who could be found throughout Russia, setting up wherever they might earn even the most modest living. The wagon's small windows glowed with warm lamplight, suggesting others were inside.

When the gypsy moved forward a few steps, intending to question Michael Strogoff further, the cottage door opened. A woman appeared, her dark silhouette framed by the warm light behind her, speaking in a dialect that Michael Strogoff recognized as a blend of Mongol and Siberian languages, the harsh consonants rolling off her tongue with practiced ease.

"Not another spy! Leave him be and come eat. Your papluka is getting cold." Her voice carried both authority and irritation as she gestured at the man.

Despite his deep aversion to spies, Michael Strogoff couldn't suppress a smile at being labeled as one. Although he maintained his neutral expression, he recognized the absurdity of the situation.

Using the same language but with a distinct accent, the Bohemian answered, his tone carrying a hint of deference mixed with amusement, "Your observation is correct, Sangarre! And also, our departure is set for tomorrow."

"Tomorrow?" Sangarre echoed, clearly taken aback, her figure stiffening in the doorway as she processed this unexpected news.

"Indeed, Sangarre," the Bohemian confirmed, spreading his arms in an expansive gesture. "Tomorrow we leave, and it's by the Father's own command that we journey to our destination! The stars themselves align for our departure."

Following this exchange, both individuals stepped inside their cottage, making sure to secure the door behind them with a heavy wooden latch that scraped against its metal housing. The sound of their continuing conversation became muffled behind the thick walls.

"Excellent!" Michael Strogoff thought to himself, a slight smirk playing at the corners of his mouth. "If these nomads want their conversations to remain private in my presence, they should consider speaking in a different tongue. Their carelessness serves me well enough."

Being of Siberian descent and having spent his early years in the Steppes, where language was as vital as breath itself, Michael Strogoff could comprehend every dialect spoken between Tartary and the Sea of Ice. The countless hours spent among traders, travelers, and tribesmen had honed this skill to near perfection. Yet he paid little attention to the precise meaning of their words, letting them wash over him like wind across the plains. After all, what reason did he have to care about the schemes of wandering Bohemians?

He headed back to his lodgings for some rest as night had fallen. On his way, he walked alongside the Volga River, its surface visible beneath the multitude of vessels that crowded its waters. The gentle lapping of waves against wooden hulls and the distant calls of night watchmen provided a soothing backdrop to his thoughts.

Within an hour, Michael Strogoff had fallen into a deep sleep on one of those firm Russian mattresses that foreigners often find uncomfortable. The bed, stuffed with dense horsehair and covered by rough-woven sheets, felt like home to his travel-hardened body. He woke at dawn the next morning, July 17th.

With five hours remaining in Nijni-Novgorod, Michael Strogoff faced what felt like an eternity. The prospect of another morning wandering the streets, as he had done the previous evening, seemed his only option. His scheduled tasks, eating breakfast, securing his bag, and having his podorojna checked at the police station, would occupy only a fraction of his wait. He calculated that even if he performed each task with deliberate slowness, he would still have three hours of idle time to endure.

Being someone who never lingered in bed after sunrise, he rose and dressed, his military habits serving him well, even in civilian life. He took special care to secure the imperial-sealed letter in its hidden pocket within his coat's lining, fastening his belt over it with practiced precision. After shouldering his packed bag, its leather worn smooth from his travels, he decided against returning to the City of Constantinople inn. Instead, planning to breakfast along the Volga's bank near the wharf where merchants were already setting up their morning trade, he settled his bill and departed.

Taking no chances, Strogoff first visited the steam-packet company's office to confirm the Caucasus would depart on schedule, finding comfort in the clerk's assured nod. There, a new thought struck him. Since the young Livonian girl was bound for Perm, she might also take passage on the Caucasus. This meant they might be travel companions, though he remained uncertain whether this prospect pleased or concerned him.

The upper town and its fortress-like kremlin, stretching two miles around and bearing similarities to Moscow's own citadel, stood deserted, its stone walls catching the early morning light. Not even the governor maintained residence there, having long since moved to more comfortable quarters in the lower town. Yet while the upper town lay lifeless as a cemetery, its empty windows staring across the landscape, the lower section bustled with activity, already alive with traders, laborers, and the daily commerce of river life.

After traversing the Volga via a pontoon bridge under Cossack horsemen's watch, Michael Strogoff arrived at the open area where he had encountered the gypsy encampment the previous evening. Near: Near the Nijni-Novgorod fairgrounds, on the outskirts, lay the location of the governor-general's makeshift residence; imperial decree required his presence throughout the fair, as the diverse crowd demanded constant vigilance.

The field was covered with stalls, set up in neat rows that created wide pathways where people could move without getting jammed together. Planners' experience in managing large gatherings was clear in the careful organization, with designated routes for foot traffic and horse-drawn carts marked by colored flags and wooden signs in multiple languages.

People organized these trading districts into distinct sections, each devoted to specific types of goods. You could find separate areas for ironwork, fur trading, wool merchants, timber sellers, textile makers, and preserved fish vendors, among others. Some creative merchants constructed their stalls using the very products they sold, building walls from tea bricks or stacks of cured meat. This unique and somewhat American-style marketing approach used the actual merchandise as both storefront and advertisement. Leather, spices, smoked fish, and fresh timber filled the air, their mingled scents accompanied by the peculiar music of haggling in dozens of languages.

A diverse crowd of Europeans and Asians filled the bustling marketplace, their voices a lively mix of negotiations and discussions as the sun rose. Goods from across the world overflowed the square in astonishing variety. Luxurious furs and glittering precious stones lay alongside delicate silks and intricate Cashmere shawls. Turkish carpets competed for attention with weapons from the Caucasus and gossamer-light gauzes from Smyrna and Ispahan. Tiflis armor stood near aromatic caravan teas, while European bronzes and precise Swiss timepieces shared space with fine Lyon velvets and sturdy English cottons. The marketplace showcased everything from practical harness to fresh produce, Ural minerals including malachite and lapis-lazuli, an array of spices and perfumes, medicinal herbs, and basic commodities like wood, tar, rope, and horn. Plump pumpkins and juicy watermelons added splashes of color to this remarkable bazaar, which seemed to gather all the treasures of India, China, Persia, the Caspian and Black Sea regions, and even goods from as far as America and Europe, all converging at this remarkable trading hub. Merchants in colorful robes and Western suits alike gestured as they bartered, their practiced hands weighing silver coins and examining goods with expert precision. The more established traders had erected semi-permanent structures with intricate wooden carvings and brass fittings, while others made do with simple canvas awnings that snapped in the morning breeze, their shadows dancing across the cobblestones below.

The scene defied description, a massive tide of humanity ebbing and flowing in all directions amid chaotic energy and clamor. While the local people and working classes displayed great animation, they were far surpassed by the visitors in their fervor. Among them were traders who had journeyed for twelve months across the expansive steppes of Central

Asia with their goods, knowing another year would pass before they saw their businesses again. The Nijni-Novgorod fair held such commercial significance that its yearly transactions reached the staggering sum of one hundred million dollars, a testament to its position as one of the world's great marketplaces.

In the open spaces between districts of this makeshift town, various entertainers gathered: mountain-dwelling gypsies read palms for gullible visitors who always frequent such gatherings, their weathered hands tracing life lines with practiced mysticism; Zingaris or Tsiganes (as Russians call these descendants of ancient Copts) performed their exotic songs and traditional dances, their colorful skirts whirling in mesmerizing patterns; foreign theater troupes presented Shakespeare adaptations to eager crowds, their makeshift stages adorned with tattered velvet curtains. Along the wide pathways, handlers led their performing bears, their massive beasts shuffling to primitive drum beats, while animal tamers in menageries wielded whips and heated irons, drawing harsh cries from their subjects that echoed through the bustling marketplace. In the central plaza's middle, surrounded by four rows of enthusiastic onlookers, "Volga sailors" sat on the ground as if aboard their vessel, mimicking rowing movements under directing their conductor's baton, he being the metaphorical helmsman of this imaginary boat, his commands carrying across the plaza like those of a true river captain. What a peculiar tradition, one that spoke to the deep connection between the Russian people and their mighty rivers!

At that moment, following an age-old tradition at the Nijni-Novgorod fair, hundreds of caged birds were released into the air above the massive crowd. Having: Having collected a few copecks from onlookers, the bird sellers unlatched their cages and freed their birds. A great flock of birds soared skyward, filling the air with cheerful songs, their wings catching the sunlight as they dispersed in all directions like scattered jewels against the azure sky.

That year, the prominent Nijni-Novgorod trade fair attracted two respected Western European journalists, Harry Blount from England and Alcide Jolivet from France. Jolivet, ever the optimist, found himself quite satisfied with the local accommodations and cuisine, leading him to write glowing reviews about Nijni-Novgorod in his journal, praising the hearty stews and fresh-baked bread served at local taverns. Blount's experience proved different, unable to secure either a meal or proper lodging, he was forced to sleep outdoors beneath the stars, with only his traveling cloak for warmth. This unfortunate situation prompted him to draft a scathing critique of the town, condemning innkeepers who turned away travelers willing to pay for even basic hospitality and shelter, noting in his dispatches how such treatment reflected on a city that prided itself on its international commerce.

With one hand tucked in his pocket and the other gripping a cherry-stemmed pipe, Michael Strogoff gave the impression of being calm and unruffled. However, anyone watching would have noticed the occasional tensing of his eyebrows, betraying his intense eagerness to depart. His fingers drummed an unconscious rhythm against the smooth wood of the pipe stem, another subtle tell that belied his outward composure.

For two hours, he wandered through the streets, finding himself drawn back to the marketplace. As he moved among the merchants and shoppers, he noticed the traders from Asia's borderlands showing clear signs of distress. Their business was declining, with many merchants whispering among themselves in their native tongues while casting furtive glances at their dwindling stocks of silk, spice, and leather goods. Another detail caught his attention. In Russia, you find military personnel everywhere. However, today was different. The soldiers, Cossacks, and other military forces were absent from the bustling market, leaving an unsettling void in the usual rhythm of commerce and surveillance. Most likely, they were confined to their barracks, anticipating imminent deployment orders, their absence speaking volumes about the gravity of the situation developing beyond the city's walls.

A flurry of military activity was clear, though not from the common soldiers. Since the previous evening, officers and aides had been rushing to and from the governor's residence on horseback in all directions, their mounts' hooves clattering against the cobblestones as they carried dispatches with increasing urgency. The heightened activity suggested something of grave importance was unfolding. Messengers traveled along the routes to both Wladimir and the Ural Mountains, their horses lathered with sweat from the relentless pace, while telegraph lines to Moscow buzzed with non-stop communications, the operators working in shifts to handle the volume of encrypted messages.

The news of the police chief's urgent summons to the governor-general's palace spread through the central square where Michael Strogoff stood, passed from merchant to merchant in hurried whispers. Word had it that a crucial message from Moscow had arrived, carried by a special courier who had ridden through the night.

"They're shutting down the fair," someone called out, the announcement sending ripples of concern through the gathered crowd.

"The Nijni-Novgorod regiment has been given marching orders," another voice announced, triggering a wave of murmurs and worried exchanges among the merchants who had traveled so far to attend the fair.

"I hear the Tartars are threatening Tomsk!" The words rang out like a gunshot, causing nearby merchants to grab at their purses and goods.

The crowd erupted with shouts of "The head of police is here!" Thunderous applause broke out across the gathering, dying down until complete stillness fell over the assembly. Women pulled their children closer, and merchants ceased their haggling mid-sentence. As the police chief made his way to the center of the square, everyone could see he was clutching an official document, its imperial seal glinting in the morning sun.

Breaking the silence, he proclaimed in commanding tones, his voice carrying to every corner of the hushed marketplace: By a decree of the Governor of Nijni-Novgorod:

First, the government prohibits all Russian citizens from leaving the province for any reason; immediate arrest will follow.

"Second: All persons of Asian descent must vacate the province within twenty-four hours, taking with them only what they can carry."

QuantumDigitalPublishing.io
Book 1 - Chapter VI

Chapter Six

BROTHER AND SISTER

These restrictions caused significant hardship for individuals and disrupted countless lives and livelihoods, the volatile political situation left no other reasonable choice for maintaining security.

The order prohibiting all Russian subjects from leaving the province served a crucial purpose; if Ivan Ogareff remained, it would make it difficult for him to join Feofar-Khan and assume a dangerous leadership role in the Tartar forces. The military authorities understood that restricting movement was essential to containing potential threats, even at the cost of civilian inconvenience.

The decree mandated that any person of Asian descent must depart from the province within twenty-four hours, allowing just enough time to gather essential belongings and make hurried travel arrangements. This sweeping order would expel all merchants from Central Asia, along with various nomadic groups like the Bohemians and gypsies, whom they suspected of having ties to the Tartars. Russian authorities viewed these diverse populations as potential security risks, each individual serving as an informant or spy in the growing network of insurgency, making their removal a matter of urgent necessity. Harsh measures reflected the administration's growing anxiety about the deteriorating situation along the frontier.

The town of Nijni-Novgorod, bustling with visitors and boasting of Russia's most vibrant commercial center, reeled from the impact of these dual proclamations. Local merchants whose ventures extended beyond Siberia found themselves stranded within the province. The first declaration was unambiguous and absolute, brooking no exceptions, individual concerns had to bow before public necessity. The second proclamation, while targeting only foreign traders of Asian descent, left them no choice but to gather their wares and retrace their journey homeward. Perhaps most severely affected were the traveling performers and entertainers, who faced an arduous journey of a thousand miles to reach the closest border, a predicament that spelled genuine hardship for these wandering artists. As vendors dismantled their stalls and packed away their goods, the bustling marketplace fell into an eerie quiet. The air was thick with whispered conversations and hurried negotiations as merchants attempted to salvage what business they could before their forced departure. Even the local taverns and inns, usually teeming with traders sharing tales over steaming cups of tea, took on a somber atmosphere as their regular patrons made preparations to leave.

Objections and cries of anguish arose in response to this extraordinary order, but the watchful Cossacks silenced these protests with

law enforcement officers, their stern faces betraying no sympathy for the desperate pleas. The massive evacuation of the sprawling grounds begun without delay, proceeding with mechanical efficiency. Vendors collapsed their canopy covers with trembling hands, theatrical structures dismantled board by board. The campfires extinguished, leaving trails of acrid smoke, and circus performers took down their rigging with practiced but heavy movements. The weary, wheezing horses that pulled the traveling wagons emerged from their temporary shelters, their hooves clattering against the worn cobblestones. Officers and military personnel, wielding whips and batons, hurried along with those who lingered, showing no hesitation in destroying the shelters even while the unfortunate nomads still occupied them, sending splinters of wood and shreds of canvas flying through the air.

Vigorous actions clarified that Nijni-Novgorod's square would become empty by nightfall, with the bustling marketplace's noise giving way to an eerie stillness that seemed to echo off the surrounding buildings like a ghostly reminder of what once was.

Nomadic tribes faced an even harsher reality beyond the initial expulsion order. Authorities prevented them from returning to their homes and from seeking refuge in Siberia's vast steppes, where generations of their ancestors had roamed across the snow-dusted plains. Their only options lay southward, toward Persia, Turkey, or Turkestan plains near the Caspian Sea, territories that promised uncertain welcome at best. The Russian authorities had established strict boundaries with unwavering severity: these displaced people could not cross the Ural River post or the mountain range that extended along Russia's frontier, creating an impenetrable wall of bureaucracy and military might. This meant they had no choice but to embark on an arduous journey of six hundred miles, traversing treacherous terrain and hostile weather, before reaching any territory where they could settle, assuming they survived the grueling exodus with their families and meager possessions intact.

As the police chief concluded reading the proclamation, a thought struck Michael Strogoff. He found it strange how the proclamation's order to expel all foreigners of Asian descent coincided with the previous evening's conversation between the two Zingari gypsies. He recalled the old man's words: "The Father himself sends us where we wish to go." Everyone knew that "the Father" was how common people referred to the emperor. This raised troubling questions in Strogoff's mind: How had these gypsies expected this decree? What prior knowledge did they possess? Where were they planning to go? Something felt amiss about these individuals, and Strogoff suspected that rather than hindering them, the government's proclamation might serve their purposes. The timing was too precise to be mere coincidence, and their confident demeanor suggested they had been preparing for this very moment.

These thoughts vanished as another consideration consumed Michael's attention. The Zingaris, their cryptic remarks, and the peculiar timing of the proclamation all faded from his mind. Instead, his thoughts turned to the young Livonian girl. "Poor child," he mused. "The border is now closed to her." He could picture her delicate features twisted with worry, her hopes of reaching her destination now dashed by the stern words of bureaucracy. The thought of her alone and stranded in this hostile environment weighed heavily on his conscience.

The Livonian maiden, who hailed from Riga, found herself in a precarious position. Being a Russian subject by virtue of her birthplace in the Baltic province, she was now bound by law to remain within Russian borders, trapped by circumstances beyond her control. Her previous travel permit, got through proper channels and at considerable expense, had become nothing more than worthless paper considering enacted regulations. With Siberian routes now closed off and military checkpoints multiplying by the day, she could not pursue her journey to Irkutsk, regardless of how urgent or important her reasons might be for wanting to reach that distant city nestled in the heart of Siberia.

Michael Strogoff pondered on this matter, his brow furrowed in concentration. He reasoned that while staying true to his crucial mission, he might find ways to assist this courageous young woman, an idea that resonated with his sense of duty and honor. Having a clear understanding of the severe risks that he, as a strong and capable man well-versed in the ways of rough travel, would face, he realized the dangers would be far more threatening for an unaccompanied young woman in these turbulent times. Her journey to Irkutsk would follow his same route through the vast Siberian wilderness, requiring her to navigate through hostile invading forces just as he planned to do. Even if she had sufficient funds for normal travel conditions, which seemed unlikely given her modest appearance, how could she manage a journey that had become both treacherous and costly, with prices for safe passage rising as dangers increased?

"Well then," he mused, "should she journey toward Perm, it's almost certain our paths will cross. I can keep a protective eye on her without her knowledge, and since she seems just as eager as I am to reach Irkutsk, she won't slow my progress. Perhaps fate has arranged this meeting for a purpose."

But thoughts have a way of flowing into one another, like tributaries joining a mighty river. Until now, Michael Strogoff had considered his actions charitable, but a new perspective dawned on him, casting the situation in an different light, one that made his pulse quicken with revelation.

He pondered, muttering to himself, his fingers drumming against the window sill. "I require her help far more than she could ever need mine. With her by my side, I'll draw less unwanted attention. A solitary traveler crossing the steppe might be suspected of being the Czar's messenger. However, if this young woman travels with me, I'll match the Nicholas Korpanoff described in my podorojna, just another ordinary merchant making his way east with a companion. She must join me. There's no other way. I must track her down, whatever it takes. She hasn't found transportation to leave Nijni-Novgorod since last evening, not with the current chaos in the city. I must search for her now. Heaven, help me find her!"

Standing amid the chaos of Nijni-Novgorod's main square, Michael scanned the crowd for any sign of the girl. The scene before him was one of utter confusion, expelled foreigners protesting their treatment, while Cossacks and government agents herded them away, creating a deafening din. Merchants packed their stalls, fearful of the growing unrest, while bewildered travelers clutched their papers close. He knew she wouldn't be found in this mayhem. The morning was still young, just past nine, and with the steamboat's departure not until noon, he had two precious hours to locate her and convince her to join him as his fellow traveler.

He made his way back across the Volga and searched through the neighborhoods beyond, finding them much less crowded. The narrow streets offered a stark contrast to the square's pandemonium, with only the occasional sound of shutters being drawn or hushed conversations behind closed doors. He visited the churches, those sanctuaries that draw in all who grieve and suffer, their ancient stone walls offering solace to the desperate and displaced. But the young Livonian woman was nowhere to be found among the scattered worshippers kneeling in prayer.

He insisted to himself that she was still in Nijni-Novgorod, and he refused to believe otherwise. He spent two more hours wandering the streets, driven by a powerful inner force left no room for weariness or conscious thought. The afternoon sun cast long shadows across the cobblestones as he checked every alley and courtyard. Yet despite his relentless efforts, he found no trace of her.

A thought came to him. Could the girl be unaware of the decree? Though he dismissed this as unlikely, since such a momentous announcement would have reached everyone's ears by now, rippling through the city like waves on the Volga. Given her keen interest in even the tiniest updates from Siberia, her constant vigilance for news of any kind, it seemed impossible that she wouldn't know about the governor's proclamation, especially since it affected her.

However, if she remained unaware, she would arrive at the quay within the hour, joining the crowd of hopeful travelers, only to have some heartless official deny her passage and dash her hopes to pieces! He had to find her before then and prevent such a cruel rejection, no matter what it took. The thought of her facing such disappointment spurred him to quicken his pace once more.

Try as he might, his search proved futile, and he lost hope of locating her. As the clock struck eleven, Michael considered showing his podorojna papers from the Czar at the police chief's office. While the proclamation didn't apply to him, since his situation had been expected, he wanted to ensure there would be no obstacles to his departure from the town.

Michael crossed back over the Volga to the district where the police chief's headquarters were located. Despite orders for all foreigners to leave the province, they still had to complete mandatory paperwork before departing, which had drawn a massive throng of people to the area. The crowd stretched down several blocks, with anxious faces peering out from beneath parasols and hat brims as they waited in the summer heat.

To prevent Russian sympathizers of the Tartar cause from sneaking across the border in disguise, strict security measures were enforced. Anyone seeking to leave required official authorization, even if turned away. Guards scrutinized documents with painstaking attention to detail, comparing signatures and seals against reference materials while questioning travelers about their destinations and purposes. The process was slow and methodical, causing tempers to flare among those who had already spent hours waiting their turn.

The police station bustled with a diverse crowd, traveling performers, Roma people, and wandering tribes mixed with traders from across Asia, including merchants from Persia, Turkey, India, Turkestan, and China, all crowding the courtyard and administrative offices. Their colorful attire and varied languages created a tapestry of cultures beneath the stern institutional walls.

The masses rushed, knowing transportation would be scarce for the throng of exiled citizens. Those who delayed risked being stranded in the city past the deadline, leaving them vulnerable to harsh treatment by the governor's officers, who were already beginning to show less patience with each passing hour.

Through his powerful arm strength, Michael managed to make his way across the courthouse, shouldering past the press of bodies and ducking under extended arms clutching papers. Getting to the clerk's window inside the office proved far more challenging, with the crush of humanity bottlenecking at the narrow doorway. Yet, with a whispered word to an inspector and the strategic placement of some roubles, he secured his passage. After escorting Michael to the waiting area, a quiet alcove away from the main crowd, the inspector left to summon a senior clerk. Michael Strogoff felt confident he would soon resolve matters with the authorities and regain his freedom of movement, though he kept his expression neutral as other waiting travelers cast curious glances his way.

As he waited, his eyes wandered around until they landed on a striking sight. A young woman slumped on a bench caught his eye; her body language betrayed deep anguish, although her face was hidden, only her profile visible against the whitewashed wall. Michael Strogoff recognized her. It was the young Livonian girl, her delicate features as memorable as they had been during their brief encounter on the train.

She had visited the police station seeking approval for her travel documents, unaware of the governor's latest directives. The officials declined to allow her papers, their bureaucratic refusal delivered with cold indifference to her obvious distress. While she had permission to travel to Irkutsk, the new mandate was absolute. It superseded all prior approvals and blocked any civilian passage into Siberian territory. Michael, thrilled to have crossed paths with her again in such an unlikely place, made his way toward the young woman, weaving between the wooden benches and scattered travelers.

Her eyes lifted, and a smile spread across her features as she recognized the familiar face of her fellow traveler. The shadow of despair that had clouded her countenance moments before gave way to a glimmer of hope. She stood up, desperate hope filling her chest as she prepared to beg for his assistance, like someone flailing in deep water, reaching for anything that might save them. Her trembling hands clasped together as she waited for him to approach.

Just then, the agent's hand landed on Michael's shoulder, his fingers pressing into the fabric of his coat. "The police chief is ready for you now," he announced in a clipped, official tone.

"Excellent," said Michael with practiced neutrality. Without acknowledging the person he'd spent the entire day searching for, without even the slightest nod or fleeting glance of comfort that might put either of them at risk, he turned and followed his guide down the crowded corridor.

The young Livonian woman slumped back onto her weathered wooden bench, watching as the only person she could turn to for help vanished into the maze of administrative offices. Her shoulders sagged with the weight of renewed despair.

Michael Strogoff returned in less than three minutes, with the agent striding by his side. He was clutching his podorojna, the document that would grant him passage through Siberia, with an air of quiet triumph. Without breaking stride, he walked over to the young Livonian woman and extended his hand toward her, his expression neutral but his eyes conveying silent reassurance.

"Sister," he said, the single word carrying the weight of a sacred promise.

The word struck her with immediate understanding, resonating through her like a bell's obvious tone. She stood up at once, as though moved by an unexpected divine insight that left no room for doubt, her previous despair melting away like morning frost in sunlight.

"Sister," Michael Strogoff said again, his voice gentle but firm, "they have given us permission to carry on our journey to Irkutsk. Would you like to accompany me?" His steady gaze conveyed the depth of protection this offer entailed.

"I'll come with you, brother," the young woman answered without hesitation, slipping her hand into Michael Strogoff's with the trust of a lifelong sibling. Her fingers trembled, but her grip was sure. Together, they stepped out of the police station and into the crisp air, leaving behind the suffocating bureaucracy that had threatened to derail both their journeys.

Chapter Seven

GOING DOWN THE VOLGA

Just before noon, the steamboat's bell called a sizeable crowd to the Volga wharf. The gathering included not just willing passengers, but also many who were traveling under duress, their faces drawn with resignation and worry. The Caucasus stood ready for departure, its boilers operating at maximum pressure, the metal sides of the vessel vibrating with contained energy. Wisps of smoke drifted from the funnel, while white vapor crowned both the escape-pipe's end and valve covers, creating a hazy curtain against the late summer sky. The police maintained a strict surveillance over the Caucasus's departure,

interrogating travelers and turning away any whose responses they found unsatisfactory, their stern faces brooking no argument.

On the quay, many Cossacks stood ready to support the agents if needed, their sabers glinting in the midday sun and their horses pawing at the wooden planks, though their intervention proved unnecessary as everyone complied without protest. At the appointed time, when the final bell tolled its deep, resonant note across the water, the steamboat's mighty engines churned the water into a frothy wake, and the Caucasus navigated between the twin sections that made up Nijni-Novgorod, leaving behind a collection of waving handkerchiefs and worried faces on the shore.

With little trouble, Michael Strogoff and his young Livonian companion secured passage aboard the Caucasus. The podorojna document, issued in the name of Nicholas Korpanoff, permitted this supposed merchant to travel through Siberia with company. They appeared as siblings journeying under official protection, their matching dark attire and reserved demeanor lending credence to the deception. Side by side at the ship's stern, they watched the troubled city grow smaller, still in upheaval from the governor's proclamation. The afternoon sun cast long shadows across the deck as smoke billowed from the steamboat's twin stacks overhead. Michael maintained his silence, asking the girl nothing, waiting for her to speak when she felt the need. Eager to flee the town where she would have remained captive if not for her unexpected guardian's timely aid, she too stayed quiet, her delicate hands gripping the ship's railing as she gazed at the receding shoreline. Yet her grateful glances spoke volumes, and the slight trembling of her shoulders betrayed the emotion she struggled to contain.

The majestic Volga River, known to ancient civilizations as the Rha, stretches three thousand miles, making it Europe's longest waterway. While its upper reaches contain somewhat unhealthy waters, they become cleaner after merging with the swift-flowing Oka River at Nijni-Novgorod, which originates in Russia's central regions. Russia's intricate network of rivers and canals resembles an enormous tree, with waterways branching throughout the empire. At the heart of this system stands the Volga as the main trunk, culminating in seventy distinct channels that empty into the Caspian Sea. Ships can travel the river from its delta all the way to Rjef, a settlement in Tver province, covering most of its impressive length. Along its banks, countless villages and towns have flourished for centuries, their church spires and wooden houses dotting the landscape like pearls on a string. The river's might has shaped not only Russia's geography but also its culture, commerce, and very identity, earning it the cherished nickname "Mother Volga" among the Russian people who depend upon its waters for sustenance and trade.

The steamboats traveling between Perm and Nijni-Novgorod cover the 250-mile journey to Kasan. These vessels benefit from the Volga's current, which adds two miles per hour to their speed, allowing passengers to watch the rolling countryside and riverside settlements glide past at a satisfying pace. However, upon reaching the junction with the Kama River just below Kasan, the boats must leave the Volga and navigate upstream on the smaller Kama to reach Perm. Even with its powerful engines, the Caucasus could only achieve ten miles per hour against the Kama's current, its paddle wheels churning against the resistant waters. With a one-hour stop in Kasan, where passengers could stretch their legs and purchase refreshments from local vendors, the complete journey from Nijni-Novgorod to Perm takes between 60 and 62 hours.

The steamship featured an excellent layout with three separate passenger classes based on social standing and wealth, each deck maintained to meet the expectations of its occupants. Having booked two premium cabins in first class, with their polished brass fittings and plush velvet furnishings, Michael Strogoff ensured his young traveling companion could withdraw to her private quarters whenever she desired, away from the curious glances of fellow passengers.

The steamship Caucasus carried a diverse array of travelers; its decks vibrated with the diverse cultures that defined trade along the great waterways. Several merchants from Asia had departed Nijni-Novgorod without delay, eager to resume their business dealings before winter's approach. The first-class section hosted an eclectic mix of passengers: Armenian traders in flowing robes and distinctive miters, their animated conversations filling the air; Jewish merchants identifiable by their pointed caps, reviewing their ledgers; wealthy Chinese passengers in their traditional attire of loose-fitting robes in blue, violet, or black silk, moving with measured grace; Turkish travelers sporting their customary turbans of finest cotton; Indian traders wearing square caps and simple cord belts, some of whom controlled much of Central Asia's commerce through ancient family networks; and Tartar merchants in braided boots and embroidered shirts that sparkled with metallic thread. They forced these traders to stow their many trunks and packages both below deck and on the main deck, creating narrow passages between towering stacks of cargo. The transportation costs for their belongings would be substantial, as regulations permitted only twenty pounds of luggage per passenger, a restriction that caused no small amount of grumbling among those whose livelihoods depended on their wares.

Aboard the Caucasus, clusters of passengers gathered near the bow, including both foreigners and Russians who had permission to return to their provincial towns. Among them were mujiks wearing their traditional caps and checked shirts beneath flowing pelisses, their weathered faces bearing witness to lives spent working the land. Volga peasants stood out in their distinctive attire: blue trousers tucked into well-worn boots, rose-colored cotton shirts cinched with cords, and felt caps pulled low against the sun. Several women dotted the crowd, dressed in floral cotton garments, colorful aprons, and vibrant headscarves that fluttered in the river breeze. These passengers, traveling third-class, seemed untroubled by their lengthy journey home, sharing bread and stories as they watched the shoreline drift past.

As the Caucasus sailed on, it passed countless vessels being towed upstream, all bound for Nijni-Novgorod with their cargo. A endless procession of wooden rafts drifted by, their rough-hewn logs lashed together with heavy rope, followed by barges so laden their sides dipped beneath the water's surface. The bargemen called out to each other across the water, their voices carrying news and greetings. However, their journey was futile because the large fair they were headed to shut down at the beginning, causing significant losses for merchants and traders.

The steamer's wake sent waves crashing against the shoreline, startling clusters of wild ducks into flight with a cacophony of alarmed calls. A few herons, disturbed by the commotion, lifted from the shallows on wide gray wings. Beyond the water's edge, sparse herds of cattle, sheep, and pigs dotted the parched pastures, which were fringed by drooping willows and trembling aspens. Here and there, weathered wooden fences marked property boundaries, their posts listing at odd angles in the dry earth. The land stretched outward in a patchwork of meager buckwheat and rye fields, rising gradually toward distant hills that lay half-tamed by cultivation. A few isolated farmhouses stood like lonely sentinels amid the crops, their chimneys sending thin wisps of smoke into the cloudless sky. The entire vista possessed a stark simplicity that would have left even the most determined landscape artist wanting, its unadorned features offering little to capture on canvas.

"We've been on the Caucasus for two hours now," said the young Livonian woman, adjusting her shawl against the river breeze as she turned to Michael. "Tell me, brother, is Irkutsk your destination?"

"Indeed it is, sister," Michael replied with a gentle nod, his eyes scanning the distant horizon. "Since we share the same path, wherever my journey takes me, you'll be welcome to follow."

"Tomorrow, brother, I'll explain why I've traveled so far from the Baltic shores, venturing beyond the Urals," she said, her voice carrying a hint of weariness that matched the pallor of her face.

"There's no need for explanations, sister," he responded, noting how her shoulders seemed to sag with an invisible burden.

"I will tell you everything," the girl said, managing a weak smile that didn't quite reach her eyes. "Sisters shouldn't keep secrets from their brothers. But I can't do it today. I'm too exhausted and heartbroken."

"Would you like to retire to your cabin to rest?" Michael Strogoff asked, concern clear in his tone as he observed her growing fatigue.

"Yes, yes; tomorrow," she murmured, her words trailing off like leaves caught in the river's current.

"Let's go then..."

He stopped mid-sentence, wanting to add his companion's name at the end, but couldn't since he still didn't know it. The omission hung between them like an unfinished bridge, reminding him how much remained unknown about his newfound traveling companion.

"Nadia," she said, extending her hand in greeting, her voice soft but steady despite her obvious exhaustion.

"Please, Nadia," Michael responded with gentle warmth, "feel free to rely on your brother Nicholas Korpanoff." With that, he guided her through the narrow corridor to the private cabin he had arranged for her, located just beyond the saloon's polished wooden doors. The small room wasn't luxurious, but it would provide the sanctuary she needed.

Michael Strogoff made his way back to the ship's deck, breathing in the crisp evening air. Keen to gather any information that might affect his travels, he positioned himself among clusters of talking passengers, his back against a weathered railing. He remained silent, not wishing to join their discussions, but his ears caught every snippet of conversation carried on the breeze. If anyone questioned him, he planned to identify himself as Nicholas Korpanoff, a merchant returning to the border region for business matters. He was determined to keep secret his special authorization to journey into Siberia, knowing that even the slightest slip could jeopardize his crucial mission.

Passengers aboard the steamer, all of them from foreign lands, seemed consumed by the day's events and the implications of the new decree. These weary travelers, still recovering from their arduous trek through Central Asia, now faced the grim reality of turning back. Though seething with frustration and dismay, they kept their emotions in check, their voices hushed. A potent mixture of reverence and dread held their tongues. Rumors circulated around that police spies might be among them on the

Caucasus, monitoring their every word. Most deemed it wiser to maintain silence, recognizing that deportation, however unpleasant, was far better than languishing in a fortress prison. As a result, the men either remained quiet or spoke in such guarded whispers that gleaning any worthwhile information proved impossible. Even those who had journeyed together for weeks now kept their distance from one another, their previous camaraderie dissolved by suspicion. The deck's atmosphere grew heavy with unspoken fears as the sun was setting, casting long shadows that seemed to mirror the dark mood of its occupants. Several merchants who had invested in their planned ventures stood apart, their faces drawn with worry as they calculated their mounting losses.

A voice caught Michael Strogoff's attention, though he had gathered no useful information from the other passengers, who grew silent when he approached. The booming voice belonged to someone speaking Russian with a distinct French accent, addressing another passenger that seemed out-of-place amid the tense atmosphere on deck.

"Well, what a surprise!" the French-accented voice exclaimed, carrying across the deck with theatrical flair. "I didn't expect to see you here on this vessel. Weren't you at that grand imperial celebration in Moscow? I believe I also spotted you in Nijni-Novgorod. The world grows smaller by the day!"

"Indeed, it is I," the second person replied, their tone suggesting they wished the conversation hadn't begun at all.

"I must say, I hadn't expected such close pursuit," the Frenchman continued, oblivious to his companion's reticence.

"I'm not pursuing you, sir; I'm moving ahead of you," came the clipped response, tinged with concealed irritation.

"Moving ahead! Moving ahead!" the Frenchman chortled with exaggerated amusement. "Let's walk side by side instead, in perfect sync, like soldiers on parade. For now, at least, shall we agree that neither of us will overtake the other? It would make our journey far more pleasant, wouldn't you say?"

"I intend to pass you," the traveler stated, brooking no argument.

"That remains to be seen when we reach the battlefield. Until then, why not travel together? We'll have plenty of time and opportunity for rivalry later," the Frenchman offered with a conciliatory gesture.

"You mean enmity," came the cold correction.

"Enemies then, if you prefer. I must say, I appreciate your precise choice of words, my dear fellow. One always knows where they stand with you," he replied with an appreciative smile that went unacknowledged.

"How could it hurt?" The words carried a note of resigned acceptance.

"It wouldn't hurt at all. If I may, I'd like to outline where we both stand in this matter," the Frenchman pressed, seizing upon this slight opening.

"Go right ahead," came the weary permission.

"You're headed to Perm just as I am?"

"Just as you are," the companion confirmed.

"And I assume you'll continue from Perm to Ekaterenburg, as that's the most secure and reliable path across the Ural Mountains?" The Frenchman's tone grew animated.

"Most likely," was the noncommittal response.

"After crossing the border, we'll find ourselves in Siberia, right in the middle of the invasion," the Frenchman concluded, his voice taking on a more serious edge.

"Indeed, we will," came the flat acknowledgment, heavy with unspoken implications.

"Well then, only at that point should we say, every man for himself, and God for..." The Frenchman left the familiar phrase unfinished.

"For me." The words came out like ice chips.

"For you alone! Fine! But since we have seven neutral days ahead of us, and since we won't be getting any news updates during our journey across this desolate stretch, why not be friends until we become competitors again?" He spread his hands in an expansive gesture of reconciliation.

"Adversaries." The correction was swift and cutting.

"Yes, that's better, adversaries. But until then, let's work together instead of trying to sabotage each other. Though I promise to keep any observations, I make to myself." His tone carried a hint of wry amusement at their verbal sparring.

"I can hear everything." The companion's words held a warning edge that suggested both awareness and suspicion.

"Do we agree?" The Frenchman persisted, undaunted by the other's coolness.

"Yes, we do." The words came, as if dragged from unwilling lips.

"May I have your hand on it?" The Frenchman's eyes sparkled with genuine warmth.

"Of course."

“Adjusting his collar, the first man stated, “I sent the order’s exact wording to my cousin at 10:17 this morning.”

"And I dispatched it to the Daily Telegraph at 10:13." The response was cool and precise.

"Well done, Mr. Blount!" He gave a slight bow of acknowledgment.

“Mr. Jolivet, your work is impressive.”

"I'll do my best to top that!" Jolivet's characteristic enthusiasm bubbled through.

"It is challenging." Blount's mouth twitched in what might have been the ghost of a smile.

"Nevertheless, I'll make the attempt." He squared his shoulders with determination, ready for whatever lay ahead.

The two journalists exchanged greetings, the Frenchman with casual warmth and an expansive gesture, the Englishman with formal reserve and a perceptible nod. Though the governor's decree didn't apply to either of them, since they were Western Europeans with proper documentation and credentials, their shared professional instincts had led them both to depart from Nijni-Novgorod at the same time. It made sense that they would choose the same transportation and route across the vast, unforgiving Siberian plains. Whether as rivals or reluctant allies, they would travel companions for the next week until their proper work began, the race to deliver the most compelling news to their respective papers. After that, may the better reporter prevail! It was Alcide Jolivet who had reached out in friendship, extending his hand with characteristic Gallic charm, which Harry Blount had acknowledged, albeit with noticeable coolness and the stiff propriety typical of his countrymen.

At dinner that very evening, the chatty Frenchman and the reserved, stern Englishman were spotted sharing a table and engaging in conversation while enjoying authentic Cliquot, priced at six roubles per bottle and crafted from local birch sap. Their unlikely camaraderie drew curious glances from other diners, who found the contrast between Jolivet's expansive gestures and Blount's measured nods rather amusing. Upon observing their animated discussion, which drifted into heated debates about European politics and the merits of their respective journalistic methods, Michael Strogoff thought to himself, "These men seem rather nosy and intrusive, I'll cross paths with them again during my journey. I'd be wise to maintain my distance." He noticed how they scrutinized each new arrival in the dining room, their practiced eyes betraying their profession's inherent curiosity.

Between dinner and evening, the young Livonian woman remained in her cabin, sound asleep. Michael chose not to disturb her rest, knowing the rigors of travel could be especially taxing on someone in her delicate state. When she emerged onto the Caucasus' deck, the day was waning, her face showing the benefits of her extended repose. The extended dusk brought welcome relief from the day's oppressive heat, and passengers embraced the cooler air, their spirits lifting as the temperature dropped. As night approached, most preferred to stay on deck rather than retreat to the saloon below, seeking escape from the stuffiness of the interior cabins. They reclined on benches, savoring the gentle breeze created by the steamer's movement through the water, their conversations growing softer as evening settled in. During this season and at this latitude, true darkness never descended, the sky maintained a perpetual twilight between sunset and sunrise, bathing the river in an ethereal blue-gray light that seemed to hover between day and night, providing enough light for the helmsman to navigate the Caucasus among the many vessels traveling the Volga's waters, from small fishing boats to other grand steamers making their way along the great river's course.

The darkness was complete between eleven and two, with only a new moon in the sky, its faint presence discernible through wisps of passing clouds. Most travelers had drifted off to slumber on the deck, and the rhythmic splash of paddles against water was the sole sound breaking the quiet, punctuated by the distant cry of a night bird along the shoreline. Michael Strogoff, kept from resting by his worries, paced back and forth near the stern, his footsteps careful and measured on the wooden planks. At one point, he wandered past the engine-room, where the muted throb of machinery provided a steady heartbeat to the night, and into the section where second and third-class passengers were quartered.

Deep in slumber, passengers sprawled across every available surface, on benches, on cargo bales, and on the deck planks, their forms visible in the dim glow of the few remaining lit oil lamps. One had to step to avoid disturbing the sleeping forms that covered every inch of space, creating a maze of humanity that required careful navigation. Most were peasant workers, their bodies hardened by years of rough living, finding adequate rest even on the unyielding wooden deck, their weather-worn faces relaxed in sleep beneath rough wool caps and shawls. Yet despite their tolerance for discomfort, they would unleash a torrent of harsh words at any careless person who kicked them awake, their rural dialects making their complaints all the more colorful.

Michael Strogoff moved to avoid waking his fellow travelers, placing each foot with deliberate care between the sleeping forms. His stroll to the boat's edge was an attempt to ward off drowsiness through gentle exercise, though the late hour made even this simple task feel clandestine. As he approached the forward deck and began ascending the forecastle steps, voices caught his attention, hushed but animated tones that carried in the still night air. He paused, noting they emanated from a cluster of passengers bundled in heavy cloaks against the river's chill. The darkness concealed their identities, though the steamer's chimney would erupt in crimson flames, sending sparks cascading over the group like a shower of glittering sequins brought to life, illuminating the outlines of their hunched forms.

Just as Michael prepared to climb the ladder, his ears caught fragments of conversation in the peculiar language he'd encountered earlier at the nighttime fair, those same harsh consonants and rolling syllables that had struck him as so foreign before. Acting on instinct, he froze in place to listen more carefully, daring to breathe lest he give himself away. The darkness beneath the forecastle concealed his presence like a protective cloak, though he couldn't make out the speakers themselves through the deep shadows. He would have to rely on what he could hear, straining his ears to catch every whispered word floating down from above.

He caught snatches of conversation that seemed trivial at first, yet they enabled him to identify the male and female voices he'd encountered earlier in Nijni-Novgorod. The distinctive cadence and pitch were unmistakable, sending a chill down his spine. This discovery heightened his vigilance, as there was a distinct possibility that these same Tsiganes, now exiled, had managed to secure passage aboard the Caucasus, perhaps with motives as dark as the shadows concealing them.

The traveler's attentiveness proved fortunate, as he caught a conversation in Tartar between two speakers, their words cutting through the ambient sounds of creaking wood and lapping waves:

"Word has it that Moscow has dispatched a messenger to Irkutsk," said one voice, the words thick with significance and contained satisfaction.

"Indeed," replied Sangarre, her tone carrying a deadly certainty that made the hidden listener's blood run cold, "but this messenger's journey will be futile, he'll either reach his destination when it's too late, or never make it there at all."

Michael Strogoff flinched upon hearing these words that were clear about him, his muscles tensing beneath his travel-worn clothes. He peered through the gathering darkness, trying to confirm whether the speaking couple were indeed the ones he had in mind, but his efforts proved futile in the ship's deep shadows.

Michael Strogoff made his way back to the vessel's stern, his footsteps careful and measured on the damp planks, choosing an isolated spot where he sat alone, his face concealed behind his weathered hands. Though he appeared to be sleeping to any who might glance his way, his mind was far from resting. Instead, he wrestled with troubling thoughts that churned like the river waters below: "Who could have discovered my journey, and what do they stand to gain from this knowledge? How many other eyes might watch my every move?" The weight of his mission seemed to press even heavier upon his shoulders with each passing moment.

QuantumDigitalPublishing.io
Book I - Chapter VIII

Chapter Eight

GOING UP THE KAMA

On July 18th, at 6:40 AM, the Caucasus docked at the Kasan quay, which lay seven miles from the city.

Located where the Volga and Kasanka rivers meet, Kasan serves as the region's primary administrative center, hosting both a Greek archbishopric and a prestigious university. The city's diverse inhabitants maintain strong ties to their Asian heritage, clear in the colorful minarets that pierce the skyline alongside Orthodox church domes. Despite the considerable distance from the docking area, throngs of people gathered at the waterfront, eager for information about events further east. The morning sun cast long shadows across the crowd as they pressed forward, their worried murmurs carrying across the water. The provincial governor had enacted regulations matching those in Nijni-Novgorod, with stringent controls on movement. A contingent of police officers and Cossacks maintained order among the masses, their uniforms stark against the civilian clothing as they facilitated movement for both arriving and departing passengers of the Caucasus while conducting thorough inspections of papers and belongings. Two distinct groups emerged on the quay: the departing Asiatic peoples facing expulsion, their faces drawn with concern as they clutched their possessions, and the mujiks whose journey ended in Kasan, relief visible in their weathered features.

Standing at the quay, Michael Strogoff observed with detachment the typical commotion that accompanies a steamship's arrival, his trained eyes scanning the organized chaos below. Dock workers scurried about with practiced efficiency, while merchants hawked their wares to weary travelers. With the Caucasus scheduled for a one-hour stopover to replenish its coal supplies, Michael remained on board, positioning himself near the ship's railing. Concern influenced his decision for the young Livonian girl, who had yet to emerge on deck, and he was reluctant to leave her unattended, given the uncertain climate that seemed to pervade the port.

The early morning sun had crept over the horizon, casting long shadows across the weathered planks of the dock, when the pair of reporters began their day, following the time-honored tradition of hunters everywhere. Upon reaching the shore, they immersed themselves in the bustling throng, each pursuing his distinct investigative style with professional determination. Harry Blount captured the scene through detailed sketches and careful observations in his leather-bound notebook, his pencil moving with precise strokes as he documented the unfolding drama at the port. Meanwhile, Alcide Jolivet relied on his razor-sharp memory as he moved through the crowd with casual grace, gathering information through countless conversations, his cheerful demeanor and quick wit drawing out details from even the most reticent sources.

Reports circulated throughout the frontier about the growing scale of both the rebellion and invasion. Getting messages from Siberia and the empire had become challenging, with many couriers disappearing along the established routes. Michael Strogoff learned all these details from travelers who had just arrived, their faces drawn with concern as they shared their accounts. Such troubling news heightened his anxiety and strengthened his desire to cross the Ural Mountains, where the vast mountain range stood as both barrier and gateway to the heart of the conflict. Once there, he could assess the validity of these rumors and prepare for any developments. Considering how he might gather more specific information from a Kasan local, something unexpected caught his attention, drawing his gaze toward the crowded docks.

The band of Tsiganes that Michael had spotted at the Nijni-Novgorod fair the previous day was now among those departing the Caucasus, their distinctive presence impossible to miss in the morning light. He watched as the elderly Bohemian and his female companion directed their troupe of performers, twenty dancers and singers between fifteen and twenty years old, as they disembarked with practiced efficiency. The young artists wore weathered cloaks draped over their sequined costumes, the fabric telling stories of countless performances and long journeys across the countryside. As the morning sun caught their garments, casting prismatic reflections across the dock, Michael realized these were the same sparkles he had noticed in the night, glinting in the firelight from the steamboat's chimney like scattered stars against the darkness.

Michael muttered under his breath, "Strange, these Romani travelers stayed hidden below deck all day, then huddled beneath the forecastle after nightfall. This secretive behavior isn't typical of their people at all." He furrowed his brow, recalling how performing troupes reveled in attention, practicing their routines on deck to draw curious onlookers.

He was now certain that the whispered conversation he'd overheard had come from that swarthy group, between the elderly Romani man and the woman he'd called Sangarre, a Mongolian name. Almost unconsciously, Michael found himself drifting toward the gangplank as the nomadic band began departing the vessel, his footsteps matching their measured pace.

The elderly gypsy man sat there, his demeanor modest for someone of his bold heritage. He seemed to shrink from noticing rather than seek it out, as if trying to fade into the weathered planks of the dock itself. The countless seasons darkened his weathered hat, which he pulled low to shade his lined features, casting deep shadows across his face. Despite the warmth, he hunched beneath an old cape that wrapped around his frame, concealing his build like armor against prying eyes. His shabby attire made it impossible to discern his physical characteristics, though occasional tremors betrayed his advanced age. Beside him stood Sangarre, a Romani woman of about thirty years. She cut an impressive figure, tall and shapely, with a dusky complexion, striking eyes that seemed to pierce through anyone who dared meet her gaze, and hair the color of honey that cascaded past her shoulders in wild waves.

The young gypsy dancers were beautiful, each displaying the distinctive facial characteristics of their heritage, high cheekbones, olive skin, and eyes that sparkled with an ancient wisdom. Among the Tsiganes, such natural beauty is common, so much so that several prominent Russian aristocrats, in their attempts to match British nobility's unconventional ways, have taken Tsigane brides from among these dancers, scandalizing Moscow's more traditional social circles. One dancer's voice carried a haunting melody with an exotic rhythm, her words flowing with the practiced ease of generations of storytellers:

"Golden strands shimmer bright
Through my dark tresses, flowing
While crimson gems shine,
Round my neck softly glowing.
Free as winds in the sky
Through vast lands I must fly"

The song continued flowing from the girl's merry lips, her bare feet moving in perfect rhythm across the worn wooden floor, but Michael Strogoff's attention had wandered elsewhere. He noticed the Tsigane woman, Sangarre, studying his face with unsettling intensity as if attempting to burn his features into her mind. Her unwavering stare made him uncomfortable, though he refused to show it.

The moment lasted only before Sangarre departed, trailing after the elderly man and his group as they disembarked, her colorful skirts swishing against the weathered planks. "That gypsy has nerve," Michael thought to himself, his jaw tightening. "I wonder, could she have recognized me from

Nijni-Novgorod? These Tsiganes possess uncanny vision, like cats peering through darkness, their eyes missing nothing of importance. Perhaps that woman identified me beneath this merchant's guise..."

Strogoff considered pursuing Sangarre and her fellow travelers, but hesitated, his hand touching the papers hidden within his coat. "Better not," he reasoned to himself, forcing his muscles to relax. "Acting rashly by confronting the elderly fortune teller and his group could expose my true identity. They've only just come ashore, and I'll be well past the border before they can cross it. True, they might travel the Kasan-Ishim route, but that path offers little comfort to travelers, with its rough terrain and sparse settlements. And my tarantass, with its sturdy Siberian steeds, will outpace any gypsy wagon on those challenging roads! Relax, Korpanoff, all is well." Yet even as he reassured himself, a shadow of doubt lingered in his mind.

By then, both the man and Sangarre had vanished from sight, melting into the bustling crowd like shadows at midday.

Kazan serves as a well-deserved gateway to Asia and functions as a vital hub for trade between Siberia and Bokhara, with two major routes starting here that traverse the Ural Mountains. Michael Strogoff made a wise decision to select the path through Perm and Ekaterinburg. This principal thoroughfare, maintained with government-funded relay stations, extends from Ishim all the way to Irkutsk, offering travelers regular opportunities for rest and fresh horses at established posts along its length.

There is another path linking Kasan to Ishim, the very one Michael had mentioned, which bypasses Perm's minor diversion. While this alternative route might be shorter, several drawbacks: the complete lack of post stations, maintained roads, and scarce settlements along the way offset its benefits. The path winds through desolate stretches where travelers must fend for themselves, often going days without encountering another soul. Michael Strogoff had chosen; assuming the gypsies would take this second route between Kasan and Ishim, as seemed likely, he stood an excellent chance of reaching the destination ahead of them, given his superior means of transport and intimate knowledge of the terrain.

As the clock struck the hour, the Caucasus' bell echoed across the water, summoning fresh travelers and alerting those already aboard. Dawn had broken at seven, and the ship, supplied with fuel, hummed with anticipation. The vessel's frame quivered as steam coursed through its pipes, signaling its readiness to depart. The deck grew busy with travelers bound for Perm from Kasan, their luggage creating a maze of trunks and bags that the crew navigated.

Scanning the crowd, Michael observed that among the two journalists, only Blount had returned to the ship. He wondered if Alcide Jolivet would appear before departure, noting how the Englishman stood apart from the other passengers, writing in his ever-present notebook with his characteristic stern expression.

Just as they were about to cast off, Jolivet came rushing up to the ship, his coat flapping behind him as he sprinted along the dock. Though the Caucasus had already begun pulling away and the gangway had been removed, such obstacles didn't deter Alcide Jolivet. With an acrobatic leap worthy of a circus performer, he landed on the vessel's deck, colliding with his competitor, who stepped aside with a disapproving grunt while maintaining his writing stance.

"For a moment there, I thought you'd miss the boat," his rival remarked, glancing up from his notebook.

"Nonsense!" Jolivet retorted, brushing off his coat and straightening his cravat with practiced flair. "I would have caught up to you, either by hiring a boat and charging it to my cousin, or by paying twenty copecks per mile to travel by post and horse. What else could I do? The telegraph office was quite a trek from the waterfront, especially in this dreadful heat."

"Did you visit the telegraph office?" Harry Blount inquired, his lips tensing as his pen stopped mid-sentence.

"That's precisely where I went!" Jolivet replied with a beaming smile, delighting in his competitor's concealed interest.

"And is it still working for Kolyvan?" Blount's voice carried a hint of urgency now.

"I can't say for certain, but I can tell you one thing: the line between Kasan and Paris is operational." Jolivet leaned against the ship's railing, savoring the moment.

"Did you manage to send a message to your cousin?" The Englishman's stern demeanor cracked.

"Most eagerly." Jolivet's eyes twinkled with mischief.

"So you'd discovered...?" Blount's notebook now hung forgotten at his side.

"Listen here, my friend, as they say in Russia," Alcide Jolivet responded with a theatrical flourish, "I'm an honest man and won't hide anything from you. The Tartars, led by Feofar-Khan, have moved past Semipolatinsk and are following the Irtish downstream. Make what you will of that information!" He punctuated his revelation with a satisfied grin.

"By Jove!" Harry Blount fumed, his jaw clenching with suppressed frustration. His rival had scooped him on crucial intelligence, likely gathered from a Kasan local, and already dispatched it to Paris. The London papers would be playing catch-up, and his editors would be livid. Without a word, Blount crossed his arms behind his back, strode away with measured steps, and dropped heavily into a seat at the vessel's stern, where he stared at the churning wake below.

The morning sun had climbed to mid-height, casting dancing reflections off the river's surface, when the Livonian girl emerged from below deck, squinting in the bright light. Michael Strogoff moved to her side and grasped her hand with brotherly tenderness. "Sister, come look at this," he said, guiding her toward the Caucasus' bow where the magnificent riverscape stretched before them.

The travelers reached the meeting point of the Volga and Kama rivers in the Caucasus region, where the waters merged in a vast confluence that had guided merchants and travelers for centuries. After following the Volga downstream for three hundred miles through the heart of Russia, they would now change course to journey upstream along the Kama for an equal distance, fighting against the river's persistent current.

The Kama River stretched wide before them, its banks adorned with lush forests that swayed in the morning breeze. The water sparkled in the sunlight, dotted here and there with white sails of merchant vessels and fishing boats plying their ancient trade. Rolling hills formed the horizon, their slopes covered with aspens, alders, and majestic oaks whose branches reached toward the cloudless sky. Gaps in the treeline revealed small villages, their wooden houses and church spires, a testament to human persistence in this wild landscape.

Yet the young Livonian woman remained unmoved by this natural splendor, her thoughts fixed on matters beyond the scenic vista. Her hand still rested in her companion's, and she turned to him with a single question, her eyes reflecting determination rather than wonder: "How far are we from Moscow?"

"Nine hundred miles," Michael stated, his voice carrying the certainty of someone well-versed in Russia's vast distances.

"Only nine hundred covered, with seven thousand still ahead," Nadia whispered, her voice tinged with concern as she contemplated the enormous journey that still lay before them. The magnitude of their undertaking seemed to weigh on her slender shoulders.

The dining bell's clear ring interrupted their exchange, its resonant tone carrying across the deck. Nadia walked alongside Michael Strogoff toward the restaurant car, their footsteps echoing on the wooden planks. She ate, choosing modest portions fitting for someone of limited means, a small bowl of soup and a crust of dark bread. Observing her restraint, Michael chose a simple meal like hers, though his physique suggested a preference for richer food. Within twenty minutes, they had returned to the deck, settling themselves at the stern where the churning wake provided both spectacle and privacy. Without hesitation, Nadia leaned close to Michael and began speaking in hushed tones meant for his ears alone, her words lost in the steady thrum of the ship's engines.

"I am an exile's daughter," she said, her fingers twisting the worn fabric of her dress. "My name is Nadia Fedor. Just a month ago I lost my mother in Riga, and now I journey to Irkutsk to be with my father in his exile." Her voice carried the weight of recent grief.

"As it happens, Irkutsk is my destination too," Michael replied, his expression softening with genuine concern. "I would be grateful to Providence if I can deliver Nadia Fedor to her father's care."

"You are kind, brother," Nadia answered, the familial term carrying a note of trust.

Michael Strogoff mentioned he had secured a special travel permit for Siberia, and that no Russian official could interfere with his journey. The document bore the imperial seal itself, though he did not elaborate on how he had obtained such a privilege.

Nadia didn't press for more details. She viewed this chance encounter with Michael to reach her father more quickly, a stroke of fortune in otherwise dark times.

'I had a permit to travel to Irkutsk,' she explained, brushing a strand of dark hair from her face, 'but the new regulations canceled it. If not for you, brother, the town would have trapped me, and I would have died there.

'And you were willing, Nadia,' Michael asked, studying her with newfound respect, 'to brave the Siberian steppes all by yourself?'

"I hadn't heard about the Tartar invasion before leaving Riga. The news only reached me when I arrived in Moscow." Her voice remained steady, though her fingers twisted in her lap.

"Yet you chose to press on?"

"I had no choice. It was my duty." The words fell from her lips like stones, heavy with conviction.

Those simple words revealed everything about her courage and determination. In them, Michael recognized the same unwavering sense of purpose that drove his own journey across the vast Russian empire.

She went on to tell them about her father, Wassili Fedor, a respected doctor in Riga whose gentle hands had healed countless patients over the years. After authorities accused him of belonging to a secret organization, charges he vehemently denied until the end, they ordered him to relocate to Irkutsk. The police who delivered this decree had escorted him across the border, giving him no chance to put his affairs in order.

With only moments to spare, Wassili Fedor hugged his ailing wife and daughter before being dragged away in tears, his medical bag left forgotten by the door. Eighteen months later, his wife passed away while being cradled by their daughter, her final whispered words a plea to find him. Young Nadia Fedor found herself without parents and destitute, their modest savings depleted by her mother's lengthy illness. She requested permission from Russian authorities to reunite with her father in Irkutsk, which they granted, perhaps seeing no threat in a lone girl's journey. She informed him of her plans by letter, choosing words that would both comfort and prepare him for her arrival. Though her funds covered the extensive journey ahead, she remained resolute, selling what few family possessions remained to gather enough rubles for the first leg of travel. She would contribute whatever effort she could muster, taking odd jobs along the way if necessary, trusting divine providence to handle the rest.

Chapter Nine

DAY AND NIGHT IN A TARANTASS

On July 19th, the steamship Caucasus made its last stop along the Kama River at Perm. This bustling provincial capital governed one of Russia's most expansive regions, with territory stretching across the Ural Mountains into Siberia. The area was rich in natural resources, with extensive mining operations extracting marble, salt, platinum, gold, and coal. Despite its strategic importance as a gateway city, Perm itself was rather unsightly and lacking in amenities, with muddy unpaved streets and simple wooden buildings dominating the landscape. However, this mattered little to Siberia-bound travelers, who came prepared from more developed regions with all their essential supplies, from preserved foods to warm clothing and medical necessities.

In Perm, Siberian travelers sell their vehicles, which often show wear and tear from the extensive journey across the plains. The city's markets buzz with activity as merchants haggle over the price of well-used carriages and worn wheels. This city also serves as a key trading point where people journeying between Europe and Asia purchase carriages, or when winter comes, sleighs. Local craftsmen maintain busy workshops, repairing and outfitting these conveyances with the sturdy features needed for the harsh terrain ahead.

Michael Strogoff had planned his route. Though a mail carrier operated across the Ural Mountains, this service was no longer running. However, even if it had been available, Strogoff would have declined it, as he wanted complete control over his travel speed without relying on others. He made the prudent decision to gain his own carriage and travel in stages, knowing that self-sufficiency would be crucial for the challenging journey ahead.

Because of strict policies targeting Asian foreigners, many visitors had already departed Perm, making transportation scarce. Michael had no choice but to use whatever means of travel others had passed over, often settling for vehicles that were serviceable but far from ideal. While still in European territory, he could show his podorojna as the Czar's messenger, which gave him priority access to horses from the postmasters and allowed him to bypass the usual waiting periods at way stations. However, once he crossed into Siberia, he would have to rely on the purchasing power of his Russian currency, a prospect that demanded careful management of his financial resources. He knew prices often doubled or tripled beyond the Urals, where the harsh conditions and limited supply networks drove up costs for even the most basic necessities.

Deciding between transportation options, the traveler had to choose between a telga and a tarantass horse drawn carriage. The telga was a basic four-wheeled wooden cart, with its components held together by sturdy ropes. Despite its basic and uncomfortable nature, one significant advantage was its ease of repair should something break down during the journey. The Russian frontier had plenty of fir trees, so people could fashion replacement axles from the forest wood when necessary. The telga was robust enough to carry the "perck-ladnoi" (special express mail service) and could handle any road condition. Though the ropes sometimes broke, causing the back half to get stuck in mud while the front portion reached the post station on just two wheels, such outcomes were acceptable given the vehicle's practical nature. Local craftsmen were well-versed in making quick repairs to these simple conveyances, often using nothing more than rope, wooden pegs, and rough-hewn planks. Even in the most remote villages, local craftsmen could repair a broken telga and make it roadworthy within hours, a crucial consideration for anyone undertaking a long journey through Siberia's unforgiving terrain.

The fortunate discovery of a tarantass saved Michael Strogoff from having to use a telga. Russian coach-builders would do well to improve upon this vehicle's design. Like the telga, the tarantass lacks springs, and wood serves as a substitute for iron throughout its construction. However, its four wheels, set eight or nine feet apart, provide reasonable stability on rough roads. The splash-board protects travelers from mud, and one can draw a sturdy leather hood over the passengers to shield them from intense summer heat and severe storms. The tarantass shares the telga's durability and ease of repair, but proves more reliable in keeping all its parts together during travel. Its wider wheelbase and reinforced axles make it well-suited for the rutted paths and unexpected obstacles common along Siberian routes.

After a meticulous search through Perm, Michael located a tarantass, the only one in the entire city. To maintain his disguise as Nicholas Korpanoff, a humble merchant from Irkutsk, he made a show of lengthy price negotiations. He haggled with the owner, a weathered old man with decades of experience selling carriages, maintaining the demeanor of someone concerned about every kopek spent. The transaction took an hour of back-and-forth bartering, punctuated by dramatic sighs and reluctant counter-offers from both parties.

At his side during the search was Nadia, who shared his determination to find suitable transportation. Though their ultimate destinations differed, both displayed an identical sense of urgency, as if driven by a single, shared purpose. Their quick strides through Perm's dusty streets and focused expressions marked them as travelers who could not afford to waste precious time.

"Michael," Nadia said, wiping perspiration from her brow as they inspected yet another stable, "you needn't worry about my comfort during our journey."

"How can I not, dear sister, when you deserve far better than these harsh traveling conditions?" His voice carried genuine concern as he tested the worn suspension of the tarantass.

"Have you forgotten I would have walked the entire way on foot to reach Father if necessary?" She straightened her shoulders, her chin lifting with determination.

"Your bravery isn't in question, Nadia. I worry some hardships might prove too taxing for a woman." Michael's eyes softened as he regarded her, noting how young she looked despite her fierce demeanor.

"I will bear whatever difficulties come, without fail," she declared, her hands clasped before her. "The day you hear me complain is the day you can abandon me by the roadside and continue on alone." The steel in her voice left no room for argument, and her gray eyes flashed with an intensity that matched her words.

Thirty minutes passed before Michael showed his travel permit, after which they hitched three post-horses to the tarantass. These shaggy beasts, with their thick coats and long legs, resembled small bears. Though not large, the Siberian horses displayed a fierce spirit, pawing at the frozen ground and tossing their heavy manes in anticipation. The iemschik, or carriage driver, followed a distinct harnessing method: he placed the biggest horse between two lengthy shafts, which ended in a decorated hoop adorned with bells and tassels. Because the cold air was filled with the horses' breath, the iemschik used ropes to tie the other two horses to the carriage steps. They completed the setup using basic, smooth string reins for steering.

Neither Michael Strogoff nor his young Livonian companion traveled with any luggage. This benefited them, as the tarantass they rode in could only accommodate two passengers plus the iemschik driver, who displayed remarkable balance on his tiny perch, his weathered hands gripping the reins with practiced ease. Michael's need for swift travel and the girl's limited means made traveling light a necessity rather than a choice, though Nadia seemed unbothered by the sparse arrangements, her earlier determination clear in her straight-backed posture.

As they reached each relay station, a new iemschik took over driving duties. The driver from their first leg of the journey was a true Siberian, as untamed in appearance as his steeds. He had cut his wild hair across his brow, and he wore a hat with upturned edges and a crimson sash. His coat featured distinctive crossed lapels, adorned with buttons bearing the emperor's seal. Upon arriving with his horses, this iemschik cast a scrutinizing look at his tarantass passengers. The complete absence of baggage caught his attention, though, he wondered where any luggage could have fit. Taking in their rather worn appearance, his expression turned to one of obvious disdain.

"Crows," muttered the driver, indifferent to who might hear, "crows, for six copecks per mile!"

"Eagles!" Michael corrected him, well-versed in the driver's coded language. "Eagles, mind you, nine copecks per mile, with extra for your trouble."

The iemschik's weathered face brightened somewhat at this promise of additional payment, though his pride as a driver remained evident in his rigid posture. He clicked his tongue and adjusted his sash, a habitual gesture among the Siberian drivers that spoke of both impatience and acceptance. The distinction between "crows", common travelers who paid the minimum fare, and "eagles", more generous passengers, was one that could differ between a leisurely pace and the swift journey Michael required.

The driver's whip cracked in response, the sharp sound echoing across the station yard as he gathered the reins with practiced efficiency.

In Russian coachman slang, passed down through generations of drivers who plied the Empire's vast network of roads, their spending habits categorized passengers. The "crow" referred to thrifty or poor travelers who paid the bare minimum, just two or three copecks per mile for horse transport at post stations, often haggling over every kopeck. In contrast, the "eagle" described generous travelers who spent and gave substantial tips, earning their preferential treatment and the drivers' genuine respect. As one might expect, the "crow" couldn't hope to travel as swiftly as the noble "eagle," for a driver's enthusiasm often matched the weight of his passenger's purse.

Nadia and Michael settled into their seats in the horse-drawn carriage, testing the worn but sturdy springs beneath them. They stowed a modest supply of food, dried meat, hard bread, and several flasks of water, in the storage compartment, preparing for potential delays between the government-maintained rest stops, which were known for their good accommodations and regular spacing along the route. With the scorching heat bearing down, they raised the carriage's leather cover, adjusting its position to maximize shade while maintaining airflow, and as noon struck, they departed Perm, leaving a dusty trail in their wake as the wheels began their rhythmic turning on the well-worn road.

The coachman's skill at maintaining his team's swift pace would have amazed any foreign travelers unfamiliar with Russian or Siberian customs. The lead horse, more robust than its companions, maintained an unwavering extended trot regardless of the terrain's incline. Its two fellow steeds seemed to know only how to gallop, adding playful bounds to their stride. The coachman never struck them, relying instead on the sharp cracks of his whip to motivate them. He would shower them with colorful phrases and invoke every saint's name when they showed proper obedience. While the simple rope reins offered little control over these spirited animals, they responded to gruffly spoken commands, "na pravo" to turn right and "na levo" to turn left more effectively than any physical guidance.

The iemschik's words shifted between sweet encouragement and harsh scolding. When pleased, he'd call out: "Forward, my precious doves! Soar ahead, my beautiful swallows! Take wing, my darling pigeons! Keep strong, dear cousin on the left! Press on, beloved father on the right!" But when dissatisfied, his tone would turn sharp and biting, unleashing a torrent of creative insults that somehow spurred the horses to even greater speeds. The animals seemed to understand the subtle variations in his voice, responding as much to his melodic intonation as to the actual words themselves. Even during the most challenging stretches of road, where loose stones threatened to upset their rhythm, the horses maintained their pace through this curious dialogue with their master.

But when the horses slowed, his tone turned cutting, each barb striking the sensitive creatures: "Move yourself, you miserable snail! Curse you, you worthless slug! I'll cook you over flames, you wretched tortoise! Your bones will feed the wolves if you don't pick up those hooves!"

The tarantass sped along at twelve to fourteen miles per hour, powered by the iemschiks' forceful shouts rather than their physical strength. Michael Strogoff felt at ease in this style of transport, having grown accustomed to its particular quirks during countless journeys across the empire's vast expanse. The constant bumps and jolts didn't bother him, he well knew Russian drivers did not try to dodge obstacles like stones, ruts, bogs, fallen trees, or ditches in their path. They believed the shortest route was always straight ahead, regardless of terrain. Though his companion risked injury from the violent lurching of the tarantass, which threatened to shake loose every bolt and board, she endured it without complaint, her hands gripping the wooden rail with quiet determination.

Nadia remained quiet for a moment, her mind working through the calculations as the vehicle bounced along the rugged road. Then, focusing on her singular goal of completing their journey, she spoke up with the precise tone of someone who had studied the route. "By my calculations, the distance between Perm and Ekaterenburg is three hundred miles. Have I calculated correctly, brother?"

"Your calculation is accurate, Nadia," Michael confirmed, adjusting his position as the tarantass hit another bump. "Once we arrive in Ekaterenburg, we'll find ourselves at the base of the Ural Mountains, on their far side. The city marks the boundary between European Russia and Siberia."

"What's the duration of the mountain crossing?" she asked, her eyes scanning the horizon as if already searching for the mountain peaks.

"It'll take two days since we won't stop moving. And when I say, Nadia," he emphasized, his voice taking on a more serious tone, "I mean that. I can't afford any delays until I reach Irkutsk. Every hour counts on this journey."

"Don't worry about me, brother," she replied with quiet determination, her chin lifting. "I won't hold you back, not even for a single hour. I'm ready to travel non-stop. The hardships of the road don't frighten me."

"In that case, Nadia," he said, studying her resolute expression, "provided the Tartar invaders haven't blocked our path, we should make it in about twenty days. Though the road ahead won't be easy."

"Have you taken this route before?" Nadia inquired, leaning forward with interest.

"Several times," he answered, his eyes distant with memory. "I remember the path."

"Wouldn't winter conditions have made our journey quicker and more certain?" she asked, considering the alternatives.

"Indeed, you could have traveled faster, but the freezing temperatures and snow would have taken quite a toll on you," Michael replied, his voice tinged with concern. "The Siberian winter shows no mercy to travelers, no matter how determined they might be."

"That's of no concern! Russia thrives in winter conditions. Our people have conquered these lands for generations!"

"Indeed, Nadia! You need extraordinary resilience to withstand such harsh conditions. I've experienced temperatures plummeting beyond forty degrees below zero in the Siberian steppes! Despite wearing my reindeer fur, I felt my heart growing numb, my muscles seizing up, and my feet turning to ice even with three layers of wool socks. I watched as my sleigh horses became encased in frost, their breath freezing at their nostrils, forming delicate crystals that sparkled like diamonds in the pale winter sun. Even my flask of brandy turned solid as stone, so hard that my blade couldn't scratch it. Still, my sleigh raced forward like a gust of wind, the runners creaking against the frozen ground beneath. The vast white plain stretched, without a single hindrance! No rivers blocked our path, just solid ice everywhere, making for clear passage and reliable travel! But the true cost of such journeys, Nadia, can only be told by those who never made it back, their bodies forever lost beneath the blinding snowstorms. I've seen powerful men, veterans of countless winter treks, brought to their knees by nature's merciless grip."

"But you made it back to us, brother," Nadia said, her voice carrying a note of admiration.

"True, though remember I'm Siberian-born. From my earliest years, I would accompany my father hunting through the endless white forests, which toughened me against such harsh conditions. Yet Nadia, when you declared that winter wouldn't have deterred you, that you'd have made the journey alone, prepared to face Siberia's brutal weather, I could only picture you collapsed in the snow, your strength giving out, never to stand again."

"Tell me, how many winters have you spent crossing the steppe?" the young Livonian woman inquired, her eyes bright with determination.

"I've been there three times, Nadia, during my journeys to Omsk," he said, rubbing his hands together as if remembering the bitter cold.

"What business took you to, Omsk?" she inquired, leaning forward.

"I was visiting my mother. She was waiting for me there," he replied, his voice growing quieter with the memory.

"Well, I'm headed to Irkutsk myself, where my father waits," she responded. "I carry my mother's last words for him, words that must not die unspoken in the frost. So you see, brother, nothing could have stopped me from making this journey."

"You possess true courage, Nadia," Michael said, studying her face with newfound respect. "The Lord Himself must be guiding your path through these frozen lands."

The iemschiks took turns throughout the day, driving the tarantass at great speed from station to station. These "highway eagles" proved themselves worthy of their mountain-dwelling namesakes, their skilled hands guiding the troika of horses over rutted paths and through treacherous mountain passes with remarkable precision. The travelers earned special treatment thanks to their generous payment for horses and liberal distribution of tips, which ensured fresh mounts were always ready upon their arrival. While the postmasters might have found it curious that a young Russian man and his sister could traverse the closed territory of Siberia after the recent decree, their documentation was impeccable and their passage rights were legitimate, bearing all the necessary stamps and signatures.

During their journey from Perm to Ekaterenburg, Michael Strogoff and Nadia discovered they weren't traveling alone. The Czar's messenger had noticed another carriage ahead of them in the early parts of their trip, a well-appointed traveling coach that seemed to maintain a consistent lead of several miles but since horses were available at the stations, he wasn't concerned about it. The vast Siberian countryside could accommodate many travelers without their paths crossing.

Travelers would stop only to eat during daylight hours. Post-houses offered both accommodation and meals. Even without an inn nearby, Russian peasant homes proved welcoming. The villages, sharing a similar appearance with their white-walled chapels topped by green roofs, were hospitable. Any traveler could approach any house, and the door would open. The moujik (peasant) would emerge with a warm smile and welcoming hand, offering bread and salt to the visitor. They would light the samovar's coals and make their guest feel at home. The host family would even give up their own space to ensure the traveler's comfort, often insisting on sleeping in the barn or kitchen while giving their best rooms to their guests. In Russian culture, people viewed strangers as relatives, "one sent by God," and even the most modest households honored this sacred obligation of hospitality.

"How long since the last carriage passed through?" Michael asked the postmaster upon arrival that evening, his boots still dusty from the road.

"About two hours, little father," came the reply from the weathered old man.

"Was it a berlin carriage?"

"No, a telga."

"How many were traveling?"

"Two passengers," the postmaster answered, stroking his gray beard.

"Are they moving quickly?"

"Like eagles!" he exclaimed, spreading his arms wide for emphasis.

"Then have fresh horses readied at once," Michael commanded, already reaching for his travel papers.

The two companions maintained their relentless pace through the night, refusing any rest despite their mounting fatigue. While the weather held steady for now, the air grew thick and charged, heavy with foreboding. They hoped to avoid any storms while crossing the treacherous mountain passes, where such weather could prove catastrophic for travelers caught exposed on the winding roads. Drawing on his experience in reading nature's warnings, Michael recognized the telltale signs of an impending clash of the elements, the unnatural stillness, the metallic taste in the air, the way the horses tossed their heads.

The darkness brought with it no disturbances, though every shadow seemed pregnant with possibility. Despite the constant shaking and rattling of the carriage over the rough terrain, Nadia found several hours of fitful rest, her head bumping against the wooden frame. They had lifted the covering to allow what little fresh air they could get in the oppressive atmosphere, though the night breeze offered scant relief from the stifling heat.

Michael remained vigilant throughout the night, his eyes never leaving the road ahead, wary of the drivers who were known to doze while on duty despite the dangers. His hand stayed close to the reins, ready to take control if needed. They maintained excellent time, pushing the horses to their limits and wasting not a moment at the posting stations or during their journey, each delay feeling like an eternity to their urgent mission.

Early in the morning, around eight o'clock on July 20th, they first spotted the Ural Mountains rising on the eastern horizon. The massive mountain range, which forms the natural border between Russia and Siberia, lay far ahead of them, its jagged peaks visible through the morning haze. They realized they wouldn't reach it until nightfall, the daunting distance serving as a stark reminder of the challenging journey still ahead. They would have to traverse the treacherous mountain passes during the darkness of the following night, a prospect that filled them with equal parts determination and unease. Throughout the day, thick clouds rolled in and blanketed the sky, making the temperature more comfortable than the previous days' sweltering heat, though the weather showed ominous signs of becoming stormy, with distant rumbles of thunder echoing across the plains.

Climbing the mountains at night was likely unwise, and Michael would have waited if given the choice. The treacherous paths would be even more dangerous in darkness, with loose stones and sheer drops impossible to spot until it was too late. At the last stop, when the iemschik pointed out thunder echoing through the rocky terrain and gestured at the blackening sky, Michael asked,

"Can you see another telga ahead?"

"Yes."

"What's our distance behind it?"

"About an hour."

"Press on, I'll triple your payment if we reach Ekaterenburg by tomorrow morning." The promise of extra coin seemed to steady the driver's nerves, though his white-knuckled grip on the reins betrayed his lingering anxiety about the journey ahcad.

Chapter Ten

A STORM IN THE URAL MOUNTAINS

The imposing Ural Mountains serve as a natural divide between Europe and Asia, stretching over two thousand miles across the continent's heart like a colossal stone wall erected by nature itself. These mountains carry two names with identical meaning, "Urals" in Tartar and "Poyas" in Russian, both translating to "belt," describing their function as a vast mountain chain that cinches the landscape like a giant's belt. This magnificent range begins at the Arctic Sea's coast, where frozen winds howl across barren peaks, and extends all the way to the sun-baked Caspian borders, creating an unbroken barrier of jagged rock and dense forest. For Michael Strogoff, these mountains presented a crucial obstacle he needed to traverse before entering Siberian Russia, a challenge that would test both his resolve and his timing. While the crossing took just one night under normal conditions, moving through well-worn passes and along established routes, the situation now looked ominous. Distant thunder rumbled like artillery fire across the peaks, heralding an approaching storm that promised no mercy. Intense electrical energy charged the atmosphere; only a massive explosion could release it. This unusual atmospheric state promised dangerous conditions, with lightning crackling between clouds and the air vibrating with tension.

To prepare for their journey, Michael secured his young fellow traveler's safety. He reinforced the hood with additional ropes, creating a criss-cross pattern above and behind to prevent it from being torn away by the wind. He strengthened the vehicle by doubling the traces and packed the nave-boxes with straw, both to reinforce the wheels and reduce the jarring movements that were inevitable while traveling in darkness. As a final measure, he installed a crossbar with pins and screws to connect the front and back sections of the tarantass, which were held together only by axles to the main body. The modifications, though time-consuming, would prove essential for the treacherous journey ahead.

Nadia climbed back into the cart, and Michael positioned himself next to her. A pair of leather curtains hung from the lowered hood, offering some shelter from the harsh wind and rain. Two large lanterns attached to the iemschik's perch cast a dim glow that illuminated their path, but served as warning beacons to prevent collisions with other vehicles. The flames within the lanterns flickered against the strengthening gusts, their dancing light creating eerie shadows that stretched and wavered across the rough terrain ahead. Despite the reinforcements, the tarantass still creaked with each gust of wind that swept down from the mountains.

Their careful preparations proved wise, as a difficult journey lay ahead. The path climbed toward the thick, menacing clouds overhead. If these clouds didn't break into rain soon, the resulting fog would make it treacherous to guide the tarantass forward, with the constant risk of plunging over one of the steep drops that lined their route. Already, wisps of mist were curling around the wheels like ghostly fingers.

Although modest in elevation, the Ural mountain range's highest peak reaches about five thousand feet. Because the summer sun melts any snow accumulating on the mountains during Siberian winters; therefore, there is no permanent snow cover. The climate supports substantial vegetation, with trees and shrubs growing quite tall, their branches often reaching out over the narrow mountain paths like grasping arms. The region attracts many workers to its abundant mineral resources, including iron, copper, and precious stone mines, their rough-hewn entrances visible as dark mouths in the mountainsides. Small settlements called "gavody" dot the area, their smoke-stained buildings clustered around mine entrances and water sources. Horse-drawn carriages can travel through the well-maintained mountain passes, though the journey is never without risk.

The task may be straightforward in pleasant weather with clear skies, but it becomes treacherous when nature unleashes its fury and the wanderer finds himself caught in its midst. Having faced mountain storms before, Michael Strogoff was well aware of their ferocity, and he suspected this one might rival the brutal winter blizzards that terrorized these peaks, storms that had claimed the lives of many less-prepared travelers.

The clouds held back their rain for now, allowing Michael to lift the leather curtains that shielded the tarantass' cabin. He peered out into the darkness, observing the roadside where strange shadows danced, cast by the flickering glow of the lanterns that swayed from their mounting hooks. In her seat, Nadia remained still with crossed arms, her gaze fixed outward, while beside her, Michael's torso stretched halfway outside the carriage as he studied both the heavens and ground below, his experienced eyes searching for any sign of the impending tempest's arrival.

An eerie stillness hung in the air, like nature itself was holding its breath. Overhead paralyzed and unable to function, dense, dark clouds loomed overhead like lungs. Only their traveling carriage, with its grinding wheels, groaning axles, and snorting horses, broke the suffocating quiet, its iron-shod hooves striking sparks from the stones and echoing like tiny thunderclaps through the desolate landscape.

No one was on the empty thoroughfare. Through the tight mountain passes of the Ural, in the ominous darkness, their carriage passed without meeting anyone, no people on foot, no riders on horseback, not a single other vehicle. The dense woods also showed no signs of life; no charcoal makers had fires glowing in the forest depths, no miners' camps appeared near any excavation sites, and not a single cabin was spotted among the thick undergrowth. Even the nocturnal creatures that filled such wilderness with their calls and rustling seemed to have abandoned their usual haunts, as if warned away by some primal instinct that humans could not perceive.

Given this unusual situation, delaying until daybreak would have been understandable. Yet Michael Strogoff couldn't justify waiting. His duty demanded he press on. Still, a troubling question nagged at him: what could drive those travelers ahead in the telga to take such a reckless risk?

The lightning started flashing across the sky around eleven o'clock as Michael kept watch. The bright flashes revealed and concealed the silhouettes of towering pines, their branches swaying in the strengthening wind. Whenever their tarantass approached the road's edge, the illuminated depths of steep ravines became visible below, yawning like hungry mouths in the darkness. As their vehicle jolted hard, they realized they were crossing crude plank bridges spanning deep chasms, with thunder echoing beneath them, the rotting wood creaking under their weight. A growing roar filled the air as they climbed higher, like the voice of some ancient mountain spirit warning them away. Mixed with these sounds were the iemschik's calls, alternating between harsh reprimands and gentle encouragement to his struggling animals, his voice growing hoarse from the constant effort. The poor beasts, more affected by the heavy air than the rough terrain, stumbled, their flanks heaving with exhaustion, no longer responding even to their shaft bells' familiar jingle, which was lost in the howling wind.

"What time will we get to the ridge's peak?" Michael asked the iemschik or carriage driver, his voice audible over the howling wind.

"If we make it at all, one in the morning," he answered, shaking his head, his weathered face creased with concern.

"Surely you've weathered mountain storms before, my friend?" Michael pressed, trying to sound more confident than he felt.

"Indeed, and God willing, this won't be my final one!" the driver replied with a grim chuckle that seemed to catch in his throat.

"Are you frightened?"

"No, not frightened. But I stand by what I said, setting out was unwise." The iemschik's knuckles whitened as he gripped the reins tighter.

"Staying behind would have been even more unwise," Michael muttered, more to himself than the driver.

"Keep going, my little doves!" the iemschik called out to his horses, his voice carrying a mixture of determination and resignation. His duty was to follow orders, not question them, no matter how treacherous the path ahead might seem.

A piercing sound cut through the tranquil air. Lightning illuminated the scene with brilliant clarity, and before the deafening thunder could finish its roll, Michael glimpsed towering pines swaying atop a distant peak. Though the storm had unleashed its fury, it remained confined to the heights above, where the gale force winds wreaked havoc. The sharp crack of splintering wood echoed as tree after tree succumbed to the hurricane's mighty gusts. A cascade of broken trunks came crashing down, sweeping across the road and plummeting over the cliff's edge two hundred feet ahead of the tarantass.

The carriage lurched to a sudden halt, its wooden frame groaning in protest as the horses stamped at the ground, their breath visible in the chilled mountain air.

"Rise up, my lovely ones!" shouted the coachman, his whip cracking above the rolling thunder. He surveyed the treacherous path ahead, his weathered face etched with concern.

Michael reached for Nadia's hand, feeling her fingers trembling in the darkness. "Sister, have you fallen asleep?"

"No, dear brother," she whispered, her voice steady despite the chaos surrounding them.

"Brace yourself, the storm is almost upon us!" another flash of lightning that cast stark shadows across their faces punctuated Michael's warning, revealing the determination in their eyes.

"I'm prepared."

Just as Michael Strogoff pulled the leather curtains closed, the tempest struck with full force, rattling the carriage windows like angry fists against glass.

The coachman sprang from his perch to grab the horses' bridles, his boots sliding in the mud as he sensed the grave danger that now threatened them all.

A gust of wind held the tarantass motionless at a bend in the road, the wooden frame creaking under nature's assault. The driver had no choice but to keep the horses facing into the wind. If the carriage were caught sideways, it would flip and plummet down the cliff face into the darkness below. The terrified horses stood on their hind legs, their eyes rolling white with fear as their handler struggled to calm them. His soothing words had given way to angry curses, each one lost in the howling wind. Nothing seemed to work. The poor beasts, dazzled by lightning and startled by the constant thunder, tossed their heads and seemed ready to snap their harnesses and bolt at any moment. The iemschik had lost control of his team, his years of experience rendered useless against nature's fury.

In that instant, Michael Strogoff leaped from the carriage and hurried to help, his coat whipping around him as he fought his way forward. With his extraordinary physical power, he succeeded, though it wasn't easy, in bringing the horses under control, his muscles straining against their panic-driven strength.

The tempest intensified at that point; the wind howling like a thousand angry wolves through the mountain passes. A massive cascade of rocks and fallen trees started tumbling down the mountainside above their position, each boulder threatening destruction as it crashed downward.

"This spot isn't safe," Michael declared, his voice audible above nature's fury.

"Nowhere is safe," replied the coachman, his courage shattered by fear, hands trembling on the reins. "This storm will send us plummeting down the mountain by the quickest route possible."

"Handle that horse, you spineless fool," Michael snapped, muscles tensing as he gripped the bridle, "I'll take care of this one."

Another violent gust that sent leaves and debris cut the conversation short, flying past them like deadly projectiles. Both men had to drop to the earth to keep from being swept away, their faces pressed against the muddy ground. Despite their best attempts, and even with the horses straining against their traces, their vehicle slid backwards with an ominous groan until an enormous tree trunk halted its path toward the steep drop-off, the impact jarring everyone inside.

"Keep your courage, Nadia!" Michael Strogoff called out, fighting to maintain his footing in the treacherous conditions.

"I am calm," the young woman from Livonia answered, her tone steady and composed despite the chaos surrounding them, her hands folded in her lap.

The deafening thunder subsided as the fierce wind rushed down into the ravine below, carrying with it loose branches and debris that whirled past them like deadly projectiles.

"Are we turning around?" the iemschik asked, his voice audible over the howling gale.

"No, we must continue forward! After this bend, the hillside will protect us from the worst of it."

"The horses are refusing to move! They sense the danger!"

"Follow my lead and pull them along. We cannot stay here exposed."

"The storm is coming back! Look at those clouds!"

"Will you follow my command?" Michael's tone grew stern.

"Is that an order?" the driver challenged, squinting through the rain that pelted his face.

"It's an order from the Father!" Michael declared, invoking the Emperor's supreme authority for the first time, knowing the weight such words carried even in this remote wilderness.

"Onward, my swift ones!" the iemschik called out, grabbing one horse's reins while Michael took hold of the other, both men leaning into the wind as they urged the frightened animals forward.

The carriage inched forward as the horses strained against the brutal wind, their muscles trembling with exhaustion and fear. The animals could no longer rear up, their spirits broken by nature's onslaught, and the middle horse, less restricted than its companions, maintained position along the road's center, providing what little stability remained. Both men and beasts struggled against the gale, losing one or two steps backward, for every three gained forward, their determination tested with each painful advance. They stumbled on the rain-slicked ground, falling and rising again in their desperate advance, clothes and harnesses soaked through to crushing weight. The carriage teetered on its wooden wheels, the entire frame groaning and threatening to shatter at any moment against the merciless assault. Extra ropes and bindings secured the hood, or canvas top, preventing the wind from tearing it away earlier and leaving them vulnerable. Michael Strogoff and the iemschik spent over two hours traversing this treacherous half-mile stretch, exposed to the storm's fury, their faces raw from the stinging rain and debris. The peril came not only from the wind's relentless assault on the travelers but also from the deadly barrage of stones and broken tree trunks hurtling through the air like nature's artillery, forcing them to duck and weave while maintaining their desperate grip on the reins.

A brilliant bolt of lightning illuminated the scene, revealing an enormous mass tumbling down the mountainside straight toward their carriage. The driver let out a terrified shout, his voice lost in the howling wind.

Despite Michael Strogoff's desperate attempts to urge the horses forward with his whip, the animals stood frozen in fear, refusing to budge. Their eyes rolled white with terror, hooves planted against the rain-slicked ground as if turned to stone themselves.

In mere seconds, the massive boulder would hurtle past their position. With horror, Michael realized the boulder would demolish the carriage and kill his companion. There wasn't enough time to pull her to safety. The distance between them was too great to cross in the precious heartbeats remaining.

In that moment of crisis, Michael felt an extraordinary surge of power course through him, every muscle and sinew charged with desperate energy. He positioned himself behind the carriage and, with impossible strength, shoved the entire vehicle clear of the boulder's deadly path, his boots scraping against the rocky ground as he strained against the weight.

The massive boulder hurtled past, striking his chest and leaving him gasping for air as if struck by artillery fire. It pulverized the stones beneath with a thunderous crack before plummeting into the dark chasm, the sound of its impact lost to the raging storm below. Fragments of shattered rock peppered Michael's face and shoulders as he stumbled backward, his lungs burning from the exertion.

"Oh, brother!" Nadia cried out, having witnessed the scene illuminated by lightning, her hands clasped against her chest in terror.

"Nadia!" Michael called back, his voice straining against the howling wind, "don't be afraid!"

"It's not myself I'm worried about!" Her words carried the tremor of contained panic.

"God watches over us, sister!" Michael's reassurance rang with conviction despite his exhaustion.

"He watches over me, brother, for He has guided you to my side!" the young girl whispered, tears mixing with the rain on her cheeks.

The momentum of the horse-drawn carriage couldn't be slowed, so the exhausted steeds continued their advance, their flanks heaving with each labored step. pulled along by Michael and the coachman, who gripped the reins with white-knuckled determination, they struggled onward toward a slim mountain passage that stretched from north to south, where they would find refuge from the storm's direct assault. At one terminus stood a massive boulder, its peak surrounded by swirling winds that tore at loose debris like hungry spirits. In the boulder's lee, there was relative stillness, a pocket of calm in the chaos; however, once caught within the tornado's reach, neither human nor animal could withstand its devastating force, which threatened to sweep them all into the abyss below.

Something sliced the tallest fir trees jutting above the barrier, as if a massive blade had sliced through their peaks, sending splintered wood and needles spiraling into the maelstrom. The tempest reached its full fury, transforming the sky into a battlefield of elements. Lightning blazed through the narrow valley in blinding sheets of blue-white radiance, while thunder rolled in an unbroken roar that seemed to shake the very foundations of the earth. Each impact made the earth shudder with increasing violence, suggesting the entire Ural mountain range might crumble from its very core, unleashing an avalanche of ancient stone.

Fortunately, they managed to position the tarantass at an angle to the storm's fury, using the natural contours of the terrain to their advantage. Yet the fierce wind currents, channeled downward by the slope like water through a funnel, proved harder to evade. These gusts struck with such force that the carriage seemed ready to shatter apart at any moment, its wooden frame creaking and groaning under the relentless assault.

Forced to abandon her seat in the vulnerable vehicle, Nadia found refuge in a mining hollow that Michael spotted using a lantern's wavering glow through the tempest. The excavation, marked by deep pickaxe strikes in the living rock, offered a secure shelter where the young woman could rest until they resumed their journey, its rough-hewn walls providing welcome protection from the howling winds that threatened to tear their world apart.

At that moment, one o'clock in the morning, the heavens unleashed a fierce downpour. Combined with the howling wind and crackling lightning, the weather turned into a terrifying tempest. The rain fell in stinging sheets, drumming against the rocky ground with such intensity that it created a deafening roar. Pressing forward was now impossible. Having reached this mountain pass, their path ahead involved descending the Ural Mountains' slopes. Attempting such a descent now, with countless mountain streams tearing apart the road and violent gusts of wind and rain swirling around them, would have been pure folly.

"The waiting is a serious matter indeed," Michael stated, his voice audible above the storm's fury. "But we must do it to prevent even longer delays later. The storm's intense fury gives me reason to believe it won't continue much longer. These mountain tempests often exhaust themselves. Dawn will break around three o'clock, and while we can't risk descending in darkness, we should be able to make the attempt after sunrise, if not easily, then at least with less peril."

"We'll wait then, brother," Nadia responded, pulling her coat tighter around her shoulders as another gust of wind howled through their shelter. "But if you're choosing to delay, don't do it just to protect me from exhaustion or danger."

"Nadia," he said, meeting her determined gaze through the shadows, "I understand your courage, but by putting us both in danger, I'm risking something far greater than just our lives. I would fail my sacred mission, a duty that must come before all else, even my own desires to press forward."

"A duty?" Nadia whispered, her voice audible above the howling wind. Her eyes searched his face with sudden intensity.

A brilliant flash of lightning shattered the darkness at that precise moment, turning night into blinding day. A deafening thunderclap followed, so close it seemed to crack the very air around them. The air grew thick with choking sulfurous fumes as a massive pine tree, struck by lightning mere yards from their carriage, erupted into flames like an enormous blazing torch, sending sparks swirling upward into the tempestuous night.

The force of impact knocked the driver down, but sprang back up without injury, brushing snow from his coat as he steadied himself against the carriage wheel.

As the thunder's final rumbles faded into the mountain valleys like distant drums, Nadia squeezed Michael's hand with sudden urgency and whispered in his ear, her breath warm against his cold skin: "Brother, do you hear those shouts?"

Chapter Eleven

TRAVELERS IN DISTRESS

A brief silence descended, then, from afar, cries pierced the stillness, their sounds carrying with remarkable clarity to the tarantass, a Russian carriage. Someone was calling for help, not far down the road.

Michael listened. Though the coachman also heard the shouts, he shook his head.

"Someone needs our help!" Nadia exclaimed.

"They are beyond help," the coachman stated.

"Why not?" Michael demanded. "Wouldn't we want others to help us if we were in their place?"

"You can't risk the carriage and horses!"

"Then I'll go on foot," Michael declared, cutting off the coachman protests.

"I'm coming with you, brother," Nadia said, rising.

"No, stay here, Nadia. Keep the coachman company. I don't want to leave him by himself."

"I shall remain here," Nadia declared with quiet determination.

"Under no circumstances must you move from this position."

"This is where you'll find me upon your return."

Michael squeezed her hand, then vanished into the inky darkness as he rounded the slope's edge.

"Your brother's judgment is faulty," the coachman commented.

"No, his judgment is sound," Nadia responded with simple conviction.

Strogoff, meanwhile, pressed forward with urgent strides. A dual purpose drove his haste, both the desire to assist the troubled travelers and a burning curiosity about their identity. He felt certain the desperate cries originated from the telga that had maintained its lead ahead of him, somehow defying the tempest that had halted others in their tracks.

Though the rainfall had ceased, the tempest continued with even greater intensity. As: The wind carried clearer cries. The tempest obscured the mountain pass where Nadia waited. The path twisted through the landscape, and the violent gusts of wind, deflected by the sharp turns, created treacherous whirlwinds that Michael could only navigate by summoning all his strength to stay upright.

Before long, he realized the travelers whose voices he'd detected were close by. Despite their proximity, the darkness prevented Michael from spotting them, though their words reached him with perfect clarity.

"Are you planning to return, you fool?" he heard someone shout, much to his astonishment.

"Wait until the next stop. You'll get a good whipping!"

"Listen here, you devil's messenger! Hey! Down there!"

"So this is what passes for transportation in these parts!"

"Indeed, they call this rickety thing a telga!"

"That wretched driver! He keeps going as if he hasn't noticed we're not with him anymore!"

"To think he would dare deceive me, a respectable English gentleman! I shall file a formal complaint with the chancellor's office and see that scoundrel hung!"

He spoke these words with intense fury, but was cut off by his companion's sudden outburst of laughter. "Now that's amusing!" the companion declared.

"How dare you laugh!" the Englishman snapped.

"Of course I dare, my dear colleague," came the reply, "and, too. I must say, I've experienced nothing so ridiculous."

At that moment, a deafening thunderclap echoed through the ravine before fading into the far-off mountain peaks. As the last rumble subsided, the cheerful voice continued: "Indeed, it's hilarious. This contraption most definitely isn't of French origin."

"Not from England either," the other person responded.

Along the road, illuminated by lightning flashes, Michael spotted two travelers about twenty yards away. They sat side by side in an unusual vehicle, its wheels sunk deep into the muddy ruts of the road.

As he drew closer, he recognized them as the two reporters he'd traveled with aboard the Caucasus. One was grinning, while the other looked at their predicament.

"Good morning!" the Frenchman called out. "What a pleasure to see you here. Allow me to introduce my dear adversary, Mr. Blount."

The British news correspondent gave a small bow, and was preparing to introduce his fellow journalist, Alcide Jolivet, as etiquette required, but Michael cut him short.

"There's no need for introductions," he said. "We've already met during our journey on the Volga."

"Oh, of course! Now I remember! Mr?"

"Nicholas Korpanoff, from Irkutsk. But tell me, what's occurred that seems to amuse you so, even though it appears to be at your companion's expense?"

"Indeed, Mr. Korpanoff," Alcide answered. "Would you believe it? Our driver has vanished with the front section of this wretched carriage, leaving us stranded in the rear portion! Here we sit in half a telga, without horses or driver. Don't you find it amusing?"

"Not in the least," the Englishman stated.

"Oh, but it is! You need to see the humor in these situations, my friend."

"And how exactly do you propose we continue our journey?" Blount demanded.

"Nothing could be simpler," said Alcide with a grin. "Just strap yourself to what's left of our wagon. I'll handle the reins and call you my sweet dove, just like a proper Russian coachman, and you can gallop away like a genuine postal steed."

"Mr. Jolivet," the Englishman said, "I find your humor most inappropriate. You're going too far with this..."

"Oh, do hush now, my good man. When you're worn out, I'll take over. And you have my permission to call me a wheezing slug and spineless turtle if I don't get you moving at breakneck speed."

Alcide conveyed all of this with such genuine cheerfulness that Michael couldn't suppress a smile. "My friends," he said, "I have a superior suggestion. We've reached the summit of the Ural mountains, so from here it's all downhill. My carriage is parked nearby, just two hundred yards back. I'll provide one of my horses to attach to what's left of the telga, and by tomorrow, assuming all goes well, we'll reach Ekaterenburg together."

"That's a magnanimous offer, Mr. Korpanoff," Alcide responded.

"You know, I'd be happy to give you spots in my carriage," Michael said, "but it's only built for two, and my sister and I take up both seats."

"That's quite alright," Alcide replied. "Between your horse and our demi-telga, we could travel anywhere."

"We'd be most grateful to accept your offer," Harry Blount chimed in. "Though that coachman..."

"Trust me, you're not the first travelers to run into this kind of trouble," Michael assured them.

"But why wouldn't our driver return?" one of them demanded. "He must realize he's abandoned us here, the scoundrel!"

"Ha! He had no clue whatsoever!"

“You mean to tell me he didn’t realize he left half his cart behind?”

"Not at all! He's driving what's left of it toward Ekaterenburg, unaware."

"Didn't I say it would be amusing, colleague?" Alcide said with a laugh.

"Well then, gentlemen, shall we?" Michael suggested. "My carriage awaits..."

"But what about the broken cart?" the Englishman interjected.

"Oh, don't worry about that, my dear Blount!" Alcide exclaimed. "It's stuck in the ground, I dare say if we left it till spring, it would sprout leaves!"

"Let's go, gentlemen," Michael Strogoff called out. "We'll retrieve the carriage together."

The Frenchman and Englishman climbed down from their seats, no longer the rear ones, as the front section had already departed, and followed Michael's lead.

As they walked, Alcide Jolivet kept up his characteristic chatter with his usual cheerful disposition. "My word, Mr. Korpanoff," he remarked, "you've helped us escape quite a predicament."

"I did what anyone would have done in the same situation," Michael responded.

"Well then, sir, you've done us a great service, and if your journey continues further, perhaps our paths will cross again, and..."

When Alcide Jolivet refrained from asking Michael about his destination, Michael volunteered the information to avoid arousing suspicion. "I'm heading to Omsk, gentlemen," he stated.

“As for Mr. Blount and myself,” Alcide responded, “we seek wherever danger, and therefore news, can be found.”

"You mean the provinces under attack?" Michael inquired, showing particular interest.

"Mr. Korpanoff. Perhaps our paths will cross there."

"I rather doubt that," Michael replied. "I have no desire to face bullets or spears. I'm far too peace-loving to venture into combat zones."

"Please accept my sincerest apologies, sir. It's regrettable that our paths must diverge ! Though perhaps fortune will smile upon us, and we might share the road together after departing Ekaterenburg, even if just for a brief while?"

Michael paused before asking, "Are you continuing to Omsk?"

"Our plans remain uncertain," Alcide responded. "Though we'll proceed to Ishim, and from there, we'll have to let circumstances guide our journey."

"In that case, gentlemen," Michael replied, "we shall be companions until we reach Ishim."

Although Michael harbored a strong preference for solitary travel, he recognized the potential for misinterpretation if he were to avoid the two journalists who happened to be charting a similar course. Since Alcide and his fellow traveler planned to stop at Ishim for a while, Michael concluded it might be beneficial to share this portion of the trip with them.

"Have you received any definite information about locating the Tartar invasion?" he inquired.

"Yes, indeed," Alcide confirmed. "All we have to go on is what was reported in Perm. The Tartar forces under Feofar-Khan have swept through Semipolatinsk province, and they've been moving down the Irtish River these past few days. If you want to reach Omsk before they do, you'll need to make haste."

"You're right about that," Michael agreed.

"Word is also going around that Colonel Ogareff managed to slip across the border in disguise. They say he'll soon link up with the Tartar commander in the rebel territory."

"But where did this information come from?" Michael pressed, troubled by this news which, true or not, affected him.

"Well, you know how news travels," Alcide responded. "Word gets around."

"So you believe Colonel Ogareff has made his way to Siberia?"

"I've heard talk that he planned to travel the Kasan-Ekaterenburg route."

"Is that so, Mr. Jolivet?" Harry Blount perked up, breaking his silence.

"Indeed it is," Alcide confirmed.

"And are you aware he traveled in disguise as a gypsy?" Blount pressed.

"Like one of the Roma people!" Michael burst out without thinking, and the memory of the elderly Bohemian traveler at Nijni-Novgorod flashed in his mind, along with their shared journey on the Caucasus and their arrival at Kasan.

"Only enough to jot down some observations about it in correspondence to my cousin," Alcide responded with a grin.

"You were quite quick during your Kasan stop," the Englishman remarked.

"Indeed, I was, my friend! While they were refueling the Caucasus, I made the most of my time gathering intelligence."

Ignoring the witty exchange between Harry Blount and Alcide, Michael's thoughts wandered to the traveling gypsies. He dwelled on the elderly Tsigane leader, whose features had remained hidden from view, and the mysterious woman at his side who had fixed Michael with such an enigmatic look. His reverie was suddenly broken by the crack of a pistol nearby.

"Quick, gentlemen!" he called out.

"Well, well," Alcide mused to himself, "our cautious merchant friend, who steers clear of gunfire, seems mighty eager to rush toward danger now!"

Racing after Michael came Harry Blount, never one to shy away from peril. Within moments, all three had reached the jutting rock formation that shielded the carriage where the road curved.

The lightning-struck pine cluster continued to blaze. Though they saw no one, Michael's instincts proved correct. A terrifying growl pierced the air, followed by another loud report.

"It's a bear!" Michael shouted, recognizing the unmistakable sound. "Nadia! Nadia!" Yanking his cutlass from his belt, he darted around the stone buttress where the young woman had said she would wait.

Fire consumed the massive pine trees, casting an eerie, flickering light across the landscape. Just as Michael approached the horse-drawn carriage, an enormous creature lumbered in his direction.

Before him stood a colossal bear. Driven from its forest home by the raging storm, the beast had sought shelter in this cavern, its regular den, which was now inhabited by Nadia.

Faced with the massive beast, the terrified horses snapped their restraints and bolted. Focusing on the coachman's actions: Abandoning Nadia to face the bear alone, the coachman pursued his fleeing horses, his concern for his animals.

Despite the danger, the young woman remained courageous and composed. unaware of her presence, the bear had turned its attention to the remaining horse. Without hesitation, Nadia emerged from her hiding place, retrieved one of Michael's revolvers from the carriage, and approached the bear before firing at point-blank range.

She darted behind the carriage as the bear, nursing a minor shoulder wound, spun to face her. But when she noticed the horse straining against its traces, ready to snap them, she knew they'd be stranded if it broke free and they couldn't recover the others. With remarkable composure, she stepped back toward the bear and, just as it lifted its paws to strike, fired her second barrel straight at it.

Michael arrived the moment he heard the news. In one leap, he reached the scene, and with another, he positioned himself between the bear and the girl. A single upward thrust of his arm, wielding his fearsome blade, brought down the massive creature. The bear collapsed, lifeless, after

Michael performed the renowned technique of Siberian hunters, a precise strike designed to preserve the animal's valuable pelt, which commanded high prices at the market.

"Tell me you're unharmed, sister," Michael said, rushing to the young girl's side.

"I'm fine, brother," Nadia answered.

The pair of reporters caught up with them. Alcide grabbed hold of the horse's reins, and with his powerful grip, brought the animal under control. He and his fellow journalist had witnessed Michael's swift action with the knife. "Well done!" Alcide exclaimed. "For someone who's just a merchant, Mr. Korpanoff, you wield that hunting blade like an expert."

"Like a true professional," Blount chimed in.

"Where I come from in Siberia," Michael replied, "we must learn to be skilled at many things."

Alcide studied him. Standing in the harsh light, his knife coated in crimson, his imposing frame towering above with one foot planted on the massive beast's body, he cut quite a striking figure.

"What a fearsome warrior," Alcide muttered to himself. Then, approaching with deep respect, he greeted the young woman.

Nadia inclined her head.

Alcide turned to face his companion. "Now there's a sister who matches her brother's courage!" he remarked. "If I were one of those bears, I'd think twice before tangling with such a brave and graceful pair."

Harry Blount maintained a rigid posture, standing apart from the others with his hat held in his hands. His companion's relaxed demeanor seemed to make Blount even more formal and uncomfortable.

Just then, the coachman returned, having caught his two runaway horses. He looked at the splendid beast sprawled lifeless on the ground, reluctant to abandon it to scavenging birds, before turning his attention to getting his team back in harness.

Michael explained to him about the stranded travelers and his plan to let them use one horse.

"Whatever you prefer," answered the coachman. "Though, mind you, that means two carriages rather than one."

"Fair enough, my good man," said Alcide, catching the driver's hint, "you'll get paid twice the usual rate."

"Then off we go, my swift beauties!" the coachman called out to his horses.

The group resumed their journey, with Nadia settling back into the carriage while Michael and his fellow travelers proceeded on foot. At three o'clock, fierce winds continued to howl through the mountain pass. By first light, they had reached the telga, which remained stuck, its wheels half-buried. The vehicle's condition made it clear why a sudden tug could split it between its front and back sections. They managed to salvage the situation by using ropes to harness one horse to what remained of the telga. The reporters climbed aboard this makeshift transport, and both carriages began moving again. All that remained was the straightforward descent down the Ural slopes.

The two carriages made their way to Ekaterenburg, with the carriage leading to the telga. The six-hour journey down the winding mountain roads was uneventful, save for the occasional glimpse of a majestic eagle soaring overhead or a curious marmot scurrying across the rocky terrain.

As they pulled up to the post-house, they spotted their former driver standing by the entrance, arms folded across his broad chest. The good-natured Russian greeted them with a warm smile, extended his calloused hand, and asked for his customary tip in a thick, gravelly voice.

The outrageous demand sent Blount into a fury, his face reddening like a ripe tomato as he clenched his fists. If the coachman hadn't backed away, he would have received a direct punch, delivered with proper British boxing technique, as payment for his audacious request for "na vodkou."

Alcide Jolivet found this display of temper hilarious, laughing harder than he ever had.

"But the poor fellow has a point!" he exclaimed. "He's right, my friend. We can hardly blame him if we couldn't keep up with his pace!"

He dug into his pocket and pulled out a few copecks. "Here, my friend," he said, offering them to the coachman. "I give these to you."

This only made Mr. Blount more furious, and he started threatening legal action against the telga's owner.

"You're talking about a lawsuit in Russia?" Alcide exclaimed. "Why, those cases drag on forever! Have you heard about that nurse who sued for twelve months' worth of infant care payments?"

"No, I haven't," Harry Blount replied.

"Well, you should've seen how old that 'baby' was by the time the court ruled in the nurse's favor!"

"And what position did he hold?" she inquired.

"He served as a Colonel in the Imperial Guard!"

The response triggered a collective burst of laughter from everyone present.

Alcide, pleased with his clever remark, retrieved his well-worn notebook and jotted down an entry he intended to include in an upcoming French-Russian dictionary he was compiling: "Telga, A Russian vehicle that begins its journey on four wheels but, owing to the appalling state of the nation's roads, arrives at its destination on two." He chuckled to himself, imagining the looks on the faces of readers who would encounter that definition. The indignant expression on Mr. Blount's face only heightened his amusement at poking fun at Russian inefficiency as he watched Alcide scribble away.

© 01/01/2025

Chapter Twelve

PROVOCATION

Ekaterinburg, despite being physically located in Asia beyond the Ural Mountains on their easternmost slopes, is part of Europe. The city falls under the jurisdiction of the Perm government, making it an administrative part of European Russia. This creates an unusual situation where a piece of what is Siberia is technically within Russia's European territory. The local population embraces this duality, often referring to their home as a bridge between continents. Street signs and official documents display both European and Asian influences, while the architecture blends classical European designs with elements inspired by the city's position as a gateway to Siberia. This geographic anomaly has helped shape Ekaterinburg's unique cultural identity, making it a distinctive melting pot where East meets West.

Ekaterenburg, established in 1723, had grown into a significant urban center where Michael and his fellow travelers would find transportation to continue their journey. The city housed the empire's primary mint and served as the administrative hub for mining operations. Its prominence stemmed from its role as the focal point of a thriving industrial region, known for its gold and platinum processing and refinement facilities.

At this time, Ekaterenburg was experiencing a significant surge in its population, with many Russians and Siberians gathering there to escape the looming Tartar threat. While finding transportation into Ekaterenburg had been challenging earlier, departing was now easy, since most people were reluctant to travel on Siberian routes during these uncertain times.

They found it easy to exchange their well-worn demi-carriage, which had carried them as far as Ekaterenburg, for a sturdy telga, a low, four-wheeled Russian wagon designed for rough terrain. Michael, however, kept his tarantass, a light, two-wheeled Russian carriage, as it had weathered the Ural crossing well and proved ideal for traversing the vast expanses ahead. All it needed was a fresh team of three hardy horses to continue their swift journey eastward toward the distant city of Irkutsk, deep in the heart of Siberia.

The road leading to Tioumen, extending as far as Novo-Zaimskoe, features mild elevations and rolling terrain, early indicators of the approaching Ural Mountains. However, beyond Novo-Zaimskoe lies the vast expanse of the steppe, a endless sea of grasslands stretching towards the horizon. The travelers could already envision the challenges that lay ahead as they ventured into this desolate yet beautiful landscape.

The journalists had planned to make Ichim their stopping point, four hundred and twenty miles distant from Ekaterenburg. From there, they would let circumstances dictate whether to continue their journey through the invaded territory together or, depending on how their journalistic instincts guided them in pursuit of news. The prospect of parting ways weighed heavily on their minds, as the bond forged through their shared experiences had become a source of strength and camaraderie in these uncertain times.

The road connecting Ekaterenburg to Ichim, passing through Irkutsk, remained Michael's sole option. However, having no interest in gathering news and wishing to steer clear of areas ravaged by the invading forces, he resolved not to make any stops along the way. The urgency of his mission weighed upon him, fueling his determination to press forward without delay.

"I'm pleased to travel alongside you," he told his fellow travelers, his voice tinged with a hint of regret, "but I must be frank. Reaching Omsk is my utmost priority. My sister and I need to reunite with our mother there before it's too late." He paused, the gravity of the situation etched on his face. "Who knows if we'll arrive before the Tartars overrun the town? Therefore, I can only pause at post-houses to switch horses. We must keep moving, both day and night, lest we risk being caught in the path of the invading forces."

"That's our plan," Blount responded, his expression resolute. "We cannot afford any delays on this perilous journey."

"Excellent," said Michael, his voice tinged with urgency. "But there's no time to waste. Find a carriage that..."

"That has back wheels," Alcide cut in with a wry smirk, "guaranteed to keep pace with the front ones."

Within thirty minutes, the determined Frenchman had secured a sturdy tarantass, and he and his companion took their seats, eager to depart. Michael and Nadia returned to their own carriage, exchanging a solemn glance as they prepared for the arduous trek ahead. As the clock struck noon, its resonant chime echoing through the streets of Ekaterenburg, both vehicles set off together, the wheels crunching against the well-trodden road, their occupants steeling themselves for the challenges that lay before them.

In the depths of Siberia, Nadia found herself traversing the expansive route to Irkutsk, her heart heavy with trepidation. Her mind was consumed with thoughts as three robust, fleet-footed horses pulled her across the exile lands where her father was forced to dwell, for an uncertain duration, far removed from their homeland. The endless steppes rolling beneath the tarantass registered in her consciousness, for her gaze remained fixed on the distant horizon, somewhere beyond which her banished father awaited, a longing ache gripping her soul. Racing at fifteen miles per hour, she remained oblivious to her surroundings and the distinct character of Western Siberia, so unlike its eastern counterpart. This region boasted few farmlands; the topsoil was barren, yet beneath the surface lay abundant treasures, iron, copper, platinum, and gold, a wealth that had drawn fortune-seekers from far and wide. The land's peculiar economy posed a simple question: why till the earth when greater riches waited below? Throughout the region, pickaxes rang out in constant labor, their rhythmic clanging echoing across the desolate landscape, while plows lay idle and forgotten, gathering dust in the arid wind.

Nadia's mind wandered from the Baikal region as she contemplated her current circumstances. The memory of her father grew dim, giving way to visions of her kind-hearted traveling companion as she'd first encountered him on the Wladimir train. She remembered his thoughtful gestures throughout their journey, his unexpected appearance at the police station to secure her release, the warm sincerity with which he'd addressed her as sister despite their forged acquaintance, his protective nature shielding her from harm during their harrowing Volga river descent. But most vivid was his heroic conduct during that frightful night amidst the raging Ural storm, when he'd braved the howling winds and lashing rain without hesitation to preserve her life at the cost of his own safety.

Nadia reflected on Michael with deep gratitude, her heart swelling with affection for this man who had become far more than a traveling companion. She felt blessed beyond measure to have found such a noble guardian, someone who combined unflinching courage with profound wisdom and selfless friendship. In his reassuring presence, she experienced a sense of complete security, knowing his protection was steadfast and unwavering no matter the peril they faced. His dedication to ensuring her safety went far beyond what even a devoted brother might offer. With the major hurdles of their harrowing adventure now overcome, completing her journey to the remote valley seemed an assured conclusion, a question of patience and perseverance until they at last reached her ancestral home.

Michael sat lost in contemplation, feeling grateful that fate had orchestrated his encounter with Nadia. This meeting served two purposes, allowing him to offer help when needed while also providing perfect cover for his true identity. He found himself admiring the young woman's steady courage. Their connection felt almost familial, as if she were his sister. What he experienced toward his capable and valiant traveling companion was more akin to deep respect than romantic attraction. He recognized in her one of those exceptional souls, pure and uncommon, that commanded universal admiration.

The perils now intensified for Michael upon entering Siberian territory. Assuming the reports were accurate and Ivan Ogareff had indeed crossed the border, every move would require utmost vigilance. The situation had shifted as Tartar scouts now patrolled the Siberian regions, their eyes ever-watchful for any suspicious activity. These merciless warriors would end both his mission and his life if his disguise fails or his role as the Czar's messenger was revealed. Michael felt the burden of his duty weighing more heavily than ever before, the stakes higher than he could have imagined when first accepting this perilous assignment. Yet he resolved to persevere, his courage and determination unwavering in the face of increasing danger.

In the second carriage, matters proceeded, the familiar dynamic between Alcide and Blount playing out as it so often did. Alcide was long-winded, constructing complete sentences with his usual flair for embellishment, while Blount's responses were terse and minimal, the man of few words offering only what was necessary. Despite their contrasting communication styles, both men remained vigilant, observing their surroundings from their unique perspectives and documenting the few uneventful happenings during their passage through Western Siberia's harsh, unforgiving territories.

At every relay station, the journalists stepped down from their coach and joined Michael. Nadia remained in the tarantass throughout the journey, only leaving when it was time for meals at the post-houses. During these breakfast and dinner stops, she would take her place at the table but kept to herself, not taking part in any discussions.

The young lady captivated Alcide, though he maintained proper decorum. Her quiet resilience impressed him in enduring the hardships of their challenging journey.

Michael found the required stops quite frustrating, and at each relay station, he worked to speed things along. He would rush the innkeepers, prod the iemschiks to move faster, and ensure the tarantass was prepared for travel. They would consume their meals much too fast for Blount's preference, as he liked to eat at a measured pace before setting off again at breakneck speed, their generous payment ensuring swift service.

Blount showed no interest in the girl during meals. He was known for his single-minded focus and preferred not to multitask. The topic of her was also one of the rare subjects he avoided discussing with his fellow traveler.

When Alcide once inquired about the girl's age, Blount responded with genuine confusion, "Which girl?"

"Nicholas Korpanoff's sister, of course," Alcide clarified.

"Oh, is that who she is?"

"No, his grandmother!" Alcide snapped back, irritated by Blount's apparent indifference. "How old would you say she is?"

"If I had been there when she was born, I might have understood."

The fields were empty of Siberian farmers, their usual occupants having retreated to safer havens. These rural people were known for their distinctive features: light complexions and solemn expressions, which one famous explorer likened to the people of Castile, though without their proud bearing. Scattered across the landscape, abandoned settlements stood as silent sentinels, signaling the advancing Tartar forces that had driven the villagers to flee northward to the plains, taking their livestock, sheep, camels, and horses, with them in a desperate bid for survival. Those nomadic Kirghiz tribes who maintained their loyalty to the old order had also moved their encampments across the Irtych River, seeking to avoid the raiders' plundering and preserve what little they could from the escalating conflict.

Fortunately, the postal service continued to operate without disruption, and telegraph messages could still be sent between locations connected to the network. Fresh horses were available at each relay station under normal terms, allowing couriers to transport mail and dispatches across the vast expanse of the steppe. The telegraph operators, those unsung heroes tasked with maintaining the vital lines of communication, forwarded each message as it arrived at their station, prioritizing only the official government communications that held sway over matters of state and military import.

The journey went well for Michael up to this point. As the Czar's messenger, he had encountered no obstacles, and he felt confident that if he could reach Krasnoiarsk, which appeared to be the furthest extent of Feofar-Khan's Tartar forces, he would beat them to Irkutsk. After departing Ekaterenburg, the two carriages traveled for twenty-four hours without incident, covering two hundred and twenty miles before reaching the small town of Toulouguisk at seven in the morning. They fed and watered the horses and then ate a quick meal before continuing across the vast steppe. Later that same day, July 22nd, they made it to Tioumen, where they would spend the night before continuing their urgent mission on behalf of the Czar at first light.

In those days, Tioumen's population had swelled to twenty thousand, twice its normal size, as refugees poured in seeking shelter from the escalating conflict. As the first Russian industrial settlement in Siberia, boasting an impressive metal-refining factory and bell foundry, the city was experiencing unprecedented bustle and strain on its resources. News correspondents scattered throughout the city, seeking information and eyewitness accounts from the displaced masses. The reports from Siberian refugees fleeing the conflict painted a grim picture of advancing devastation. They revealed that Feofar-Khan's forces were advancing through the Ichim valley, leaving a trail of burned villages and pillaged settlements in their wake.

They confirmed the disturbing rumors that the traitorous Colonel Ogareff would soon join, or perhaps had already joined the Tartar leader's ranks, lending his strategic expertise to the enemy's cause. These developments suggested military campaigns in Eastern Siberia would intensify in the coming days. In response, the steadfast Cossacks under Tobolsk's government were conducting rapid marches toward Tomsk, determined to intercept and cut off the Tartar forces before they could advance further into the heart of the empire.

The travelers arrived at Novo-Saimsk as the clock struck midnight, leaving behind the undulating landscape with its tree-covered hills, the last vestiges of the Ural Mountains. This marked a pivotal transition, for they were now entering the true Siberian steppe, stretching all the way to the outskirts of Krasnoiarsk in an unbroken expanse.

The terrain transformed into an immense, featureless plain, a sweeping grassland that extended to the horizon in every direction, where earth met the sky in a perfect circle as precise as if drawn by mathematical instruments. In this vast, uninterrupted expanse, only the regimented telegraph poles broke the monotony, their wires singing in the wind like an aeolian harp played by unseen hands. The only sign of the road's presence was the fine dust clouds kicked up by the tarantass' wheels, creating a white ribbon that stretched into the distance, disappearing into the infinite flatness. Without this dusty trail to guide them, the travelers might have believed themselves alone in an endless wilderness, adrift in a sea of grass with no landmarks or reference points to steer by.

The group, led by Michael, continued their swift journey. Their driver, the iemschik, spurred the horses onward, making them race across the terrain as if they had wings. With no barriers or hindrances in their path, the tarantass carriage maintained its direct course toward Ichim, where the two journalists planned to make their stop, assuming circumstances didn't force them to change their intended route.

Novo-Saimsk and Ichim were one hundred and twenty miles apart, a distance they could cover before eight o'clock the following evening, provided they maintained a steady pace. The iemschiks, those hardy drivers of the Siberian steppe, while unsure if their passengers were nobility or high-ranking officials, treated them with the deference deserving of such status, if only for their generous tips of "na vodkou", that ubiquitous offering of vodka that greased the wheels of travel across the vast Russian expanse. As the tarantass rattled over the rutted trail, Michael and his companion settled in for the long haul, the endless grasslands stretching out before them like an ocean of wind-rippled green.

The next day, July 23rd, as they drove their carriages within thirty miles of Ichim, Michael's keen eyes spotted another vehicle ahead, visible through the dusty haze kicked up by the churning wheels. His horses, being fresher than those of the traveler ahead, would soon catch up to them at their current pace. The vehicle wasn't a tarantass or the ubiquitous telga favored by peasants, but a post-berlin, a lighter, swifter carriage built for speed over long distances. It showed unmistakable signs of a lengthy journey, its once gleaming varnish dulled by the relentless Siberian elements. The postillion was whipping the horses, maintaining their gallop only through harsh treatment and constant shouting of indecipherable urgings. This berlin couldn't have come through Novo-Saimsk; it must have joined the Irkutsk road using one of the lesser-known paths that crisscrossed the steppe, those ancient trails known only to the most seasoned Russian travelers.

When they spotted the berlin in the distance, their immediate instinct was to overtake it and reach the relay station first, ensuring they would secure fresh horses before the other travelers. A quick command to their iemschiks, and their tarantasses caught up to the swifter berlin, the horses' hooves thundering across the dusty steppe.

Michael Strogoff took the lead in the pursuit, his carriage inching ever closer to the berlin. As his vehicle drew alongside, someone leaned out of the berlin's window, the wind whipping at their cloak. Before he could make out any details of the mysterious person, he sped past in a blur, but a commanding voice rang out with one stern word that cut through the cacophony: "Stop!"

The three vehicles thundered onward, with the berlin falling behind the pair of tarantasses. Far from slowing, the chase intensified as the berlin's horses, roused by their competitors' speed and presence, found renewed vigor and kept pace for several minutes. All three carriages vanished into a thick dust cloud kicked up by the pounding hooves, from which came the sharp snap of whips cracking through the air and the angry shouts of the drivers urging their mounts on. The cloud billowed and shifted like a living thing as the pursuit raged within its dusty confines, the horses' breath rasping amid the rumble of spinning wheels over the hard-packed earth.

Michael and his group maintained their lead, which could prove crucial if the relay station had limited horses available. The station might struggle to supply enough horses for two carriages, let alone three. This would force the trailing berlin to wait, allowing Michael's caravan to extend its advantage even further.

Thirty minutes later, the berlin had fallen so far behind that it appeared as a tiny dot where the steppe met the horizon, the dust cloud that once enveloped the chase now dissipating in the distance. Michael's driver cracked his whip with renewed vigor, the horses straining against their harnesses as they thundered across the vast, rolling expanse of the steppe, kicking up clods of dirt in their wake as they raced to put even more ground between themselves and their pursuers.

On that evening, two carriages arrived in Ichim as the clock struck eight, their wheels kicking up plumes of dust in the dying light. Reports about the Tartar invasion grew dire with each passing hour. The advance guard now threatened the town, and just two days prior, forces compelled local officials to withdraw to the relative safety of Tobolsk, abandoning

Ichim. The streets stood silent and deserted, not a single officer or soldier remaining within the town's bounds to offer protection or reassurance to those few civilians who had chosen not to flee.

When Michael Strogoff reached the relay station, his first priority was securing fresh horses. He was relieved to have outpaced the berlin. Unfortunately, only three horses were in suitable condition for harnessing, as the remaining animals had just returned exhausted from a lengthy journey.

Since the two correspondents planned to remain in Ichim, they didn't need to concern themselves with transportation arrangements and had their carriage stored. Within ten minutes, Michael received word that his tarantass was prepared for departure.

"Excellent," he replied.

He turned to face the two reporters. "Gentlemen, we must now part ways."

"But Mr. Korpanoff," Alcide Jolivet interjected, "You can spare an hour in Ichim?"

"I'm afraid not," he answered. "In fact, I intend to depart from the post-house before that berlin we outpaced catches up to us."

"Are you concerned the traveler might compete with you for horses?"

"I'd prefer to avoid any confrontation."

"In that case, Mr. Korpanoff," said Jolivet, "allow us to express our gratitude once more for your help, and for the pleasure of your company during our journey."

"Perhaps we'll cross paths in Omsk in the coming days," Blount mentioned.

"That's likely," Michael replied, "as I'm heading there."

“Well then, have a safe journey, Mr. Korpanoff,” Alcide said, “and may you not encounter any more telgas.”

Both reporters extended their hands to Michael, intending to give him a warm handshake, when they heard the sound of an approaching carriage. The door burst open, and in stepped a man.

Standing there was the Berlin traveler, a commanding figure of military bearing who appeared to be in his forties. Broad shoulders marked his imposing frame and a sturdy build, topped by a resolute head adorned with thick mustaches that merged into his reddish whiskers. His attire consisted of an unadorned uniform, with a cavalry saber at his hip and a short-handled whip gripped in his hand. A stern expression creased his weathered features, and his piercing gaze swept over the room, assessing the occupants with a practiced eye honed from years of military service. An aura of authority radiated from his very presence, commanding respect and obedience from those around him.

"I need horses," he declared with the unmistakable authority of someone used to giving orders.

The postmaster responded with a deferential bow, "I have none available, sir."

"I must have them."

"It simply can't be done," the postmaster asserted, his brow furrowing with concern.

The traveler's eyes narrowed, his jaw tightening. "In that case, how do you explain the horses I noticed being prepared for the carriage outside?"

The postmaster swallowed hard, his gaze darting toward Michael Strogoff. "Those belong to him," he explained with a deferential gesture.

The traveler's expression hardened, his mouth setting in a grim line. "Remove them at once!" he commanded, his authoritative voice brooking no opposition. An edge of impatience crept into his tone as he surveyed the room.

Michael stepped forward, his shoulders squared. "I've already arranged for those horses," he stated, meeting the traveler's gaze without flinching.

"That's irrelevant! I require them," the traveler snapped, his eyes flashing with irritation. "Hurry up; I'm pressed for time."

Drawing a steadying breath, Michael responded, "I'm equally short on time." He struggled to maintain his composure, his jaw clenching as he fought to keep his voice level.

Nadia stood close by, composed, but her heart pounding as internal anxiety gripped her over the confrontation that would have been better avoided.

"That's enough!" the traveler declared, his voice cutting through the tension like a knife. Moving toward the postmaster with purposeful strides, he demanded with a menacing motion of his hand, "Have those horses hitched to my berlin."

The harried postmaster found himself in a quandary, unsure whether to follow Michael's legitimate claim or the other traveler's improper request. His questioning gaze fell on Michael, who possessed the lawful authority to challenge such unreasonable demands. Yet the postmaster could do nothing. He could not ignore the forceful demands of an armed traveler.

For a brief moment, Michael weighed his options, his brow furrowing as he considered the potential consequences of each course of action. He was reluctant to present his podorojna papers, as doing so would draw unwanted notice and reveal his identity as an imperial courier. Surrendering his horses would set back his journey, a delay he could ill afford with the pressing importance of his mission. Yet he also recognized that becoming embroiled in a confrontation, especially one involving violence, could jeopardize his vital mission and put innocent lives at risk. Michael's jaw clenched as he wrestled with the tough decision, aware that the tense situation could escalate at any moment.

The two journalists watched him, prepared to back him up if he sought their help. Michael's heart pounded in his chest, but he fought to maintain an outward sense of calm and composure.

"I will keep my horses in my carriage," Michael stated, maintaining the modest tone befitting a store owner from Irkutsk. He hoped this reasonable stance would defuse the tense situation.

The stranger stepped toward Michael and gripped his shoulder, his fingers digging into Michael's flesh. "Is that so?" he growled, his breath hot and sour. "You refuse to surrender your horses to me?"

"That's correct," Michael replied, holding the stranger's gaze despite the menacing proximity.

"Very well then. The horses will go to whoever proves stronger. Prepare yourself, I'll show no mercy!" With a sudden motion, the stranger unsheathed his blade, the steel glinting in the dim light.

Nadia rushed forward without hesitation, positioning herself between Michael and the armed stranger, her own hand resting on the hilt of her sword. The two journalists, Blount and Alcide Jolivet, moved forward as well, ready to intervene and defend their comrade.

"I won't engage in combat," Michael stated, crossing his arms over his chest in a gesture of resolute non-violence. He had no intention of being drawn into an unnecessary confrontation that could derail his vital mission.

The stranger's eyes narrowed, his expression a mixture of confusion and outrage. "You refuse to fight?" he spat, tightening his grip on his weapon.

"Yes," Michael replied, his voice level and unwavering.

"Even after that, you still refuse?" the traveler shouted in disbelief. Then, catching everyone off guard, he swung the whip handle and struck Michael's shoulder with a sharp crack. The blow made Michael's face drain of color and he staggered back a step, grimacing in pain. His fists clenched, every fiber of his being yearning to strike back at his attacker and defend his honor. But through sheer force of will, he held himself in check, his jaw clenched tight. A fight now would mean more than just lost time, it could derail his entire vital mission and put everything at risk. Better to sacrifice a few hours and endure the indignity than risk the collapse of all he had worked towards. And yet, to stand there and endure such humiliation in front of his companions, to be branded a coward... it took every ounce of Michael's restraint.

"Come on then, you lily-livered milksop, fight back if you're not a complete craven!" the traveler taunted again, his words growing even more crude and hostile as he sensed Michael's internal struggle. The cruel lash of his tongue was almost as painful as the blow from the whip handle.

"No," Michael stated, his gaze unwavering as he met the other man's eyes, refusing to be cowed despite the stinging ache from the blow. He would not retaliate, no matter how greatly the insults stung his pride. To do so would only vindicate the bully's taunts about his lack of courage.

"Bring the horses now, you useless layabout!" the man snarled, his face reddening with rage at Michael's stoic defiance. He stormed out of the stables, boots kicking up dust in his wake.

The postmaster, who had witnessed the entire confrontation, trailed after him, shaking his graying head at Michael with an exasperated shrug as if to say "I cannot fathom why you didn't defend yourself."

Michael's passive response to the unprovoked attack unsettled the small cluster of reporters watching this exchange. They struggled to understand how such a capable-looking young man in his prime could accept being struck without demanding swift retribution. Uncomfortable with the tense situation they had stumbled into, they offered Michael brief, awkward nods of... what? Sympathy? Admiration for his restraint? It was impossible to discern their intentions. Then they withdrew, with the eldest among them, Jolivet, turning to make a low comment to Harry Blount as they departed, no doubt dissecting what they had just witnessed.

"How could someone so masterful at hunting Ural bears show such weakness? Can a person be brave one moment and craven the next? It defies understanding," Jolivet muttered, his brow furrowed in consternation as he grappled to reconcile the young man's composed demeanor with the tales of his wilderness exploits.

after, the sound of turning wheels and cracking whips showed the berlin carriage, now pulled by the tarantass's sturdy horses, was speeding away from the station and back toward the heart of the city, leaving the unsettling scene behind. The rhythmic clatter of hooves on cobblestone faded into the cacophony of St. Petersburg's bustling streets.

Nadia and Michael were now alone in the room, she maintaining her composure while he trembled, a visceral reaction he could not seem to control no matter how he willed his body to stillness. The Czar's messenger sat, his arms folded across his chest in a defensive posture, as still as carved marble save for the faint quivering of his hands. His face, once pale, had taken on a new hue that spoke not of embarrassment but of something else: fear, perhaps, or a dawning realization of truths he had never contemplated.

Nadia knew only the weightiest of reasons could have compelled him to endure such degradation from that man. Forces he could comprehend laid low on his once unyielding pride, beating the arrogance from him. She approached him now, just as he had come to her at the Nijni-Novgorod police station those many months ago when their paths had first intersected.

"Let me take your hand, brother," she whispered, her voice hushed yet resonant with an undercurrent of quiet strength. Extending her fingers, she offered a lifeline to anchor him against the turbulence that threatened to sweep him away.

Then, with the tender touch of a mother soothing a frightened child, she reached up and brushed away the tear that had formed in his eye, a solitary droplet of sorrow trailing down his ashen cheek. In that simple gesture, she conveyed a world of empathy and compassion, a balm against the anguish that contorted his features.

© 01/01/2025
QuantumDigitalPublishing.io

Chapter Thirteen

DUTY BEFORE EVERYTHING

Nadia understood, with a woman's intuition, that Michael Strogoff was driven by hidden purposes. She sensed he served something greater than himself, and that in this moment, he had set aside his own feelings, even his justified anger at being wronged in the service of his duty.

Nadia felt a profound respect and admiration for the man before her. Though she did not know the details of his mission, it was clear that Michael was willing to sacrifice his own desires and personal grievances for the sake of a higher calling. His unwavering dedication was both humbling and inspiring. She saw no need to question Michael about any of this. The simple gesture of offering her hand to him had already expressed everything that words could have conveyed between them. An unspoken understanding passed between their souls in that moment, a silent promise to stand together against the trials that lay ahead, no matter the cost.

Michael remained silent all the evening. Because the postmaster couldn't supply fresh horses until the next morning, they had to spend the entire night at the house. Nadia could profit by it to take some rest, and a room was therefore prepared for her.

The young girl would no doubt have preferred not to leave her companion, but she felt he would rather be alone, and she made ready to go to her room.

Just before heading to bed, she felt compelled to approach Michael and bid him goodnight. Nadia moved towards him, her steps soft upon the wooden floor. "Brother," she murmured, the word tinged with a melancholic affection. He responded only with a dismissive wave of his hand, his gaze remaining fixed on some indistinct point in the distance. With a heavy sigh that seemed to carry the weight of their shared burdens, she departed from the room, leaving him to his solitary vigil.

Sleep eluded Michael Strogoff that night. Rest would have been impossible, even for the briefest moment. The spot where the lives of his mother and father had ended loomed large in his mind's eye, an indelible stain upon his memory. The path forward remained shrouded in uncertainty, fraught with perils yet unknown. Still, he steadied his resolve, allowing the embers of determination to burn ever brighter within his breast. For the sake of Mother Russia, he would not falter.

"For the homeland and the Almighty," he whispered, concluding his nightly devotion. The words hung in the still night air, a solemn vow imbued with profound resolve.

A burning curiosity consumed him about his mysterious assailant, their identity, origin, and destination remained unknown. Yet, he remembered their face that he knew he would recognize them, even years later, should they ever meet again? He seared the details of their features and the intensity of their gaze into his memory, an unsettling reminder of the dangers ahead.

Michael Strogoff summoned the stationmaster, his eyes heavy from the sleepless night. An old-school Siberian emerged, regarding the young traveler with concealed disdain as he awaited the inevitable questions. The man's weathered face betrayed a lifetime of hardship and toil in this unforgiving land. His eyes narrowed suspecting this outsider.

"Are you from around here?" Michael inquired, his voice tinged with weariness from the long journey.

"Indeed," came the curt reply, the stationmaster's gruff demeanor betraying little warmth or hospitality.

"Are you familiar with the person who stole my horses?" Michael pressed, undeterred by the man's brusque manner.

"Not at all," the Siberian stated, his eyes revealing nothing.

"Was that your first time seeing him?"

"It was."

"What's your impression of him?" Michael persisted, determined to glean whatever insights he could.

"Someone who commands respect and obedience," the stationmaster said, his gaze hardening as he studied the young traveler. Michael's intense stare bore into the Siberian, but the man remained unflinching, impervious to the scrutiny.

"How dare you pass judgment on me?" Michael burst out, his frustration mounting at the man's enigmatic responses.

"I do dare," the Siberian replied, squaring his shoulders as if bracing for a confrontation. "Some actions demand a response, even from a simple merchant." His words carried the weight of hard-earned wisdom, a lifetime of experience in this unforgiving land.

"A physical response?" Michael challenged, his brow furrowing.

"Yes, young fellow. I'm both old and strong enough to say that to your face." The station master's voice was filled with a strong and quiet confidence born of years spent enduring the harsh Siberian elements. Clearly, nothing would cow or intimidate this man, despite Michael's status and intentions.

Michael went up to the postmaster and laid his two powerful hands on his shoulders.

Then in a calm tone, “Be off, my friend,” said he: “be off! I could kill you.”

The postmaster understood. “I like him better for that,” he muttered and retired without another word.

On the morning of July 24th, at eight o’clock, they harnessed three strong and sturdy horses to the waiting tarantass, ready for the journey ahead. Michael Strogoff and Nadia took their places, and Ichim, with its disagreeable remembrances, was soon left far behind.

At different points during the event, Michael made his way to the postmaster and firmly grasped the man’s shoulders with his powerful hands.

Speaking with eerie calmness, he said: "Leave now, my friend. Leave before I end your life."

The postmaster grasped Michael's meaning. "I respect him more for that," he murmured as he withdrew silently.

When morning came at eight o'clock on July 24th, they hitched three sturdy horses to the tarantass. Michael Strogoff and Nadia settled into their seats, leaving behind Ichim and its unpleasant memories.

During their travels, they made their way between relay posts until reaching Abatskaia at four in the afternoon, another fifty miles along their route. Here, they encountered the Ichim, a major tributary flowing into the Irtych River, which proved more challenging to cross than their earlier passage over the Tobol. The waters of the Ichim rushed swiftly at this crossing point, churning and foaming as they cascaded over rocks and debris. Winter journeys across Siberian rivers were straightforward, as the waterways froze several feet thick, allowing travelers to pass almost without noticing they were crossing a river. The frozen riverbeds lay hidden beneath an unbroken blanket of snow stretching across the steppe, a pristine white expanse broken only by the tracks of sleds and the occasional stunted tree. Summer crossings, however, often presented significant obstacles, with raging currents and slippery embankments posing risks to both man and beast. They needed careful guidance to get the tarantass across the rushing Ichim river without mishap.

Frustrating Michael, the Ichim crossing consumed two full hours, wasting precious time. His anxiety and sense of urgency increased because of the boatmen's troubling reports about the Tartar invasion. Scouts serving Feofar-Khan, the fearsome leader of the nomadic horde, had been spotted along both shores of the lower Ichim in the southern regions of Tobolsk province, placing the city of Omsk in imminent danger. Disquieting word spread of a recent battle between Siberian and Tartar forces near the great Kirghese horde's border, a clash that ended for the outnumbered Russians. Their troops' subsequent withdrawal had triggered a mass exodus of local peasants fleeing the province to escape the invaders' path.

The boatmen described in grim detail the Tartars' savage acts, looting villages, the theft of livestock, burning homes and crops, and the wanton slaughter of any who dared resist. Such brutality and disregard for human life typified the nomads' approach to warfare, as they sought to crush all opposition through sheer force and the ruthless application of terror. With the Tartars drawing ever closer, Michael could only pray they would reach Omsk before the dreaded horde descended upon the city like a ravenous wolf among the flock.

In their panic, the entire population scattered at Feofar-Khan's approach. Michael Strogoff's primary concern wasn't for his own safety, but that the mass exodus from cities would leave him with no way to continue his journey. His urgent need to reach Omsk consumed his thoughts. If he could arrive there enough, he might manage to outpace the Tartar scouts who were advancing through the Irtych valley, and find a clear route to Irkutsk.

As the tarantass traversed the river, it marked the terminus of what military strategists called the "Ichim chain", a series of wooden watchtowers and small fortifications stretching four hundred miles along Siberia's southern border. These outposts, once manned by Cossack units, had served as a defensive line against Kirghese and Tartar incursions. The Muscovite authorities, blinded by hubris and believing that they had subjugated these nomadic peoples, withdrew the garrisons, leaving the fortifications unmanned, a grave miscalculation that left them defenseless when most needed. Invading forces had already reduced several of these strongholds to smoldering ruins, and the boatmen directed Michael's attention to ominous smoke clouds rising on the southern horizon, grim harbingers signaling the inexorable advance of the Tartar horde.

The ferry deposited their tarantass on the Ichim's right bank, and they continued their rapid trek across the vast, undulating steppe. Though Michael Strogoff maintained a stoic demeanor, speaking little, he remained ever-vigilant and devoted to ensuring Nadia's comfort, doing what he could to ease her burden during their relentless journey across the unforgiving terrain. The young woman, for her part, never uttered a word of protest or complaint, wishing only that their sturdy horses could move with even greater swiftness. She sensed that her enigmatic companion's urgency to reach the city of Irkutsk exceeded even her own burning desire to be reunited with her father, and oh, what a daunting, endless distance still stretched before them!

The thought struck her that Michael's mother could be in grave danger if the Tartars took Omsk where she lived. This would explain why her son was so desperate to reach the city, putting his very life at risk with each passing day. Nadia's heart went out to the noble courier, imagining the anguish he must feel at being unable to protect his own flesh and blood.

Finally, unable to contain her curiosity any longer, Nadia mentioned his elderly mother, Marfa, complaining about her vulnerability during these troubled times of violence and upheaval. "Since the invasion began," she inquired, her eyes full of empathy, "have you heard anything from your mother? I can only imagine how worried you must be for her safety."

"No news, Nadia. The last message I received from my mother was positive. Marfa is a resilient woman from Siberia. Despite her years, she maintains her inner strength and fortitude. She understands what it means to endure hardship." A wistful look crossed Michael's weathered features as he spoke of his elderly parent, the worry for her safety etched into the creases around his eyes.

"I will meet her, brother," Nadia responded, placing a comforting hand on his arm. "If you call me sister, then I am Marfa's daughter, too." She offered him a warm smile, hoping to ease his concerns.

When Michael remained silent, his brow furrowed in contemplation, she ventured: "Is it possible your mother escaped from Omsk before the invasion? Perhaps she found refuge elsewhere?"

"I believe so, Nadia," Michael answered, his voice tinged with cautious optimism. "With any luck, she's made it to Tobolsk by now. Marfa despises the Tartars and their brutality, she would never allow herself to be captured without a fierce fight. And she knows these steppes like the back of her weathered hand. Marfa wouldn't think twice about taking her trusty walking stick and following the winding path of the Irtych River to safety. She's traveled every inch of this province over the decades, there isn't a single hidden trail or secluded grove she doesn't know intimately. She and my father explored this entire region countless times in their youth, and I often joined them as a young boy on their adventurous journeys across the vast Siberian wilderness. Yes, Nadia, I'm confident my resilient mother has managed to escape the horrors of Omsk."

Nadia nodded, relieved by his reassurance. "When will you see her again?" she asked.

Michael's expression hardened with determination. "When I return from the battlefield and drive these Tartar invaders from our lands once and for all. Only then can I embrace her again."

"But if she's still trapped in Omsk, you could spare an hour to visit her before we march?" Nadia ventured, her eyes full of concern.

"I won't visit her," Michael stated, his jaw clenched with resolve.

"You're refusing to see her?" Nadia asked, her brow furrowed in disbelief.

"Yes, Nadia," Michael responded, his breathing heavy as he struggled to continue answering her persistent inquiries. An internal battle raged within him, torn between his love for his mother and the duty that now consumed his every waking thought.

"You're saying no? But brother, what likely reason could you have for not seeing your mother if she's still in Omsk?" Nadia pressed, her eyes pleading for an explanation that could justify such a heartless decision.

"What reason?" Michael burst out, his voice so altered by anguish that Nadia flinched. "The same reason that forced me to endure that scoundrel's presence with such cowardice..." His words trailed off, unable to complete the thought as the memories of that fateful night flooded his mind, the night that had changed the course of his life and set him on this perilous path of vengeance.

"Try to be at peace," Nadia whispered to her brother, her gentle words a balm to his tormented soul. "There's only one thing I understand, or perhaps I don't understand it so much as sense it. I believe your actions are now guided by an obligation even holier than the bond between mother and child, if such a thing is possible." Her eyes shone with a profound empathy, an unspoken acknowledgment of the immense weight he carried.

Nadia fell quiet after that, respecting the sacred nature of Michael's burden. From then on, she avoided any discussion that might touch upon his unique circumstances, recognizing the toll it took on him to even contemplate the events that had set him on this perilous path. She understood he carried a private anguish, one that demanded her utmost respect and compassion. And so she honored his silence, offering the solace of her steadfast presence as he navigated the treacherous waters of his quest for justice and retribution.

On the morning of July 25th, as the first pale rays of dawn crept across the horizon, the clock struck three, heralding the tarantass's arrival in Tioukalmsk after a grueling eighty-mile journey from the banks of the Ichim. Although the travelers arranged for fresh horses, their progress stalled when the driver, concerned, hesitated to leave. With a grave tone, he warned of the ever-present threat posed by marauding Tartar bands, who prowled the vast steppe like hungry wolves, eager to seize any unsuspecting travelers, horses, or vehicles that dared to cross their path. The ominous caution cast a pall over the group, yet they steeled their resolve, determined to press on despite the looming perils that awaited them in the wilderness beyond Tioukalmsk's walls.

The only way Michael could overcome the driver's resistance was by offering a substantial payment, as he wanted to avoid showing his travel papers in this situation, like many others. Since the telegraph had sent the latest imperial decree to all Siberian regions, a Russian with special exemption from these orders would have attracted unwanted notice, something the Czar's messenger needed to avoid at all costs. The driver's reluctance either stemmed from trying to exploit Michael's urgency for more money, or from genuine concerns about the journey ahead into the vast, unforgiving steppe, where danger lurked behind every rise and fold of the land. Michael's urgency and the weight of his mission compelled him to agree to the iemschik's demands, though he did so with a furrowed brow and a silent prayer that no further obstacles would impede their progress.

The team made excellent progress in their tarantass, covering fifty miles to reach Koulatsinskoe by 3 PM. The sturdy vehicle, with its pliable suspension and broad wheels, proved well-suited for traversing the undulating terrain of the steppe. Within the next hour, they arrived at the Irtych River, leaving them just fourteen miles from Omsk, their next major waypoint on the long road eastward.

The mighty Irtych River stands as one of Asia's major northern waterways, carving a serpentine path through the continent's heart. Beginning in the majestic Altai Mountains, it traces a southeastern to northwestern route, traveling four thousand miles before joining with the mighty Obi River in a glacial runoff and snowmelt. Along its banks, nomadic tribes have made camp for centuries, following the ebb and flow of the seasons across the vast Siberian expanse.

The rivers in the Siberian basin were at their peak during this season, and the Irtych's waters had risen, swollen with the recent snowmelt from the Altai peaks. The calm flow had transformed into a fierce torrent, the current churning and eddying as it rushed over submerged rocks and sandbars, making any crossing treacherous. Even the strongest swimmer would find it impossible to traverse such roiling rapids, and using a ferryboat carried significant risks of being capsized or swept away.

Despite these dangers, Michael and Nadia remained resolute, refusing to let any obstacle deter them from their eastward journey. Michael suggested a cautious approach: he would first transport the tarantass and horses across the swollen river, concerned that their combined weight might compromise their safety if they attempted the crossing all together. Once he had secured the carriage on the opposite bank, he would return with the small rowboat to bring Nadia across, sparing her from the perils of fording the turbulent waters.

The young woman shook her head, unwilling to accept Michael's cautious proposal. A delay of one hour was too much in her estimation, she wouldn't let concern for her own safety cause such a significant holdup in their eastward journey. With a determined glint in her eyes, Nadia insisted they all cross the raging river together, tarantass and horses included.

Getting everything aboard the small ferryboat proved challenging, as the swollen riverbanks kept the vessel from coming close to shore. Still, with thirty minutes of determined effort from Michael, Nadia, and the crew, they managed to load the bulky tarantass carriage and all three of their sturdy horses onto the precarious craft. Once the intrepid travelers had climbed aboard as well, they pushed away from the muddy bank with poles and set off across the roiling rapids, the ferryboat rocking with each churning swell.

The boat glided through the water for several minutes, the sturdy craft riding the powerful current with ease. They encountered a favorable spot where a lengthy peninsula jutted from the shoreline, creating a gentle eddy that made the crossing straightforward and calm. The pair of boatmen, seasoned veterans of these treacherous rapids, maneuvered their vessel using extended poles, guiding it through the swirling eddies. But as they approached midstream, the water's depth increased, the riverbed sloping away beneath them. Eventually, they could touch bottom with their poles, leaving only about twelve inches of the stout wooden shafts exposed above the surface, which made navigation challenging as they lost their primary means of propulsion and steering. From their position in the boat's rear, Michael and Nadia observed the boatmen's frantic efforts, concerned about potential delays and the prospect of being swept off course by the relentless flow.

"Watch out!" warned one boatman to the other, his voice cutting through the rush of the river.

He had shouted because their vessel was changing course, the current seizing it in a powerful grip. Having drifted into the main flow, the boat was being pulled downstream, the swirling eddies tugging and twisting at the sturdy hull. The boatmen worked their poles, muscles straining as they braced the stout wooden shafts against notches cut beneath the boat's edge. Through sheer force of effort, they managed to resist the relentless force of the river while steering diagonally toward the right shoreline.

Though they expected to make landfall about three to four miles downstream from their intended destination, this mattered little, as long as passengers and animals could disembark onto dry land. The pair of sturdy, weathered oarsmen, further motivated by the promise of twice their usual payment from the wealthy travelers, felt confident they could navigate this challenging stretch of the mighty Irtych River through skill and perseverance.

They didn't expect an unavoidable accident that was beyond their control. Even their dedication and expertise couldn't have differed in this situation. A freak occurrence, an act of nature no mortal could foresee or prevent, was about to unfold before their very eyes.

The current caught their vessel in the middle of the stream, equidistant from both banks, drifting downstream at about two miles per hour, when Michael stood up and stared upstream, squinting against the glare of the sun on the water. He spotted multiple boats approaching their position from upstream, propelled by both oars and the river's relentless current. As the crafts drew nearer, Michael's expression turned to one of grave concern, for the vessels were military, bearing the colors and crests of an elite imperial regiment.

Michael tensed up, letting out an involuntary cry as the blood drained from his face.

"What's wrong?" the girl asked, her voice tight with sudden dread.

But before Michael could answer, one boatman shouted in terror, pointing an accusatory finger upstream,

"Tartars! The Tartars are coming for us!"

Sure enough, a small fleet of sleek boats filled with armed and armored enemy soldiers was closing the distance, propelled by the combined efforts of oarsmen and the river's relentless current. Within minutes, they would catch up to the laden ferry that had no chance of outrunning their lighter craft.

The panic-stricken boatmen cried out, letting their long poles drop into the water with resigned futility. But Michael refused to surrender.

"Stay strong, friends!" he called out in a firm voice that brooked no argument. "I'll give you fifty roubles each if we make it to the far bank before those Tartar dogs catch us!"

The boatmen redoubled their efforts at these words, digging their long poles into the riverbed with renewed vigor, but it became clear they couldn't outrun the approaching Tartars' lighter craft.

There was little chance the Tartars would let them pass unmolested across the river. Indeed, they had every reason to fear what these notorious bandits and raiders might do if they caught the ferry's occupants.

"Stay calm, Nadia," Michael said in a low voice, his eyes narrowing as he assessed the dire situation. "But be prepared for anything."

"I'm ready," Nadia answered, her hand tightening around the hilt of the dagger concealed beneath her cloak.

"Even to jump into the water if I give the word?" Michael pressed.

"Just say when," she replied without hesitation.

"Trust in me, Nadia." Michael reached out and gave her hand a reassuring squeeze.

"I trust you completely!" she affirmed, staring at him with unwavering faith.

The Tartar vessels had closed to within a hundred feet by now. They carried a contingent of Bokharian troops who were scouting the area around the frontier city of Omsk, no doubt on the lookout for any suspicious river traffic.

The vessel was still a short distance from land, the shoreline close yet far. The crew redoubled their efforts, muscles straining as they dug the oars deep into the murky waters, with Michael lending his considerable strength to the cause, grabbing an oar and pushing with extraordinary power. Landing with the carriage and what few horses remained might give them a sliver of a chance to escape the clutches of the approaching Tartars, who were advancing on foot across the riverbank.

But their desperate attempts to outrun their pursuers proved futile, the distance too great to overcome. "Saryn na kitchou!" came the guttural battle cry from the lead boat, the harsh Tartar words slicing through the air like a blade. Rebels and defiant groups use "Saryn na kitchou!" as a cry to catch and subdue all in their path. And here they were, referring to the Tartars coming after them. Michael knew this command well. It demanded immediate and unconditional surrender, with victims expected to prostrate themselves before their captors. The staccato eruption of gunfire shattered the oppressive silence when neither he nor his stalwart crew surrendered; bullets wounded two of the remaining horses.

The ferryboat jolted as the boats crashed into it; the impact reverberating through the wooden hull. Splinters flew in every direction as the vessels ground together, the cacophony of splintering timber and shouts filling the air.

"Quick, Nadia!" Michael called out, preparing to leap into the churning waters in a desperate bid for freedom. His muscles tensed as he steadied himself on the rocking deck.

Just as Nadia moved to follow his lead, a Tartar lance lanced out, burying itself in Michael's side with a sickening crunch. A guttural cry tore from his lips as he pitched forward, sent plunging into the turbulent river. He raised his hand above the churning waters, fingers clawing at the empty air, before vanishing beneath the relentless current that dragged him away into the depths.

Nadia's scream of anguish cut through the chaos, but before she could dive in after him, rough, calloused hands seized her by the arms and dragged her, thrashing wildly, into one of the Tartar boats. The ferrymen lay dead, their vessel abandoned to drift aimlessly downstream, while the ruthless invaders continued their grim journey down the Irtych River, their prize clutched tightly in their grasp.

© 01/01/2025

Chapter Fourteen

MOTHER AND SON

Tomsk, another city in the region, surpasses Omsk in size and population, though Omsk serves as the administrative capital of Western Siberia. In Omsk, living in a stately mansion near the center of the administrative district, the Governor-General, who oversees this first section of Asiatic Russia, maintains their residence. Two distinct areas make up the city: one, planned with whitewashed buildings housing government officials and administrators, and Siberian merchants; The merchant quarter, with its wooden houses and traditional architecture, presents a stark contrast to the more European-styled administrative district, though both areas share the same harsh climate that characterizes this remote outpost of Russian civilization.

Numbering between twelve thousand (12,000), and thirteen thousand (13,000), residents, the city's population is modest, befitting its role as a regional administrative center. Although the city possesses defensive walls, they are earthworks only, offering inadequate protection, a common but dangerous compromise in frontier settlements lacking stone and skilled masons. Understanding this vulnerability, the Tartars launched an aggressive assault on the city, managing to capture it after besieging it for just a few days, their mounted forces overwhelming the makeshift fortifications.

The defending forces at Omsk numbered only 2,000 soldiers, who fought with great courage despite being outnumbered. However, the attacking forces pushed them back from the commercial district, as they fought street by street through the wooden buildings, and they had to withdraw to seek shelter in the upper section of the city, where the more substantial government buildings offered better defensive positions.

In this location, the Governor-General had established a defensive position alongside his military personnel. They transformed Omsk's upper district into a makeshift fortress, creating what resembled an improvised "kreml" where they managed to maintain their defense, though with little expectation of receiving the reinforcements they were promised. The narrow streets were barricaded with overturned wagons and furniture from nearby buildings, while sharpshooters took positions in the upper windows of the sturdier structures. The Tartar forces, advancing along the Irtych, grew stronger daily with new troops arriving from the steppes, their campfires dotting the riverbank like countless burning eyes in the gathering darkness. But an even greater threat came from their commander, a man who had betrayed his homeland. This leader was Colonel Ivan Ogareff, whose notorious reputation matched his exceptional boldness in the face of any challenge. His intimate knowledge of Russian military strategy and the city's layout made him an especially dangerous adversary, one whose very name caused whispers of concern among the defending troops.

Ivan Ogareff was a formidable military commander who combined sophisticated military training with the ruthless tactics of Tartar warlords. His maternal Mongolian heritage influenced his preference for cunning warfare, using misdirection and carefully laid traps. He excelled in espionage and infiltration, employing various disguises and deceptions. His moral flexibility allowed him to use whatever means necessary to achieve his goals, including falsehoods when helpful. Known for his merciless nature and experience as an executioner, he served as the perfect lieutenant to Feofar-Khan in their brutal campaign. The soldiers spoke of his ability to appear out of nowhere, striking at the most vulnerable points with devastating precision. His strategic genius lay not just in conventional warfare, but in psychological manipulation, spreading rumors and discord that could tear apart even the most unified resistance. Those who had witnessed his handiwork firsthand told tales of elaborate schemes that would unfold like deadly puzzles, leaving his opponents reeling long before the final blow was struck.

Ivan Ogareff had already seized control of Omsk by the time Michael Strogoff reached the Irtych riverbank. Ogareff was intensifying his assault on the town's upper district, knowing he needed to move on to Tomsk, where the Tartar forces had gathered their main army. His troops swept through the streets, crushing any remaining pockets of resistance with ruthless efficiency.

Several days earlier, Feofar-Khan had captured Tomsk, establishing it as the launching point from which the invaders, now controlling Central Siberia, would advance toward Irkutsk. The city's strategic position and well-stocked armories made it an ideal base of operations, while its network of roads leading eastward would facilitate the rapid movement of troops and supplies. The Tartar banners now flew from every major building, a stark reminder of how quickly the region had fallen to the invading forces.

Ivan Ogareff's true target was Irkutsk, the crown jewel of eastern Siberia. His treacherous scheme involved approaching the Grand Duke using an alias, earning his trust through calculated displays of loyalty, and betraying both the city and the Duke to the Tartars. Such a strategic victory would guarantee the invaders' control over all of Asiatic Siberia, from the Ural Mountains to the Pacific coast, cutting Russia's empire in half. The Czar had discovered this plot through his network of spies and informants and, in response, had dispatched a courier carrying crucial intelligence to thwart it. This explained the courier's strict orders to travel through enemy territory in complete secrecy, concealing his true identity at all costs, for even the slightest hint of his mission would put both his life and the fate of Irkutsk in grave danger.

He had executed his mission until now, but would he be able to see it through to the end? The weight of Russia's fate pressed upon his shoulders with each passing moment.

Though wounded, Michael Strogoff had survived. He swam while keeping himself hidden from view, fighting against the current's relentless pull and ignoring the searing pain from his injuries. Eventually reaching the riverbank on the right side, he dragged himself through the muddy shallows. There, he collapsed among the dense shrubs, his strength depleted, his sodden clothes clinging to his exhausted frame as he struggled to catch his breath in the gathering darkness.

Consciousness returned to reveal he was lying in a peasant's cabin. A kind Russian farmer had found him and nursed him back to health. He had no sense of how many days he'd spent under this generous Siberian's care. As his eyes fluttered open, he saw the man's friendly bearded face hovering above, filled with concern. 'Rest your voice, little father,' the peasant said. 'You don't have the strength yet. Let me explain where you are and what has happened.'

The cabin was modest but warm, with rough-hewn wooden walls and a small iron stove in the corner that filled the single room with the comforting scent of burning pine. Dried herbs hung from the rafters, and through the single window, Michael could make out the silhouettes of birch trees swaying in the wind. A weathered icon of Saint Nicholas hung above the bed where he lay, watching over his recovery with painted eyes that seemed to hold both wisdom and mercy.

The peasant described to Michael Strogoff everything he had seen during the violent encounter, how the Tartar vessels had stormed the ferry, ransacked the coach, and slaughtered the crew. The old man's voice trembled as he recounted the savage efficiency of the attack, the screams that had echoed across the water, and the way the morning mist had turned crimson with blood.

Michael Strogoff had stopped listening, his thoughts turning inward as an icy dread settled in his stomach. Discreetly reaching beneath his clothes, his fingers found the emperor's letter still tucked against his chest, the parchment crackling against his skin. He exhaled with quiet relief, though the weight of his mission seemed heavier than ever considering what he'd just heard.

But there was something else weighing on his mind, something that made his heart clench with worry. "I was traveling with a young woman," he said, his voice hoarse with concern.

"They haven't killed her," said the peasant, seeing the worry etched in his guest's haggard face. "They took her in their boat and continued downstream along the Irtych. She's just one more prisoner being taken to Tomsk with the others, they've been gathering up civilians all along the river these past few days!"

Michael Strogoff couldn't speak, his throat constricting with a mixture of relief and fresh anxiety. He pressed his hand against his chest to steady his racing heart, feeling the precious letter crinkle beneath his palm. Yet despite all these hardships, despite separating from his traveling companion, his sense of duty remained unwavering, like steel tempered in fire. "Where am I?" he asked, forcing himself to focus on his immediate situation.

"On the right bank of the Irtych, about five miles from Omsk," the peasant answered, gesturing toward the north where the city's spires would be visible on a clearer day. "The main road runs parallel to the river, but I wouldn't recommend traveling on it just now."

“How could I have ended up in such a weakened state?”

"You took a lance to the head, but it's healing now," the peasant explained, dabbing at Michael's forehead with a damp cloth. "Rest for a few days, sir, and you'll be fit to travel. You fell into the river, but thankfully the Tartars didn't search you. Your money's still safe in your pocket. The current swept you right to my doorstep."

Michael Strogoff clasped the peasant's rough, weathered hand. Then, with a sudden determination that made him wince from the effort, he asked, "Tell me, friend, how long have I been here in your home?"

"Three days."

"Three days wasted!" Michael's voice cracked with dismay.

"You've been unconscious the whole time. The fever only broke last night."

"Do you have a horse you could sell me?" He struggled to sit up straighter on the straw pallet.

"You want to leave?" The peasant's eyes widened with concern.

"Right now."

"I'm sorry, sir, but I have no horses or carriages. The Tartars took everything when they came through! They didn't leave so much as a mule in the entire village. They stripped us clean, like locusts through a wheat field!"

"I'll walk to Omsk and find a horse there," he declared, already pushing himself to his feet despite his obvious weakness.

"Rest a few more hours first. You'll be stronger for the journey," urged the peasant, reaching out as if to steady him. "The road is treacherous, even for those in good health."

"Not even one hour!" Michael's voice held an edge of steel that brooked no argument.

"Very well then," the mujik conceded, seeing it was pointless to argue with his guest's determination. "I'll guide you myself as far as the main road. Besides," he added, lowering his voice to above a whisper, "the Russians still have a powerful presence in Omsk, you might slip through unnoticed if you're careful."

"My friend," Michael Strogoff replied, gripping the peasant's weathered hand with surprising strength, "may Heaven bless you for your kindness to me!"

"Only fools expect earthly rewards," the mujik responded, already reaching for his worn walking stick and threadbare coat.

Staggering from the hut's doorway, Michael Strogoff nearly collapsed, saved only by the mujik's quick support. His vision swam and darkened at the edges as waves of dizziness washed over him. The crisp outdoor air helped restore his senses, and he touched the head wound, thankful his fur cap had absorbed much of the impact. Blood had matted his dark hair, but the gash wasn't deep. Being the determined man he was, such a minor injury wouldn't stop him. He'd endured far worse in his years of service. His mind focused on one thing alone: reaching far-off Irkutsk. He knew he must pass through Omsk without delay, regardless of the dangers that awaited him there.

"May God watch over my mother and Nadia!" he whispered, his breath forming small clouds in the frosty morning air. "I must put them from my thoughts now! Their safety depends on my success."

Michael Strogoff and his peasant companion made their way into the bustling trading district in the lower section of Omsk. The defensive earthen walls surrounding the area had many gaps and openings created when the raiders accompanying Feofar-Khan's forces had broken through. Inside the city itself, Tartar troops filled the streets and public squares, moving about like colonies of busy insects. However, one could observe they were under strict military control, quite foreign to their usual ways. Rather than wandering, they moved into armed groups to protect against any unexpected attacks. Their boots crunched against broken glass and debris as they patrolled, weapons held at the ready. The morning sun glinted off their polished sabers and the metal tips of their spears, creating an intimidating display of force. Local merchants who would have had their stalls open at this hour instead peered from behind shuttered windows, the usual clamor of commerce replaced by the rhythmic marching of soldiers and occasional barked commands in their harsh foreign tongue.

They converted the sprawling central plaza into a makeshift military encampment, where two thousand (2,000), Tartar soldiers now rested under heavy guard. Their mounts remained saddled while tethered, prepared for immediate departure at a moment's notice. Steam rose from the horses' flanks in the cool morning air as they stamped, their riders sprawled nearby on bedrolls or huddled around small cooking fires. Omsk served as a brief stopover for these Tartar horsemen, who had their sights set on the prosperous eastern Siberian plains, where wealthier cities promised richer spoils from raiding.

The elevated quarter above, which continued to resist Ivan Ogareff's forces despite their fierce attacks, overshadowed the commercial district. The Russian flag still waved atop its fortified walls, a testament to the defenders' successful repulsion of multiple assaults. Scorch marks and impact craters scarred the ancient stonework, while makeshift barricades of overturned carts and furniture blocked the narrow streets leading up to the stronghold. The defenders had proven remarkably resourceful, using everything from boiling oil to improvised explosives to keep the invaders at bay.

With sincere devotion, Michael Strogoff and his companion paid their respects, a gesture filled with justifiable honor, their heads bowed in quiet reverence before the symbols of their homeland's resilience.

Having intimate knowledge of Omsk's layout, Michael Strogoff chose less crowded pathways through the town, weaving through shadowy alleyways and forgotten courtyards that most visitors never discovered. This wasn't because of concerns about recognition. Only his elderly mother, still living there, would have known his true identity beneath his weathered traveler's disguise. Yet he had made a solemn vow to avoid her, and he intended to keep it, no matter how his heart ached at the thought of passing so near without a word. He hoped she had already sought refuge in some remote corner of the steppe, far from the chaos and destruction that threatened to engulf the city.

The mujik knew a postmaster who, if well paid, would not refuse at his request either to let or to sell a carriage or horses. There remained the difficulty of leaving the town, but the breaches in the fortifications would, of course, facilitate his departure.

The peasant was leading his guest to the posting-house when Michael Strogoff halted and ducked behind a protruding wall in a narrow street, his movements swift and silent as a shadow. The weathered stone felt cool against his back as he pressed himself against it.

"What's wrong?" the startled peasant asked, his weathered face creasing with concern.

"Quiet!" Michael whispered, pressing his finger to his lips, his eyes alert and watchful. Just then, a military unit emerged from the main square into the street they had been walking along, their horses' hooves clattering against the cobblestones.

Leading the group of twenty mounted soldiers was an officer in plain uniform, his bearing rigid and purposeful. Though he scanned both sides of the street with keen eyes, sweeping his gaze across doorways and alleyways, he failed to spot Michael Strogoff, who had hidden himself just in time behind the ancient stonework. The soldiers' weapons gleamed in the light as they passed by, unaware of the courier's presence.

The troops galloped down the cramped alleyway, showing no regard for the townspeople. Those unfortunate enough to be caught in their path leaped aside, pressing themselves against weathered walls or diving into doorways. A few terrified screams rang out, silenced by jabbing spears, and the street emptied in moments, leaving only scattered market goods trampled in the dust.

After the riders had vanished around the distant corner, their thundering hoofbeats still echoing off the buildings, Michael Strogoff asked, his face drained of all color and his fingers clenched at his sides, "Who was that, commander?"

"Ivan Ogareff," the Siberian answered in a deep voice filled with loathing, spitting the name as if it were poison on his tongue.

"Ha!" burst out Michael Strogoff, unable to contain his rage. The officer before him was none other than the traveler who had attacked him at Ichim's posting station. Though the encounter had been brief, Strogoff realized this was also the aged Zingari whose suspicious conversation he had overheard in the bustling marketplace of Nijni-Novgorod. Strogoff's mind raced as he connected the dots, realizing this man must be a dangerous adversary who had been tracking him for some time.

Ivan Ogareff was indeed the man Michael Strogoff had suspected. By disguising himself as a Zingari and blending in with Sangarre's traveling group, Ogareff had escaped from Nijni-Novgorod after meeting with his accomplices. He had the complete loyalty of Sangarre and her Zingari companions, who served as his paid informants and carried out his schemes without question. Ogareff was the mysterious voice who had spoken those puzzling words that Michael Strogoff heard at the fairground that night, plotting against the Czar under cover of darkness. He had traveled aboard the Caucasus with the Bohemian group, maintaining his elderly disguise among the dancers and fortune-tellers, and then taken an alternate path from Kasan to Ichim, crossing the treacherous passes of the Urals getting to Omsk, where he now wielded considerable power with the local authorities.

Having spent only three days in Omsk, Ivan Ogareff lagged behind schedule. If not for their unfortunate encounter at Ichim and the three-day delay along the treacherous waters of the Irtych River, where flooding had made crossing impossible, Michael Strogoff would have outpaced him on the journey to Irkutsk.

One could only imagine how much suffering a different fate might have prevented! A different fate could have spared the now ruined towns and villages and the families torn apart by conflict from such devastation. Now, more than ever, Michael Strogoff needed to stay hidden from Ivan Ogareff's calculating sight. Yet when the inevitable confrontation would come, he stood ready to face the traitor, even if by then Ogareff controlled all of Siberia from the Ural Mountains to the Pacific shores.

The peasant and Michael made their way to the posting station, keeping to the shadows of buildings and avoiding the suspicious glances of patrolling soldiers. Once night fell, they could slip through one gap in Omsk's defenses, where the wooden palisades had begun to rot and crumble. Getting another carriage to replace their tarantass was out of the question, none were available for purchase or hire in the war-ravaged city. But Michael Strogoff had no need for a carriage anymore, being alone now, his heart heavy with thoughts of Nadia's fate. A horse would serve his purpose, and, one was available, a sturdy, spirited animal with a dark bay coat and alert eyes that Michael, being an expert rider trained in the imperial courier service, could handle even in the most challenging conditions.

At four in the afternoon, Michael Strogoff found himself waiting at the posting station, studying maps and planning his route while the autumn sun crawled westward. To pass the fortifications, he needed darkness, and wishing to remain unseen from Ogareff's spies who might watch, he stayed inside and took some refreshment, a simple meal of black bread and dried meat that did little to lift his spirits but would fuel his journey ahead.

The crowded public room buzzed with discussions about incoming Muscovite forces. Word had spread that troops would march not to Omsk but to Tomsk, their mission being to wrest the town from Feofar-Khan's Tartar control. The air was thick with tobacco smoke and the sharp scent of kvass, while merchants and travelers huddled in corners, their voices a mix of worry and speculation about the brewing conflict.

Though Michael Strogoff listened, he remained silent amid the chatter, his weathered hands wrapped around a cup of cooling tea as he absorbed every detail of the conversations swirling around him. Then a voice pierced the air, a cry that shook him to his core, two words that thundered in his ears: "My son!"

There stood his mother, old Marfa, trembling yet smiling at him, her lined face illuminated by the dim lamplight that filtered through the station's grimy windows. She tucked her gray hair beneath a worn headscarf, and her work-hardened hands clutched at her shawl. As she reached out her arms, Michael Strogoff rose from his seat, ready to embrace her, his heart pounding with both joy and dread at this unexpected reunion.

The threat of responsibility and the grave risk to both his mother and himself in this chance encounter made him freeze. His self-control was so complete that his face remained completely still. The public room held twenty people, and among them could be informants. After all, wasn't it common knowledge in town that Marfa Strogoff's son served as one of the Czar's messengers?

Michael Strogoff remained motionless.

"Michael!" his mother called out.

"Who might you be, madam?" Michael Strogoff said, his steady voice faltering.

"Who am I? Can it be that you don't recognize your own mother?"

"You must have me confused with someone else," Michael Strogoff responded with icy detachment. "A chance likeness has misled you."

The elderly Marfa approached him with halting steps and stared into his eyes, her weathered face inches from his own. "Are you not the son of Peter and Marfa Strogoff?" she asked, her voice quavering with emotion.

Michael Strogoff would have sacrificed everything to embrace his mother at that moment, to feel her familiar warmth against his chest just once more. But he knew that if he gave in, all would be lost, his mission, his oath, and both their lives. The weight of his duty pressed down upon him like a physical force. With supreme self-control, he shut his eyes, unable to bear the sight of his beloved mother's face contorted with pain, each line of anguish cutting him to his core. He pulled his hands away from her searching, trembling fingers, though every fiber of his being screamed to grasp them tightly. "I'm afraid I don't understand what you're talking about, good woman," he said, taking a step backward, his boots scraping against the wooden floor.

"Michael!" his elderly mother called out once more, her voice cracking with desperation and years of longing.

"I'm not Michael. You are mistaken! I am Nicholas Korpanoff, a store owner from Irkutsk," he declared, each word feeling like broken glass in his throat, the lie tasting bitter on his tongue.

Without warning, he rushed from the public room, shouldering past startled onlookers, as his mother's words echoed one last time: "My son! My son!" The anguished cry followed him down the corridor like a ghost that would forever haunt his memories.

Michael Strogoff summoned all his willpower to depart, his hands trembling and heart pounding against his ribs like a caged bird desperate for freedom. He missed seeing his elderly mother collapse onto a bench in near-unconsciousness; her weathered frame crumpling like autumn leaves. Though the postmaster rushed to help her, his concerned hands steadying her shoulders, she managed to gather her strength and sit up, her breath coming in ragged gasps. A sudden realization struck her with the force of a physical blow. Her own son had denied knowing her! She couldn't accept this possibility, couldn't reconcile the loving boy she'd raised with the stranger who'd stood before her. And there was no chance she had mistaken someone else for him, she was certain it was Michael she had just seen, would know those eyes anywhere, even if they now held a coldness that pierced her soul. If he had pretended not to recognize her, there must have been a compelling reason, something that forced him to act this way, some grave circumstance that demanded such cruel deception. Then, maternal instinct taking over, a single haunting thought consumed her, gnawing at her conscience like a hungry wolf: "Could I have brought about his downfall?"

"I've lost my senses," she declared to those questioning her, wringing her hands in apparent distress. "My vision must be playing tricks! This youth cannot be my son. The voice is all wrong, the mannerisms too foreign. Let's put this behind us, or I'll start seeing him in every face I encounter, haunting me like a ghost."

Barely ten minutes later, an officer of Tartar descent entered the station, his boots clicking against the wooden floor. "Are you Marfa Strogoff?" he inquired, his dark eyes scanning the waiting area with practiced efficiency.

"Yes, that's me," the elderly woman answered, her voice steady and her expression so composed that anyone who had observed her earlier encounter with her son would have thought her a different person. The trembling hands and desperate eyes were gone, replaced by an almost regal bearing.

"Follow me," the officer commanded, turning on his heel without waiting for acknowledgment.

Marfa Strogoff strode behind the Tartar soldier. Within moments, someone brought her to the main square where Ivan Ogareff awaited, already informed of everything.

Sensing there was more to the situation than met the eye, Ogareff fixed his gaze on the elderly Siberian woman and demanded, "What is your name?"

"Marfa Strogoff," she answered, her voice betraying no emotion.

"Do you have a son?" Ogareff's eyes narrowed as he studied her face.

"Yes." The word came out clear and crisp.

"Is he a courier for the Czar?"

"Yes." Her shoulders remained squared, her posture unwavering.

"Where is he?"

"In Moscow."

"Have you heard from him?"

"No."

"How long has it been?"

"Two months."

"Then who was that young man you called your son earlier at the posting-house?" Ogareff's tone grew sharper, more accusatory.

"A young Siberian I mistook for him," replied Marfa Strogoff, her weathered face a mask of weary resignation. "He's the tenth man I've thought was my son since the town filled with strangers. I keep seeing him everywhere." She allowed a tremor to enter her voice, just enough to suggest the desperation of a mother's longing.

"Then this young man wasn't Michael Strogoff?"

"No, it wasn't Michael Strogoff." Her words rang hollow in the tense air between them.

"Listen here, old woman. You know I can torture you until you tell me the truth?" Ogareff leaned forward, his shadow falling across her face like a dark promise.

"I've already told you the truth, and no amount of torture will make me say otherwise." She met his gaze without flinching, her hands clasped in her lap.

"This Siberian wasn't Michael Strogoff?" Ivan Ogareff demanded again, his fingers drumming an impatient rhythm against the wooden table between them.

"No, it wasn't him," Marfa Strogoff repeated, her voice carrying the weight of maternal conviction. "Do you think I would deny my own son, given to me by God himself, for any reason in this world? A mother's heart cannot lie about such things."

With a malevolent glare, Ivan Ogareff studied the elderly woman who dared to defy him, his eyes narrowing as he traced the lines of determination etched into her weathered face. He was certain she had identified her son as the young Siberian traveler, despite her unwavering denials. That this son had first denied his mother, only to have her reject him, suggested something of grave importance, a orchestrated deception that only heightened his suspicions. This convinced Ogareff that the man calling himself Nicholas Korpanoff was none other than Michael Strogoff, the Czar's messenger, traveling under an alias and carrying out a crucial mission, one that Ogareff wanted to uncover. Without hesitation, he pushed back from the table and commanded his men to pursue him, his voice cutting through the tense atmosphere like a blade.

"Take this woman to Tomsk," he ordered, gesturing toward Marfa. "Keep her under close watch."

As his soldiers hauled her away, her head still held high in silent defiance, he muttered under his breath, his words dripping with venom, "When the time comes, I'll make that old witch talk. Every mother has her breaking point."

© 01/01/2025

Chapter Fifteen

THE MARSHES OF THE BARABA

Fortune had smiled upon Michael Strogoff's swift departure from the posting-house. Ivan Ogareff's commands had reached every entry point around the city without delay, with detailed descriptions of Michael distributed to all commanding officers to prevent his escape from Omsk. However, Michael had already slipped through a gap in the fortifications; his mount was now thundering across the open steppe, and the odds of successful flight were tipping in his favor. The hoofbeats of his Siberian horse echoed across the darkening plains as he urged the beast onward, its muscled flanks heaving with each powerful stride. Behind him, the lights of Omsk grew dimmer with each passing minute, and the vast expanse of wilderness ahead promised both refuge and peril. Timing his escape had been crucial. Had he delayed even a quarter hour more, the tightening noose of Ogareff's surveillance would have sealed his fate.

Michael Strogoff departed from Omsk at 8:00 PM on July 29th, the fading summer sun casting long shadows across the city's weathered walls. Located midway between Moscow and Irkutsk, Omsk marked the halfway point of his journey, though the most treacherous stretches still lay ahead. He needed to reach Irkutsk in ten days or fewer to stay ahead of the advancing Tartar forces, a timeline that grew more daunting with each passing hour. Unfortunately, the unexpected encounter with his mother had compromised his secret identity, a moment of filial devotion that might yet prove costly. Now Ivan Ogareff knew well that a Czar's messenger had passed through Omsk in route to Irkutsk, and his spies would already spread word along the road ahead. Given the crucial nature of the dispatches Michael Strogoff carried, he realized they would spare no effort to apprehend him, dispatching their fastest riders and most ruthless agents to intercept him before he could reach his destination.

Little did he realize that Marfa Strogoff had been captured by Ivan Ogareff, and she might pay the ultimate price for her uncontrollable display of emotion upon encountering her son. Perhaps it was a blessing that he remained unaware. Would he have had the strength to endure such devastating news? The weight of such knowledge might have shattered even his iron resolve, forcing him to choose between duty to empire and devotion to family.

Michael Strogoff spurred his horse onward, his own restless urgency flowing into the animal. He asked just one thing of his steed: to carry him to the next station, where he could get a faster mount. The beast's labored breathing and foam-flecked flanks told him it was nearing exhaustion, but there could be no rest until they reached the safety of the imperial post station. Every league gained was another minor victory in this desperate race against time and treachery.

The night had stretched on, and by twelve o'clock, he had covered fifty miles before stopping at Koulikovo station. He confirmed his fears when he found the station without horses and carriages. Tartar patrols had swept through the steppe highway, leaving nothing behind. Everything of value had been taken or commandeered from both the villages and posting-houses. Michael Strogoff could manage to secure minimal provisions for himself and his horse, settling for a handful of dried meat and a small measure of grain that had been overlooked in a dusty corner.

Conserving his horse's strength had become crucial, as finding a replacement seemed unlikely in these circumstances. The animal's coat was dark with sweat, its flanks heaving with each labored breath. Yet, convinced that riders had been sent to chase him, he felt compelled to maintain his lead. Every moment of delay could mean the difference between success and capture. After allowing his horse a brief hour's rest, during which he kept vigilant watch from the shadows of the deserted station, he set off again across the vast steppe, guided only by starlight and his unwavering sense of direction.

Wonderful weather had favored the journey thus far. The climate remained bearable, and moonlight illuminated the brief night's characteristic of this season, making travel across the steppe possible. Michael Strogoff moved with unwavering certainty, his mind sharp despite his troubled thoughts. He advanced toward his destination as if drawn by a visible beacon on the horizon. His only pauses came at occasional bends in the path, where he would stop to let his horse catch its breath. Sometimes he would dismount to give his steed brief relief, or press his ear to the earth, listening for any horses galloping across the steppe. Finding nothing suspicious, he would continue his journey, his muscles tense with vigilance. The cool night air carried the faint scent of wild grasses and distant wood-smoke, while overhead, the stars wheeled in their eternal dance, serving as both compass and timekeeper. Each mile covered brought both satisfaction and anxiety, satisfaction at the progress made, yet anxiety over the vast distance still remaining. His water supply was holding steady, though he rationed it carefully, knowing well the scarcity of reliable sources in these parts.

At nine o'clock on the morning of July 30th, Michael Strogoff moved through Touroumoff station and ventured into the Baraba's marshy terrain, his boots sinking with each determined step into the soft, waterlogged earth.

The next three hundred miles would present formidable natural challenges, treacherous bogs that could swallow a horse whole, swarms of mosquitoes that tormented both man and beast, and deceptive patches of solid ground that could give way without warning. Though well aware of these obstacles, he felt absolute certainty in his ability to overcome them, drawing upon years of experience traversing similar landscapes and an iron resolve that had served him well throughout his career.

The immense Baraba wetlands serve as a natural basin for rainfall that cannot drain into either the Obi or Irtych rivers. With its clay-based ground preventing water absorption, this extensive lowland becomes treacherous to traverse during warmer months. Yet this challenging terrain provides the only route to Irkutsk, where travelers must navigate a path through many ponds, pools, lakes, and swamps. Adding to the journey's perils, these stagnant waters release harmful vapors under the sun's heat, making the passage both exhausting and hazardous. The few local inhabitants who manage to survive here have learned to read the subtle signs of safer passage, certain reeds, slight variations in ground coloration, and the behavior of water birds that avoid the most dangerous areas. But for those unfamiliar with these wetlands, each step forward requires careful consideration and a measure of faith, as what appears solid from above may prove to be nothing more than a thin crust concealing treacherous depths below.

Going through the dense prairie grass, Michael Strogoff urged his horse forward. Unlike the grazed grasslands of the steppe where vast Siberian herds roamed, this terrain featured towering vegetation reaching heights of five to six feet. The damp soil and summer heat had transformed the landscape into a jungle of massive swamp plants. Thick canes and rushes created an intricate maze of vegetation, forming an impassable barrier below. Throughout this wild tangle bloomed countless flowers, their vivid colors painting the landscape in brilliant hues, purple loosestrife stretching toward the sky, delicate white water lilies floating in the scattered pools, and golden marsh marigolds dotting the wettest areas. The air hung heavy with the sweet perfume of these blooms, mingling with the earthy scent of decomposing vegetation. His mount's hooves struck harder ground with a hollow sound, suggesting hidden cavities beneath the surface, while other areas were very soft under their weight, forcing both rider and horse to proceed with heightened caution.

Among the dense thicket of reeds, Michael Strogoff's form had vanished from view of the marshy roadside. The startled water birds that erupted skyward in raucous clouds could only trace his presence, disturbed from their resting places along the path as he thundered past on horseback, concealed by the towering stalks that rose high above him. The rhythmic splashing of his mount's hooves through shallow pools and the swaying motion of the reeds in his wake offered fleeting hints of his passage, like ripples spreading across the surface of a pond. Herons and egrets took flight with indignant squawks, their long legs trailing behind them as they sought refuge deeper in the marsh, while smaller birds darted between the stems in confused, chirping masses.

The path was easy to follow, winding through the marshy landscape. Sometimes it cut straight through thick clusters of wetland vegetation, while at other times it meandered along the edges of enormous pools of water, some so vast they could be called lakes, stretching several miles in each direction. Where the route encountered stagnant waters, travelers would find not bridges but precarious platforms, stabilized with thick clay layers. These makeshift crossings, some extending over three hundred feet, would sway and wobble so much that passengers in horse-drawn tarantasses often felt as queasy as if they were at sea. The wooden planks creaked beneath hooves and wheels, their surfaces slick with algae and morning dew, while beneath them dark water seeped through gaps in the weathered boards. Occasionally, pieces of these ancient crossings would break free and drift away into the marshland, requiring constant maintenance by local villagers who would venture out in flat-bottomed boats to make repairs with whatever timber they could salvage from the surrounding wilderness.

Across stable ground and treacherous terrain alike, Michael Strogoff rode at full speed, his horse jumping over gaps between the decomposing planks. Yet despite their swift pace, neither rider nor mount could evade the relentless biting of the winged pests that swarmed throughout these swamplands. Clouds of mosquitoes and biting flies descended upon them in waves, finding every exposed patch of skin and even penetrating through the weave of his traveling clothes. The horse tossed its head in constant irritation, nostrils flaring against the assault, while sweat-dampened flanks trembled with the effort of maintaining their breakneck pace across such hazardous footing.

In summer, anyone crossing the Baraba must wear special protective gear: horsehair masks with fine wire mesh that extend over their shoulders and wrap around their torsos. Yet even with these safeguards, most travelers emerge with red welts covering their faces, necks, and hands, the skin raised and angry from countless bites. The air seems alive with invisible needles, and one might think that even a suit of armor cannot shield against these flying pests, so determined are they to find any gap or seam through which to attack. Humans and swarms of insects, crane flies, gnats, mosquitoes, horse-flies, and countless microscopic creatures, battle for control of this harsh landscape; the insects' numbers seem to multiply with each passing hour of daylight. Though invisible to the naked eye, these insects make their presence known through merciless stinging, to which even the toughest Siberian hunters have never grown accustomed, forcing even the most hardened veterans indoors during the worst of the swarm seasons.

The stallion beneath Michael Strogoff bolted forward in agony, tormented by the swarm of poisonous insects as if countless spurs had been driven into his flesh. Maddened with pain, the beast thundered across mile after mile at the velocity of a railway engine, whipping his sides with his tail and trying to outrun his tormentors through sheer speed. The horse's muscles rippled and strained beneath its sweat-darkened coat as it charged headlong through the punishing terrain.

Only a rider of Strogoff's exceptional skill could have maintained his seat through the horse's wild plunges, sudden halts, and desperate leaps to escape the relentless attackers. Having pushed beyond physical anguish into a state of singular focus, Strogoff was driven by one guiding purpose: to reach his destination regardless of the cost. Through this frenzied gallop, his mind registered only the landscape rushing past in a blur behind him. His knuckles had gone white from gripping the reins, every muscle in his body tensed to expect the horse's next frantic movement while clouds of the vicious insects continued their pursuit, undeterred by the breakneck pace.

Deep in the Baraba region, where summer brought pestilence and disease, an unexpected sight emerged: human settlements scattered among towering reeds. The inhabitants of these Siberian hamlets, from young children to weathered elders, survived wrapped in animal hides, their faces bearing the marks of harsh living. They tended to their meager flocks of sheep, protecting them from the relentless swarms of insects by creating a barrier of smoke. Day and night, they maintained fires of green wood, the acrid smoke drifting across the endless marshland, a necessary shield for their livestock's survival. These resilient people had adapted to nature's cruelest challenges, their homes built on elevated ground to avoid the worst of the flooding, their daily routines dictated by the endless battle against the biting hordes. The damp air carried not just the smell of smoke but also the pungent aroma of herbs they burned to further repel the insects, creating a haze that hung like a protective veil over their isolated community.

Noticing his exhausted horse was about to collapse, Michael Strogoff stopped at a desolate village, its handful of wooden houses standing silent in the gathering dusk. Setting aside his own weariness, he tended to the beast, massaging its wounds with warm grease as Siberians do, paying special attention to the chafed areas beneath the saddle and around the bit. After feeding the horse well and ensuring its comfort in a makeshift stable fashioned from an abandoned shed, he attended to his own needs, restoring his energy with a quick meal of bread, meat, and a glass of kwass from his dwindling supplies. Within an hour or two, as the first stars began appearing in the darkening sky, he was back on the endless road to Irkutsk, pressing forward with urgency, knowing each moment of rest had cost him precious time he could ill afford to lose.

Traveling through the rugged Siberian terrain, Michael Strogoff reached Elamsk at four in the afternoon on July 30th, his clothes coated in dust from the long journey. His faithful horse needed a full night's rest, as the exhausted creature could not journey any further without risking collapse, its flanks heaving with each labored breath. Like all the villages they had passed through before, Elamsk, with its weathered wooden buildings and suspicious inhabitants, offered no alternative means of transportation, there were neither carriages to hire nor fresh horses available in the stables, which stood empty save for a few scrawny farm animals. The sight of yet another depleted outpost added to Strogoff's growing concern about the delays plaguing his mission.

Michael Strogoff accepted he would need to spend the night in Elamsk, allowing his horse twelve hours to recover its strength. He thought back to his orders from Moscow, to journey across Siberia in secret, reaching Irkutsk without letting speed compromise his mission's success. This meant careful management of his remaining method of transportation was necessary for him. The weight of his responsibility pressed upon him as he secured lodging at the village's only inn, a cramped establishment that smelled of stale beer and wood smoke.

The following day, Michael Strogoff departed Elamsk just as the first Tartar scouts were spotted ten mile behind on the Baraba road. He ventured back into the marshy terrain. Though the path was flat and easy to traverse, it wound, making the journey longer. The surrounding landscape of endless pools and marshes made it impossible to take any shortcuts or alternate routes. Tall reeds swayed in the morning breeze, and occasional water birds took flight at his approach, their wings cutting through the heavy mist that clung to the wetlands. The soft ground beneath his horse's hooves served as a constant reminder that one wrong step could mire them both in the treacherous bog.

Michael Strogoff continued his journey the following day, August 1st, covering another eighty miles before reaching the town of Spaskoe at noon. By two in the afternoon, he made it to Pokrowskoe; the buildings emerging like gray shadows through the hazy summer air. His mount, exhausted from the trek since leaving Elamsk, had reached its limit, its flanks heaving and coat dark with sweat.

At Pokrowskoe, Strogoff had no choice but to stop for the rest of the day and throughout the night to allow for essential rest. The horse's labored breathing and trembling legs clarified that pushing further would risk losing his only means of transportation. Setting off again the next morning across the flooded terrain, where patches of standing water reflected the pale sky above, he pressed on until he arrived in Kamsk at four in the afternoon on August 2nd, having covered fifty miles in that leg of his journey. The town's wooden buildings and modest church spire were a welcome sight after the desolate marshlands.

The village of Kamsk stood as a solitary oasis of life amidst a desolate region. Unlike its surroundings in the Baraba, Kamsk remained viable and wholesome, persisting at the heart of an otherwise uninhabitable expanse. Despite the widespread displacement triggered by Tartar forces, the townspeople had stayed put, believing their central location would afford them adequate warning should danger approach. The village's elevated position on a gentle rise allowed its inhabitants to survey the surrounding marshlands, providing an additional measure of security that had helped maintain their resolve.

Michael Strogoff found himself unable to gather any intelligence during his time there. Had the Governor known the true identity of this supposed Irkutsk merchant, he would have sought him out. Yet Kamsk's remote position had isolated it from the turmoil gripping Siberia, leaving it disconnected from the serious developments unfolding across the region. The villagers went about their daily routines with an almost surreal normalcy, tending to their gardens and livestock as if the political upheaval threatening the empire was nothing more than a distant rumor carried on the wind.

Staying out of sight, Michael Strogoff made every effort to minimize his presence. But mere discretion wasn't sufficient anymore, he yearned for complete invisibility. His experiences had taught him valuable lessons, making him cautious about his current situation and what lay ahead. As a result, he kept to himself, avoiding the village streets and remaining confined within the walls of his chosen inn. The small, dimly lit room became both his sanctuary and his prison, its wooden shutters drawn against prying eyes. He took his meals at odd hours when few others were about, speaking only when necessary and in the muted tones of a man accustomed to blending into shadows. Even his footsteps became measured and deliberate, each movement calculated to draw minimal attention from the inn's other occupants.

The rider had grown quite fond of his horse and had no desire to trade him for another mount. He trusted the animal's capabilities. It had been a fortunate purchase in Omsk, and the kind-hearted peasant who had helped him acquire it from the postmaster had done him an invaluable favor. The bond between Michael Strogoff and his horse had strengthened over time, and the sturdy beast seemed to adapt well to their arduous journey. The animal's steady gait and unflagging endurance had proven invaluable during their long days of travel, and its calm demeanor in the face of unexpected challenges had saved them both more than once. With adequate rest periods of several hours each day, Michael was positive his loyal companion could carry him beyond the territories under siege.

Throughout the evening and night of August 2nd, Michael Strogoff stayed within the confines of his lodging, a quiet inn at the town's edge, far from prying eyes and unwanted attention. He spent the hours reviewing his plans and tending to his horse in the attached stable, ensuring both their needs for the coming day's journey were well met. The distant sounds of the town's nightlife penetrated the thick walls of his refuge, allowing him the solitude he required.

Drained, he retired to his quarters after ensuring his steed was well-tended, yet his rest was restless. His experiences since leaving Moscow had revealed the gravity of his task. The rebellion had reached alarming proportions, made even more dangerous by Ogareff's betrayal. As his gaze fell upon the imperial seal adorning the letter, a document that held the key to easing such widespread suffering and securing peace in this war-torn region, Michael Strogoff felt an overwhelming urge to race across the steppe. He yearned to cover the distance to Irkutsk as swiftly as a bird in flight, to soar like an eagle above all hindrances, to move with the speed of a tempest at a hundred miles per hour, all to stand before the Grand Duke and declare: "Your highness, a message from his Majesty the Czar!"

Sleep eluded him as his mind raced with thoughts of the treacherous path ahead. Each time he closed his eyes, visions of burning villages and rebel encampments flickered behind his eyelids. The weight of responsibility pressed upon his chest, making even the soft bed feel as unyielding as stone. Through the small window of his quarters, the faint glow of distant fires served as a stark reminder of the chaos spreading across the land. His fingers traced the edges of the sealed letter tucked within his coat, its presence both a comfort and a burden that would allow him no true rest this night.

The following morning at six, Michael Strogoff resumed his journey, his muscles still aching from the previous day's rigors. This leg of the trip passed with no problems, owing to his careful vigilance and constant awareness of his surroundings. The terrain, though difficult, offered few surprises, and he encountered only the occasional merchant wagon heading in the opposite direction. Upon reaching Oubinsk, he allowed his horse to rest through the night, tending to the animal's needs and ensuring it had fresh hay and clean water, as he planned to cover the hundred miles between Oubinsk and Ikoulskoe in a single stretch the next day. He set out at first light, the morning mist still clinging to the ground like a ghostly shroud; however, to his dismay, the conditions in the Baraba region had grown even more challenging than before, with muddy paths that threatened to swallow careless hooves and low-hanging branches that required constant vigilance to navigate.

The torrential rains from recent weeks had transformed the lowland between Oubinsk and Kamakore into a vast water basin, turning what should have been solid ground into treacherous wetlands that seemed to mock his urgent mission. The landscape was an endless succession of marshes, ponds and lakes stretching as far as the eye could see, with deceptive patches of firm ground that often gave way to ankle-deep mud. One massive body of water, Lake Tchang, bearing a Chinese name from traders who had long used these routes, required travelers to navigate around its swollen shores for over twenty miles , a painstaking journey at best that involved picking paths through waterlogged grassland and avoiding deeper pools hidden beneath the surface. Michael Strogoff found himself delayed by these challenging conditions, though the setbacks tested his patience, each detour and careful step feeling like precious minutes slipping away from his mission. His earlier decision to forgo taking a carriage in Kamsk had proven wise, as his horse could traverse areas that would have been impassable to wheeled vehicles, its sure-footed instincts helping to detect and avoid the most dangerous spots in the waterlogged terrain.

The night fell as Michael Strogoff reached Ikoulskoe at nine o'clock, where he decided to rest until morning. This secluded Baraba village remained untouched by news of the ongoing conflict. Its unique position between the split Tartar forces, with one branch heading toward Omsk and the other toward Tomsk, had so far shielded it from the invasion's devastation. The villagers went about their simple routines, tending to livestock and small gardens, oblivious to the turmoil that raged beyond their borders.

The challenging terrain would soon be behind him. For barring any setbacks, Michael Strogoff would leave the Baraba behind tomorrow and reach Kolyvan. From there, only eighty miles would separate him from Tomsk. His next moves would depend on the situation, and he would choose to bypass Tomsk, assuming the reports of Feofar-Khan's occupation were accurate. He spent the evening studying his maps by candlelight, plotting alternative routes that might allow him to circumvent the city while still maintaining his heading toward Irkutsk. The thought of being so close to his destination, yet facing such a formidable obstacle, weighed heavily on his mind as he prepared for what promised to be another demanding day of travel.

As Michael Strogoff traveled through the peaceful villages of Ikoulskoe and Karguinsk in the Baraba region, he couldn't help but worry about what awaited him on the Obi River's right bank. The threat from hostile forces there seemed likely to be far greater. If necessary, he was prepared to leave the established route to Irkutsk, even though venturing across the steppe would mean risking a journey without reliable supplies or clear paths to follow. Despite these dangers, he knew he had to press forward without wavering. The contrast between these tranquil settlements, with their simple wooden houses and gentle farmland, and the uncertainty that lay ahead weighed on his mind. He observed the villagers going about their daily routines, tending to their gardens and livestock, untouched by the brewing conflict. Yet the distant sound of birds taking sudden flight or an unexpected movement in the tree line would put him on alert, his senses heightened by the knowledge that each mile brought him closer to hostile territory.

As Michael Strogoff emerged from the final stretches of the Baraba around three-thirty in the afternoon, his horse's hooves began striking the familiar firm, arid ground of Siberia once again, the rhythmic clatter a welcome change from the treacherous marsh terrain he'd endured for days.

His journey had begun in Moscow on July 15th. Now, on August 5th, twenty days had elapsed since he set out, including the three-day delay while stranded along the Irtych River, where rising waters and debris had made crossing impossible despite his desperate attempts to find passage.

He still had a thousand miles ahead of him before reaching Irkutsk, a daunting distance that would take him through some of the empire's most unforgiving territories. The thought of the vast expanse yet to cover made his muscles ache, but there was no time to dwell on physical discomfort.

© 01/01/2025
QuantumDigitalPublishing.io

Chapter Sixteen

A FINAL EFFORT

Michael understood all too well why he dreaded encountering the Tartars in the vast plains beyond the Baraba. The trampled fields, marked by countless hoofprints, provided clear signs of the hordes' passage. One could say of these invaders what was often said of the Turks: "In the wake of their advance, not even grass survives." The earth itself seemed to have been scraped clean, with broken fence posts and scattered debris the only reminder that crops had once grown here.

Taking in the scene, Michael recognized the need for extreme vigilance while crossing this territory. In the distance, wisps of smoke rose against the horizon, marking where villages and homesteads continued to burn. The acrid scent carried on the wind told of destruction both fresh and days old. He wondered whether these fires were set by advance scouts, or if the Emir's primary force had already pushed deeper into the province. The location of Feofar-Khan himself remained a mystery. Had he already reached the Yeniseisk government? Michael couldn't plan a proper strategy without answers to these crucial questions. The landscape appeared abandoned that he questioned whether he could find even a single local Siberian to provide the information he needed. Even the birds had fled, leaving an eerie silence broken only by the whisper of wind through the charred ruins.

Michael traveled for about two miles, encountering no one. He searched for an occupied dwelling, but found every building abandoned and empty, their doors hanging open like hungry mouths, windows staring at the desolate road.

Then he spotted smoke rising from a humble cottage hidden by trees. The thin gray wisps curled against the sky like desperate fingers reaching for help. Drawing closer, he discovered an elderly man some distance from the burned structure, surrounded by crying children. His weathered face was streaked with soot and anguish as he tried to comfort the little ones. A young woman, his daughter and the children's mother, knelt on the ground, staring at the devastation before her. Her clothes were singed and torn, her dark hair matted with ash. She cradled an infant of just a few months at her breast, though soon she would have no milk left to feed the baby. The child's weak cries joined the chorus of despair from its older siblings. Everything around them spoke of complete destruction and despair, scorched walls still radiating heat, the remains of a simple life scattered and smoking in the yard, precious family possessions reduced to cinders and ash.

Michael made his way over to the elderly man, stepping around the smoldering debris that littered the ground between them.

"May I ask you something?" Michael inquired, his voice gentle but urgent.

"Go ahead," the elder responded, his weathered face etched with grief.

"Did Tartar forces come through here?"

"Indeed, you can see my home burning," the old man gestured at the flames still consuming what remained of his dwelling.

"Was it their full army or just a smaller group?"

"The entire army, look around. They've destroyed every field in sight. Not a single stalk of wheat remains standing."

"And was the Emir leading them?"

"Yes, the Emir, that's why the Obi runs red with blood. His presence always brings the worst destruction."

"Has Feofar-Khan made it to Tomsk?"

"He has." The old man's voice was hollow.

"What about Kolyvan? Have his forces reached there?"

"Not yet. Kolyvan still stands unburned. But it won't be long, mark my words."

"I appreciate your help. Is there anything I can do for you?"

"No." The elder turned away, shoulders slumped in defeat.

"Then I'll take my leave."

"Farewell, stranger," the old man murmured, already lost once more in contemplation of his ruined life.

Michael pressed twenty-five roubles into the trembling hands of the destitute woman, who could only stare back in wordless gratitude, tears welling in her weathered eyes, before he urged his mount forward with sharp spurs. The horse snorted and pranced sideways before settling into motion.

His mind was crystal clear on one crucial point: Tomsk must be avoided at all costs. The path to Kolyvan remained viable, as the Tartar forces hadn't yet reached that far. Yes, that would be his course, to rest, regroup, and prepare for the grueling journey ahead. There was no alternative but to cross the Obi, strike out on the Irkutsk road, and give Tomsk a wide berth. The very thought of encountering Feofar-Khan's forces made his jaw clench with determination.

With this fresh route mapped in his mind, Michael knew every moment was precious. Without hesitation, he spurred his horse into a steady, ground-eating gallop, heading toward the Obi's left bank, still forty miles away. Questions plagued him: Would he find a ferry waiting? Or had the marauding Tartars destroyed every vessel, leaving him no choice but to brave the river's waters on horseback? The weight of his mission pressed upon him as the afternoon sun beat down on his shoulders.

This point quite exhausted the horse, its labored breathing and sweat-dampened flanks testament to their hard journey, and Michael planned to use it only for this portion of the journey before getting a fresh mount at Kolyvan. That town would serve as a new beginning, as his journey would take on a distinct character afterward. While traveling through ravaged territories remained treacherous, if he could bypass Tomsk and take the road to Irkutsk through the still-intact province of Yeniseisk, with its dense forests and scattered settlements, he could complete his journey within days.

The arrival of night brought welcome relief from the day's heat, the temperature dropping as stars peppered the vast sky above. By midnight, profound darkness had settled over the steppe, transforming familiar shapes into mysterious shadows. Only the rhythmic sound of hoofbeats broke the silence, accompanied by Michael's gentle words of encouragement to his horse, soft murmurs that seemed to float away into the endless night. The darkness demanded extreme caution to avoid straying from the road, which was flanked by various pools and streams feeding into the Obi, their surfaces catching glimmers of starlight. Michael maintained a careful pace, relying both on his keen eyesight that could pierce the darkness and his horse's proven instincts, developed through countless hours of navigating similar terrain.

Michael had just dismounted to get his bearings when an unusual rumbling sound drifted across the darkened steppe from the west. The noise carried the unmistakable rhythm of multiple horses' hooves drumming against the parched earth somewhere in the distance. Following an old hunter's technique, he dropped to one knee and pressed his ear to the ground, straining to interpret the vibrations.

"Must be a cavalry unit moving along the Omsk road," he thought, his jaw tightening with concern. "They're moving fast. The sound's getting louder with each passing moment. But are they Russian troops or Tartars?"

He listened again, his experienced ear analyzing every nuance of the approaching thunder. "Yes, they're moving at a quick trot, perhaps twenty or thirty horses at least. My horse won't be able to outrun them, not after the distance we've already covered today. If they're Russians, I'll ride to meet them. They could provide valuable intelligence. But if they're Tartars, I'll need to stay clear of their path. The question is, how? There's nowhere to hide in this open steppe, not a tree or rocky outcrop in sight."

Looking around through the darkness, he made out a shadowy mass about a hundred paces ahead on the road's left side. "A copse!" he thought. "Hiding there could be dangerous if they're searching for me, but I have no other option. At least it's better than being caught in the open."

Within moments, Michael had led his horse by the bridle to a small larch of wood that the road cut through. Beyond it lay a treeless expanse of bogs and pools, dotted with stunted bushes, gorse, and heather. The air grew damp and heavy with the scent of rotting vegetation. The terrain on both sides was impossible to traverse, a maze of treacherous mud and half-hidden sinkholes, meaning the patrol would have to pass through this wooded section. They were following the main road toward Irkutsk. He ventured about forty feet in before encountering a stream flowing beneath the undergrowth, its gentle gurgling audible above the rustle of leaves. The darkness was so complete here that Michael had no fear of being spotted unless they conducted a thorough search of the woods. Even the moon's light couldn't penetrate the dense canopy above. After securing his horse to a tree near the stream, taking care to choose a spot where the animal could drink if needed, he crept back to the road's edge to listen and determine what manner of travelers approached. His boots made no sound on the carpet of fallen needles.

Michael had just settled into his hiding spot behind several larch trees when he noticed a dim glow emerging, with brighter, flickering lights moving above it in the darkness. The orange flames cast eerie, dancing shadows against the tree trunks.

"They're carrying torches," he thought, retreating deeper into the dense undergrowth with the stealth of a hunter. His heart pounded as he moved, each step placed to avoid any telltale snap of twigs.

The riders slowed their horses as they neared the wooded area. They seemed to use their lights to examine every bend in the road, the torch flames wavering with each methodical sweep. Their weapons glinted in the firelight, suggesting they were well-armed.

This development worried Michael, who crept closer to the creek's edge, prepared to dive in should the need arise. The water's soft gurgle reminded him it would be cold if he had to use it as an escape route.

The group stopped when they reached the woodland's crest. All fifty or so riders climbed down from their horses, their boots hitting the ground with muted thuds. Around twelve of them held torches aloft, illuminating the path ahead, the combined light creating a bright pool that pushed back the forest's darkness. Their serious expressions and purposeful movements suggested they weren't mere travelers, but men on a mission.

Michael watched with relief as the soldiers made no move toward the copse, choosing instead to set up a temporary camp nearby for rest and sustenance. They removed their horses' saddles, letting the animals feed on the lush grass that blanketed the area. The men sprawled alongside the road, taking out provisions from their knapsacks for a much-needed meal. A few of them stretched their legs and rubbed their sore muscles, while others gathered in small clusters, speaking in hushed tones that didn't quite carry to where Michael hid. The aroma of dried meat and hard bread wafted through the air as they settled in, their weapons kept within arm's reach despite the casual atmosphere. Even at rest, there was an underlying tension in their movements, a readiness that spoke of men expecting trouble at any moment.

Michael identified the approaching horsemen as an Omsk contingent, Usbeck mounted troops with Mongol ancestry. Concealed in the high grass, Michael observed them, trying to discern their words. These formidable soldiers were tall, with hardened, intimidating countenances and weathered faces that spoke of countless days under the harsh steppe sun. Their headgear consisting of traditional "talpak" hats crafted from black sheep's wool, while their feet bore distinctive yellow riding boots featuring elevated heels and pointed tips that echoed medieval styles. The leather of their boots was well-oiled and creased from long hours in the stirrups. woven belts of red leather, each adorned with intricate patterns that marked their rank and tribal affiliations, secured their close-fitting military attire. Each warrior's battle gear included a protective shield burnished to a dull sheen, and the curved blade kept razor-sharp, plus a flintlock rifle attached to their mount with well-maintained leather straps. Colorful capes flowed from their wide shoulders, the fabric rippling in the breeze like battle standards, lending vivid touches to their warrior-like bearing. Their horses, sturdy steppe breeds with powerful haunches and thick necks, moved with the fluid grace that came from years of partnership between mount and rider.

The Usbeck steeds grazed near the forest's edge, sharing their masters' hardy bloodline. Though smaller in stature than their Turcomanian cousins, these mounts possessed extraordinary vigor and moved only at a gallop, knowing no other pace. The demanding terrain suited their compact frames and powerful legs, and their thick winter coats protected them from the bitter steppe winds.

The unit operated under a pendja-baschi, an officer commanding fifty warriors, who was assisted by a deh-baschi, a leader of ten. Both officers were distinguished by their helmets, partial suits of mail, and the small trumpets secured to their saddle-bows, marking their positions of authority. Their armor gleamed with careful maintenance, decorated with brass studs and elaborate engravings that spoke of their elevated status. The trumpets, crafted from polished brass and wrapped with dyed leather cords, could pierce through the din of battle with their sharp, commanding notes.

The commander had no choice but to grant his weary troops respite after their grueling march across the steppes. As he and his lieutenant made their way through the sparse woods, they passed a clay pipe between them filled with "beng," the potent cannabis plant used throughout the region to make hashish. The pungent smoke curled in the still air as they walked. Hidden behind a fallen log just yards away, Michael Strogoff could distinguish every word of their conversation in Tartar, a language he had learned during his years as a courier.

His ears perked up at their first words. They were discussing him, their voices carrying in the quiet forest.

"That courier can't be far ahead," the commander said, exhaling a cloud of sweet-smelling smoke. "And there's no way he could have taken any path except through the Baraba. The marshlands would force him along the primary route."

"Is he even gone from Omsk?" the deh-baschi questioned, scratching his beard. "He could still hide somewhere in the city, waiting for us to pass by."

"Let's hope so. That way, Colonel Ogareff's dispatches would never make it to where they're meant to go." He spat into the dirt with obvious disdain.

"I've heard he's local, from Siberia," the deh-baschi continued, lowering his voice as if sharing a secret. "If that's true, he'd know these lands well. He might have left the Irkutsk road, planning to get back on it later. These Siberians are crafty with their backwoods routes."

"But we'd still be ahead of him," the pendja-baschi countered, adjusting his weapons belt. "We rode out of Omsk an hour after he did, taking the quickest route and riding hard. Our horses are the finest in the regiment. Either he's still in Omsk, or we'll beat him to Tomsk and stop him there. Either way, he won't make it to Irkutsk. The Colonel's orders were quite clear about that."

"That tough-looking Siberian woman must be his mother," remarked the deh-baschi, scratching at his beard. "She had the same stubborn look in her eyes."

Michael's heart pounded at these words, his fingers tightening on his reins until his knuckles went white.

"Indeed," the pendja-baschi replied, a cruel smile playing across his weathered face. "She kept insisting the supposed merchant wasn't her son, but it was futile. Colonel Ogareff wasn't fooled; as he said, he'll know just how to make the old crone talk when the moment's right. He has ways of loosening even the most determined tongues."

Each word struck Michael like a physical blow, leaving him dizzy with dread. His identity as the Czar's courier had been discovered! Mounted soldiers would intercept him now, their nets closing in from every direction. And most devastating of all, his mother was now captive to the Tartars, with the ruthless Ogareff vowing to force information from her whenever he pleased! The thought of what torments that monster might inflict on her made his blood run cold.

Michael was aware of the loyal Siberian woman's willingness to die protecting him. Though he had thought his hatred for Ivan Ogareff couldn't grow stronger, a fresh surge of loathing filled his heart as the traitor who had betrayed their homeland now threatened to inflict pain on his mother. The very thought of Marfa suffering at Ogareff's hands made his jaw clench until his teeth ached.

As Michael listened to the two officers talking, he learned that a battle was about to take place near Kolyvan between Russian forces advancing from the north and the Tartar army. Reports showed that a small Russian contingent of two thousand soldiers had reached the lower Obi River and was moving toward Tomsk. If true, these troops would soon clash with Feofar-Khan's dominant forces and face certain defeat, leaving the invaders in complete control of the road to Irkutsk. The officers spoke with such confidence about their superior numbers that Michael's heart sank. The

Russian soldiers were marching straight into a massacre, unaware of the overwhelming force that awaited them.

Someone had placed a bounty on Michael's head, according to information he gleaned from the pendja-baschi's words. The orders expressly stated that Michael was to be captured, dead or alive, and anyone delivering him would receive a reward.

Time was of the essence. He needed to outpace the Usbeck cavalry on the road to Irkutsk and place the Obi River between them. This meant he had to make his escape before the camp disbanded, while the soldiers were still settling in for their brief rest.

Once Michael reached this conclusion, he set his mind to carrying it out with the same iron determination that had sustained him through his journey thus far.

Little time was available. The pendja-baschi planned only a brief hour's rest for his men, despite their horses being as exhausted as Michael's own mount, having had no fresh replacements since leaving Omsk. The animals' labored breathing and drooping heads testified to their fatigue.

With dawn approaching within the hour, Michael had precious little time. He would need to use the cover of darkness to slip from the small forest and speed along the road. Though the night would provide some concealment, attempting such an escape seemed impossible given the vigilant guards and the open terrain that lay ahead. Still, he had no choice but to try.

Michael refused to act rashly, taking time to carefully consider his options. Analyzing his surroundings, he concluded that escape through the rear of the wood was impossible. A wide and deep stream of treacherous muddy waters blocked that path. Below the water's surface lay an unstable, mucky bottom that would not support weight. Only one route remained available: the high-road. He would need to quietly skirt the wood's perimeter to reach it, then push his valiant horse to its absolute limits in a desperate gallop. The faithful creature would collapse upon reaching the Obi's banks, where Michael would then have to cross the mighty river either by boat or swimming. This was the daunting challenge before him.

The sight of such peril only strengthened his resolve and bravery. His jaw set as he mentally mapped the treacherous path ahead, calculating distances and timing with the precision of a military strategist. The cool night air seemed to sharpen his senses, and the weight of his responsibilities pressed upon him like a physical force.

With his life, his mission, his homeland, and his mother's wellbeing hanging in the balance, there was no room for doubt. Every fiber of his being focused on the task ahead, his muscles tensing in anticipation of the moment when he would need to act. The fate of his beloved Russia might well depend upon his success or failure in the next few crucial hours.

Time was of the essence. A faint stirring had begun among the soldiers, with several riders patrolling the road before the forest's edge. Though most troops still rested beneath the trees, their mounts were working their way deeper into the woods, their hooves crunching on fallen leaves and broken twigs.

The thought of commandeering one of their horses crossed Michael's mind, but he dismissed it, those steeds would be just as exhausted as his own, if not more so after their long march. Better to rely on his faithful companion, which had already proven invaluable throughout this perilous journey. His horse remained well-concealed behind dense brush, still undetected by the Usbecks, who hadn't ventured this far into the forest. The animal stood, its breath creating small clouds in the cool air, as if understanding the need for absolute silence in these tense moments.

Michael crept through the grass to reach his horse, which was lying down among fallen pine needles. He stroked its damp neck and whispered soothing words into its twitching ears, getting it standing and making no sound. The animal's muscles trembled beneath his touch, but it remained steady. By now, the torches had burned out, leaving them in total darkness beneath the towering larch trees. After securing the bit with practiced fingers, Michael checked the saddle straps and stirrups before leading his horse away from their hiding spot. The well-trained animal followed, placing each hoof with deliberate care, not making even the slightest sound against the soft forest floor.

Several Usbeck horses lifted their heads and began moving toward the forest's edge, their nostrils flaring as they caught unfamiliar scents on the night breeze. Michael gripped his revolver, its familiar weight offering some comfort as he prepared to shoot any Tartar who came near. His finger rested on the trigger, heart pounding in his chest. Fortunately, no alarm was raised, and he reached the corner where the woods met the road, the shadows of the forest canopy providing welcome cover from any watchful eyes.

Intending to remain unseen, Michael planned to wait until he was around two hundred feet past the corner before mounting. His heart was still racing from the close call with the sentries, and he knew this next part would require perfect timing. His plans were foiled when, just as he emerged from the wood, one of the Usbeck's horses caught his scent. The horse whinnied and started trotting down the road, its hooves clattering against the packed earth. Its owner chased after it and, spotting a dark figure moving in the low light, called out, "Look out!"

The warning cry sent all the men at the bivouac scrambling to their feet and rushing to get to their horses. Curses and shouts in their native tongue filled the air as they stumbled over their bedrolls in the darkness. Michael mounted his horse and galloped away, the animal's powerful muscles bunching beneath him as they shot forward into the night. Behind him, the detachment's two officers were barking orders in harsh voices, urging their men to give chase.

Michael detected a report and felt something pierce his tunic, the sharp sting of a bullet grazing his shoulder. He remained focused forward, saying nothing as he spurred his horse onward, pressing his body low against the animal's neck. With one powerful leap, they cleared the thick tangle of undergrowth and galloped at full speed toward the Obi, the horse's hooves thundering against the hard-packed earth.

His pursuers' fumbling with their mounts gave him a slight advantage as the Usbek horses remained unsaddled, buying him precious moments. But within two minutes, he could hear multiple sets of hoofbeats closing the gap behind him, the rhythmic drumming echoing through the pre-dawn stillness.

The first light of dawn was now spreading across the landscape in pale fingers of gray, making distant shapes more distinct against the retreating darkness. Michael glanced back and saw a lone rider gaining on him, the man's silhouette growing larger with each passing moment. It was the deh-baschi, who had outpaced his men thanks to his superior mount, a magnificent Arabian stallion whose long strides ate up the ground between them.

Without hesitation, Michael leveled his revolver with deadly precision, his arm steady despite the jarring motion of his galloping mount. His shot found its mark. The Usbeck officer clutched his chest and toppled from his saddle, crumpling to the earth in a lifeless heap, his fine Arabian rearing as its master fell.

The remaining horsemen thundered forward, their weapons glinting in the pre-dawn light. Paying no heed to their fallen commander, they urged each other on with fierce battle cries that pierced the morning air, their spurs biting into their mounts' flanks as they closed the gap between themselves and their quarry. The thunder of hooves seemed to shake the very ground.

For thirty desperate minutes, Michael managed to stay just beyond the Tartars' reach, weaving across the terrain to break their pursuit. But he could feel his horse's strength failing beneath him, foam flecking its heaving flanks as each labored stride brought them closer to disaster. His heart pounded with the terrible certainty that any moment could bring a fatal stumble on the treacherous ground.

Dawn was breaking, though the sun still lurked below the horizon, painting the clouds above in shades of violet and amber. In the growing light, a pale strip of land stretched out two miles ahead, marked by a scattered line of trees whose branches swayed in the morning breeze, their only hope of sanctuary from the relentless pursuit.

The Obi River stretched across the landscape, running from southwest to northeast, its surface distinguishable from the surrounding steppe as its bed melded with the flat terrain, the water's sluggish current marked only by occasional ripples catching the early light.

Michael faced repeated gunfire but managed to dodge the bullets, twisting in his saddle as the lead whistled past. When soldiers pressed too close, he returned fire with his revolver, dropping several Usbeck attackers who fell with angry shouts from their comrades, their bodies tumbling from their mounts into the trampled grass. But time was against him. His horse was reaching its limits, its breathing now ragged and uneven. Though he made it to the riverbank, the Usbeck force had closed to within fifty paces, their weapons raised and ready.

The Obi's waters lay empty before him, not a single vessel in sight that could carry him across, nothing but the endless expanse of dark water stretching into the distance like a great serpent across the plains.

"One last push, my brave friend!" Michael called to his horse as he spurred it into the river, whose width stretched half a mile across, the icy water soaking through his boots as they plunged into the current.

The rushing waters made forward progress impossible. Michael's mount struggled to find purchase on the riverbed, hooves slipping on smooth stones and treacherous mud. He had no choice but to attempt the treacherous swim across, though the current raged like a tempest, its icy fingers clawing at both horse and rider. Such a daring crossing spoke volumes of Michael's extraordinary bravery, born of desperation and an iron will to survive. Though the soldiers had reached the riverbank, they balked at entering the churning waters, their hesitation visible even from a distance.

Raising his rifle, the pendja-baschi aimed at Michael in the stream, his expert eye accounting for wind and current. The shot rang out, sharp and definitive, striking Michael's horse in its flank. The relentless current swept the wounded, screaming animal away, its dark blood staining the surrounding water.

Michael freed himself from the stirrups and struck out for the far shore, his arms cutting through the frigid water with determined strokes. Bullets rained around him like hail, sending up small geysers where they struck the river's surface, yet he managed to reach the opposite bank and vanish into the protective cover of the reeds, their tall stalks closing behind him like a curtain.

Chapter Seventeen

THE RIVALS Modern English PBHC

Exhausted but momentarily safe, MICHAEL faced a dire predicament. His loyal horse had perished in the river's depths, leaving him stranded and wondering how to press onward with his journey.

He stood alone, without food or supplies, in a land ravaged by invasion and crawling with the Emir's scouts. Despite being far from his destination, his resolve remained unshaken. "By Heaven, I will get there!" he declared defiantly. "God will protect our sacred Russia."

The Usbeck cavalry had given up their pursuit, unwilling to brave the river's crossing. Now on firm ground, Michael paused to contemplate his next move. Though Tomsk lay under Tartar control and had to be avoided, he needed to locate a town or posting station to acquire a horse. Once mounted, he planned to abandon the main road, only rejoining the Irkutsk route near Krasnoiarsk. From there, if swift enough, he hoped to find clear passage, intending to traverse the Lake Baikal provinces in a southeasterly direction.

Setting off eastward, Michael followed the Obi for two versts until he spotted a picturesque settlement perched on a modest hill. Several churches with distinctive Byzantine domes in green and gold punctuated the gray skyline. This was Kolyvan, a summer refuge for officials and workers from Kamsk and neighboring towns seeking escape from the Baraba's unhealthy climate. According to recent intelligence available to the Czar's courier, Kolyvan remained free of invaders. The Tartar forces had split into two columns, advancing left toward Omsk and right toward Tomsk, leaving the area between untouched.

Michael's strategy was straightforward: reach Kolyvan ahead of the Usbeck horsemen who would follow the opposite bank of the Obi to the ferry. There he would obtain fresh clothing and a horse before continuing toward Irkutsk across the southern steppe.

At three in the morning, Kolyvan lay silent and seemingly deserted. The local inhabitants had apparently fled northward to Yeniseisk province, knowing they could not resist the approaching invasion.

The sound of distant gunfire caught Michael's attention as he strode quickly toward Kolyvan. He halted, clearly identifying the deep boom of artillery mixed with the sharp crackling of muskets.

"Artillery and musket fire!" he exclaimed. "The Russian forces must be engaging the Tartar army. I must reach Kolyvan before they do!"

The battle sounds grew louder, and a haze began forming to Kolyvan's left—not smoke, but the distinctive white clouds created by artillery fire.

On the Obi's left bank, Usbeck cavalry had positioned themselves to watch the battle's outcome. Michael felt safe from them as he rushed toward the town.

The gunfire intensified and drew closer, transforming from a general roar into distinct shots. As the smoke thinned periodically, it became clear the fighting was moving southward. Kolyvan appeared to face an attack from the north, but Michael couldn't determine whether Russians or Tartars held the town.

When he was just half a verst from Kolyvan, flames erupted from the town's buildings, and a church steeple collapsed amid smoke and fire. The battle had reached Kolyvan's streets. Michael questioned whether to seek shelter there. Could he avoid capture? Would he manage another escape like in Omsk? After a moment's hesitation, he considered finding a smaller town and acquiring a horse at any cost. This seemed his best option, so he left the Obi and headed right of Kolyvan.

The battle intensified, with flames now consuming an entire quarter of the town's left side.

As Michael ran across the steppe seeking tree cover, he spotted Tartar cavalry approaching from the right. Unable to continue in that direction and with the horsemen advancing quickly, he faced limited options.

Then he noticed a solitary house among dense trees, which he might reach undetected. Exhausted and hungry, Michael had no choice but to seek shelter there and find sustenance, whether offered or taken.

He rushed toward the building, which stood about half a verst away. As he drew closer, he recognized it as a telegraph office, with two wires extending east and west, and a third leading toward Kolyvan.

Given the circumstances, he expected the station to be deserted. Even if it was, Michael could shelter there and wait for nightfall before venturing across the steppe dotted with Tartar scouts.

He burst through the door.

Inside the dispatch room sat a single clerk—a remarkably composed man who seemed utterly unaffected by the chaos outside. He waited patiently at his wicket, ready to serve any customers who might appear.

"What news?" Michael gasped, his voice ragged from exhaustion.

"None," replied the clerk with a smile.

"Are the Russians fighting the Tartars?"

"So they say."

"Who's winning?"

"I couldn't say."

Such extraordinary composure amid such turmoil seemed almost unbelievable.

"Is the telegraph line still intact?" Michael asked.

"It's cut between Kolyvan and Krasnoiarsk, but still functioning between Kolyvan and the Russian border."

"For government use?"

"For the government when they need it. For anyone else who can pay. Ten copecks per word, whenever you're ready, sir!"

Michael was about to explain that he needed no telegraph—only bread and water—when the door flew open again.

Fearing Tartar soldiers, Michael prepared to escape through the window, but only two men entered. Neither looked like Tartar warriors. One clutched a penciled dispatch, and hurrying past his companion, approached the unflappable clerk's window.

Michael was astounded to recognize these unexpected visitors: Harry Blount and Alcide Jolivet, the two reporters. Once traveling companions, they were now rivals competing for battlefield stories.

They had departed Ichim shortly after Michael but had reached Kolyvan first, following the same route—Michael's three-day delay at the Irtych had cost him precious time. After witnessing the clash between Russians and Tartars outside town, they had fled just as fighting erupted in the streets, racing to the telegraph office to dispatch their competing reports to Europe, each hoping to scoop the other.

Hidden in the shadows, Michael observed the scene unfold, able to witness everything without detection. This was his chance to gather crucial information about whether he could enter Kolyvan.

Blount had managed to reach the telegraph window first, leaving his competitor behind. Alcide Jolivet, unusually agitated, stood nearby tapping his foot impatiently.

"Ten copecks per word," announced the clerk.

Without hesitation, Blount placed a substantial stack of roubles on the counter, while Jolivet watched in disbelief.

"Very well," the clerk said, then began transmitting the message with remarkable composure: "Daily Telegraph, London.

"From Kolyvan, Government of Omsk, Siberia, 6th August.

"Engagement between Russian and Tartar troops."

The clerk's clear voice allowed Michael to hear every word of the English correspondent's report.

"Russians repulsed with great loss. Tartars entered Kolyvan today." The message concluded there.

"My turn now," Jolivet called out eagerly, ready to send his dispatch to his cousin.

But Blount had other plans. He intended to maintain his position at the window, ensuring he could report events as they unfolded. He refused to yield to his colleague.

"You've finished!" Jolivet protested.

"I have not," Blount replied calmly.

He proceeded to write additional lines, which the clerk read aloud in his steady voice: "John Gilpin was a citizen of credit and renown; a train-band captain eke was he of famous London town."

Blount was cleverly reciting childhood verses to maintain his position and prevent his rival from taking over. Though this tactic might cost his newspaper a fortune in roubles, it would secure them the breaking news. France would simply have to wait.

Jolivet was furious, though under normal circumstances he might have admired such tactical thinking. He tried unsuccessfully to convince the clerk to prioritize his dispatch.

"This gentleman has the right," the clerk stated pleasantly, indicating Blount with a smile. He continued transmitting Cowper's famous verses to the Daily Telegraph.

While the transmission continued, Blount stepped to the window, using his field glass to survey the situation around Kolyvan. He soon returned to add to his message: "Two churches are ablaze. The fire spreads rightward. 'John Gilpin's spouse said to her dear, Though wedded we have been these twice ten tedious years, yet we no holiday have seen.'"

Alcide Jolivet was seething with frustration at his rival, the Daily Telegraph's correspondent, whom he wished he could throttle.

He interrupted the clerk again, who remained unperturbed and simply stated, "He has every right to do so, sir - at ten kopeks per word."

Blount had just delivered this news to be telegraphed: "Russian refugees fleeing the town. 'Away went Gilpin—who but he? His fame soon spread around: He carries weight! he rides a race! 'Tis for a thousand pound!'" He then turned to give his competitor a teasing look.

This only increased Jolivet's irritation.

Meanwhile, Blount had returned to watch through the window, this time genuinely absorbed by the unfolding scene. Seizing this opportunity after Blount's message was sent, Jolivet quietly took his place at the counter. Following his rival's example, he placed a substantial pile of rubles down and submitted his dispatch, which the clerk read aloud: "To Madeleine Jolivet, 10, Faubourg Montmartre, Paris.

"From Kolyvan, Government of Omsk, Siberia, 6th August.

"Refugees fleeing town. Russians defeated. Tartar cavalry in fierce pursuit."

As Blount returned, he heard Jolivet finishing his telegram by singing mockingly:

"Il est un petit homme, Tout habille de gris, Dans Paris!"

Like his rival had done, Jolivet had incorporated a playful Beranger verse.

"Well, well!" remarked Blount.

"Indeed," Jolivet responded.

The situation in Kolyvan had become dire. The battle was drawing closer, with gunfire continuing without pause.

Suddenly, the telegraph office shook violently as a shell burst through the wall, filling the room with dust.

Alcide was just completing his message when this happened. In one fluid motion, he stopped writing, rushed to grab the shell with both hands, hurled it out the window, and returned to the counter.

The shell exploded outside five seconds later. With remarkable composure, Alcide wrote: "A six-inch shell has just breached the telegraph office wall. Expecting more of similar caliber."

Michael Strogoff was now certain the Russians had been forced out of Kolyvan. His only option left was to escape across the southern steppe.

At that moment, another burst of gunfire erupted near the telegraph office, with bullets shattering all the window glass. Harry Blount collapsed, struck in the shoulder.

"Even at this critical moment, Jolivet was preparing to add a final note to his dispatch: 'Harry Blount of the Daily Telegraph has fallen beside me, struck by—' when the unflappable clerk announced with perfect composure: 'Sir, there's been a break in the wire.' Then, stepping away from his station, he calmly picked up his hat, brushed it with his sleeve, and with his perpetual smile, vanished through a small door that Michael hadn't noticed before.

Tartar troops had encircled the building, leaving Michael and the journalists with no escape route.

Alcide Jolivet, still clutching his now-futile dispatch, rushed to Blount's motionless form on the ground. He courageously hoisted his colleague onto his shoulders, intending to make a break for it. But he had waited too long!

They were captured, and in that same moment, Michael, caught off guard as he attempted to escape through the window, was seized by the Tartars!

Michael Strogoff - Book II - Illustrated

Juan José Piedra

QuantumDigitalPublishing.io

Chapter One

A TARTAR CAMP

At a day's journey from Kolyvan, several miles past Diachinks town, a vast plain extends, dotted with towering trees, pines and cedars stretching toward the horizon. During warmer months, Siberian shepherds graze their abundant flocks in this section of the land, their bells echoing across the grasslands as sheep and goats feast on the rich vegetation. However, at this time, the approaching danger had driven away every nomadic resident. Yet the plain was far from empty. It was bustling with an ominous activity.

Fearsome Emir Feofar-Khan, at the heart of his Tartar army, commanded a landscape dotted with white tents like sprouting mushrooms, his pavilion a pinnacle of power. The next day, August 7th, saw the arrival of captives from Kolyvan, where Russian forces had failed to halt the invaders' advance despite their valiant resistance. The Russian army had suffered devastating losses, of the two thousand troops who had faced the enemy's twin columns extending from Tomsk and Omsk. Only a few hundred survived, their defeat marking another victory in the Tartars' relentless march westward.

The situation looked grim. Imperial control seemed to have crumbled beyond the Ural frontiers, though this setback would prove temporary, as Russian forces would prevail against the barbaric invaders. For now, though, the invasion had penetrated deep into Siberia's heart, spreading through rebellious territories both east and west like wildfire through dry grass. Irkutsk, Asiatic Russia's capital, stood vulnerable to its insufficient garrison, its walls a thin line of defense against the surging tide of invaders. Without timely reinforcements from the Amoor and Takutsk provinces, their troops still days or weeks away on forced marches through treacherous terrain, the city would fall to the Tartars, leaving the Grand Duke, the Emperor's own brother, at the mercy of Ivan Ogareff's vengeance.

Had Michael Strogoff succumbed to his hardships, worn down by the endless classes of hostile territory? Had the mounting calamities since the Ichim incident, each more devastating than the last, broken his iron spirit? Was he ready to admit defeat, to surrender to the overwhelming odds that seemed to multiply with each passing day, believing his mission was impossible and his orders futile in the face of such widespread devastation?

But Michael belonged to that rare breed who persists until their last breath, who finds strength in adversity and courage in despair. He yet drew air; the imperial message remained secure in his possession; none had penetrated his disguise. He found himself among countless prisoners being herded like beasts by the Tartars, stumbling through dust and mud beneath the merciless sun. Each step toward Tomsk brought him closer to Irkutsk. He maintained his position ahead of Ivan Ogareff, a minor victory that sustained his resolve.

"I must make it!" he vowed, his jaw clenching with determination.

After what happened at Kolyvan, his thoughts focused on a single goal: freedom! How could he slip away from the Emir's guards? Every moment brought fresh scrutiny from the watchful Tartar soldiers, their curved sabers glinting in the harsh light as they prowled the edges of the prisoner column.

The sight of Feofar's encampment was breathtaking, a sprawling city of tents that stretched across the plain like a sea of silk and canvas, banners snapping in the wind.

Countless tents made of hide, felt, and silk sparkled under the sunlight like gems scattered across the steppe. Tall plumes adorned their pointed peaks, fluttering among flags, banners, and streamers of every imaginable hue, from deep crimson to brilliant azure. The most lavish tents belonged to the Seides and Khodjas, the khanat's most distinguished figures, their dwellings adorned with intricate patterns and precious ornaments that spoke of wealth and power. A distinctive pavilion, decorated with a horse's tail emerging from an array of woven red and white poles, marked the exalted status of these Tartar leaders, its shadow stretching long across the trampled grass. Beyond stretched thousands of Turcoman tents, known as "Karaoy," which were transported on camelback, their dark shapes dotting the landscape like islands in a vast sea.

The massive encampment housed 150,000 troops, split between cavalry and infantry, all united under the Alamanes banner that rippled in the wind. The Tadjiks stood out among these forces as the quintessential representatives of Turkestan, distinguished by their classical features, fair complexion, tall stature, and dark hair and eyes that seemed to hold the mysteries of the ancient silk road. Making up the largest portion of the Tartar military, they came in equal numbers from the khanats of Khokhand and Koundouge as from Bokhara, their diverse origins clear in the subtle variations of their dress and weaponry. The air hummed with the sounds of their different dialects mixing, creating a constant murmur that drifted across the camp like music.

Interspersed among the Tadjiks were warriors from various neighboring peoples. The short-statured, red-bearded Usbecks, similar to those who had chased Michael, stood alongside flat-faced Kirghiz warriors who resembled Kalmucks. These Kirghiz bore an array of weapons: Asian-made lances, bows and arrows, sabers, matchlock guns, and the deadly "tschakane", a short-handled ax known for inflicting fatal wounds. Their skill with these diverse weapons matched their fierce battle reputation; each warrior carried three or four different weapons.

The Mongol soldiers presented a distinctive appearance with their medium build, black hair braided into back-hanging pigtails, circular faces, dark complexions, and sparse beards. Blue nankeen, trimmed with black plush leather, composed their clothes. Their attire also included sword-belts with silver buckles, braided coats, and fur-edged silk caps adorned with three trailing ribbons. The ribbons, dancing in the wind like serpents, served as markers of rank and experience, their colors and patterns telling stories of battles fought and victories won. Supple leather and metal studs reinforced their boots, suiting them for riding and fighting on foot, a testament to their versatility as warriors.

The army's diversity extended to dark-skinned Afghans with their weathered faces and battle-hardened expressions, Arabs displaying the classic features of ancient Semitic peoples - aquiline noses and deep-set eyes, and Turcomans with their distinctive pupilless-appearing eyes that seemed to reflect the vast steppes of their homeland. All these varied peoples served together under the Emir's banner, a flag that symbolized destruction and pillage across the lands it conquered.

Within the ranks of these independent warriors were several slave soldiers of Persian origin, led by their own countrymen as officers. Feofar-Khan's military forces highly regarded these Persian units for their disciplined approach to warfare and the mastery of both bow and blade. Their reputation for unwavering loyalty, even in captivity, had earned their positions of trust.

The army's composition was further diversified by Jewish servants, distinguished by their cord-bound garments and small dark cloth caps worn in place of the turban (which their faith prohibited). They moved through the camp, maintaining supplies and tending to essential logistics. Hundreds of "kalenders", religious beggars dressed in tattered clothing and leopard also supplemented the ranks of skins, their wild appearance masking their fervent dedication to both faith and combat. These wandering warriors carried curved daggers beneath their ragged garments and were known for their fearless charges into battle. This diverse assembly of peoples and tribes, each bringing their own fighting traditions and survival skills, formed the Tartar army.

The scene was a masterpiece of visual splendor that would challenge even the most talented painter to capture its full magnificence, a tableau that seemed to blend earthly wealth with divine authority.

Feofar's grand pavilion dominated the encampment. Luxurious silk, cascading in elegant folds and secured with ropes and gold tassels, adorned the tent; the tassels' metallic sheen caught the sunlight like frozen streams. Tall, graceful plumes crowned its peak, swaying like elegant fans in the breeze, their shadows dancing across the dyed fabric below. The majestic shelter stood in a spacious clearing, embraced by towering birch and pine trees whose ancient trunks seemed to stand guard over this temporary palace. A gleaming lacquered table, embellished with precious gems of sapphire and ruby that sparkled like morning dew, sat before the tent, supporting the holy Koran. Master artisans designed its sacred pages from delicate gold leaf, executing each letter and flourish with exquisite precision. The Tartar standard flew overhead, displaying the Emir's coat of arms in its quartered design, the fabric snapping in the mountain air as if proclaiming its master's authority to the heavens themselves.

The ornate tents of Bokhara's highest officials formed a precise semicircle around the mountain clearing, each dwelling marked by distinctive pennants that fluttered in the crisp air. Among these distinguished residents was the master of stables, who held the unique privilege of accompanying the Emir on horseback right into the palace courtyard, a right guarded and passed down through generations. Nearby dwelt the grand falconer, keeper of the royal hunting birds, and the "housch-begui," keeper of the royal seal whose touch could transform a mere document into imperial law. The artillery commander, known as "toptschi-baschi," also maintained his quarters there, his tent marked by crossed bronze cannons above the entrance. The council head, the "khodja," enjoyed special honors, like receiving the prince's kiss and appearing with an untied girdle, signifying great trust and intimacy. Verses from the Koran distinguished the religious authority rested with the "scheikh-oul-islam," leader of the Ulemas, embroidered in gold thread along its edges. The "cazi-askev" handled military disputes when the Emir was away, wielding power over life and death in matters of martial discipline. Completing this circle of power was the chief astrologer, whose primary duty involved consulting the stars whenever the Khan contemplated moving, his tent adorned with celestial symbols and charts mapping the heavens' secrets.

The Emir remained secluded in his tent when the prisoners arrived at the camp, choosing not to appear behind its embroidered curtains. This was likely a blessing, as even the slightest gesture or command from him could have sparked a massacre among his zealous followers. By maintaining his distance, he embodied the mysterious power of Eastern monarchs, whose very invisibility inspired both awe and terror among their subjects, a tradition dating back to the great Khans of antiquity.

The captives faced a grim fate. Guards would herd them like cattle into a crude enclosure ringed by sharpened stakes, where they would endure harsh treatment, meager rations of moldy bread and brackish water, and the full force of the elements while awaiting Feofar's judgment. The Tartar soldiers took particular pleasure in tormenting these captured enemies, prodding them with spear butts and showering them with jeers in their guttural dialect.

Michael Strogoff proved to be the most compliant and composed among them. He submitted to being guided, knowing they were taking him to his intended destination under safer conditions than if he had traveled alone from Kolyvan to Tomsk. His calm demeanor and apparent acceptance of his fate drew suspicious glances from the guards, who were accustomed to more resistance from their captives. Attempting an escape before reaching Tomsk would have risked encountering the Tartar scouts patrolling the steppe, their mounted units sweeping across the grasslands like hungry wolves searching for prey. The easternmost boundary of Tartar control lay at the eighty-fifth meridian, which intersected Tomsk, creating an invisible line between captivity and freedom that consumed Strogoff's thoughts. Once beyond this meridian, Michael believed he would be clear of enemy territory and could journey through Genisci to reach Krasnoiarsk before Feofar-Khan's forces could spread into the province.

Michael silently repeated, "Once at Tomsk" to himself, trying to suppress his mounting impatience, his fingers tapping against his leg as he walked. "Just a few minutes more and I'll be past the outposts. Twelve hours gained on Feofar and Ogareff would give me enough of a head start to Irkutsk." The thought of outpacing his enemies gave him a grim satisfaction, though he kept his face neutral as the guards prodded the group forward.

What troubled Michael most deeply was the thought of Ivan Ogareff being present in the Tartar encampment. Beyond the risk of being identified, he sensed this traitor was the one person he had to outrun. He realized that once Ogareff's forces merged with Feofar's, it would create a complete invasion force that would sweep toward Eastern Siberia's capital as one overwhelming unit. These thoughts consumed him, and he listened for any trumpet signals that might herald the Emir's lieutenant's arrival, his shoulders stiffening at every distant sound carried on the wind.

Thoughts of his loved ones weighed heavily on his mind - his mother imprisoned in Omsk, and Nadia, now held captive aboard the Irtych boats just like Marfa Strogoff. He felt powerless to help either of them. The possibility that he might never see them again made his heart sink with despair. His jaw clenched as he imagined their faces, wondering if they still held hope, if they were being treated, if they had enough food and water. The burden of their fates pressed down on him like a physical weight, making each step forward feel like an act of will against his desire to turn back and attempt their rescue, however foolish and impossible such an action might be.

Within the same Tartar encampment where Michael Strogoff was being held, his former traveling companions, Harry Blount and Alcide Jolivet, were also being held captive. Though aware that the telegraph office had captured them all and that guarded walls now confined them together, Michael kept his distance. Their opinion of him since the Ichim incident meant little to him now. He preferred solitude, wanting the freedom to act if needed, and thus maintained his isolation from his onetime acquaintances. He sometimes glimpsed them across the compound, huddled together in earnest discussion, no doubt planning their next newspaper dispatches should they ever regain their freedom. The two journalists seemed to have formed an unlikely alliance in their captivity, their previous professional rivalry set aside in the face of their shared predicament. Michael found a bitter irony in how circumstances had pushed the competitive reporters together while driving him further into self-imposed seclusion.

During the journey from Kolyvan to the camp, Harry Blount depended on Jolivet's unwavering support. After being wounded and falling at Jolivet's side, Blount kept pace with the other prisoners only by leaning on his companion's arm for several hours. Though he attempted to declare his status as a British subject, the barbaric captors showed no concern, responding only with threatening jabs from their weapons. Left with no choice, the Daily Telegraph's correspondent had to endure the same harsh treatment as everyone else, though he resolved to lodge a formal protest and demand recompense later. The journey proved especially difficult because of his painful wound, and without Jolivet's constant aid, Blount would not have survived the march to reach the camp. Each stumbling step sent waves of agony through his injured leg, and the freezing wind cut through his inadequate clothing like knives. Jolivet, despite his own exhaustion, maintained a steady stream of quiet encouragement in his peculiar mix of French and English, helping to keep Blount's mind focused on placing one foot in front of the other rather than dwelling on the growing infection he could feel taking hold in his wound.

The correspondent Jolivet, ever practical in his outlook, had done everything possible to boost his companion's physical and mental condition. Once they were inside the enclosure, his immediate priority was to check Blount's injury. He helped remove Blount's coat and discovered that the bullet had grazed the shoulder, though the surrounding skin was an angry red from exposure and strain.

"Nothing serious," he assured him, prodding the area with experienced fingers. "Just a surface wound. You'll be fine after I dress it a few times. The inflammation will subside."

"But who will dress it?" Blount inquired, his British reserve clear, even through his obvious discomfort.

"I'll take care of that myself," Jolivet responded, already rolling up his sleeves.

"Oh? You have medical training?" Blount's skepticism was obvious in his voice.

"Every Frenchman knows a bit about medicine," Jolivet replied with confidence, a familiar twinkle returning to his eye. "We learn it somewhere between wine-tasting and philosophy."

Alcide ripped his handkerchief in two, fashioning one piece into lint and the other into bandages with practiced movements. After drawing water from a well in the center of the enclosure, its rusty chain creaking in protest, he cleaned the wound and applied the damp cloth to Harry Blount's shoulder, his touch gentle but assured.

"Water is my treatment of choice," he explained, dabbing at the wound's edges. "It's the most effective pain reliever we know for wounds, and it's now the most widely used. Can you believe it took doctors six thousand years to figure this out? Yes, a full six thousand years, give or take! Such a simple solution, right under our noses the whole time."

"Much appreciated, Monsieur Jolivet," Harry said as he reclined on the cushion of dried foliage that his companion had prepared for him beneath a birch's cooling shadow. His face had already showed signs of relief from the treatment.

"Oh, think nothing of it! You'd do the same for me," Jolivet replied, adjusting the makeshift bandage with practiced care.

"I wouldn't be so certain," Blount replied with frank honesty, though a hint of amusement played at the corners of his mouth.

"Don't be absurd, you fool! Every Englishman has a generous heart," Jolivet declared, patting his handiwork with satisfaction. "It's written into your constitution."

"Perhaps, but what about the French?" Blount countered, his eyes twinkling despite his apparent discomfort.

"Ah, the French, they're savages, if that's what you want to call them! But their saving grace is their Frenchness itself. Now, let's drop this topic, or better yet, let's have complete silence. You must rest," Jolivet insisted, his tone growing more stern with each word.

Despite needing rest for his wound, Harry Blount, the Daily Telegraph correspondent, couldn't keep quiet. The journalist in him was far too restless to succumb to silence.

"M. Jolivet," he inquired, shifting against the tree trunk, "what do you think? Have our recent dispatches made it past the Russian lines?"

"I don't see why not," Alcide replied, busying himself with organizing his travel pack. "I'm certain my dear cousin is already well-informed about everything that happened at Kolyvan."

For the first time addressing his companion, Blount asked, his professional curiosity getting the better of him, "How many copies of her dispatches does your cousin distribute?"

Alcide chuckled, a knowing gleam in his eye. "My cousin is quite the private person," he said, adjusting his cravat with deliberate care. "She doesn't appreciate being discussed and would be upset to think she's keeping you from the rest you need."

"I have no interest in sleeping," the Englishman retorted with concealed impatience. "What's your cousin's take on the situation in Russia?"

"The situation may look dire for now. But damn! The Russian government has such might - they can't be worried about some barbarian invasion," he said, waving his hand as if brushing away an annoying insect. "We will crush these Tartars like all the others before them."

"Even the mightiest empires have fallen because of overconfidence," Blount countered, betraying a hint of the typical English skepticism toward Russia's ambitions in Central Asia. His fingers drummed against his knee as he spoke.

"Please, let's avoid politics," Jolivet interjected, adjusting his position with a slight wince. "Doctor's orders. It's terrible for shoulder wounds - almost as bad as making you fall asleep. And I've had quite enough of both for one day."

"Then let's discuss what our next move should be," replied Blount, leaning forward with renewed intensity. "I don't plan on being these Tartars's prisoner any longer than necessary, Mr. Jolivet."

"Good heavens, neither would I!" Jolivet exclaimed, his voice dropping to a whisper despite their relative privacy. "The accommodations are up to standard."

"Should we make a run for it when we get the chance?" Blount's eyes darted toward the tent entrance as he spoke.

"Yes, if we can't find another way to get free." Jolivet rubbed his wrists where the ropes had chafed them earlier.

"Have you thought of something else?" Blount asked, eyeing his companion with a mixture of skepticism and hope.

"Of course. We're not combatants; we're neutral parties, and we can demand our release. Any civilized army would recognize that fact."

"From that savage Feofar-Khan?" Blount scoffed, shaking his head at the notion.

"No, he wouldn't grasp the concept," Jolivet replied, drumming his fingers on his knee. "But from his second-in-command, Ivan Ogareff."

"That man's a scoundrel." Blount spat the words with obvious distaste.

"True enough, but he's a Russian scoundrel. He understands you can't ignore human rights, and keeping us serves no purpose for him. Still, I'm not keen on asking that man for any favors." Jolivet grimaced at the thought.

"Where is that man? I haven't spotted him anywhere in the camp," Blount pointed out, peering through the tent flap again.

"Don't worry, he'll show up. It's inevitable. He needs to meet with the Emir. With Siberia split in half now, Feofar's forces are just waiting for his arrival before they march on Irkutsk." Jolivet's voice took on a grim tone as he considered the implications of such a military advance.

"And once we're free, what's our next move?" Blount asked, touching the makeshift bandage on his arm.

"We'll keep up our mission, trailing the Tartars until we can make our way to the Russian forces. We can't back down now, we're just getting started. You've already earned your battle scars for the Daily Telegraph, while I have faced no hardship yet for my publication. Though I must say, this entire ordeal has given me enough material for a dozen articles." He paused, studying his companion's face. "Ah, look at that," Alcide Jolivet said, "he's drifted off. Nothing that a few hours of rest and some cold compresses won't fix. These Englishmen are built like tanks. Perhaps getting knocked around by those guards was a blessing in disguise, forcing him to get some sleep."

During Harry Blount's rest period, Alcide maintained a vigilant watch nearby, his notebook at the ready, filling it with detailed observations. His pencil moved swiftly across the pages, capturing not only the events but also the charged atmosphere of uncertainty that hung over the camp. He intended to share these notes with his colleague, ensuring Daily Telegraph readers would receive comprehensive coverage that reflected both their perspectives. Recent events had forged an unexpected alliance between the two men, dissolving their previous professional rivalry into something resembling genuine friendship and mutual respect. Ironically, what Michael Strogoff feared most had become the journalists' greatest hope, Ivan Ogareff's arrival would provide them with the story they sought, a tale of intrigue and conflict that would captivate their readers back home. This put their interests in direct opposition to Strogoff's objectives, creating an unspoken tension that none of them acknowledged. Recognizing this conflict, and mindful of several other concerns about maintaining his cover and protecting his mission, Strogoff kept his distance from his former traveling companions, taking care to remain out of their sight whenever they crossed paths in the crowded encampment.

The situation remained unchanged for four days. The captives received no word about the Tartar camp dismantling. Under constant surveillance, they faced an impenetrable ring of guards, both on foot and on horseback, monitoring them around the clock. Their meager rations arrived twice daily, charred goat intestines or portions of "kroute," a tart cheese crafted from sheep's milk. This cheese, when mixed with mare's milk, creates the Kirghiz specialty known as "koumyss," a staple that even their captors seemed to relish.

Violent storms, lashing rain, and howling winds tore through the camp like angry spirits, turning the weather brutal. The prisoners, lacking any protection save what threadbare garments they still possessed, endured these harsh elements without relief, huddling together in desperate attempts to preserve warmth. The toll was especially heavy on the injured women and children, with several succumbing to their conditions despite the valiant efforts of their fellow captives to share what little they had. Their captors added to their degradation by forcing them to dig graves for their dead, refusing even this basic duty and watching with cruel indifference as grieving families struggled with frozen ground and inadequate tools to bury their loved ones.

During this difficult time, Alcide Jolivet and Michael Strogoff labored in their assigned sections of the compound. Being strong and in good health, they endured the harsh conditions better than most others and could withstand the challenges they faced. Their guidance and support proved invaluable to their fellow prisoners, who were suffering and losing hope. Through quiet words of encouragement and minor acts of help, they helped maintain what little dignity remained among the captives, sharing their meager rations with the weakest and organizing small work groups to improve their desperate situation.

Could these circumstances continue? Would Feofar-Khan, content with his initial victory, delay his advance on Irkutsk? These concerns seemed likely to materialize. However, events unfolded differently. On August 12th, the situation Jolivet and Blount expected, yet Michael dreaded, transpired. As dawn broke, an unusual stirring among their captors created a palpable tension that spread through the compound like an icy wind, leaving the prisoners to wonder what fresh torment awaited them.

Across the desolate plains echoed the cacophony of trumpets, drums, and cannons. A massive dust cloud billowed across the Kolyvan road as Ivan Ogareff led his army of thousands into the encampment of the Tartars, their horses' hooves pounding the earth like rolling thunder. The air grew thick with the metallic scent of weaponry and the acrid smoke of gunpowder as column after column of mounted warriors emerged from the haze, their standards snapping in the wind and their armor glinting in the morning light.

Chapter Two

CORRESPONDENTS IN TROUBLE

The vast army of the Emir advanced under Ivan Ogareff's command. His forces, comprising both mounted soldiers and foot soldiers, had taken part in the capture of Omsk. Ogareff had failed to seize the elevated citadel where the governor and his troops had taken shelter, he chose not to linger. The fortified position had proven too strong for a direct assault, and a prolonged siege would have delayed his broader objectives. Determined to press forward with the campaign to conquer Eastern Siberia, he stationed a defensive force in Omsk, gathered additional troops from those who had taken Kolyvan, and merged his strengthened forces with Feofar's army. The combined might of their forces stretched across the horizon like a dark tide.

The troops under Ivan Ogareff's command stopped at the camp perimeter, their weapons gleaming in the fading light. Their leader did not instruct them to set up camp, as he intended to push straight through to Tomsk with minimal delay. The soldiers remained mounted or stood at attention, awaiting orders to continue their march. This strategic town would serve as a crucial base for their upcoming military operations, its position and resources, making it an ideal staging ground for further conquest.

Along with his military force, Ogareff was transporting a group of Russian and Siberian captives taken during the battles at Omsk and Kolyvan. Harsh conditions confronted these prisoners; instead of placing them in the full main enclosure, guards forced them to remain unprotected on the outskirts, without adequate food or protection from the elements. The relentless march wounded many, and their injuries went poorly treated, while others showed signs of exhaustion. Their fate remained uncertain, would Feofar-Khan have them imprisoned once they reached Tomsk, or would he order their execution, as Tartar leaders did when prisoners became burdensome? Only the unpredictable Emir knew what he had planned for these unfortunate souls.

Trailing behind the army that had marched from Omsk and Kolyvan was the usual collection of vagrants, bandits, traveling merchants, and nomadic peoples, the typical hangers-on that follow military forces on campaign. These opportunists set up their own makeshift camps each night, trading goods and information, offering services to soldiers, and scavenging what they could from the army's wake. Some were spies, others survivors trying to profit from the chaos of war, but all contributed to the swelling mass of humanity that stretched for miles behind the dominant force.

These followers stripped the land bare wherever they went, leaving almost nothing in their wake - not a stalk of wheat in the fields, not a head of livestock in the pastures. The army had no choice but to keep advancing, if only to find enough food to sustain the soldiers, pushing ever forward like a swarm of locusts across the steppes. The army plundered the entire territory between Ichim and the Obi, exhausting all resources down to the last root vegetable and dried grass blade. In the Tartars' path lay only barren wasteland, a desolate stretch of earth that would take years to recover its former fertility.

Moving from the western regions, a notable Tsigane band stood out among the arriving gypsies, the same group that had journeyed with Michael Strogoff to Perm, their colorful wagons and fierce horses drawing wary glances from other travelers. Among them was Sangarre, the ruthless spy who served Ivan Ogareff with unwavering loyalty, her dark eyes missing nothing as she surveyed the countryside. While Ogareff made his way to Ichim, Sangarre led her band through the province's southern territory to reach Omsk, gathering intelligence and marking the movements of Russian forces along their circuitous route.

Sangarre proved invaluable to Ogareff's operations. Her gypsy group could slip unnoticed into any location, acting as his eyes and ears throughout the occupied territories. Through this network, Ogareff maintained a constant awareness of developments deep within the conquered provinces. He rewarded this surveillance, knowing well the strategic advantage it provided him.

The Russian officer had once rescued Sangarre when she found herself entangled in a grave situation. The debt of gratitude remained forever etched in her mind, leading her to pledge unwavering loyalty to him. Her dedication went beyond mere obligation, she had developed an almost fanatical devotion to Ogareff's cause, directing her fellow Tsigane with ruthless efficiency. They moved like shadows through villages and military outposts, their aimless wandering concealing a orchestrated web of espionage. Local authorities, who might have otherwise questioned their presence, often dismissed them as simple nomads, never suspecting the crucial intelligence flowing through their network.

Ivan Ogareff, upon choosing the path of betrayal, recognized how he could use this woman's dedication. Sangarre would carry out any command he issued without question, executing his will with a single-minded focus that bordered on obsession. Beyond mere gratitude, an unexplainable force drove her to become subservient to the traitor, having been bound to him since he first arrived in Siberian exile, where their paths had crossed amid the harsh winter winds.

A loyal associate, Sangarre, who lived as a nomad without ties to any nation or family, had offered her services to the invaders that Ogareff had unleashed upon Siberia. She moved through the land like a phantom, her dark eyes missing nothing, her network of informants growing with each passing day. She possessed remarkable cunning and fierce determination, showing neither mercy nor forgiveness to those who stood in her way. Her ruthlessness made her a formidable ally in Ogareff's campaign, and her reputation alone often extracted information from those who might otherwise resist.

After arriving in Omsk with her fellow travelers, Sangarre had remained at Ogareff's side, her dark presence like a shadow that never wavered. She knew about Michael and Marfa Strogoff's meeting and shared Ogareff's concerns about a courier traveling for the Czar, her instincts telling her there was more to this situation than met the eye. With Marfa Strogoff in her custody, Sangarre could employ cruel methods to extract information from the prisoner, methods she had perfected through years of practicing her dark craft. However, Ogareff had not yet decided it was time to force the old Siberian woman to speak, preferring to let fear and isolation do their work first. So Sangarre waited, keeping Marfa under constant surveillance, studying her every movement and word, trying to catch any mention of the word "son," her keen ears attuned to even the slightest whisper or mumbled prayer. Despite her vigilance, Marfa's silence remained unbroken, a testament to the old woman's iron will.

When the trumpets first sounded, their brass notes echoing across the encampment, a group of high-ranking officers, accompanied by an impressive contingent of Usbeck cavalry in their distinctive armor and flowing robes, advanced to the camp's entrance to welcome Ivan Ogareff. Upon meeting him, they showed him profound respect, bowing and speaking in reverent tones, and requested his presence at Feofar-Khan's quarters, where matters of great importance awaited discussion.

Maintaining his characteristic composure, Ogareff responded to their courtesies with cold detachment, his face a mask of calculated indifference. His attire was plain, yet exuded an air of rebellious pride. He continued to wear his Russian military uniform, its brass buttons gleaming in the harsh light.

Just as he prepared to enter the camp, Sangarre emerged from among the officers like a shadow taking form, stopping in front of him. Her presence caused several nearby horses to stamp. "Nothing?" Ogareff inquired, his voice barely above a whisper.

"Not a thing," she replied with apparent frustration.

"We must wait."

"Will we soon make the elderly woman reveal what she knows?" Sangarre's fingers twisted at her sleeve as she spoke.

"Indeed, we will, Sangarre," Ogareff answered with quiet certainty.

"Tell me when she'll talk."

"Once we arrive at Tomsk."

"And that journey ends..." she pressed, leaning closer.

"Three days from now," he cut her off.

A mysterious light flashed in Sangarre's dark eyes before she walked away, her silhouette melting into the shadows between the tents. Ogareff dug his spurs into his mount's sides with unnecessary force, causing the horse to snort in protest, and, trailed by his contingent of Tartar officers who maintained a respectful distance, made his way toward the Emir's pavilion, where the silk banners snapped in the rising wind.

The high-ranking Tartar leader Feofar-Khan sat awaiting his lieutenant in his opulent tent, surrounded by braziers that filled the air with sweet-scented smoke. His council gathered around him: the keeper of the royal seal, his face lined with age and wisdom; the stern-faced khodja in his dark robes; and several senior military officers with their curved sabers at their sides. Ivan Ogareff arrived on horseback, dismounted with practiced ease, and stepped inside, the tent flap rustling behind him.

At forty years old, Feofar-Khan cut an imposing figure, tall and pale-skinned, with fierce features, malevolent eyes that seemed to pierce through men's souls, and a thick black beard that cascaded down his chest like silk. His battle attire was a dazzling display of wealth and power: a coat of mail inlaid with gold and silver that caught the lamplight, a jewel-encrusted cross-belt and scabbard that spoke of plundered riches, boots fitted with golden spurs that clinked as he moved, and a helmet crowned with sparkling diamond plumes that trembled with his slightest motion. Yet despite all this finery, his appearance struck one as more peculiar than majestic for a Tartar ruler, a self-indulgent Sardanapalus who held absolute power over his subjects' lives and fortunes, and wielded that power with capricious cruelty.

As Ivan Ogareff entered, the high-ranking officials remained in their positions atop cushions adorned with golden thread and intricate Eastern motifs. However, Feofar stood up from an ornate divan at the rear of the tent, where a luxurious Bokharian carpet with a thick velvet pile covered the ground, its deep crimson and azure patterns telling ancient stories of conquest and glory.

The Emir moved toward Ogareff with calculated grace and given upon him a significant kiss, one whose importance was unmistakable to all who witnessed it. This gesture elevated Ogareff to the head of the council, placing him in authority even above the learned scholar, whose weathered face betrayed a flicker of displeasure at this unexpected honor.

Feofar then broke the silence, his voice carrying the weight of absolute authority through the perfumed air. "There's no need for me to interrogate you," he declared, settling back onto his divan with fluid ease. "Speak freely, Ivan. Everyone here is most eager to hear what you have to say." His jeweled fingers traced idle patterns on the arm of his seat as he waited, the assembled dignitaries leaning forward almost imperceptibly in anticipation.

"My lord," said Ogareff, conveying his message with the ornate flourishes typical of Eastern speech, "I bring vital information." He continued in the Tartar tongue, his voice dropping to a conspiratorial timbre that made the assembled dignitaries lean closer still. "My lord, now is the time for action, not idle talk. You've witnessed my achievements leading your forces. We've secured both the Ichim and Irtych frontiers, and your Turcoman cavalry now water their steeds in what are now Tartar-controlled rivers. The Kirghiz tribes have rallied to Feofar-Khan's banner, swelling our ranks with their fierce warriors. Your armies can now advance either eastward toward the rising sun, or westward toward its setting."

"And should I follow the sun's path?" inquired the Emir, his expression remaining inscrutable beneath his jeweled turban, fingers still tracing those meaningless patterns.

"To follow the sun's path," Ogareff replied, drawing himself up with contained excitement, "means to strike at Europe itself, to conquer the Siberian territories of Tobolsk all the way to the Ural Mountains. The very heartland of Russian power lies vulnerable before us."

"What if I venture forth to confront this celestial messenger?"

The Tartars target Central Asia's most prosperous regions, including Irkutsk, for inclusion in their rule.

"What of the forces under the Sultan of St. Petersburg?" asked Feofar-Khan, using this peculiar title to refer to the Russian Emperor. His fingers drummed against the ornate arm of his chair, a steady rhythm that matched the tension in the air.

"They pose no threat," Ivan Ogareff assured him, his scarred face twisting into a confident smile. "Our attack came without warning; Irkutsk and Tobolsk will fall to your control before Russian reinforcements can arrive. The Czar's military crushed at Kolyvan, and they shall meet the same fate wherever they dare face your forces. Their scattered remnants flee before our advance like leaves before a storm."

"What direction should we take to serve the Tartar mission?" inquired the Emir after a thoughtful pause, his calculating gaze fixed on the detailed maps spread before him like a tapestry of conquest.

"We must advance eastward, toward the rising sun," Ivan Ogareff replied with conviction, tracing his finger along the map's eastern territories. "Let our Turcoman steeds graze upon the eastern steppes until their hooves shake the very foundations of Russian power. We shall capture Irkutsk, the eastern provinces' crown jewel, and with it claim a hostage more valuable than any territory, the Grand Duke himself, the Czar's own brother, who cowers behind its walls."

This was Ivan Ogareff's scheme, crafted through years of festering resentment. His passionate words revealed his true nature, he seemed cut from the same cloth as Stephan Razine, the infamous pirate who had terrorized Southern Russia during the 1700s, with similar dreams of chaos and revenge. Ogareff's deepest desire was to capture and eliminate the Grand Duke, thus satisfying his burning hatred that consumed him like a fever. Seizing Irkutsk would deliver all of Eastern Siberia into Tartar hands, from the Ural Mountains to the Pacific shores.

“Do it as you say, Ivan,” Feofar declared, drumming his jeweled fingers against the wooden table.

"What are your commands, Takhsir?" Ogareff asked, his head bowed in deference.

"We shall move our headquarters to Tomsk today," the Emir pronounced, rolling up the maps with deliberate precision.

Ogareff bowed, his scarred face concealing a triumphant smirk, and departed with the administrative officer to carry out the Emir's instructions, their boots echoing against the wooden floor as they left.

Just as he prepared to mount his horse to return to the outposts, chaos erupted from the prisoners' section of the camp. Several shouts pierced the air, followed by the crack of two or three gunshots, the sounds echoing off the wooden barracks. Perhaps some captives had attempted to escape or start an uprising, something that would require immediate and harsh response to maintain iron discipline among the ranks.

Ivan Ogareff and the administrative officer strode toward the commotion, their faces dark with contained fury. Within moments, two men burst through the gathering crowd, their clothes torn and muddy, having overpowered the guards who tried to restrain them with rifle butts and bare hands. All the other surrounding Tartar soldiers raised their weapons, ready to fire.

Lacking further information, and adhering to standard procedure, the administrative officer ordered the prisoners' deaths; however, Ogareff's intervention prevented the execution. Because these prisoners' manner and dress, different from the local captives, revealed their foreign nature to the Russian, who ordered them brought for questioning, his cold eyes studying their features.

Harry Blount and Alcide Jolivet stood before Ivan Ogareff. Earlier, they had insisted on seeing him upon his arrival at the camp, but the soldiers had denied their request with rough shoves and harsh words. What followed was chaos. A scuffle broke out when Blount attempted to push past a guard, the journalists attempted to flee through the gathering crowd, and shots rang out, the bullets whistling past their ears and kicking up dirt at their feet. Their lives would have ended there in the dusty camp thoroughfare had the Emir's lieutenant not stepped in, raising his hand to halt the execution.

The lieutenant studied these unfamiliar prisoners with scrutiny, noting their European dress and bearing. Though they had witnessed the violent encounter at the Ichim post-house where Ogareff had struck Michael Strogoff, the cruel traveler had paid no mind to anyone else present in that common room too focused on his own dark purposes to notice the watching journalists huddled in the shadows of the crowded space.

The two men, Blount and Jolivet, identified him, prompting Jolivet to whisper with contained revulsion, "Well, well! So the Colonel Ogareff we see here is none other than that brute from Ichim!" He then leaned closer to his companion, his breath hot against Blount's ear as he murmured, "Please handle this conversation, Blount. I'd be grateful. Something about seeing this Russian colonel in a Tartar camp turns my stomach. Though I owe him my life, I don't trust myself to look him in the eye without revealing my disgust. The very sight of him makes my blood run cold."

With these words, Alcide Jolivet composed his features into a mask of supreme, disdainful indifference, drawing himself up with the practiced hauteur of a Parisian gentleman who has encountered something unpleasant.

Ivan Ogareff may have noticed the prisoner's contemptuous demeanor, but he gave no sign, his face remaining as impassive as carved stone. "Your names, gentlemen?" he inquired in Russian, his voice cool and measured, lacking its characteristic harshness, though an undercurrent of menace lingered beneath the polite words.

"We're reporters from British and French newspapers," Blount stated, his clipped English accent lending authority to the simple declaration.

"I assume you have documentation to verify your credentials?" Ogareff's eyes narrowed as he studied their faces, searching for any sign of deception.

"These letters from the British and French chancelleries confirm our authorization in Russia," Blount declared, withdrawing the preserved documents from his leather satchel.

Ivan Ogareff examined the papers Blount presented, turning them over in his gloved hands and scrutinizing the official seals. "You're requesting permission to cover our military campaign in Siberia?" he asked, his tone neutral.

"All we want is freedom of movement," the British journalist replied curtly, his stance rigid and professional despite the tension in the air.

"Consider it granted, gentlemen," Ogareff responded, handing the papers back with practiced precision. "I look forward to reading your coverage in the Daily Telegraph." A ghost of a smile played at the corners of his mouth.

"The cost is sixpence per issue, delivery included," Blount stated with remarkable composure, as if discussing subscription rates in a London drawing room. He then rejoined his associate, who seemed to endorse his handling of the situation, a slight nod passing between them.

Showing no sign of annoyance at the journalist's impertinence, Ivan Ogareff mounted his steed with fluid grace and, taking his position at the front of his military escort, vanished into a swirling cloud of dust kicked up by dozens of hooves.

"Tell me, Jolivet, what's your impression of Colonel Ivan Ogareff? Who commands the Tartar forces?" Blount inquired once the soldiers were well out of earshot, brushing dust from his sleeve.

"My dear friend," Alcide responded with a sardonic grin, adjusting his cravat with theatrical flair, "I must say the administrator displayed quite an elegant form when he signaled for our execution. Such impeccable posture, is truly the mark of a gentleman."

Ogareff's motives aside, the two correspondents now found themselves unrestrained, able to move throughout the war zone. Rather than part ways, they stayed together, their previous antagonism having transformed into genuine camaraderie. Their shared experiences had forged a bond between them, erasing their former competitive spirit. Harry Blount remained grateful for his companion's help, though the latter never mentioned it. This newfound friendship enhanced their reporting capabilities, benefiting their readership from both the Daily Telegraph and Le Constitutionnel.

"Now that we're free," Blount inquired, adjusting his wire-rimmed spectacles with a thoughtful expression, "what's our next move?"

"You might as well take advantage of it," Alcide responded, pulling out his leather-bound notebook and studying the scrawled maps within. "We should head to Tomsk and observe the situation there firsthand."

"Until we can reconnect with a Russian regiment, I assume? Hopefully that won't be long," his companion replied, squinting at the distant horizon where dust clouds still marked Ogareff's departure.

"Exactly, my dear Blount. We mustn't become too comfortable among the Tartars. The civilized army has the advantage here. These Central Asian invaders have nothing to gain and everything to lose, while the Russians will push them back. It's a matter of time," Alcide declared with the confident air of a seasoned war correspondent who had witnessed countless similar conflicts.

While Ivan Ogareff's arrival had granted freedom to Jolivet and Blount, it posed a serious threat to Michael Strogoff. If chance brought the Czar's courier face-to-face with Ogareff, he would surely recognize Michael as the traveler he had treated so harshly at the Ichim post-house. Though Michael had restrained himself from responding to that insult, unlike how he might have reacted in different circumstances, any recognition would draw unwanted attention to him and complicate executing his mission. The memory of that confrontation still burned in his mind, making him all too aware of how precarious his position had become.

The situation had its drawbacks. Yet his presence brought one welcome development, the command to break camp and move headquarters to Tomsk. This aligned with Michael's deepest wishes. As mentioned before, he aimed to reach Tomsk by blending in with the other captives, reducing his chances of being spotted by the many scouts patrolling the town's outskirts. However, with Ivan Ogareff's unexpected appearance, he questioned whether his original strategy remained viable or if he should attempt an escape during the transfer instead. The chaos of moving an entire camp might provide opportunities, but it would also mean increased vigilance from the guards. Every option carried its own risks, and Michael knew one wrong choice could doom not only himself but his vital mission to warn Irkutsk.

The plan to continue on would have held firm in Michael's mind if not for the news that Feofar-Khan and Ogareff were already moving toward the town, accompanied by thousands of mounted warriors. "Perhaps it's best to bide my time," he reasoned. "Unless fortune presents an extraordinary chance to break free. The dangers are considerable on this side of Tomsk, but once I push beyond it, I'll have cleared the easternmost Tartar positions within hours. Just three more days of endurance, Lord willing!" His muscles tensed at the thought, but he forced himself to maintain an appearance of defeated resignation.

Watched by a large contingent of Tartar guards, the prisoners faced a grueling three-day trek across the steppe. The journey stretched one hundred and fifty kilometers from their camp to their destination, a manageable distance for the Emir's well-provisioned troops but a brutal ordeal for the captives, weakened by hunger and hardship. The bodies of those who couldn't survive the journey would soon mark the path they would take. Already, the elderly and infirm among them cast desperate glances at the horizon, knowing their chances of reaching Tomsk were slim.

The sun blazed overhead at two o'clock on August 12th, without a cloud in sight, when the toptschi-baschi commanded the group to begin their journey. The harsh rays beat down on the assembled crowd, and the dry grass crackled beneath their feet as they shuffled into formation.

Having gained horses, Alcide and Blount had already departed for Tomsk, where fate would bring together the key figures in this tale, their hoofbeats fading into the distance as dust clouds marked their progress across the barren landscape.

Among the captives in Ivan Ogareff's Tartar camp was an elderly woman who remained silent, keeping to herself and avoiding the other prisoners. She never uttered a sound, resembling a living monument to sorrow, her weathered face bearing the deep lines of untold hardships. This woman received close supervision, with the gipsy spy Tsigane Sangarre watching her, her dark eyes never straying far from her charge, though the old woman seemed oblivious to this surveillance. Despite her advanced years, she was forced to march alongside the other prisoners on foot, receiving no mercy or special consideration for her age, her steps growing more labored with each passing hour.

In their midst stood a young woman, placed there by fate's merciful hand to provide solace and aid. Among the other captives, this beautiful yet quiet girl had appointed herself as guardian to the elderly prisoner, moving with grace despite the harsh conditions. Though they exchanged no words, the young woman stayed beside the old woman, offering her support on difficult terrain and sharing her meager water ration whenever needed. Yet as time passed, the girl's straightforward gaze, modest demeanor, and the unspoken bond that forms between fellow sufferers melted Marfa Strogoff's reserve, creating a silent alliance against their shared misfortune.

Nadia, for this was indeed her name, returned to the mother the same care she had once received from the son. Her natural compassion guided her actions twofold. By dedicating herself to the older woman's care, Nadia's youth and beauty found shelter beneath the protective mantle of the elderly prisoner's age, shielding her from unwanted attention in these dangerous times.

The silent pair, a grandmother and granddaughter, commanded a certain respect from the crowd of suffering, embittered people around them. Even the most hardened among their fellow captives would step aside to let them pass, perhaps reminded of their own mothers or daughters left behind.

Tartar scouts captured Nadia along the Irtych and transported her to Omsk with other unfortunate travelers. There she remained a prisoner, sharing the same fate as all others taken by Ivan Ogareff, including Marfa Strogoff. The girl's quiet strength never wavered, even as the harsh conditions of their captivity tested the limits of human endurance.

Only Nadia's remarkable strength of spirit kept her from collapsing under these twin blows. The halting of her journey and Michael's death had left her oscillating between despair and agitation. She faced the anguish of being separated, perhaps, from her father, just when her determined efforts had brought her so close to him. Adding to her sorrow was the loss of her brave companion, whom Providence seemed to have sent to guide her. She couldn't banish from her thoughts the image of Michael Strogoff being struck by a lance before her eyes and vanishing into the Irtych's waters, his body swept away by the merciless current while she stood helpless on the shore.

Was it possible for such a noble person to meet such an end? Why would God not intervene if this virtuous soul, driven by an honorable mission, was destined for such a tragic fate? Her sorrow soon gave way to fury, burning hot in her chest. She recalled the humiliating incident at the Ichim relay station, where her companion had shown remarkable restraint in the face of cruel provocations. The memory made her blood surge with indignation, and her hands clenched at her sides as she relived those moments of helpless anger.

"Who shall seek justice for one who can no longer seek it himself?" she wondered, her whispered words carrying the weight of both a prayer and a promise. The question echoed in her mind, unanswered but persistent, as she gazed through the bars of her prison toward the distant horizon.

Deep within, she declared, "Let it be me!" The words burst forth with fierce determination, though she spoke them only to herself. Had Michael shared his secret with her before his passing, despite her being a young woman, she might have been able to complete the unfinished mission of her brother, whom the Lord had claimed . The weight of this lost opportunity pressed heavily upon her conscience.

Nadia, lost in her own reflections, noticed the hardships of her imprisonment, the cold stone walls, the meager rations, the endless hours of silence. A twist of fate placed her alongside Marfa Strogoff, and she remained unaware of the woman's true identity. How could she know that this elderly fellow prisoner was the mother of the man she knew only as

Nicholas Korpanoff? The weathered lines on Marfa's face held no clue to their connection. Marfa couldn't understand that this young woman beside her was her son's connection, and owed him an unrepayable debt of gratitude. They sat together in their shared confinement, each harboring secrets that might have changed everything had they only known.

What caught Nadia's attention about Marfa Strogoff was how they both endured their misfortunes with similar resilience. The elderly woman's steadfast demeanor in the face of daily trials and her indifference to physical discomfort could only stem from an emotional anguish that matched Nadia's own. This understanding was correct. An unspoken connection formed between them, as Nadia recognized in Marfa the same deep suffering that lay beneath the surface. The young girl's proud spirit admired this dignified way of handling hardship. Rather than offering help, Nadia provided it, leaving Marfa neither the burden of accepting nor declining help. Whenever the path grew challenging, Nadia was there for support. During food distribution, while the older woman would remain still, Nadia would share her meager rations with her, often placing the better portions near Marfa's hands when the guards weren't looking. This arrangement helped them endure the grueling journey across the harsh terrain, where each step seemed to drain more of their strength. With Nadia's support, Marfa could keep pace with the prisoner-guarding soldiers without suffering the fate of many other unfortunate captives who were bound to saddle-bows and pulled along this trail of misery, their feet bloody and raw from being dragged across the unforgiving ground.

The aged Marfa Strogoff could only exclaim, "May the Lord bless you, dear child, for your kindness to me in my twilight years!" These heartfelt words marked their sole exchange for some time, hanging in the air like a fragile thread connecting their shared misfortune.

Though the days stretched before them like centuries, both women remained quiet about their circumstances, finding solace in their silent companionship amid the harsh realities of their journey. Marfa, exercising careful discretion, shared minimal details about herself, avoiding any mention of her son or their fateful encounter, her weathered face masking the pain of secrets held close.

Nadia, too, kept to herself, though her composure gave way under the weight of her burdens. One day, as they huddled together during a brief rest, her emotions spilled forth as she recounted everything, from leaving Wladimir to witnessing Nicholas Korpanoff's last moments, her voice trembling with the raw memory of those events.

The elderly Siberian woman listened with strong attention as her young friend spoke, her lined face betraying a flash of recognition that she concealed. "Nicholas Korpanoff, you say?" she inquired, her voice carrying an unusual urgency. "Please, tell me more about him. In all my years, I've known only one person who might act in such a way. Are you certain that was his name? Think, my dear." Her gnarled fingers gripped her worn shawl as she waited for the answer.

"He was honest with me about everything else," Nadia responded, her fingers tracing patterns on the rough wooden table between them. "Why would he lie about his name? Everything about him spoke of honor and truth."

Driven by a strange inner feeling that seemed to quicken her aged heart, Marfa Strogoff pressed on with her questions, leaning forward in her chair.

"You mentioned his bravery, child. Did you witness this courage yourself?" she asked, her eyes searching Nadia's face.

"Brave doesn't describe him," Nadia declared with conviction, her cheeks flushing with remembered admiration. "He faced dangers that would have broken lesser men."

Marfa whispered to herself, her voice stirring the air, "That's exactly how my son would have behaved."

"Did you not mention," she continued, her voice growing stronger, "that he remained undaunted and unshaken by any challenge? That his gentle strength made him like both a brother and sister to you, watching over you with a mother's care?"

"Yes, that's true," Nadia confirmed, clasping her hands together. "He was everything to me, brother, sister, and mother, all in one! Through the darkest nights and coldest days, he never wavered."

"And he protected you fiercely, like a lion?" Marfa's voice quavered with suppressed emotion.

"Indeed, he did!" Nadia exclaimed, rising from her seat in enthusiasm. "Like a lion, an authentic hero! Nothing could stop him when danger threatened."

'My son, my son!' thought the elderly Siberian woman, her heart pounding beneath her worn dress. But aloud she said, maintaining her composure with visible effort, "Yet you mentioned he endured a terrible insult at the post-house in Ichim?"

"He endured it," Nadia replied, lowering her eyes, her fingers twisting the fabric of her dress.

"Endured it!" Marfa whispered with a shudder, her weathered hands trembling in her lap.

"Mother, please," Nadia pleaded, leaning forward with earnest intensity, "don't judge him! He carried a secret, a secret that only God can judge right now! There was purpose in everything he did."

Marfa lifted her head, her eyes searching Nadia's face as if trying to peer into her very soul, studying every minute expression that crossed the young woman's features. I'm curious. Did his public embarrassment cause you to despise Nicholas Korpanoff?

"No," Nadia answered, her voice filled with conviction despite its gentleness. "I was in awe of him, even though I couldn't comprehend his actions. Never had I felt he deserved more respect than at that moment. His dignity seemed to grow even as others tried to diminish it."

The old woman fell quiet, considering this for a moment, her fingers tracing the worn wooden arm of her chair.

"Was he a tall man?" she asked, breathing as she waited for the answer.

"Yes, very tall," Nadia confirmed, straightening her posture as if the mere memory made her stand prouder.

"And his looks?" the old woman pressed, her voice gentle, almost caressing the words. "Tell me, my dear girl."

A blush crept across Nadia's cheeks, coloring them like rose petals at dawn. "He was... very handsome. Noble in bearing, with eyes that could pierce your very soul."

"My son!" the old woman cried out, throwing her arms around Nadia with surprising strength. "It was my son, I tell you! My Michael!"

"Your son?" Nadia gasped in astonishment, her hands trembling as they clutched the fabric of her dress. "Your son?"

"Let me understand this, my dear," Marfa said, her weathered fingers reaching out to grasp Nadia's hands. "This man who traveled with you, who protected you, he had a mother. Did he ever mention her?"

"His mother?" Nadia's eyes softened with remembrance, a gentle smile playing at her lips. "He spoke of her, just as I spoke of my father. He loved her. Sometimes, on frosty nights by the fire, he would tell me stories of her strength and kindness."

Marfa's voice trembled with emotion, her grip tightening. "Nadia, you're describing my son. Everything you say matches what I know in my heart."

She leaned forward, her eyes bright with desperate hope. "Surely he was traveling to Omsk to see this mother he cherished so much?"

"No," Nadia replied, the weight of truth heavy in her voice, "he wasn't."

"What?" Marfa exclaimed, her voice rising as she pulled back, color draining from her face. "How dare you say he wasn't!"

"Let me explain: Despite what I've said, I realize that Nicholas Korpanoff had compelling reasons, unknown to me, for traveling through the region in complete secrecy. His very survival depended on it, and more importantly, his honor and duty were at stake. There were things far greater than personal desires driving his journey."

"Yes, duty, an overwhelming sense of duty," the elderly Siberian woman responded, her weathered hands clasping together. "The kind that forces someone to give up everything, including perhaps a last embrace with their mother. Nadia, there's so much you don't know, so much I didn't understand until now. You've helped me make sense of it all, like pieces of a puzzle falling into place. But while you've illuminated the shadows in my heart, I cannot do the same for yours. If my son chose not to share his secret with you, I must honor that silence. Please forgive me, Nadia; I can never repay your kindness in bringing me this understanding."

"Mother, I'm not asking you to tell me anything," Nadia replied, reaching out to touch the older woman's arm with gentle reassurance.

Understanding dawned on the elderly Siberian woman, everything made sense now, including her son's behavior toward her at the Omsk inn, his distant manner and careful words. Without question, the young girl's traveling companion had been Michael Strogoff himself, concealing his identity as the Czar's courier because of his secret mission through enemy territory. The pieces fit together with painful clarity, explaining both his presence in Siberia and his necessary deception.

"My courageous son," Marfa thought to herself, her weathered hands clasping in her lap. "I shall guard your secret. No amount of torture could make me reveal you were the one I encountered in Omsk. Not even to ease this child's pain."

With just a few words, Marfa could have repaid Nadia's kindness and devotion. She could have disclosed that her companion Nicholas Korpanoff, or rather Michael Strogoff, hadn't died in the Irtych River after all, since she had met and spoken with him several days after that incident. The truth burned in her throat like a coal, demanding release.

But she held her tongue, keeping silent, knowing the gravity of her son's mission and the lives that might depend on her discretion. Instead, she said, her voice gaining strength with each word, "Keep hope alive, my child. Misfortune won't defeat you. You'll be with your father. I feel it in my heart. And perhaps the one who called you sister still lives. God wouldn't let such a brave companion perish. Hold on to hope, dear child! Look at me, I wear this mourning dress, but not yet for my son." Her eyes gleamed with the conviction of one who knew more than she could say.

Chapter Three

BLOW FOR BLOW

The current circumstances had brought Marfa Strogoff and Nadia together. The old Siberian woman now comprehended their connection, and while Nadia remained unaware that the companion she mourned was still alive, she had at least discovered her link to the woman she now called mother. Nadia felt blessed to serve as a surrogate child to this woman who believed she had lost her son, finding solace in their shared grief and mutual support during these dark times.

Yet both women remained oblivious to one crucial fact: Michael, who had been taken prisoner in Kolyvan, was traveling in the same group of captives, heading toward Tomsk alongside them, separated by mere yards yet distant in the chaos of their forced march.

The captives delivered by Ivan Ogareff joined those already imprisoned in the Emir's Tartar encampment. These victims, a mix of Russian and Siberian military personnel and ordinary citizens, formed a massive column stretching several miles long, their footsteps raising clouds of dust in the summer heat. The most potentially threatening prisoners were bound in chains and shackles, the iron clanking with each weary step. The group included both women and children, many youngsters strapped to saddles, their faces streaked with tears and dirt, while the women were forced to march on foot or driven forward like livestock, their expressions haunted by exhaustion and despair. Mounted guards maintained strict order in the column, brandishing whips and rifle butts at any sign of rebellion or weakness, and none dared fall behind, save for those who collapsed, never to stand again, their bodies left as grim markers along the harsh Siberian road.

Because of these circumstances, Michael Strogoff found himself positioned among the front lines of those departing the Tartar encampment, with the Kolyvan captives. This placement made it impossible for him to interact with the prisoners who had arrived at the camp from Omsk after him. As a result, he remained unaware that his mother and Nadia were part of the convoy, while they too did not know he was marching ahead of them. The trek from the camp to Tomsk proved devastating, with many perishing under the brutal treatment of soldiers who drove them forward with whips and spears, showing particular cruelty to those who stumbled or pleaded for water. The soldiers forced the captives across the steppe on a path made even more suffocating by the dust kicked up from the Emir's advance guard, the chalky clouds stinging their eyes and coating their parched throats. Their commanders ordered them to maintain a swift pace, allowing very few breaks, only when the mounted officers needed to water their horses or adjust their equipment. Though covered as quickly as possible, the hundred-mile journey beneath the scorching sun felt endless to the suffering prisoners, each step bringing fresh agony to their blistered feet and exhausted bodies, while the horizon seemed to stretch before them, offering no hint of respite or salvation.

The region stretches eastward from the Obi River to where the Sayanok Mountains jut out their rocky spur, a harsh expanse of desolate terrain that seems to mock any attempt at human passage. This barren landscape offers little vegetation, with only occasional withered shrubs dotting the endless plain, their branches twisted and bleached by relentless winds and merciless sun. The soil supports no farming, lacking the essential water that the exhausted prisoners craved during their grueling march, their tongues swollen and lips cracked from dehydration. To find any flowing water, they would have needed to travel fifty miles east, right to the mountain foothills, a detour that seemed an impossible dream to the suffering column.

In those mountains runs the Tom, a modest tributary that flows past Tomsk before joining one of the major northern rivers, its waters cutting through ancient valleys carved by centuries of persistent flow. That route would have provided plentiful water, more hospitable terrain, and milder temperatures, sheltered from the worst of the steppe's punishing heat by towering rock faces and scattered pine forests. However, the convoy commanders had strict instructions to take the most direct path to Tomsk, their orders brooking no argument or deviation. The Emir feared Russian forces from the northern provinces might outflank and isolate his position if he deviated from the shortest route, a strategic concern that outweighed any humanitarian considerations for his captives' welfare.

There was no point in describing the torment of those wretched captives. Countless prisoners died on the open plains, leaving their remains to scatter across the steppe until the cold season brought the wolves to devour the remaining bones. The guards seemed indifferent to the mounting death toll, viewing their charges as little more than cargo to be delivered.

Just as Nadia aided the elderly Siberian, Michael did what he could to support his weaker fellow prisoners, despite his own circumstances. He moved among them, offering words of hope to some and physical help to others, continuing until a guard's spear forced him back to his designated position in the line. His quiet defiance earned him both admiring glances from the other prisoners and suspicious stares from the guards.

What kept him from attempting to flee?

He had waited until he could traverse the steppe. His plan to reach Tomsk "courtesy of the Emir" remained unchanged, and his reasoning was sound. Watching the many patrols that swept across the plain sometimes to the south, sometimes to the north, he knew he wouldn't make it even two kilometers before being caught. Tartar cavalry seemed to materialize everywhere, like insects emerging from the soil after a storm. Attempting to escape under such circumstances would have been impossible. The guards maintained constant vigilance, knowing their lives would be forfeit for even the smallest lapse in attention. They watched their prisoners with the desperate intensity of men who knew their own survival depended on preventing any escape.

As night fell on August 15th, the convoy arrived at Zabediero, a small village thirty miles from Tomsk. The settlement's few wooden buildings cast long shadows in the fading light, their windows dark and unwelcoming.

Armed guards prevented the prisoners from dashing toward the Tom River, keeping them in formation until proper arrangements were made. Even though the river's fierce current could have aided an escape attempt by the more daring captives, the authorities had implemented rigorous security measures. They had commandeered boats from Zabediero and positioned them across the river, creating an impassable barrier. Vigilant sentries who paced along their assigned routes, their rifles gleaming in the twilight surrounded the camp it, on the village outskirts,.

Michael Strogoff assessed the situation, considering his own escape. After examining their predicament, he concluded breaking free was impossible under such tight security. Unwilling to risk capture in a futile attempt, he bode his time. Despite: Guards, with torches placed at regular intervals, eliminated shadows that might have offered concealment, providing no comfort in the growing darkness. The sound of the rushing river, its waters unreachable, mocked the held prisoners.

Along: The army ordered its prisoners to make camp along the Tom River for the night. Planning: The Emir planned a grand military celebration to mark the Tartar headquarters' establishment in Tomsk, delaying his troops' entrance into the important city. While Feofar-Khan had taken control of the fortress, most his forces remained camped outside its walls, awaiting their ceremonial entry, their campfires dotting the landscape like fallen stars.

Ivan Ogareff, having arrived at Tomsk with the Emir the previous evening, departed for the Zabediero camp where he would spend the night in prepared quarters. The next day, he would lead the Tartar army's rear-guard, a position that allowed him to maintain his watchful eye over both the prisoners and his own troops. At dawn, the cavalry and infantry would march to Tomsk, where the Emir planned to welcome them with the lavish ceremony typical of Asian rulers, complete with flowing banners and the thunderous beating of war drums.

Once the camp was established, guards let the exhausted prisoners, who had endured three days of travel and suffered from severe thirst, drink and rest. Many collapsed on the spot, their legs too weak to carry them further. The sun had already dipped below the horizon when Nadia, supporting Marfa Strogoff, reached the Tom's riverbank. They had struggled to make their way through the crowds gathered at the water's edge, but at last quenched their thirst, the cool water bringing momentary relief to their parched throats.

The elderly woman leaned down toward the pristine stream while Nadia dipped her hand in the water and brought it to Marfa's parched lips. After helping the older woman, Nadia quenched her own thirst, cupping the water in both hands. The cool waters restored their vigor, washing away some of the day's exhaustion from their bodies. Without warning, Nadia jerked upright, letting out an involuntary gasp that drew curious glances from nearby prisoners.

There stood Michael Strogoff, mere paces away. The setting sun's dying light illuminated his figure, casting long shadows across his weather-worn features and travel-stained clothing.

Michael flinched at Nadia's outcry, his shoulders tensing. Though startled, he maintained enough self-control to remain silent, knowing any word might betray him. Yet when his gaze fell upon Nadia, he recognized his mother beside her, and his hands trembled ever.

Realizing he couldn't maintain his composure much longer during this unexpected encounter, he shielded his eyes with his hands and strode away, pushing through the crowd of prisoners still gathered at the riverbank.

Nadia moved to pursue him, her feet already carrying her forward, but the elderly Siberian woman caught her arm and whispered in her ear, "Remain here, my child! There are too many eyes watching."

"It's him!" Nadia exclaimed, her voice thick with emotion, her hands clasped against her chest. "He's alive, mother! It's him! I can believe my eyes!"

"That's my son," Marfa replied with practiced calm, though her heart raced beneath her composed exterior, "that's Michael Strogoff, and notice how I remain still, not taking a single step toward him! Follow my lead, my daughter. Our actions now could mean life or death."

Michael felt his heart surge with the most powerful emotion he had ever experienced, threatening to overwhelm his maintained facade. Before him stood his mother and Nadia, looking worn but unbroken by their ordeal!

Divine providence had brought together these two prisoners, forever linked in his heart, in their shared misfortune. Each step of their separate journeys had led to this moment. He wondered if Nadia knew his true identity, studying her face from afar for any sign. Yes, he had seen Marfa's restraining gesture when she held Nadia back from rushing to him. Marfa had understood everything, and was protecting his secret with the fierce devotion only a mother could muster.

Throughout that long, sleepless night, the urge to reunite with his mother tempted Michael. The urge to embrace her weathered form and clasp his young friend's hand was almost overwhelming, gnawing at his resolve with each passing hour. Yet he understood that even the smallest misstep could prove catastrophic to them all. He had made a solemn vow not to see his mother, and he would honor it despite the agony it caused. Once they reached Tomsk, since escape was impossible that night, he would have to depart without embracing the two people who meant everything to him, leaving them vulnerable to countless dangers that haunted his thoughts.

Michael wished to believe that this unexpected encounter at the Zabediero camp would bring no harm to either himself or his mother. However, he remained unaware that Sangarre the gypsy, Ogareff's spy, had witnessed a portion of their brief interaction, her keen eyes missing little despite the gathering gloom.

The mysterious Tsigane stood a short distance away on the riverbank, her eyes fixed on the elderly Siberian woman as they had been so many times before, studying every minute change in Marfa's bearing and expression. Michael had vanished before she could spot him, but she hadn't missed how the mother had held Nadia back, nor the telling expression in Marfa's eyes, that flash of recognition and desperate restraint that spoke volumes to one trained in reading such subtle signs.

Now she was certain, Marfa Strogoff's son, who carried messages for the Czar himself, was here among the captives in Zabediero, trapped with Ivan Ogareff's other prisoners. Though Sangarre couldn't identify him by sight in the sea of faces before her, she knew without question he was present, like a wolf knowing its prey was near even if hidden. She did not locate him just then, the darkness and the vast crowd of people made such a search futile, but her patience was as endless as the Siberian steppes themselves.

Spying on Nadia and Marfa Strogoff would prove futile. The two women were on their guard, their faces betraying nothing, making it impossible to gather any information that might incriminate the Czar's courier. The Tsigane, the gypsy spy, decided her best course was to inform Ivan Ogareff without delay. Slipping away like a shadow through the gathering dusk, she left the camp and arrived at Zabediero within fifteen minutes, where armed guards escorted her to the lieutenant's quarters. Ogareff, who had been pacing, granted her an immediate audience.

"What news do you bring, Sangarre?" he inquired, his eyes glinting with anticipation.

"Marfa Strogoff's son is here in the camp," she stated with quiet confidence.

"As our prisoner?"

"Yes, as a prisoner," she confirmed, her voice carrying a note of triumph.

"Ah!" Ogareff exclaimed, his thin lips curling into a cruel smile, "Now I shall know..."

"You'll learn nothing, Ivan," the Tsigane cut in, her dark eyes flashing, "for you wouldn't recognize him if you saw him."

"But you know him; you've seen him, Sangarre?" Ogareff demanded, leaning forward.

"I haven't seen him myself, but his mother's unconscious reaction revealed everything. The signs were unmistakable."

"Could you be wrong?"

"I'm certain of it," she replied with unwavering conviction.

"The capture of this messenger is of utmost importance to me," Ivan Ogareff declared, his fingers drumming against the wooden table between them. "If his letter from Moscow reaches the Grand Duke in Irkutsk, the Grand Duke will be warned, and my chance to strike will be gone forever."

The intensity in Ogareff's voice was unmistakable. His agitation revealed just how desperately he wanted to get this letter, and beads of sweat had formed on his upper lip as he spoke. Each word carried the weight of his mounting frustration and anticipation. Sangarre remained composed despite Ogareff's insistent questioning, her stillness a stark contrast to his nervous energy. "I'm certain, Ivan," she replied, her unwavering gaze meeting his.

"But there are thousands of prisoners here, Sangarre, and you've admitted you don't recognize Michael Strogoff," he pressed, rising halfway from his chair as if the very thought of searching through countless faces was too much to bear.

"No," the Tsigane replied with fierce delight, her dark eyes glittering with malicious satisfaction, "I have not met him myself. But his mother will know him. Ivan, we must compel his mother to reveal the truth. She cannot hide her reaction when she sees him."

"Tomorrow she will tell us everything!" Ogareff declared, slamming his fist on the wooden table. He then held out his hand to the Tsigane, who kissed it, a customary gesture of respect among Northern peoples, carrying no connotation of servility. The candlelight cast long shadows across his face as a cruel smile played at the corners of his mouth.

Later, Sangarre made her way back to the camp, her silent footsteps ghosting across the frozen ground as she located Nadia and Marfa Strogoff, and kept watch over them through the night. Despite their exhaustion, neither the elderly woman nor the young girl could find sleep, tossing on their thin blankets. Worry consumed their minds, each passing hour bringing fresh waves of anxiety. They knew Michael was alive but captured, imprisoned somewhere among the masses of other unfortunates. The burning questions remained: Had Ogareff recognized him? If not, how long until he did? Nadia could think only of the joy that he whom she had believed dead still lived, her heart racing whenever she recalled his face. Marfa, however, looked beyond the present moment with mounting dread, her weathered hands clasped in her lap. She was terrified by Ogareff's cold-blooded nature and worried about her son's vulnerability.

Under the cover of darkness, Sangarre had approached the two women and spent several hours listening to them, her form indistinguishable from the shadows that cloaked the camp. She detected no sound, not even a whisper between the prisoners. Out of caution, neither Nadia nor Marfa Strogoff uttered a single word to each other, communicating only through subtle glances and the occasional brush of hands. The following morning, August 16th, around ten o'clock, trumpet blasts echoed across the camp, their harsh notes shattering the morning stillness. The Tartar troops took up their positions, moving with practiced efficiency into neat rows.

Accompanied by many Tartar officers, their uniforms gleaming in the morning sun, Ivan Ogareff entered. His expression was darker than ever, and his furrowed forehead suggested a simmering anger ready to explode at any moment, like storm clouds threatening to unleash their fury.

From within a cluster of captives, Michael Strogoff observed the man's arrival, his muscles tensing. He sensed impending danger, knowing that Ivan Ogareff had discovered Marfa was Michael Strogoff's mother. The weight of this knowledge pressed down on him like a physical burden.

Ivan Ogareff dismounted from his horse with fluid grace that belied his murderous intent, as his soldiers formed a wide circle around him, their weapons at the ready. Sangarre approached with cat-like stealth and reported, her voice barely above a whisper, "There is nothing to tell."

Without responding, Ogareff signaled to one of his officers, his cold eyes never leaving the crowd. With whips and spears, the soldiers drove the prisoners into position around the camp. A sharp crack of leather against flesh accompanied cries of pain and protest. Facing: With armed guards forming an impenetrable wall behind them, their bayonets glinting in the harsh light, the çaptives had no chance of fleeing.

A tense quiet fell over the scene, broken only by the occasional shuffle of feet and muffled sob. At Ogareff's gesture, Sangarre moved toward the crowd with predatory purpose, making her way to where Marfa stood among the prisoners, her dark eyes scanning faces as she went.

The elderly woman from Siberia noticed her approach and understood what was about to unfold, her weathered face betraying no fear. A look of disdain crossed her features, hardening the lines around her mouth. She then bent close to Nadia and whispered, her breath warm against the girl's ear, "Pretend you don't recognize me anymore, child. No matter what happens, no matter how difficult this becomes, stay silent - don't react at all. This is about him, not about me."

Just then, Sangarre studied her, eyes narrowed with calculating intensity, before placing her hand on the old woman's shoulder like a spider settling on its prey.

"What is it you want?" Marfa demanded, her voice carrying across the tense silence.

"Come with me!" Sangarre ordered with cruel satisfaction, then forced the elderly Siberian forward with rough hands, leading her to where Ivan Ogareff stood in the center of the open space. Michael lowered his gaze to hide the fury that blazed in his eyes, his fingers curling into tight fists at his sides.

Marfa positioned herself in front of Ivan Ogareff, straightened her posture with quiet dignity, folded her arms across her chest, and stood waiting. Her weathered face remained impassive, a mask of stone.

"Are you Marfa Strogoff?" Ogareff demanded, his voice sharp as steel, cutting through the air between them.

"Yes," the elderly Siberian woman answered with unwavering composure, meeting his gaze.

"Do you stand by your words from three days ago during your interrogation at Omsk?" His eyes glittered with dangerous intent.

"No!" The word rang out clear and firm.

"Then you deny knowing that your son, Michael Strogoff, the Czar's courier, passed through Omsk?" Ogareff leaned forward, studying her face for any sign of deception.

"I know nothing of it." Her voice remained steady, betraying nothing.

"And that man you claimed to recognize as your son - you now say he wasn't your flesh and blood?" His tone dripped with concealed mockery.

"He was not my son." Each word fell like ice from her lips.

"You haven't glimpsed him among the captives since then?" Ogareff pressed, circling her like a predator.

"No." The single syllable carried the weight of finality.

"If someone pointed him out, would you know him?"

"No."

Her resolute response rippled through the assembled crowd, drawing murmurs of disbelief. Several prisoners shifted, their chains rattling in the tense silence that followed.

Ogareff's face darkened with rage, his hand jerking upward in a menacing gesture. His fingers curled into a tight fist as veins bulged at his temples, betraying the fury that threatened to overwhelm his calculated demeanor.

"Hear me well," he snarled at Marfa, leaning so close she could feel his hot breath on her face. "Your son is here, and you will identify him to me this instant."

"No."

"Every single prisoner from Omsk and Kolyvan will march before your eyes," he growled, pacing before her with measured steps. His boots crunched against the gravel, punctuating each word. "For each man who passes without you revealing Michael Strogoff, you'll feel the bite of the knout across your back." He snapped his fingers, and a guard stepped forward, uncoiling the dreaded leather whip with deliberate slowness. The metal tips caught the sunlight, glinting with malevolent promise.

Ivan Ogareff saw that, whatever might be his threats, whatever might be the tortures to which he submitted her, the indomitable Siberian would not speak. To discover the courier of the Czar, he counted, then, not on her, but on Michael himself. He did not believe it possible that, when mother and son were in each other's presence, some involuntary movement would not betray him. To seize the imperial letter, he would have ordered all prisoners searched, had he so desired. It was thus not only the letter which the traitor must have, but the bearer himself. His calculating mind had already planned the perfect trap, one that would exploit the most basic of human weaknesses: the bond between mother and child.

Nadia listened and understood Michael Strogoff's true identity and his motivation for traveling incognito through Siberia's occupied territories. Her heart raced as the pieces fell into place, his careful demeanor, his unwavering determination, and his mysterious mission made perfect sense.

She prayed that Michael's iron will would prove stronger than Ogareff's cruel machinations.

Following Ivan Ogareff's command, the prisoners walked single file past Marfa, who stood motionless as marble, her face betraying no emotion whatsoever. Years of hardship had taught her well how to mask her feelings, even in this moment of ultimate test.

Her son came near the end of the line. As he approached his mother, Nadia closed her eyes, unable to bear the sight of what might transpire between them. While Michael maintained an calm demeanor, his fingernails dug into his palms that they drew blood, the physical pain a welcome distraction from the emotional torment that threatened to overwhelm him.

Mother and son, his keen eyes searching their faces for any hint of recognition, any telltale flicker that would confirm his suspicions baffled Ivan Ogareff.

Sangarre, close to him, said one word, her dark eyes glittering with malice: "The knout!"

"Yes," cried Ogareff, who could no longer restrain himself, his frustration boiling over into rage; "the knout for this wretched old woman, the knout to the death!"

A guard approached Marfa with a threatening weapon, the leather strips of the knout trailing behind him as he walked. She knew the punishment that awaited her would be severe, but remained resolute, understanding the gravity of her choice. The weight of the Czar's mission, carried by her son, far outweighed her own safety. She would not speak, no matter the cost, even if every lash stripped away not just flesh but life itself.

Two soldiers forced Marfa to her knees, hustling her shoulders down against the hard ground. Though fear coursed through her veins, she held firm to her convictions, her weathered face a mask of determination, knowing she was making the ultimate sacrifice for what she believed in. She remained dignified, back straight and head held high, even as they prepared to carry out their grim task.

The Tartar soldier straightened his posture, muscles tensing as he gripped the knout, awaiting orders. "Begin!" commanded Ogareff, his voice thick with malicious satisfaction. The whip cut through the air with a menacing hiss, leather strips whistling as they descended.

But before it could strike, a mighty hand seized the Tartar's arm mid-swing, arresting the brutal momentum. Michael had lunged forward from the crowd, unable to bear witness to such cruelty against his own mother. Though he had endured Ogareff's lash at the Ichim relay without retaliation, maintaining his disguise through that torment, seeing his mother about to suffer the same fate broke his maintained restraint. Ivan Ogareff had achieved his aim, drawing out his quarry.

"Michael Strogoff!" he exclaimed, eyes gleaming with vindictive pleasure. Stepping closer, he sneered, savoring the moment, "So, the man from Ichim?"

"The same!" Michael declared, his voice resonating with fury. In one fluid motion, he grabbed the knout from the startled soldier and delivered a fierce slash across Ogareff's face, the leather strips leaving angry red welts. "That's for your blow!" he proclaimed, satisfaction clear in his tone.

"Justice served!" shouted an anonymous voice from within the crowd, echoing the feeling many onlookers.

A score of soldiers descended upon Michael like wolves upon prey, weapons drawn and faces twisted with rage, and death seemed mere moments away as they closed in from all sides.

But Ogareff, who on being struck had uttered a cry of rage and pain, stopped them with an upraised hand. "I reserve this man for the Emir's judgment," he said, dabbing at the bleeding welt across his face. "Search him! Every pocket, every seam!"

In Michael's breast pocket, the soldiers discovered a letter bearing the imperial arms.

Alcide Jolivet himself spoke the words, "Well repaid!" "Par-dieu!" said he to Blount, wiping sweat from his brow as they watched from the crowd's edge. "They are rough, these people. Acknowledge that we owe our traveling companion a good turn. Korpanoff or Strogoff is worthy of it. Oh, that was fine retaliation for the minor affair at Ichim."

"Yes, retaliation," replied Blount, adjusting his spectacles with a grimace; "but Strogoff is a dead man. I suspect that, for his own interest at all events, it would have been better had he not possessed quite so lively a recollection of the event."

"Would you have his mother die from the whip?" Alcide demanded, his face flushing with emotion.

"How does his outburst help either his mother or sister?" Blount countered, his British pragmatism clear in every word.

"All I know is I'd have done the same in his shoes," Alcide responded, his hands clenching into fists at his sides. "Observe that gash on the Colonel!"

"This would make quite the story for our papers," Blount remarked, dabbing at his own minor wounds with a handkerchief, "if only Ivan Ogareff would share what's written in that letter."

After stopping the blood flowing from his face with a strip of linen, Ivan Ogareff broke the seal with trembling fingers. He studied the letter, reading it multiple times as if trying to extract every detail from its contents, his eyes narrowing with each pass over the critical message.

He then ordered Michael to be bound with thick hemp ropes and taken to Tomsk with the other captives under heavy guard. Taking command of the Zabediero forces with a triumphant air, he marched toward the town where the Emir waited, accompanied by the thunderous sound of drums and trumpets echoing across the windswept plains. The column of soldiers stretched far into the distance, their boots raising clouds of dust as they advanced.

Chapter Four

THE TRIUMPHAL ENTRY

TOMSK, founded in 1604, in the heart of the Siberian provinces, is one of the most important towns in Asiatic Russia. Tobolsk, above the sixtieth parallel; Irkutsk, built beyond the hundredth meridian, have seen Tomsk increase at their expense, its influence growing over the centuries.

As mentioned, Tomsk is not the capital of this important province. It is at Omsk that the Governor-General of the province and the official world live, conducting their administrative duties from grand government buildings. But Tomsk is the most considerable town of that territory, with bustling streets and a thriving marketplace. The country being rich, the town is so likewise, for it is in the center of fruitful mines that yield gold, silver, and precious stones in abundance. In the luxury of its houses, its arrangements, and its equipages, it might rival the greatest European capitals. Ornate mansions and elegant shops line the wide streets; these would not look out of place in Moscow or St. Petersburg. It is a city of millionaires, enriched by the spade and pickax, and though it has not the honor of being the home of the Czar's representative, it can boast of including in the first rank of its notables the chief of the merchants of the town, the principal grantees of the imperial government's mines, whose influence extends far beyond the city's boundaries.

But the millionaires have left now, and except for the crouching poor, the town stood empty to the hordes of Feofar-Khan. At four o'clock the Emir made his entry into the square, greeted by a flourish of trumpets, the rolling sound of the big drums, salvoes of artillery and musketry. The echoes of martial music bounced off the abandoned mansions, a mocking reminder of the city's former grandeur.

Feofar mounted his favorite horse, which carried on its head an aigrette of diamonds. The Emir still wore his uniform, its gold braiding glinting in the afternoon sun, the medals on his chest clinking with each movement. A many staff accompanied him, and beside him walked the Khans of Khokhand and Koundouge and the grand dignitaries of the Khanats, their silk robes rustling as they strode forward with measured steps, their faces stern with conquest.

At the same moment, the chief of Feofar's wives, the queen (if that title applies to the Bokharan sultana), appeared on the terrace. But, queen or slave, this woman of Persian origin was beautiful, her presence commanding immediate attention from all who beheld her. Contrary to the Mahometan custom, and no doubt by some caprice of the Emir, she had her face uncovered, revealing features that seemed carved from the finest alabaster. Her hair, divided into four plaits, fell over her dazzling white shoulders, concealed by a veil of silk worked in gold, which fell from the back of a cap studded with gems of the highest value. The intricate embroidery of the veil caught the sunlight, creating a ethereal halo around her form. Under her blue-silk petticoat, fell the "zirdjameh" of silken gauze, and above the sash lay the "pirahn," each layer of fabric moving with fluid grace as she walked. Jewels adorned her from head to toe; gold beads strung on silver threads, chaplets of turquoises from the famed Elbourz mines, and necklaces of cornelians, agates, emeralds, opals, and sapphires—her dress appeared to be crafted of precious stones. Her neck, arms, hands, waist, and feet sparkled with thousands of diamonds, worth countless millions of roubles, reflecting every ray of the afternoon sun.

The Emir and the Khans dismounted, as did the dignitaries who escorted them. All entered a magnificent tent erected on the center of the first terrace, its billowing silk panels adorned with intricate golden embroidery that caught the waning daylight. As usual, they placed the Koran on a decorated mahogany pedestal before the tent.

Feofar's lieutenant did not make them wait, and before five o'clock the trumpets announced his arrival with a piercing blast that echoed across the terrace. With practiced military precision, Ivan Ogareff, nicknamed "the Scarred Cheek," dismounted before the Emir's tent in his distinctive Tartar officer's uniform, complete with medals and braiding. A party of soldiers from the Zabediero camp accompanied him. They lined the sides of the square, reserving a space for the sports, marked by colorful pennants fluttering in the breeze. A large scar, cut across the traitor's face, was visible; the puckered flesh recalled a violent past encounter.

Ogareff presented his principal officers to the Emir, who, without departing from the coldness which composed the main part of his dignity, received them in a way which satisfied them they stood well in the good graces of their chief. His calculating eyes moved from one face to another, measuring each man's worth with the detached assessment of one accustomed to command.

At least so thought Harry Blount and Alcide Jolivet, the two inseparables, now associated together in the chase after news. After leaving Zabediero, they had proceeded to Tomsk, pushing their horses hard through the rugged terrain. The plan they had agreed upon was to leave the Tartars as soon as possible, and to join a Russian regiment, and, if they could, to go with them to Irkutsk. All that they had seen of the invasion, its burnings, its pillages, its murders, the charred remains of villages and the haunted eyes of survivors, had sickened them, and they longed to be among the ranks of the Siberian army. Jolivet had told his companion that he could not leave Tomsk without making a sketch of the triumphal entry of the Tartar troops, if it was only to satisfy his cousin's curiosity, though his hands trembled at the thought of documenting more devastation; but the same evening they both intended to take the road to Irkutsk, and being well mounted on fresh horses gained at considerable expense, hoped to distance the Emir's scouts who patrolled the surrounding countryside.

Alcide and Blount mingled therefore in the crowd, to lose no detail of a festival which ought to supply them with a hundred excellent lines for an article. They admired the magnificence of Feofar-Khan, his wives adorned in silk and precious gems, his officers in their gleaming armor, his guards with their curved sabers, and all the Eastern pomp, of which the ceremonies of Europe can give not the least idea. But they turned away with disgust when Ivan Ogareff presented himself before the Emir, his traitorous smirk concealed beneath a show of deference, and waited with some impatience for the amusements to begin.

"You see, my dear Blount," said Alcide, adjusting his collar in the sweltering heat, "we have come too soon, like honest citizens who like to get their money's worth. All this is before the curtain rises, it would have been better to arrive only for the ballet."

"What ballet?" asked Blount, wiping his brow with a handkerchief.

"The compulsory ballet, to be sure. But see, the curtain is going to rise." Alcide Jolivet spoke as if he had been at the Opera, and taking his glass from its case, he prepared, with the air of a connoisseur, "to examine the first act of Feofar's company." His attempt at levity masked the unease they both felt at being present for such a grotesque display of conquest.

A painful ceremony was to precede the sports. In fact, the triumph of the vanquisher could not be complete without the public humiliation of the vanquished. Soldiers whipped several hundred prisoners, forcing them forward with bent backs and exhausted faces. They would march past Feofar-Khan and his allies before being crammed with their companions into the dark, suffocating prisons in the town.

In the first ranks of these prisoners figured Michael Strogoff, his head held high despite his circumstances. As Ogareff had ordered, a file of soldiers who kept their rifles trained on him with particular vigilance guarded him. His mother and Nadia were there also, forced to witness whatever was to come.

The old Siberian, although energetic enough when her own safety was in question, was pale, her weathered hands trembling as she watched her son. She expected some terrible scene. The Emir had brought her son before him for good reason. She therefore trembled for him, knowing the cruel nature of their captors. Ivan Ogareff wouldn't forgive being whipped, and his revenge would be merciless. No doubt, the captors would inflict some frightful punishment, familiar to Central Asian barbarians, on Michael. Ogareff had protected him against the soldiers because he well knew what would happen by reserving him for the justice of the Emir, savoring and expecting his revenge like a fine wine.

The mother and son could not speak together since the terrible scene in the camp at Zabediero. Marfa longed to ask her son's pardon for the harm she had done him, for she reproached herself with not having commanded her maternal feelings. If she had restrained herself in that Omsk post-house, encountering him, Michael would have passed unrecognized, and she would have avoided all these misfortunes. The weight of this guilt pressed heavily upon her heart with each passing hour.

Michael thought that if his mother was there, Ogareff had brought her to make her suffer by witnessing his punishment, or perhaps Ogareff had reserved a frightful death for her. The thought of his mother being forced to witness whatever torments awaited him was more unbearable than any physical pain he might endure. His imagination conjured up horrific scenarios, each more terrible than the last, as he contemplated their fate.

As to Nadia, she only asked herself how she could save them both, how come to the aid of son and mother. As yet she could only wonder, but she felt she must above everything avoid drawing attention upon herself, that she must conceal herself, make herself insignificant. Perhaps she might at least gnaw through the meshes which imprisoned the lion. At any rate, if given an opportunity, she would seize it and sacrifice herself for Marfa Strogoff's son. Her heart raced with determination even as her mind struggled to form a concrete plan of action.

In the meantime the greater part of the prisoners were passing before the Emir, and as they passed each had to prostrate himself, with his forehead in the dust, in token of servitude. Slavery begins by humiliation. When the unfortunate people were too slow in bending, the rough guards threw them to the ground, their bodies making dull thuds against the hard earth. Some cried out in pain, while others remained eerily silent, their spirits already broken by their circumstances.

Alcide Jolivet and his companion could not witness such a sight without feeling indignant. Their hands clenched at their sides as they watched the degrading spectacle unfold before them.

"It is cowardly, let us go," said Alcide, his voice tight with contained anger.

"No," answered Blount, though his face had grown pale; "we must see it all."

"See it all!, ah!" cried Alcide grasping his companion's arm with such force that Blount winced.

"What is the matter with you?" asked the latter.

"Look, Blount; it is she!"

"What she?"

"The sister of our traveling companion, alone, and a prisoner! We must save her," Jolivet exclaimed, his voice trembling with desperate urgency.

"Calm yourself," replied Blount, placing a restraining hand on his colleague's shoulder. "Any interference on our part in behalf of the young girl would be worse than useless. We would only bring more suffering upon her."

Alcide Jolivet, who had been about to rush forward with reckless determination, stopped in his tracks, his muscles still tense with the desire to act. Nadia, who had not perceived them, her features being half hidden by her disheveled dark hair, passed in her turn before the Emir without attracting his attention, her steps measured.

However, after Nadia came Marfa Strogoff; and as she did not throw herself in the dust like the others, the guards pushed her with the butts of their rifles. She fell with a painful cry.

Her son struggled so violently that the soldiers who were guarding him could hardly hold him back, their faces reddening with effort. But the old woman rose, her dignity intact despite her trembling limbs, and they were about to drag her on, when Ogareff interposed, raising his hand and saying, "Let that woman stay!"

As to Nadia, she regained the crowd of prisoners, melting into their midst like a shadow. Ivan Ogareff had taken no notice of her, his attention focused elsewhere.

Michael was then led before the Emir, and there he remained standing, his bearing proud and defiant, without casting down his eyes.

"Your forehead to the ground!" cried Ogareff, his voice cutting through the tense silence.

"No!" answered Michael, the single word ringing with unmistakable resolve.

Two soldiers endeavored to make him bend, grabbing his shoulders, but they were themselves laid on the ground by a powerful buffet from the young man's fist, the blow sending them sprawling in the dust.

Ogareff approached Michael with deliberate steps, his face contorted with rage. "You shall die!" he said, his hand moving to the hilt of his sword.

"I can die," answered Michael, standing even straighter despite his bonds; "but your traitor's face, Ivan, will not the less carry forever the infamous brand of the knout." His words rang through the courtyard, ensuring all present heard the accusation.

At this reply Ivan Ogareff became livid, the blood draining from his features until his skin took on an almost ghostly pallor. His fingers twitched at his sides, containing his fury.

"Who is this prisoner?" asked the Emir, in a tone of voice terrible from its very calmness. His dark eyes moved between the two men, studying their mutual hatred with cold interest.

"A Russian spy," answered Ogareff, his voice dripping with venom. In asserting that Michael was a spy he knew the sentence pronounced against him would be terrible. A slight, cruel smile played at the corners of his mouth as he spoke.

The Emir made a sign at which all the crowd bent low their heads, their foreheads touching the dusty ground in complete submission. Then he pointed with his hand to the Koran, which was brought him by a robed attendant on a silk cushion. He opened the sacred book with measured reverence and placed his finger on one of its pages, his expression unreadable as stone.

It was chance, or rather, according to the deeply-held beliefs of these Orientals, God Himself who was about to decide the fate of Michael Strogoff. The people of Central Asia give the name of "fal" to this ancient and sacred practice. After having interpreted the sense of the verse touched by the judge's finger, they apply the sentence whatever it may be, accepting it as divine will made manifest.

The Emir had let his finger rest on the page of the Koran, the weight of destiny hanging heavy in the air. The chief of the Ulemas then approached with measured steps, his robes rustling in the tense silence, and read in a loud, resonant voice a verse which ended with these ominous words, "And he will no more see the things of this earth."

"Russian spy!" exclaimed Feofar-Kahn in a voice trembling with fury, his eyes blazing with a mix of triumph and rage. "You see what is going on in the Tartar camp. Then look while you may, for these moments shall be your last with sight." His words cut through the air like a blade, carrying both judgment and menace.

Chapter Five

LOOK WHILE YOU MAY!

Michael stood before the Emir's throne at the base of the terrace, his arms restrained behind him by thick iron chains that bit into his wrists. His mother, broken by both mental and physical anguish, had collapsed to the ground, her weathered hands covering her face, unable to watch or listen to what was unfolding in this cruel spectacle.

"Observe while you still can," Feofar-Khan declared, extending his arm toward Michael with a flourish of his jewel-encrusted sleeve. Ivan Ogareff, well-versed in Tartar traditions, understood the grave implications of these words, as evidenced by the brief cruel smile that crossed his face before he took his position beside Feofar-Khan. His hand rested on the hilt of his sword, a gesture of casual dominance.

The sound of a trumpet pierced the air, its harsh brass notes echoing off the stone walls and signaling the start of the entertainment. "The ballet is about to begin," Alcide remarked to Blount with bitter irony in his voice, "though these barbarians, unlike us, present it before the major performance." His fingers drummed against his thigh as he watched the scene unfold.

A group of dancers flowed into the clearing in front of the Emir's pavilion. Michael, following his orders, observed it all, his trained eyes missing no detail of the spectacle before him. The performance featured an exotic blend of Tartar musical instruments: the doutare, a guitar with an elongated neck that produced haunting melodies; the kobize, resembling a violoncello with its deep, mournful tones; and the tschibyzga, a long flute made of reed that whistled like desert winds. The deep voices of singers merged with the sounds of wind instruments, tom-toms, and tambourines, creating a hypnotic rhythm that seemed to pulse through the ground itself. Above them all, an unusual aerial symphony played out as a dozen kites, each with strings attached to their centers, hummed in the wind like celestial harps, their silk surfaces catching the late afternoon light.

The dancers took the stage, all of Persian descent and now free to perform as they chose, having once been in bondage. These artists had held official roles in Teheran's court ceremonies, where they had danced for shahs and princes, but when the new ruling dynasty came to power, they faced exile and scorn, forcing them to pursue their art elsewhere among less discriminating audiences. They displayed their heritage through traditional Persian attire, their costumes shimmering with abundant jewels that caught and scattered light with every movement. Their ears were decorated with small, gem-encrusted golden triangles that tinkled as they moved, while their necks and ankles were covered with silver bands marked with dark patterns that spoke of ancient traditions and forgotten stories.

The dancers moved with elegant precision, performing both solo and ensemble pieces. While their faces remained visible, they draped delicate veils over their heads, creating an effect like mist passing across their luminous eyes, reminiscent of clouds drifting past stars. Several of these Persian performers wore pearl-decorated leather belts with small triangle-shaped pouches attached. These ornate pouches, adorned with gold filigree and tiny bells that chimed with each step, contained elongated strips of crimson silk inscribed with Koranic verses. The performers would stretch these bands between them, creating a passage beneath which other dancers would weave, their movements fluid like water flowing through ancient stone channels. As each dancer passed under a particular verse, they would either bow down to touch the ground or leap skyward, acting out the sacred text's instructions as if seeking to join the heavenly beautiful, pure, and eternal companions in Mohammed's paradise, their gestures infused with both reverence and yearning.

What grabbed Alcide's attention was the surprising lack of energy among the Persian dancers. Instead of displaying their usual passionate nature, they moved with an unexpected restraint, as if holding something back beneath their practiced smiles. Unlike the passionate Egyptians, their movements were flowing and elegant, like willow branches in a soft breeze.

As the performance concluded, a harsh voice cut through the air like a whip crack:

"Watch while you still can!"

These words, echoing the Emir's command, came from a tall, lean Tartar who served as Feofar-Khan's executioner. His angular features were as sharp as the impressive curved Damascus blade he wielded behind Michael. The weapon was one of those masterpieces crafted by the renowned weaponsmiths of Karschi and Hissar, its surface rippling with the distinctive water-pattern that marked its superior quality.

The guards behind him, their faces illuminated by its orange glow carried a tripod holding. Instead of smoke, a subtle haze enveloped the dish, created by burning some fragrant resinous material he had scattered across the top, filling the air with an exotic, almost narcotic sweetness.

Following the Persian performers came another group of dancers that Michael knew all too well. The reporters seemed to recognize them too, as Blount remarked to his colleague with a knowing grimace, "Those are the Tsiganes from Nijni-Novgorod."

"Indeed they are," Alcide replied, his voice tinged with suspicion. "I suspect their talents for observation earn them more than their dancing skills. Those women's eyes miss nothing, and their ears catch every whisper."

By all indications, Alcide Jolivet was correct in his assessment that these performers were working as the Emir's spies, gathering intelligence through their innocent entertainment at celebrations and gatherings across the region.

In the front row stood Sangarre, a Tsigane woman in her exotic and striking attire, layers of colored silks adorned with jingling coins and intricate embroidery that caught the lamplight enhanced whose extraordinary beauty.

Though motionless like a statue among the dancers, Sangarre's presence commanded attention, her dark eyes scanning the crowd with predatory intensity. Around her, the other performers moved in steps that blended dance traditions from their ancestral journey - incorporating movements from Turkey, Bohemia, Egypt, Italy, and Spain. The rhythmic clash of cymbals worn on their arms and the resonant beats of finger-played "daires" tambourines, the hypnotic music building accompanied their passionate performance to a feverish crescendo as their bare feet traced ancient patterns across the floor.

Sangarre, holding one of those tambourines which she played between her hands with practiced grace, encouraged this group of wild dancers with subtle nods and piercing glances. A young Romani boy, about fifteen years old, stepped forward from the shadows. He held a "doutare" (a traditional string instrument) which he played by plucking the strings with his fingernails, creating haunting melodies that seemed to float on the night air. He sang, his voice carrying both youth's sweetness and an ancient sorrow. During each verse, with its unique rhythm and plaintive tone, a female dancer would position herself next to him and stand motionless, listening, as if carved from stone. But whenever the chorus came from the young singer's lips, she would resume her dance with renewed vigor, filling his ears with the sound of her tambourine and the clash of her cymbals, her feet moving in perfect time. After the final chorus, the rest of the dancers encircled the Romani boy in their spiraling dance, their movements growing wild and mesmerizing.

Gold coins cascaded from the Emir and his entourage like metallic rain, showering down from officials of every rank who sat on cushioned divans around the performance space. The pieces clinked against the dancers' cymbals with musical precision, mixing with the fading notes of doutares and tambourines in a symphony of wealth and excess.

"They spend like thieves," Alcide whispered to his companion, his voice tinged with both admiration and disgust.

A hush descended, broken only when the executioner placed his calloused hand on Michael's shoulder and repeated those ominous words, each utterance more chilling than the last, his breath visible in the cooling air.

"Look while you may," he intoned, the words carrying across the clearing like a death knell.

The executioner had sheathed his blade, Alcide noted with keen interest, the polished steel disappearing into worn leather with practiced ease. The man's movements were deliberate, almost ceremonial in their precision.

Dusk was settling in as the sun vanished beyond the horizon, its last rays painting the clouds in bruised purples and deep crimsons. Twilight crept across the landscape, while the cedar and pine forest transformed into an impenetrable wall of darkness, the ancient trees seeming to lean inward, witnesses to what was about to unfold. In the distance, the Tom's waters merged with the gathering gloom, becoming indistinguishable from the encroaching night, its surface now black as pitch, reflecting neither stars nor the last remnants of day.

A multitude of torch-bearing slaves, numbering in the hundreds, flooded into the square, their flickering lights creating an undulating sea of flame that cast wild, dancing shadows across the stone. With Sangarre at their head, her dark eyes flashing with fierce pride, the Tsiganes and Persians emerged once more before the Emir's throne, performing their different dance styles in striking contrast to one another. The Tsiganes moved with passionate abandon while the Persians maintained their elegant precision. The Tartar musicians played with even fiercer intensity, their wild melodies intertwining with the singers' deep, throaty calls that seemed to emerge from some ancient place. Above, the grounded kites took flight again, each one carrying a multicolored lantern that swayed and bobbed in the night air, their harp strings resonating more powerfully in the breeze as they soared through the illuminated night sky, creating an ethereal chorus high above the revelry below.

The scene intensified as a unit of Tartar soldiers joined the festivities, their ornate uniforms gleaming with gold thread and polished metal in the torchlight. They merged into the frenzied dances, launching into a remarkable display that spoke of both military discipline and savage joy. Armed warriors moved across the ground wielding unsheathed sabers and elongated pistols, their boots striking the earth in perfect rhythm as they performed intricate steps while discharging their weapons into the air. Each thunderous shot triggered a cascade of percussion, the deep rumble of tambourines, the low growl of daires, large drums and the sharp twang of doutares two string guitars resonating in response, building to a crescendo that seemed to make the very air vibrate with sound and fury.

A spectacular display unfolded as the dancers moved with their arms dusted in metallic-based pigments, creating streams of crimson, emerald, and azure light in the traditional Chinese style. The performers appeared to dance within their own personal fireworks show, their fingertips trailing ghostly ribbons of light through the night air. While reminiscent of ancient military dances performed among bare blades, this Tartar spectacle took on an even more magical quality as colored flames twisted like serpents above the dancers, making their costumes appear trimmed with living fire. The scene transformed into a dazzling array of sparks, shifting and recombining with each graceful movement of the performers, creating ephemeral patterns that hung suspended in the darkness before dissolving into stardust.

The Parisian journalist, despite his presumed immunity to theatrical spectacles given how far modern stagecraft had advanced, found himself impressed. Alcide Jolivet made a subtle nod of approval, the gesture that, back in Paris between Boulevard Montmartre and La Madeleine, would have translated to "Quite impressive indeed." His practiced cynicism forgotten, he leaned forward to better observe the mesmerizing display before him.

In an instant, responding to a signal that cut through the night like a blade, the fantasia's lights extinguished all at once. The dancing stopped, and the performers vanished from sight as if they had never existed, leaving only ghostly afterimages dancing in viewers' vision. As the ceremony concluded, only torches remained to illuminate the plateau that moments before had blazed with spectacular brightness, their steady flames now seeming somehow mundane compared to the magical display that had preceded them.

At the Emir's imperious gesture, Michael was dragged to the center of the square, his chains rattling against the cobblestones.

"Blount," Alcide asked his associate in a low voice, his face ashen, "will you stay to witness how this ends?"

"Absolutely not," Blount responded with a shudder, already turning away from the grim scene unfolding before them.

"I doubt the Daily Telegraph subscribers are interested in reading about an execution done in the Tartar style?" Alcide's attempt at professional detachment masked his revulsion.

"Only your own readers!" Blount's voice cracked.

"What a shame," Alcide remarked, observing Michael's proud bearing even in chains. "Such a brave warrior deserved to die in combat!"

"Is there any way we could rescue him?" Blount inquired, his hands clenching into helpless fists.

"None whatsoever!" The finality in Alcide's tone left no room for hope.

The journalists reflected on Michael's past kindness to them, now understanding the hardships he had endured while staying true to his mission. Surrounded by the merciless Tartars, they found themselves powerless to help him. Unable to bear the thought of witnessing the torment awaiting their unfortunate friend, they retreated to the town, their footsteps heavy with regret. Within the hour, they had set out for Irkutsk, their horses pushing hard through the gathering dusk, determined to join their Russian allies in what Alcide had already dubbed "the campaign of revenge."

Meanwhile, Michael stood defiant, meeting the Emir's imperious gaze without flinching. His face showed nothing but contempt when he looked at Ivan Ogareff. Though prepared to face death, he remained unwavering, without displaying even the slightest trace of fear. His shoulders were squared, his bearing that of a soldier facing his destiny with honor intact.

The crowd gathered in anticipation around the square, including Feofar-Khan's personal guards, for whom executions were another form of entertainment. They would soon disperse to seek their pleasures in drink once their morbid curiosity was satisfied. Some were already placing wagers on how long the prisoner would maintain his composure, their coarse laughter echoing across the stone courtyard.

With a gesture from the Emir, the guards forced Michael forward until he stood at the terrace's base. His boots scraped against the rough ground as they shoved him into position. With icy contempt, Feofar addressed him, “You sought to observe our movements, Russian spy.”

Fate, cruel in its twist, had in store for Michael not death, but the permanent darkness of blindness; a punishment perhaps more devastating than death itself. His fate was sealed: he would be robbed of his sight. For a courier whose very mission depended on his ability to see, whose duty required him to witness and report, this sentence was precise in its cruelty.

Yet upon hearing the Emir's brutal decree, Michael's spirit remained unbroken. He stood motionless, his eyes wide, as if trying to burn every image into his memory. He knew better than to beg for mercy from these merciless men, such an act would be beneath him. The thought never crossed his mind. Instead, his thoughts dwelled on his failed mission, on his beloved mother, and on Nadia, whose face he would never again behold. Still, he maintained his composure, refusing to let his inner turmoil show. Then, a powerful urge for retribution seized him. "Ivan," he declared in a voice cold as steel, "Ivan the Traitor, my last gaze shall be reserved for you!"

He shrugged his shoulders, a smirk playing across his weathered face, but Michael refused to face him during the blinding. Instead, his mother Marfa stood before him, her lined face a map of worry and determination.

"Mother!" he exclaimed, his voice cracking with emotion. "Yes, let my last sight be of you, not this villain! Stay where you are, I want to gaze upon your beloved face one last time before darkness takes me forever... Let me remember every detail, every line that tells the story of your love and sacrifice."

The elderly woman approached, her steps measured and dignified despite the trembling of her hands. Her eyes, brimming with unshed tears, locked onto her son's face with fierce maternal pride.

"Remove her!" Ivan commanded, his voice sharp with irritation. His hand slashed through the air in an imperious gesture that brooked no argument.

Two guards moved to grab her, but she backed away with surprising agility for her age, maintaining her position several steps from Michael. Her weathered hands trembled but remained raised in a protective gesture.

The executioner emerged from the shadows, his face impassive beneath his hood as he brandished a glowing white saber he had just retrieved from the chafing-dish. Steam rose from the blade in the cool air, its heat visible in waves. His intention was obvious, to blind Michael using the brutal Tartar method of passing a heated blade before the eyes, a punishment designed to inflict maximum suffering while preserving life.

Michael remained still as stone, offering no resistance against his bonds. In these last moments of sight, his gaze fixed on his mother, drinking in her image with desperate intensity as if trying to burn her features into his memory forever. His entire existence concentrated into this last look, memorizing every line of her face, every silver strand of hair.

Marfa Strogoff stood with arms outstretched toward her son, her eyes wide with horror at the impending brutality. Her lips moved in silent prayer as the blazing blade swept across Michael's field of vision with a terrible hiss.

A heart-wrenching scream pierced the air, echoing off the stone walls of the square as his elderly mother collapsed unconscious, her body crumpling like a marionette with cut strings. Michael Strogoff had been blinded, his world forever darkened by the searing metal.

The Emir and his entourage withdrew from the square with measured steps, satisfied with the day's cruel spectacle, leaving only Ivan Ogareff and the torch bearers behind in the growing shadows. The flickering flames cast grotesque shapes across the cobblestones as evening approached. Would this villain seek to further torment his victim with one last act of cruelty, or was the day's barbarism complete?

Ivan Ogareff approached Michael with deliberate slowness, his boots scraping against the rough cobblestones with each calculated step. Sensing his enemy's presence, Michael straightened his posture, his jaw clenched despite the lingering agony from the heated blade. With theatrical flourish, Ogareff retrieved the Imperial letter from his pocket and unfolded it, the parchment crackling in the evening air. In a display of savage mockery, he held the document before Michael's blinded eyes, sneering, "Read it now, Michael Strogoff. Read it and deliver its contents to Irkutsk. I, Ivan Ogareff, am the true Courier of the Czar."

Having delivered his cruel taunt, the traitor tucked the letter into his breast pocket with a satisfied pat. Without a backward glance, he strode away from the square, the torch bearers following in his wake, their shadows dancing across the weathered stone walls.

In the desolate square, Michael stood mere steps from where his mother lay lifeless, the evening chill settling around them like a shroud. The sounds of revelry and celebration echoed from afar, while Tomsk blazed with light and festivity, its revelry a stark contrast to the darkness that now defined his world.

Listening in the empty silence, his other senses already beginning to sharpen, Michael inched his way toward where his mother had collapsed. His hands found her form, trembling as they traced her familiar features, and he lowered himself close, pressing his face near hers to detect any flutter of life. His lips moved in hushed words, a mixture of prayer and plea.

Whether Marfa lived still and could hear her son's whispered voice remained uncertain - she gave no response, no sign, not even the faintest breath against his cheek. Michael pressed a kiss to her forehead and silver hair before rising, his heart heavy with a grief he dared not yet embrace. Cautiously, he began making his way toward the square's edge, his foot testing each step, his hand reaching out for guidance in the darkness that had become his world.

In that moment, Nadia appeared, emerging from the shadows like a guardian angel. She moved toward her companion, using a knife to slice through the bonds restraining Michael's arms, her movements quick and precise. Being blind, he couldn't know who had freed him, as Nadia worked in silence, her presence known only through the sawing motion at his wrists and the gradual loosening of his bonds.

Only when finished did she speak, her voice thick with emotion: "Brother!"

"Nadia!" Michael whispered her name twice, relief flooding through him at the sound of her familiar voice.

"Come, brother," Nadia said, taking his arm with gentle determination. "While your eyes rest, use mine. I shall guide you to Irkutsk, through every step and every obstacle that lies ahead."

Chapter Six

A FRIEND ON THE HIGHWAY

HALF an hour afterwards, Michael and Nadia had left Tomsk.

In the chaos of that night, many prisoners managed to slip away from their Tartar captors, both officers and soldiers. The celebrations of their victory had led to reckless indulgence, with wine and spirits flowing through the camp. Among those who escaped was Nadia, who was captured but broke free when her guard stumbled away to join a rowdy gathering. She made her way back to the square just as Michael was being brought before the Emir, her heart pounding with each cautious step. Hidden within the crowd, pressed between weather-worn peasants and merchants, she witnessed the horrific scene in its entirety. She remained composed, not uttering a single sound when the burning blade passed before her companion's eyes, though her fingernails dug deep crescents into her palms. Through sheer force of will, she stayed still and silent, even as those around her gasped and turned away. When the elderly Siberian woman collapsed unconscious, Nadia's heart stopped, the sound of the woman's fall echoing in her ears like thunder. But a sudden flash of purpose renewed her determination, cutting through her horror like a blade through darkness. She made a solemn vow to herself: "I shall become his eyes and guide him," the promise burning in her chest as fiercely as her desire for revenge.

After Ogareff left, Nadia pressed herself against the cold stone walls, melting into the shadows and waiting with the patience of a hunter until the last echoes of footsteps faded from the square. Michael remained alone, a figure of tragic isolation, dismissed by passersby who now regarded him as nothing more than a pitiful blind man. Her throat tightened as she watched him crawl to his unconscious mother, press a tender farewell kiss to her weathered forehead, then rise to his feet.

Moments later, their hands found each other in silent understanding, and together they descended the treacherous incline. Following the high, craggy banks of the Tom River to the town's periphery, fortune smiled upon them as they discovered a crumbling section of the perimeter wall, just wide enough to slip through.

The vast expanse before them offered only one route eastward, the well-worn road to Irkutsk stretching into the distance. There could be no confusion about direction, no possibility of wrong turns in this desolate landscape. Time pressed heavily upon them, for they knew that once the Emir's scouts shook off their drunken stupor the next day, they would swarm across the steppes like locusts, choking off all escape routes. Their head start was paramount. It seemed almost inconceivable how Nadia endured that punishing night march between August 16th and 17th. What hidden wellspring of strength sustained her through such an ordeal? How did her feet, torn and weeping blood from the merciless pace, continue their relentless forward motion? The feat bordered on miraculous. Yet the truth, when dawn broke the following morning, twelve hours after their desperate flight from Tomsk, she and Michael had reached Semilowskoe, having conquered an extraordinary thirty-five miles of harsh terrain.

Michael remained silent. Rather than Nadia holding onto him, he was the one who kept a firm grip on her hand throughout the night. Yet thanks to her gentle, trembling guidance, he had maintained his usual walking pace, navigating the treacherous terrain without serious mishap.

They found Semilowskoe deserted, with most of its residents having fled. Only two or three houses showed any signs of life, thin wisps of smoke curling from their chimneys into the morning air. The townspeople had loaded all their valuables and necessities into wagons and departed, leaving behind an eerie stillness that hung over the empty streets. Despite their desire to press on, Nadia needed to stop for a while. Both travelers needed to eat and rest their weary bodies, their strength depleted from the grueling journey.

The girl guided her companion through the town until they reached its outskirts, their footsteps echoing in the abandoned lanes. They discovered an abandoned dwelling with its entrance ajar, the door creaking in the morning breeze. Inside, a weathered wooden bench occupied the center of the room, positioned near the tall stove common to all homes in Siberia. The air was stale and thick with dust, but it offered welcome shelter. Without exchanging words, they took their seats, their exhausted bodies grateful for the respite.

Nadia studied her companion's features with unprecedented intensity, taking in every line and shadow of his face. Her gaze held something deeper than mere thankfulness or compassion, something that made her heart ache with unspoken emotion. Had Michael been able to see her expression, he would have recognized in those gentle, sorrowful eyes an infinite well of loyalty and affection, a devotion that transcended their dire circumstances.

The scorched eyelids of the sightless man drooped halfway, concealing his eyes. His pupils had grown large, while the once-bright blue of his iris had deepened to a darker shade. Though his eyebrows and lashes were singed, his piercing gaze appeared unchanged to observers.

Michael extended his hands outward, his fingers trembling in the dim light.

"Nadia, are you there?" he called out, his voice betraying a hint of vulnerability.

"I'm right here beside you," she answered with gentle reassurance. "And I won't leave your side, Michael. Not now, not ever."

When Nadia spoke his name for the first time, Michael's body tensed. A shiver ran through him as he realized she now knew everything about his identity, his mission, his true purpose, everything he had fought to keep hidden.

"Nadia," he said, his voice tight with emotion, "we must part ways!"

"Part ways? What do you mean, Michael?" Her voice quavered with disbelief and hurt.

"I can't hold you back from your journey! Your father is expecting you in Irkutsk! You need to get to him!" His words came out, almost desperately, as if trying to convince himself as much as her.

"My father would never forgive me if I abandoned you now, not after everything you've done for me!" she declared with fierce determination, her loyalty clear in every word.

"Think of your father, Nadia, only your father!" Michael insisted, his hands clenching at his sides. "He needs you safe, whole!"

"You need me more than he does right now, Michael," Nadia responded, taking a step closer to him. "Are you giving up on reaching Irkutsk?"

"Never!" Michael exclaimed, his voice filled with unwavering determination, echoing against the walls. "Not while breath remains in my body!"

"But you don't have the letter anymore!" Her words hung heavy in the air between them.

"The letter Ivan Ogareff stole from me! No matter, Nadia! They branded me a spy, so a spy I shall become!" His jaw set with grim resolve. "I'll journey to Irkutsk and report everything I've witnessed, everything I've heard. I swear this sacred oath! One day, I shall confront that traitor face to face! But I must reach Irkutsk before he does, before more damage is done."

"Yet you speak of parting ways, Michael?" She touched his arm.

"Nadia, they've stripped me of everything!" His voice cracked with raw anguish. "My dignity, my purpose, my very sight!"

"I still have some roubles, and my sight remains!" Her voice grew stronger with each word. "Let me be your eyes, Michael. I'll guide you to places you cannot reach alone! Together we are stronger than apart."

"How will we travel?" He asked, uncertainty creeping into his voice.

"By foot," she answered, her chin lifted with determination.

"How will we survive?" His fingers brushed against the empty coin purse at his belt.

"We'll beg if we must," she declared without shame. "Whatever it takes."

"Then let us depart, Nadia." He extended his hand, seeking hers.

"Yes, Michael, let's go." She clasped his hand, their fingers intertwining with shared purpose.

Having endured hardships together, the young pair stopped referring to each other as siblings. Their shared troubles had strengthened their bond into something deeper, more profound than mere family ties. Following a brief rest of sixty minutes beneath the shade of a gnarled oak tree, they ventured out into the dusty afternoon. While in town, Nadia had got some tchornekhleb (a bread made from barley) and meod (a Russian honey drink) from sympathetic merchants. She'd gained these without payment, having relied on charity and the kindness of strangers, though the shame of begging still burned in her cheeks. These modest provisions helped ease Michael's hunger and quench his thirst after their long journey. Nadia ensured he received most their meager supplies, watching him with careful attention. He consumed the bread she offered and drank from the container she raised to his mouth with trembling hands.

"Have you taken your share, Nadia?" he questioned repeatedly.

"I have, Michael," the young woman would answer each time, forcing warmth into her voice to mask her deception, though she was surviving on the remnants he didn't consume, her own stomach growling in protest.

Michael and Nadia departed from Semilowskoe and resumed their challenging journey toward Irkutsk. Nadia displayed remarkable endurance in the face of exhaustion, her feet blistered and aching with each determined step forward. If Michael had seen her condition, the pallor of her skin, the dark circles beneath her eyes, the way she sometimes stumbled, he might have lost his resolve to continue. However, Nadia remained silent about her struggles, swallowing her discomfort, and Michael, hearing no complaints, maintained a relentless pace he couldn't help but sustain. What drove him? Was he still hoping to stay ahead of the Tartars? His situation was dire, traveling on foot, without money, and blind. If he were to lose Nadia, his sole guide and anchor in this darkness, his only option would be to collapse beside the road and meet a tragic end. Yet, if through sheer determination he could reach Krasnoiarsk, there might still be hope. The governor there, once Michael revealed his identity, would provide the means for him to complete his vital journey to Irkutsk.

Michael walked, deep in contemplation, his fingers intertwined with Nadia's. Their connection transcended mere physical touch, it was a lifeline of mutual trust and dependency that made words seem unnecessary in the vast Siberian wilderness. Michael would request, "Talk to me, Nadia," seeking reassurance in the gentle melody of her voice.

"What need is there, Michael? Our thoughts are already one," she would respond, masking the exhaustion in her voice, her fingers tightening around his.

Yet there were moments when her strength would falter, her heart appearing to skip a beat, her legs growing unsteady, her arms falling limp at her sides as she lagged behind. The harsh Siberian terrain seemed to drain what little energy remained in her weary body. At such times, Michael would halt, turning his sightless gaze toward her as if willing himself to see through the darkness that enveloped him. His chest would rise with deep emotion, and then, offering her even greater support than before, he would press onward with renewed determination, drawing from some hidden reserve of strength.

While trudging through their endless hardships, fate smiled upon them that day with something that promised to lighten their burden. After two hours of walking from Semilowskoe, their boots heavy with mud and their clothes damp with sweat, Michael came to an abrupt halt, his head tilted slightly as he listened.

"Can you see anyone on the path?" he asked, his voice barely above a whisper.

"Not a living soul," Nadia answered, scanning the desolate landscape before them.

"I think I hear something approaching from behind. We'll need to conceal ourselves if it's the Tartars. Keep your eyes sharp!" His grip on her hand tightened as he spoke.

"One moment, Michael!" Nadia called out, stepping back to where the road curved rightward, her eyes searching for any suitable hiding place among the scattered rocks and sparse vegetation.

Michael Strogoff stood in silence, straining his ears to listen, his body tense and alert like a hunter tracking prey.

Nadia quickly returned with news: "There's a cart coming. A young man's driving it," she reported, out of breath from her brief reconnaissance.

"Is he by himself?"

"Yes, alone. No other travelers that I can see for miles."

For a moment, Michael considered his options. Should he seek cover, or attempt to secure passage in the approaching transport, if not for himself, then at least for his companion? He felt strong enough to grasp the wagon and push it along if needed, as his legs remained sturdy. However, he worried about Nadia, who was forced to walk since their Obi crossing eight days ago, and must be reaching her limits. The harsh journey had taken its toll on them both, but she had shown remarkable resilience. He remained still, watching, his hand resting on his belt.

The wagon soon reached the intersection, its wooden wheels creaking with each rotation. It was an old, weathered wagon, a kibitka, as locals called it, with room for three passengers. While kibitkas required three horses for pulling, this one had just a single steed, a long-haired Mongolian horse with an long tail. This breed was well-known for its exceptional endurance and bravery, perfectly suited to the harsh conditions of the steppes. The animal's muscular frame and alert ears suggested it was still in its prime, despite the rather decrepit state of the vehicle it pulled.

A young Russian man was guiding the vehicle, accompanied by a shaggy-coated Siberian hunting dog that trotted alongside. His calm, friendly face, weathered by the elements but still youthful, put Nadia at ease. He moved, careful not to push his horse too hard on the uneven terrain. Looking at his relaxed demeanor and easy posture on the driver's bench, one would never guess he was traveling on a path that Tartars could overrun at any moment.

Nadia, still holding Michael's hand, stepped aside onto a patch of trampled grass to let the kibitka pass. The driver brought his vehicle to a halt with a gentle tug of the reins, and smiled at the young girl, the corners of his eyes crinkling with genuine kindness.

"Where might you be heading like this?" he asked with genuine curiosity, his eyes wide and sincere beneath the brim of his well-worn fur cap.

When Michael heard the man speak, something stirred in his memory, he knew that voice from somewhere, like a half-forgotten tune. A wave of relief washed over him as he placed the familiar sound, his worried expression softening, tension draining from his shoulders.

"And just where might you be headed?" the young fellow asked again, directing his question to Michael, leaning forward on his perch.

"Our destination is Irkutsk," Michael answered, his voice steady despite their circumstances.

"Oh! my good man, you realize there are countless kilometers between here and Irkutsk?" the driver exclaimed, gesturing at the vast landscape before them.

"I'm well aware," Michael replied with quiet determination.

"And you plan to walk?" The incredulity in his voice was unmistakable.

"Yes, walk."

"You perhaps, but what about the young lady?" He glanced at Nadia.

"She's my sister," Michael stated, deciding it prudent to maintain this description of Nadia, his tone leaving no room for discussion.

"Your sister, you say! Well, take my word for it, she'll never manage the journey to Irkutsk!" The driver shook his head in disbelief, his weathered face creasing with concern.

"My friend," said Michael as he moved closer, his voice dropping to an urgent whisper, "we've been stripped of everything by the Tartars. I don't have even a single copeck for you, but please, take my sister in your cart. I'll walk alongside it, I'll run if I must, and won't slow you down at all!" His words carried the weight of desperate sincerity.

"No, brother!" Nadia burst out, her voice trembling with emotion as she grabbed Michael's arm. "I won't do it! Please, sir ,my brother cannot see!" The words tumbled out before she could stop them, her protective instinct overriding their careful pretense.

"He's blind?" the young man asked, deeply affected by this revelation.

"The Tartars burned his eyes!" Nadia cried, raising her hands in a pleading gesture, tears threatening to spill down her cheeks.

"Burned his eyes! Oh, you poor soul! Listen, I'm headed to Krasnoiarsk. Why don't both of you ride in my kibitka? We can squeeze together, and there's room for all three of us. My dog won't mind walking, and though we won't travel fast since I'm careful with my horse, we'll get there enough," he offered, his voice full of genuine compassion.

"Tell me your name, friend," Michael requested, turning his face toward the sound of the young man's voice.

"I'm Nicholas Pigassof," he replied.

"That's a name I'll carry with me always," Michael responded with heartfelt gratitude.

"Climb in, dear blind friend. Your sister can sit next to you in the back of the cart, while I'll take the front to steer. We've lined the bottom with fresh birch bark and straw, it's quite cozy, like a bird's nest. Move aside, Serko!" Nicholas called to his faithful companion.

The dog obeyed, jumping down with a soft thud. He was a Siberian breed with gray fur, medium-sized with a friendly, pattable head, and devoted to his master. His intelligent eyes watched the newcomers with gentle curiosity as they prepared to board the cart.

Soon after, Michael and Nadia settled into the kibitka. Michael reached out, searching for Pigassof's hands. "Ah, you want to shake hands!" Nicholas said. "Here they are, my friend, hold them as long as you like. They're rough and calloused, but honest working hands."

The carriage continued forward, with Nicholas's horse maintaining a steady pace with no whip. The animal seemed to know the route by heart, its hooves striking a familiar rhythm against the packed earth. While Michael's journey wasn't moving any faster, at least Nadia could rest a bit in relative comfort.

The young girl was so exhausted that the gentle rocking of the carriage soon lulled her to sleep, a deep slumber that showed just how drained she was. Her head drooped until it rested against Michael's shoulder. Together, Michael and Nicholas carefully arranged her on the straw bedding, making sure she was secure and wouldn't roll with the cart's movement. Nicholas felt great sympathy for her condition, and though Michael shed no tears, it was only because the hot iron that had blinded him had dried up his ability to cry.

"Such a lovely girl," Nicholas commented, glancing back at his passengers. "She reminds me of my daughter at that age."

"Indeed," Michael replied, his face turned toward where Nadia lay sleeping.

"These dear ones try to show such strength, little father. They're brave souls, but in the end, they're still delicate creatures. Have you traveled from afar? Your clothes suggest quite a journey."

"A very long way."

"You poor souls! The burning of your eyes, it must have caused terrible pain! I can not imagine such suffering."

"Yes, terrible," Michael responded, turning toward Nicholas's voice as if he could still see him, his scarred face twitching at the memory.

"Didn't you cry?"

"I did." The words came out clipped and raw.

"I would have cried too. Imagine never being able to see your loved ones again. Though they can still see you, maybe that's something to hold onto! A small blessing in such dark times."

"Yes, maybe it is." Michael paused, his head tilted. "Listen, my friend," he went on, his voice taking on an intent quality, "are you sure we haven't met somewhere before?"

"You, sir? Never."

"Your voice sounds familiar to me." Michael leaned forward, his unseeing eyes searching.

"Well!" Nicholas said with a smile, adjusting his grip on the reins, "he recognizes my voice! Perhaps you're asking to figure out where I'm from. I'm from Kolyvan."

"Kolyvan?" Michael echoed, his face brightening with recognition. "Then that's where I met you, weren't you working at the telegraph office?"

"Could be," Nicholas answered, his tone neutral. "I was employed there. I handled the telegraph messages."

"And you remained at your station until the very end?"

"Well, that's when you need to be there!" Nicholas declared with unwavering conviction.

"I remember the day when a Brit and a Frenchman were arguing, waving roubles around, fighting for a spot at your window. The Englishman was sending some verses." Michael's voice carried a hint of amusement at the memory.

"That might have happened, but I can't recall it," Nicholas replied with practiced indifference.

"Really? You don't remember?"

"I never read the messages I transmit. Since I'm supposed to forget them anyway, it's easier to not know them." Nicholas's words came out clipped and precise, like a well-rehearsed response.

The response revealed much about Nicholas Pigassof's nature, his disciplined loyalty to duty and careful discretion. The kibitka continued its journey at a steady rhythm, with Michael wishing they could go a little faster. However, both Nicholas and his horse were set in their ways, following a routine they had no desire to change. Their pattern was consistent: two hours of travel followed by one hour of rest, continuing this way through day and night. During these breaks, the horse would graze in whatever patch of grass it could find, while the travelers shared meals alongside the loyal Serko, who always seemed to know when mealtime approached. Their kibitka carried enough provisions to feed twenty people, packed into every available space, and Nicholas, with characteristic generosity, shared his supplies with his two guests, whom he assumed were siblings traveling together through circumstance.

Refreshed after resting for a day, Nadia found her strength returning, the color coming back to her cheeks and her appetite improving with each meal. Nicholas tended to her needs with great care and attention, offering extra blankets during the frosty nights and ensuring she had the most comfortable spot in the kibitka. Though their progress was unhurried, they advanced and under good conditions, the weather remaining mild for their journey. During the night drives, Nicholas would drift off to sleep, his loud and steady snoring revealing his untroubled mind, his head nodding with each breath and the motion of the cart. In these moments, one might have caught glimpses of Michael's hand reaching for the reins, urging the horse to pick up speed, confusing Serko, who remained silent about these occurrences, though his intelligent eyes followed each subtle movement. Whenever Nicholas stirred from his slumber, the pace would return to its usual amble, but by then the kibitka had already covered several additional miles, their progress hastened under the cover of darkness.

On their journey, the travelers crossed several rivers and passed through many settlements in Siberia. They traversed the Ichirnsk River and moved through a series of villages including Ichisnokoe, Berikylokoe, and Kuskoe, each one more desolate than the last, with shuttered windows and abandoned market squares. Their path then led them across the Marunsk River and its namesake village, followed by Bogostowskoe. They reached the Ichoula, a small stream marking the boundary between Western and Eastern Siberia, its waters running clear and swift between moss-covered banks. The landscape alternated between vast, empty moors stretching to the horizon, where the wind whispered through the tall grass, and dense fir forests that seemed to go on forever, their dark branches creaking in the breeze. The entire region was deserted, with most villages standing empty, their wooden houses creaking in the wind. Local peasants had retreated beyond the Yenisei River, believing its wide waters might block the advancing Tartar forces, taking with them whatever possessions they could carry on their backs or load onto carts.

The kibitka arrived in Atchinsk on August 22nd, having covered two hundred and fifty miles from Tomsk, the wheels worn and muddy from the difficult terrain. They still needed to traverse another eighty miles to reach Krasnoiarsk, a journey that would take them through even more challenging territory as summer waned into early autumn.

The journey had been uneventful, though the constant rocking of the kibitka over uneven ground tested their endurance. Throughout their six days together, Nicholas maintained his characteristic composure, while Michael and Nadia remained anxious, their thoughts drifting to the inevitable moment when their fellow traveler would part ways with them.

Through Nicholas and the young girl's descriptions, Michael experienced the landscape they journeyed across. They took turns painting verbal pictures of their surroundings, allowing him to envision whether they were passing through dense forests or open plains, if there huts dotting the steppe, or if any Siberians ere visible nearby. Nicholas, talkative by nature, kept up a constant stream of commentary, describing everything from the way morning dew glistened on tall grass to the patterns of migrating birds overhead, and his unique perspective on things often brought smiles to his companions' faces. During these long hours of shared observation, the three travelers grew more comfortable with one another, and on one such conversation, Michael inquired about the weather.

"It's fair for now, little father," Nicholas replied, tugging at his thick wool collar, "though we'll be feeling winter's first bite soon enough. Perhaps these conditions will drive the Tartars to seek winter shelter during the harsh months ahead, when the steppes become treacherous with ice and snow."

Michael gave a skeptical shake of his head, his jaw tightening almost imperceptibly.

"Don't you agree, little father?" Nicholas pressed, leaning forward in his seat. "Do you think they'll advance toward Irkutsk despite the coming cold?"

"I'm afraid they will," Michael replied, his voice carrying a weight of certainty.

"Yes... you're right; they have that villainous man with them who won't let them dawdle. Have you heard of Ivan Ogareff?" Nicholas's cheerful face darkened at the name.

"I have."

"You know betraying one's homeland is unforgivable! To turn against Mother Russia herself!"

"Yes... it's unforgivable..." Michael responded, striving to maintain his composure while his fingers clenched against his knee.

"Little father," Nicholas continued, studying his companion's face with growing curiosity, "you seem rather calm when Ivan Ogareff name is mentioned. As a Russian, your blood should boil at the mere sound of his name."

"Trust me, friend, my hatred for him runs deeper than yours ever could," Michael said, each word measured and heavy with an intensity that silenced his talkative companion.

"That's impossible," Nicholas objected, his voice rising with indignation. "No, it can't be! When I think of Ivan Ogareff and the damage he's inflicting on our holy Russia, I become so enraged that if I ever got my hands on him," His fists clenched, knuckles whitening with the force of his emotion.

"If you got your hands on him, friend?" Michael's tone was soft, almost inviting.

"I believe I would kill him." Nicholas declared, chest puffing with patriotic fervor.

"And I know I would," Michael replied with quiet certainty, his words carrying the weight of steel and absolute conviction.

Chapter Seven

THE PASSAGE OF THE YENISEI

As darkness descended on August 25th, Krasnoiarsk appeared on the horizon, its scattered lights twinkling like distant stars. Eight days had passed since leaving Tomsk, the journey marked by caution and weariness. The journey could have been quicker, but Nicholas's lack of rest had prevented them from pushing their horse harder, the animal already showing signs of fatigue from the constant travel. Under different circumstances, another driver and fresh mounts could have covered the same distance in just sixty hours across the Siberian terrain.

The threat of Tartars had subsided, giving them a brief respite from constant vigilance. The road behind their kibitka remained clear, with not a single scout in sight across the vast steppes. This unusual calm suggested something significant had prevented the Emir's forces from advancing toward Irkutsk, though the reason remained uncertain. Recent events had taken an unexpected turn in the region's volatile political landscape. A assembled Russian force from Yeniseisk had attempted to reclaim Tomsk but, finding themselves outnumbered against the massive Tartar army, were forced to withdraw in anarchy. Feofar-Khan commanded a formidable army of two hundred and fifty thousand men, combining his own battle-hardened troops with those from the Khanats of Khokhand and Koun-douze, creating an overwhelming force that swept through the territory. Reinforcements: Without reinforcements from the west, the Russian government lacked the forces in Siberia to counter the threat and halt the invasion. Irkutsk's very existence is threatened, as the Tartar army might march on the city at any moment. On August 22nd: Although isolated from recent news, Michael was unaware that the battle of Tomsk had occurred This explained why the Emir's advance forces hadn't reached Krasnoiarsk by the 25th, giving them this temporary window of safety.

Despite being unaware of what had transpired since he left, Michael Strogoff took comfort in knowing he had a lead of several days over the Tartars, giving him reasonable confidence he would reach Irkutsk before them, even though the city lay another six hundred miles ahead through challenging terrain and unpredictable weather.

In Krasnoiarsk, a town of twelve thousand inhabitants nestled along the Yenisei River, Michael expected securing new transportation. As Nicholas Pigassof planned to remain there, Michael would need to find both a replacement guide and a faster vehicle, one better suited to the tough roads ahead. He was confident that, after presenting himself to the town's governor and verifying his status as the Czar's Courier, he could arrange swift passage to Irkutsk. He intended to bid farewell to the helpful Nicholas Pigassof and depart with Nadia, whom he was determined to deliver to her father, no matter the obstacles they might face. Though Nicholas had stopped in Krasnoiarsk, he had specified this was contingent on finding work there that would allow him to serve the government as faithfully as before. True to his conscientious nature, having stayed at his Kolyvan post until the very end despite mounting dangers, he now sought another government position where he could be of use. "I cannot accept wages I haven't earned," was his principle, a motto that had guided him throughout his years of service.

The traveler decided that if Krasnoiarsk, likely still connected to Irkutsk by telegraph, didn't need his help, he would journey onward to Oudinsk or even Siberia's capital. Should he choose the latter destination, he would continue accompanying the siblings. Indeed, they could hope to find someone more reliable or devoted to their cause, especially given the perilous nature of their journey through the harsh Siberian wilderness.

Their horse-drawn carriage was now half a mile from Krasnoiarsk. Wooden crosses, markers common near the town's entrance, dotted both sides of the road, their weathered forms casting long shadows in the fading light. As evening settled in at seven o'clock, the silhouettes of churches and houses perched on the Yenisei's elevated banks stood against the darkening sky, their forms mirrored in the river's dusky waters below. The last rays of sunlight painted the scene in muted shades of purple and gold.

"What's our location?" Michael asked his sister, leaning forward to peer through the gathering gloom.

"About half a mile before we reach the first buildings," Nadia answered, her voice tinged with both weariness and anticipation.

"Could everyone be sleeping?" Michael wondered aloud. "I can't hear a single sound." The unusual stillness made him uneasy, as even the smallest towns buzzed with some activity at this hour.

"I don't see any lights at all," Nadia said, scanning the horizon intently, "not even smoke rising from chimneys. At this time of year, they should at least have fires burning for warmth."

"What an odd town!" Nicholas remarked from his perch on the driver's seat. "It's silent, and apparently they all turn in early! Even the dogs are quiet, which is most unusual."

A sense of dread crept into Michael's heart, settling like a cold weight in his chest. He hadn't told Nadia that he'd pinned all his hopes on Krasnoiarsk, where he'd expected to find what he needed to complete their journey. The supplies they carried wouldn't last forever, and winter was approaching fast. He was worried that, once again, his expectations would prove false.

Nadia sensed his thoughts, though she couldn't understand why he remained so determined to reach Irkutsk after someone stole the Imperial letter. When she mentioned this to him one day during their arduous journey, he stated, "I made a vow to reach Irkutsk," in a tone that brooked no further discussion.

However, to complete his mission, he needed to secure faster transportation once they reached Krasnoiarsk. Their current pace was far too slow. "My friend," he called out to Nicholas, shifting in his seat, "what's causing our delay?"

"I'm trying not to disturb the townspeople with my carriage's racket!" Nicholas replied with forced cheerfulness, then gave a gentle snap of his whip to urge his horse forward along the darkening road.

The desolate High Street of Krasnoiarsk lay before them. Once dubbed the "Northern Athens" by Madame de Bourboulon, the city now stood eerily empty of its Athenian character. Silence now fell on the once elegant, wide, pristine streets, devoid of carriage sounds. Impressive in their architectural splendor, the grand wooden buildings cast shadows over deserted walkways where no footsteps fell. Siberian beauties in Parisian fashions were missing from the beautiful park carved from a birch forest to the Yenisei's banks. No longer did the cathedral's mighty bell ring, nor did church chimes fill the air. This once-vibrant city had transformed into a ghost town, stripped of all signs of life. Even the marketplace, bustling with merchants hawking their wares and housewives haggling over prices, stood abandoned, its wooden stalls collecting dust.

Prior to the telegraph lines being cut, the Czar's office had transmitted its final directive to Krasnoiarsk. Everyone, from the governor and military forces to ordinary citizens, were commanded to abandon the city, taking with them any valuable or useful items that might aid the Tartar forces. They were to seek sanctuary in Irkutsk. This evacuation order extended to all settlements in the province, as the Russian government's strategy was to leave nothing but empty land for the advancing enemy. The unquestioning obedience to the orders explains why Krasnoiarsk now stands deserted. Windows were shuttered, doors were locked, and even the city's archives and administrative documents had been carefully packed away and transported eastward, leaving behind nothing but hollow buildings and memories of better days.

The trio, Michael Strogoff, Nadia, and Nicholas, tiptoed through the empty town streets, their shadows stretching long against the abandoned buildings in the fading light. A sense of numbness had overtaken them, and their footsteps echoed against the cobblestones, the only sounds breaking the eerie silence of the abandoned city. Though Michael kept his emotions hidden behind his stoic expression, inside he seethed with frustration at his continued streak of misfortune and his thwarted plans, each setback feeling like another obstacle in his urgent mission.

"Oh, what terrible luck!" Nicholas lamented, gesturing at the shuttered shops and vacant houses. "How can I find work in such a desolate place? Not a soul remains to employ me!"

"You should continue traveling with us," Nadia suggested, her voice gentle but firm. "It would be unwise to stay here alone."

"Yes, I suppose I must!" Nicholas agreed, brightening somewhat at the prospect. "I expect the telegraph line between Oudinsk and Irkutsk is still functioning. At least there's that hope. So then, shall we get going, little father?"

"We should wait until tomorrow," Michael suggested, his face turned away as if listening to distant sounds.

"Indeed," Nicholas agreed. "We'll need daylight to navigate the Yenisei crossing! The river can be treacherous even in the best conditions!"

"To see!" Nadia whispered under her breath, thinking of her sightless companion with a pang of sympathy.

Nicholas caught her words and turned to Michael, his expression falling as realization dawned. "I apologize, little father," he said, embarrassed. "How thoughtless of me, day or night makes no difference to you, does it? I sometimes forget about your... condition."

"Please, friend, don't blame yourself," Michael responded, his hand moving to cover his eyes, fingers brushing against the rough fabric that concealed them. "With you guiding me, I can manage just fine. The darkness has been my companion for so long now. Take some hours to rest now. Nadia needs sleep too. We'll resume our journey tomorrow!"

Finding shelter proved easy for Michael and his companions. The first dwelling they entered stood vacant, like all the neighboring homes, its wooden door creaking in the night wind. Inside, they discovered only scattered piles of leaves, brittle and brown, that rustled beneath their feet. Their horse, having no better options, made do with this meager sustenance, pawing at the floor for better morsels. The group still had supplies remaining in their kibitka, allowing everyone a portion of food, simple fare of dried meat and hard bread that they shared in companionable silence. Later, after kneeling in prayer before a small icon of the Panaghia mounted on the wall, its lamp still casting a weak glow that flickered against the weathered timber walls, Nicholas and the young woman drifted off to sleep while Michael kept vigil, unable to find rest himself. His acute hearing picked up every subtle sound of the night, the whisper of wind through cracks, settling old wood, and the steady breathing of his sleeping companions.

At first light on August 26th, the carriage made its way through birch forests, heading for the Yenisei's shores. Michael's mind was troubled. The river posed a significant challenge, if the Tartars' advance had prompted the destruction of all vessels, as he suspected, how would they manage to cross? He was well acquainted with the river Yenisei's formidable nature: its vast expanse and powerful currents. Even under normal circumstances, using designed ferries for passengers, carriages, and horses, the crossing consumed three hours, with boats struggling to reach the far bank. Now, with no ferry service available, the question loomed: how could they transport the kibitka across these waters?

The first rays of dawn were appearing as their horse-drawn cart arrived at the elevated left shoreline, where a broad pathway through the park ended. From their position, thirty meters above the Yenisei River, they had a commanding view of its expansive flow. The cool morning air carried the distant sound of rushing water and the earthy scent of damp soil and river vegetation. Their horse stamped, steam rising from its flanks in the crisp morning air.

"Can you spot any vessels?" inquired Michael, his eyes darting from side to side, a futile habit, given his blindness. His fingers gripped the wooden seat, knuckles white with tension as he strained his other senses to compensate for his lack of sight.

"The morning's still too dim, brother," Nadia answered, squinting into the grayness. "There's a heavy mist hanging over everything, the river isn't visible yet. The fog's so thick it looks like a white blanket draped across the water."

"Though I can hear its rushing waters," Michael noted, his head tilted slightly as he focused on the sound. "The current seems stronger than usual today."

A thunderous roar emerged from within the dense fog as the swollen waters cascaded below, sending occasional spray into the air that merged with the morning mist. The three companions stood waiting for the misty veil to lift, knowing the sun would soon break through and scatter the morning vapors, its warmth already beginning to penetrate the gloom.

"What's happening?" Michael inquired, his fingers drumming against his knee.

"The fog is drifting away," Nadia answered, her voice carrying a note of relief. "It won't be long before everything clears."

"Can you see the water's surface yet?"

"Not yet." She leaned forward, straining her eyes.

"Just wait a moment, little father," Nicholas said, placing a reassuring hand on Michael's shoulder. "This will all vanish soon. Look, there's a breeze coming! It's pushing the fog away. I can already make out trees on the hills across from us. The mist is dissolving, floating off into nothing. The sun's warm rays are burning through all this haze. Oh, what a magnificent sight this is! Such a shame you cannot witness this beautiful scene, my poor friend!".

Michael scanned the horizon before turning to his companion, his face etched with concern. "Do you see a boat?"

"I see nothing of the sort," Nicholas replied, shaking his head.

"Look carefully, my friend, check both banks, as far as you can see," Michael urged, his voice carrying a note of desperate hope. "A raft, perhaps? Even a small canoe?"

Nicholas and Nadia leaned forward, clutching the bushes along the cliff's edge as they peered down at the waters below, their fingers digging into the coarse bark. Their vantage point offered a sweeping view, the wind tugging at their clothes as they searched. Here, the Yenisei River sprawled to nearly a mile wide, splitting into two channels of different sizes where the current rushed through, its waters churning and frothing around submerged rocks. Several islands dotted the space between these channels, lush with alders, willows, and poplars, like green vessels anchored in the flowing water, their leaves dancing in the breeze. Beyond: Rising beyond, the eastern shore showed forested hills wearing a purple crown in the light, each ridge distinct against the sky. Stretching in both directions, the mighty Yenisei presented a magnificent panorama extending fifty miles into the distance, where water and sky appeared to merge in a hazy embrace.

No watercraft were present in the area; the riverbanks were empty where boats usually gathered. Following instructions from military command, every vessel had been removed or demolished, leaving only weathered posts and frayed ropes swaying in the wind. The Tartars could not advance toward Irkutsk unless they brought materials to construct a pontoon bridge, as the Yenisei River formed an impassable barrier, its rushing waters a natural defense line.

"Wait," Michael said, his eyes scanning the distant shoreline. "I recall a small dock upstream, near the edges of Krasnoiarsk where vessels dock. Let's explore the riverbank in that direction, perhaps we'll find an overlooked boat."

Nadia grasped Michael's hand, her fingers tightening with renewed hope, leading them along the suggested route. She hoped to find a vessel, whether a boat or barge, substantial enough to transport either their kibitka or at least themselves across the churning waters. Michael stood ready to brave the crossing at a moment's notice, his determined expression matching the urgency of their mission. After twenty minutes of hurried walking along the rocky shoreline, dodging fallen branches and scrambling over moss-covered stones, the trio arrived at a small quay, where buildings lined both sides down to the water, creating what appeared to be a village extension beyond Krasnoiarsk proper, its wooden structures weathered by years of river mist and seasonal storms.

Their hearts sank at the sight before them. The shoreline stood deserted, no boats, no barges at the modest wharf, not even enough materials to construct a raft capable of bearing three passengers. When Michael questioned Nicholas about their options, the latter's response crushed their hopes: he deemed the crossing impossible under these circumstances, gesturing at the barren stretch of weathered planks and empty moorings.

"We'll make it across!" Michael declared, his voice carrying over the rush of the river waters with unwavering conviction.

They continued their thorough search. The group inspected the deserted houses along the shoreline, all abandoned just like the rest of Krasnoiarsk. The doors needed a gentle push to open, their hinges creaking from disuse and exposure to the elements. These were the dwellings of poor folk, stripped bare save for the occasional broken piece of furniture or tattered scrap of cloth. Nicholas explored one cottage, while Nadia ventured into another, their footsteps echoing through the empty rooms. Even Michael moved about, feeling his way through different houses, hoping to discover something useful among the scattered debris and abandoned belongings.

After Nicholas and Nadia had unsuccessfully searched their respective cottages and were ready to abandon their efforts, their spirits dampened by each empty dwelling, they heard Michael calling out to them. They rushed to the riverbank, their boots clattering against the worn wooden planks, and spotted him standing in a doorway, his silhouette framed by the dim interior of yet another fisherman's home.

"Quick, over here!" he called, waving them forward with urgency. Nicholas and Nadia hurried toward him and followed him inside the cottage, ducking beneath the low doorframe into the musty interior.

"What's all this?" Michael inquired, gesturing toward a pile of items stacked in the corner near a weathered wooden table.

"Those are containers made of leather," Nicholas replied, running his hand over the smooth, well-oiled surface of the nearest one.

"Are they filled?"

"Indeed, filled with koumyss. How fortunate we've found them to supplement our supplies!" Nicholas lifted one to test its weight.

Koumyss, a beverage produced from either mare's or camel's milk through a process of fermentation, provides substantial nourishment and can even produce intoxicating effects. Nicholas and his fellow travelers were quite pleased with their find, knowing how valuable such provisions could be on their journey.

"Keep one," Michael instructed, his voice firm with decision, "but drain the rest."

"Right away, little father." Nicholas began moving the containers into a more organized arrangement.

"These will be useful for crossing the Yenisei." Michael's fingers traced the leather's seams.

"What about the raft?"

"The kibitka will serve as our raft, it's lightweight enough to stay afloat. Plus, we can use these containers to help keep both it and the horse buoyant. The leather will provide extra flotation when we need it most."

"That's clever thinking, little father!" Nicholas said. "With God's blessing, we'll make it across... though we might not manage a straight path, given how swift the current runs! The spring melt makes the waters treacherous."

"What does it matter?" Michael replied, running his hand along the cart's wooden frame. "Once we're across, we can find the way to Irkutsk from the other bank. The road is well-marked on that side."

"Let's get to work then," Nicholas said, emptying the bottles with practiced efficiency.

They kept one bottle of koumyss, but used the rest, sealing in the air, to create a flotation device. Working in the fading daylight, they secured two bottles to each side of the horse to help it stay afloat. The animal shifted as they worked, but Nicholas's gentle words kept it calm. They attached two more bottles to the shafts to keep them level with the cart's body, which had now become a makeshift raft. They completed the task quickly, double-checking each knot and seal.

"Are you frightened, Nadia?" Michael asked, noticing her intent study of the rushing water.

"No, brother," the girl answered, lifting her chin with quiet determination.

"And you, friend?"

"Me?" Nicholas exclaimed, his weather-worn face breaking into a broad grin. "Why, this is like a dream come true, floating along in a cart! We Siberians can make a boat out of anything!"

The riverbank's muddy shore, smoothed by seasons of flowing water, was ideal for easing the kibitka into the water. Cautiously, the horse pulled the vehicle forward until it floated, Serko paddling alongside, creating small ripples.

They wisely removed their footwear and securing it in the cart, the three travelers sat in the kibitka as the water lapped around them; however, thanks to floating bottles, it only reached their ankles. Beneath them, the wooden planks creaked with each gentle wave. Michael handled the reins with steady hands, following Nicholas's guidance to steer the horse at a careful angle, avoiding overexertion against the river's flow. With effort, the animal's powerful muscles strained to maintain its course, avoiding a direct fight against the current. Initially, the journey downstream was smooth, the morning sun glinting off the water, and within minutes they passed Krasnoiarsk's waterfront, where a few early risers watched their unusual passage. Carried northward by the current, landfall became certain well below the town, a fact of little concern given their intended destination. Despite their makeshift vessel, the crossing would have been straightforward had the current remained steady. However, many whirlpools dotted the river's surface like hungry mouths, and despite Michael's best efforts to navigate between them, one of these swirling vortexes caught hold of the kibitka.

The small vehicle was in grave peril. Instead of drifting along, it now spun in circles, tilting toward the whirlpool's heart, reminiscent of a circus performer's calculated rotations. Their steed struggled to keep its nostrils above the churning waters, fighting against the very real threat of drowning, its eyes wide with terror as it thrashed against the merciless pull. Even Serko, the faithful dog, was forced to scramble into the carriage for safety, his wet fur pressed against the wooden planks as he whimpered.

Michael understood all too well the dire situation they faced. He could feel their vessel being pulled inward along an ever-tightening spiral, with no apparent means of escape. The wooden frame creaked with each rotation, water sloshing over the sides and pooling around their feet. How desperately he wished for his sight in that moment, to better navigate this treacherous trap, but such wishes were futile. Beside him, Nadia remained wordless, her hands gripping the cart's edges with white-knuckled intensity as their transport tilted ever more steeply toward the vortex's consuming center. The roar of the water grew louder with each passing second, drowning out even the panicked breathing of their horse.

Was Nicholas blind to the dire circumstances? Did his calm demeanor stem from stoic composure, fearless bravery, or mere apathy toward danger? Perhaps he viewed life as the Eastern philosophers did, as a brief stay at an inn, where one must check out on the sixth day, regardless of desire. Whatever the reason, his cheerful expression remained unwavering, his rosy cheeks still bearing that persistent smile, even as death itself seemed to beckon from the depths below.

The kibitka swirled in the churning waters, its horse spent, foam flecking from its quivering muzzle as it fought against the inexorable pull. Michael sprang into action, his movements decisive and purposeful. Shedding any restrictive clothing, letting his heavy coat and boots fall where they may, he plunged into the water and seized the panicked horse's bridle with iron determination. The icy current bit into his flesh, but he paid it no mind. With tremendous effort, his muscles straining against the relentless force of the water, he guided the animal free from the deadly whirlpool's grip. Once back in the main current, the kibitka resumed its downstream journey, water streaming from its wooden sides.

"Victory!" Nicholas cried out, throwing his arms wide as if embracing their salvation.

After two hours of grueling navigation from the dock, their battered vehicle had made it across the river's treacherous main channel, landing on a welcoming island over six miles downstream from where they began, the wooden kibitka creaking in protest as it dragged against the gravelly shore.

Once there, the horse, sides heaving and nostrils flaring, pulled the cart up the steep riverbank, and they allowed their valiant steed an hour to recover its strength. During this respite, they dried their sodden clothes and shared what remained of their provisions. After crossing the island beneath a canopy of stunning silver birch trees, their branches swaying in the afternoon breeze, they reached the bank of the Yenisei's narrower branch.

This crossing proved far less challenging; the river's second channel lacked the dangerous whirlpools of the first, though the water still churned with considerable force around them. However, the swift current still pushed them off course, carrying them five miles downstream before they could reach the far shore, the horse's hooves at last finding purchase on solid ground. They had drifted eleven miles from their original starting point, the journey having carved a great arc through the mighty river's expanse.

As the travelers crossed these vast Siberian rivers, still unbridged and formidable barriers to easy travel, each crossing had brought its share of troubles for Michael Strogoff. The Tartars had attacked their boat on the Irtych while he traveled with Nadia, the memory of bullets whistling past their heads still fresh in his mind. During the Obi crossing, he had escaped pursuing horsemen after his horse was shot, forced to abandon the dying animal and swim the final distance through the frigid waters. By comparison, their passage over the Yenisei had been uneventful, though no less demanding of their strength and determination.

"It wouldn't have been half as exciting," Nicholas declared as they stepped onto the river's far bank, wringing water from his sodden sleeves, "if it hadn't been such a challenge."

"What we found challenging," Michael Strogoff replied, scanning the distant shore they'd left behind, "may prove impossible for the Tartars to accomplish. Even the most skilled horsemen must respect nature's obstacles."

Chapter Eight

A HARE CROSSES THE ROAD

The messenger Michael Strogoff had reason to believe his path to Irkutsk would be unobstructed. He had outpaced the Tartar forces, who remained held up in Tomsk, and by the time the Emir's troops reached Krasnoiarsk, they would discover only an empty town. Since there was no way to cross between the shores of the Yenisei River, it would take several days to construct a pontoon bridge, a challenging task to accomplish in the best of conditions, let alone during a military campaign. For the first time since his confrontation with Ivan Ogareff in Omsk, the Czar's courier felt his anxiety ease, and he thought his journey might continue without further impediments, though experience had taught him to remain vigilant.

The stretch of road linking Krasnoiarsk to Irkutsk was well-maintained, standing out as the finest section of the entire route. Travelers enjoyed smoother passage here, with majestic trees providing welcome shade from the scorching sun that had tormented them across the steppes. In places, vast forests of pine and cedar stretched for a hundred miles, their branches swaying in the mountain breeze. Though no longer the boundless horizon of the steppe, a baron dessert, this fertile region lay vacant, its silence broken only by the occasional cry of a distant bird. They encountered nothing but abandoned settlements along their way, their wooden houses standing like silent sentinels. The Siberian farmers were gone, leaving behind a desolate landscape, not by nature's hand, but by imperial decree that had commanded their evacuation ahead of the advancing invasion.

The weather was pleasant, though the nighttime chill lingered in the morning air, slow to dissipate even as the sun climbed higher. As September approached, daylight hours grew shorter in this elevated region, the sun setting earlier each evening and rising later each dawn. The autumn season here was brief, despite being at the same latitude as Edinburgh and Copenhagen, around the fifty-fifth parallel, where fall stretched for months. Winter seemed to arrive almost without warning in this part of Siberia, descending like a heavy curtain across the landscape. Extreme temperatures characterized these harsh Asiatic Russian winters; sometimes the mercury plunged to an astounding 42 degrees below zero, a temperature even the hardiest locals found unbearable.

The group enjoyed favorable weather as they traveled, with no storms or rain to impede their progress. The clear skies and moderate temperatures made their journey almost pleasant. Both Nadia and Michael had regained their strength since departing from Tomsk, their previous exhaustion fading away as their bodies adjusted to the rigors of constant travel.

Nicholas Pigassof was thriving, feeling better than ever before. His cheeks had taken on a healthy ruddy glow, and his step had become more vigorous with each passing day. He viewed their journey not as a hardship but as an enjoyable expedition, a welcome use of his mandatory time off. The fresh mountain air and daily exercise had done wonders for his constitution, and he often hummed as they walked.

"I must say," he declared, "this beats spending twelve hours daily hunched over a stool, operating that telegraph machine! My back feels ten years younger already!"

The duo had convinced Nicholas to push his horse harder. Michael had achieved this by telling Nicholas that he and Nadia were rushing to reunite with their father, who was in exile in Irkutsk. While they needed to be careful not to exhaust the horse, especially since finding a replacement might prove impossible in these remote regions, they could still maintain a decent pace. By allowing the horse to rest every ten miles, they could cover forty miles within a day. The horse was well-suited for such a journey, being from a hardy breed known for its endurance in the harsh Siberian climate, and the route offered plenty of lush grass for grazing, ensuring the animal stayed well-nourished throughout their trek. Given these favorable conditions, they felt justified in asking the horse to increase its speed without risking its health.

Nicholas accepted all their reasons with enthusiastic understanding. The situation of the two young people about to join their father in exile touched him. He had seen nothing so moving in all his years of service. Smiling at Nadia, his eyes crinkling with genuine emotion, he said, "Oh, what joy Mr. Korpanoff will feel when he sees you, when he opens his arms to embrace you! If I make it to Irkutsk, which seems now, would you allow me to witness that reunion? You will, won't you? It would warm my heart to see such a happy moment."

Then, suddenly slapping his forehead with a sharp crack that startled them both, he added, "But oh! I forgot! What sorrow he'll feel when he discovers his poor son is blind! Ah! Such is life, joy and sadness always mixed, like light and shadow on a summer's day!"

Consequently, as a result, the kibitka's wheels turned over the rough terrain, now traveling faster, nearly eight miles per hour, according to Michael's careful calculations. Sensing: Sensing their passengers' urgency, the horses maintained a brisk pace despite the challenging road conditions.

Arriving: In the early hours of September 4th, just as dawn broke over the horizon, the carriage arrived at Biriousensk, having crossed the small Biriousa River whose waters flowed beneath. Nicholas was relieved by this arrival, as he had noticed their food supplies dwindling to low levels over the past few days. Luckily, he discovered several "pogatchas", traditional cakes made with fat from sheep, baking in an oven, their rich aroma filling the air, along with a considerable amount of cooked rice. This lucky find came at just the right time, as they needed to replace the koumyss, a fermented drink they had stocked up on while in Krasnoiarsk, which had run out during their journey.

The group resumed their travels later that day, following their brief stop. They were now within three hundred miles of Irkutsk. The Tartar advance forces remained unseen. Michael Strogoff felt optimistic that he would face no further interruptions and could reach the Grand Duke within eight to ten days at most, assuming the roads remained passable and weather favorable.

Just as they were departing Biriousinsk, a hare darted across their path in front of the kibitka, its brown fur a blur against the dusty road. "Ah!" Nicholas called out, jerking back on the reins.

"What's wrong?" Michael asked, reacting with the heightened awareness typical of a sightless person responding to unexpected sounds. His hands gripped the side of the cart.

"Did you notice that?" Nicholas asked, his cheerful expression turning gloomy, the color draining from his rosy face. He added, "Oh, but of course you couldn't have seen it, and that's probably for the best, my friend!"

"I saw nothing," Nadia said, glancing around with confusion at Nicholas's sudden change in demeanor.

"That's fortunate! Very fortunate! But I, I saw it!" Nicholas's voice trembled with genuine concern.

"What did you see?" Michael inquired, his sightless face turned toward the driver's voice.

"A hare ran across our path!" Nicholas replied, crossing himself with his free hand.

According to Russian folklore, a hare crossing one's path is considered an omen of impending misfortune, a sign that dark forces were at work. Being as superstitious as most Russians, those who spent their lives on the road, Nicholas brought the kibitka to a halt and muttered a quick prayer under his breath.

Michael could sense his companion's unease, though he didn't share the same superstitious concerns. "You needn't worry," he said, a gentle smile crossing his face. "Such omens only have the power we give them."

"Perhaps you and she have nothing to worry about, little father," Nicholas replied, his fingers still gripping the reins, "but I do! My grandmother always said a crossing hare means the devil himself is watching."

"Whatever happens is meant to be," he added with resigned determination, then urged his horse forward with a soft click of his tongue. Despite his gloomy predictions and frequent backward glances, they made it through the day without incident, though Nicholas remained quiet.

The kibitka came to a stop at noon on September 6th in Alsalevok village. Like the surrounding countryside, the village was completely abandoned, with only the whisper of wind through empty doorways and the occasional creak of shutters to break the eerie silence. While there, Nadia discovered two sturdy hunting knives with sharp blades, the kind used by Siberian hunters for skinning game and survival in the wilderness, lying on a doorstep. She kept one knife for herself and gave the other to Michael, who tucked it away in his clothing, both recognizing that such tools might prove invaluable on their journey.

The gloomy mood still clung to Nicholas. The bad omen had shaken him far more deeply than anyone might have expected. Once known for his constant chatter, unable to stay quiet for even thirty minutes, he now sank into prolonged silences that Nadia struggled to break. Their kibitka raced along the road at full speed, yes, full speed! Nicholas had abandoned his usual careful treatment of the horse, now sharing Michael's urgent desire to reach their destination. Despite his fatalistic nature and acceptance of fate, he wouldn't feel safe until Irkutsk's walls protected them. His reaction wasn't unusual among Russians, many would have shared his fears, and some would have even turned back after seeing a hare cross their path.

As they traveled onward, his keen observations, which Nadia relayed to Michael, suggested their hardships weren't over yet. While the natural resources around Krasnoiarsk had remained untouched, the woodlands they now encountered showed clear signs of destruction by fire and blade, showing that a substantial military force had moved through the area. Charred stumps dotted the landscape where healthy trees had once stood, and deep ruts carved into the earth spoke of heavy wagons and artillery pieces being dragged through. Even the underbrush had been stripped away in places, likely used for campfires by an army on the move. Nicholas's experienced eye could read these signs like a book, and the story they told made him pull his coat tighter around himself despite the mild temperature.

When they reached a point twenty miles from Nijni-Oudinsk, the unmistakable evidence of recent destruction pointed to the Tartar forces. The damage went beyond mere trampled fields and felled trees. The scattered homesteads along their route stood empty, some destroyed, others charred by fire. Their walls bore the telltale pockmarks of bullet impacts, and broken window frames gaped like hollow eyes beneath scorched eaves. Household belongings lay strewn across muddy yards, testament to hasty departures or violent looting.

Tension gripped Michael as the evidence became undeniable. Fresh tracks confirmed Tartar riders had indeed traversed this route, yet these couldn't be from Emir's forces, such a group would have been spotted. This raised alarming questions: what unknown raiders had appeared, and through which hidden steppe trails had they connected with the main Irkutsk road? The Czar's messenger now faced the daunting prospect of confronting mysterious new adversaries. His military training told him these raiders were skilled in stealth operations, moving swiftly and striking without warning, a far more dangerous proposition than facing conventional forces in open combat.

The fearful thoughts remained locked in his mind, as he chose not to burden Nicholas and Nadia with his concerns. His determination to press forward remained steadfast until they encountered a impassable barrier. As they continued their journey the following day, signs of recent military movement became clear. Wisps of smoke rose on the distant horizon, dark plumes that stained the otherwise clear Siberian sky. They guided the kibitka forward with great caution, every creak of the wooden wheels setting their nerves on edge. They passed through abandoned villages where several houses still smoldered, the fires set within the past twenty-four hours. The acrid smell of burnt timber and thatch hung heavy in the air, while scattered belongings in the dirt told of hasty departures.

Finally, on September 8th, their progress came to an abrupt halt when the horse refused to move another step, its ears pinned back and nostrils flaring with obvious distress. Serko's fierce barking pierced the air, the dog's hackles raised as he faced the road ahead with uncharacteristic aggression.

"What's wrong?" Michael called out, his hand instinctively moving to his belt as he scanned the surroundings for danger.

"There's a dead body!" Nicholas shouted back, jumping down from the kibitka. It was the corpse of a peasant, disfigured and already lifeless, his simple homespun clothing stained dark with blood. Nicholas made the sign of the cross, muttering a quick prayer under his breath. With Michael's help, he gripped the body under the arms and moved it to the roadside, laying it beneath a scraggly bush. He wished he could give the poor soul a proper burial to protect it from the wild animals of the steppe, but Michael wouldn't allow them to spare the time.

"We must go, my friend!" he urged, his voice tight with contained urgency. "We can't afford even an hour's delay!" And with that, they drove the kibitka onward, the wheels crunching over scattered stones.

During their journey toward Nijni-Oudinsk, Nicholas and his companions encountered a grim scene, the road was littered with dozens of victims, their bodies scattered across the landscape in groups of twenty or more, some still clutching makeshift weapons or lying over fallen loved ones.

They had no choice but to continue along this route until it became too dangerous to proceed without risking capture by the invading forces. Though the path grew treacherous, with deep ruts and debris making travel difficult, they couldn't deviate from it. Each village they passed through showed escalating signs of destruction and bloodshed, with evidence of recent violence still fresh, doors hanging from hinges, wells fouled, livestock scattered and dead. Gathering any details about what had transpired proved futile, not a single survivor remained who could recount the tragic events that had unfolded, leaving only the silent testimony of the devastation around them.

As the day drew toward late afternoon, around four o'clock, Nicholas spotted the distinctive high steeples of Nijni-Oudinsk's churches piercing the sky. Strange wisps of vapor, not natural clouds, swirled around the towers, their shifting patterns casting eerie shadows across the landscape below.

Nicholas and Nadia studied the scene before sharing their findings with Michael, their eyes straining to make sense of the unsettling sight before them. They faced a crucial decision. A deserted town would offer safe passage, but if the Tartars had somehow seized control, an unexpected yet possible scenario given recent events, they would need to avoid Nijni-Oudinsk at all costs. The risks of encountering enemy forces in such a confined space were too great to ignore.

"Move forward with caution," Michael Strogoff commanded, his voice tight with tension, "but keep moving!"

After traveling about a mile across rough terrain, they stopped abruptly, the horses stamping nervously beneath them.

"Look!" Nadia cried out, her face pale with dawning horror. "Those aren't clouds, it's smoke! Brother, the town is on fire!" The dark plumes now visible against the afternoon sky left little doubt about the grim situation that awaited them ahead.

The terrible truth was undeniable. Bright flashes pierced through the thickening haze as it billowed skyward, casting an eerie orange glow across the landscape. But who was responsible for this destruction? Could it be the Tartars? Or perhaps Russian forces following the Grand Duke's commands? Was this part of the Czar's strategy to deny the Emir's army any shelter, burning everything from Krasnoiarsk to the Yenisei River? Michael wrestled with what action to take, his jaw clenched tight as he weighed their dwindling options.

Uncertain at first, he evaluated the situation, scanning the horizon for any sign of movement. Though traversing the unpaved steppe would pose significant challenges, with its treacherous terrain and lack of water sources, he concluded it was preferable to risking another Tartar capture. Just as he prepared to suggest leaving the road to Nicholas, a gunshot cracked through the air from their right, shattering the tense silence. A bullet whizzed past, striking the kibitka's horse in the head, killing it instantly. The animal crumpled without a sound, its weight causing the carriage to lurch violently.

Before they could react or even cry out in alarm, about twelve mounted warriors surrounded them, their weapons drawn and faces obscured by dark cloth wrappings. In mere moments, Michael, Nadia, and Nicholas found themselves captive, their hands bound with coarse rope as they were taken toward the burning town of Nijni-Oudinsk, the acrid smoke growing thicker with each step.

Despite this second assault, Michael maintained his composure. His blindness made self-defense impossible, but even with functioning eyesight, he wouldn't have fought back. Such resistance would have meant certain death for him and his fellow travelers. Though his vision failed him, his hearing remained sharp, allowing him to comprehend the attackers' conversation, their voices carrying through the smoke-laden air.

Their speech patterns revealed them to be Tartar soldiers, their harsh consonants and distinctive inflections unmistakable to Michael's trained ear. Their discussion made it clear they were scouts advancing ahead of the major invasion force, gathering intelligence about the territory's defenses and population centers.

From the current discussion and fragments of dialogue he caught afterwards, Michael gathered the following information: the Emir, who was held up somewhere past the Yenisei River, dealing with logistical challenges of moving his massive army did not command the soldiers. Instead, they belonged to a separate third division, comprising of Tartars from the Khokland and Koondooz territories, fierce warriors known for their skilled horsemanship and ruthless efficiency. This force met up with Feofar's main army somewhere near Irkutsk, creating a pincer movement that would make defending the city impossible.

The invading column, acting on Ogareff's guidance, had taken a route along the Altai Mountains' base to ensure successful conquest of the Eastern provinces. As they advanced, they left destruction in their wake, burning villages and destroying infrastructure, reaching the upper Yenisei River. Understanding the Czar's defensive measures at Krasnoiarsk, they deployed a fleet of boats to help Feofar's forces cross the river and continue their march toward Irkutsk. The crossing took several days, with local fishing vessels commandeered to ferry troops and supplies. After establishing this crossing, the column moved downstream along the Yenisei valley until intersecting the main road near Alsalevsk. From this small settlement onward, they unleashed a devastating campaign of destruction, characteristic of Tartar military tactics, burning crops, poisoning wells, and leaving nothing behind that could sustain pursuit or resistance. The town of Nijni-Oudinsk fell to their onslaught after a day of fighting, and now fifty thousand Tartar warriors had positioned themselves outside Irkutsk, their campfires dotting the landscape like malevolent stars as they awaited reinforcement from the Emir's approaching army.

The situation had grown dire for this remote region of Eastern Siberia and the small group of soldiers protecting its principal city, their resources already stretched thin by the harsh winter and dwindling supplies.

One might expect Michael to have fallen into despair given these circumstances. Yet remarkably, his resolve remained unshaken, and he repeated only one phrase with determination: "I will get there!" His voice carried the same steadfast conviction it had held since departing Moscow, despite the mounting obstacles.

The small group reached Nijni-Oudinsk thirty minutes after fleeing from the Tartar cavalry's assault. Michael Strogoff led the way, accompanied by Nadia and Nicholas, while their loyal canine companion trailed behind at a distance, whimpering at the acrid smoke filling the air. With the town engulfed in flames and the last raiders preparing to depart, remaining there was impossible. The wooden buildings crackled and spat embers into the darkening sky as they burned. The captors forced their prisoners onto horseback and departed, their rough handling betraying their nervousness about lingering too long. Nicholas maintained his characteristic resignation, his weathered face showing accepting a man long accustomed to life's hardships, while Nadia's confidence in Michael remained unwavering, her eyes fixed on him with complete trust. Michael himself appeared detached, though he stayed vigilant for any chance to break free, his muscles tense beneath the ropes that bound him.

The Tartar soldiers discovered one prisoner was sightless, and their cruel nature drove them to mock their helpless captive. As they rode, Michael's horse, lacking guidance, veered off course, disrupting the formation. This behavior prompted the soldiers to heap abuse and harsh treatment upon Michael, causing Nadia deep anguish and filling Nicholas with rage. Yet, they could not intervene, unable to communicate in Tartar, and their pleas for mercy went unheeded. The soldiers soon devised an even crueler torment, deciding to switch Michael's mount for a blind horse. Their motivation became clear when Michael caught their whispered suspicion: "Maybe this Russian isn't really blind!"

Forced onto the horse, Michael had the reins thrust into his grasp. The mob drove the animal into a frenzied gallop through a barrage of whips, stones, and shouts. Like its rider, the horse was blind, careening into trees and veering off the path. These violent collisions and tumbles could have proven fatal. The soldiers' raucous laughter echoed through the wilderness as both beast and man struggled to maintain their balance, the horse's hooves slipping on loose rocks and roots. Michael gripped the saddle with his knees, his face betraying no emotion despite the blood trickling from fresh cuts on his face and arms. The blind horse's terrified whinnies pierced the air as it stumbled forward, guided only by the cruel shouts and threatening weapons of their tormentors.

Yet Michael remained stoic, never uttering a sound of protest. When his mount fell, he waited for it to rise again, his face an expressionless mask despite the fresh bruises forming on his body. Others would haul the horse back to its feet, cursing and shoving as they did so, eager to resume their cruel sport. Watching this barbaric display, Nicholas struggled to help his companion but was kept down and beaten for his attempts to intervene, his captors' fists leaving him doubled over in pain.

The entertainment would have continued, much to the Tartars' delight, if not for a tragic turn of events. On September 10th, the sightless steed bolted, its hooves thundering against the rocky ground as it charged toward a deep chasm, perhaps thirty or forty feet in depth, that lay beside the path, its jagged walls promising certain doom.

When Nicholas attempted to pursue, others restrained him, their iron grips leaving bruises on his arms. With no one to guide it, the horse plunged into the pit, its terrified scream echoing off the canyon walls as it took its rider down to the bottom. Nicholas and Nadia released an anguished scream, their voices joining the horse's dying cry as they feared their companion had met his death.

On rushing to help him, they discovered Michael had leaped clear of the saddle at the last possible moment and was unharmed, though his poor horse lay with two broken legs, its sides heaving with labored breaths, beyond saving. They abandoned the animal to a slow death, its agony unrelieved in the cold shadow of the ravine, while Tartar riders bound Michael with rough rope to a saddle and forced him to continue on foot across the treacherous terrain.

Yet still he uttered no word of protest or complaint. He kept pace, not needing the rope that bound him, his face set in grim determination as his boots found purchase on the uneven ground. He remained true to his nature as "the Man of Iron", just as General Kissoff had described him to the Czar!

As darkness fell on September 11th, the military group made its way through Chibarlinskoe village, its weathered wooden houses casting long shadows in the dying light. What happened there would prove fateful. The Tartar cavalry, who had stopped to rest, were drunk on fermented mare's milk and local spirits as they prepared to resume their journey, their raucous laughter echoing through the village streets. Until that moment, Nadia had been fortunate to receive decent treatment from the soldiers, but now one of them, emboldened by drink, subjected her to harassment.

Though Michael couldn't witness the offensive act or identify the perpetrator, Nicholas observed everything from his position among the guards, his hands clenching into fists at the sight. Without hesitation or apparent forethought, Nicholas approached the offender with deadly purpose in his stride. Before the man could react or defend himself, Nicholas grabbed a pistol from the soldier's holster and fired into his chest, the report of the shot shattering the evening's quiet.

Upon hearing the report echo through the evening air, the commanding officer rushed to the scene, his boots kicking up dust as he ran. Though the soldiers were ready to kill Nicholas on the spot, their rifles already raised and fingers on triggers, their officer signaled otherwise with a sharp wave of his hand. Following his command, they bound Nicholas with rough rope, draped him over a horse's back like a sack of grain, and the entire unit departed at full gallop, their hoofbeats thundering into the growing darkness.

Michael, who had been gradually chewing through his bonds throughout the chaotic scene, felt the fibers give way when the horse lurched forward over uneven ground. His captor, dulled by drink and focused on the commotion ahead, continued riding without noticing his prisoner's escape into the shadows of the roadside brush.

In the aftermath, Michael and Nadia remained behind, finding themselves alone on the deserted road, with only the settling dust and the distant sound of retreating horses to mark the violent events that had just transpired.

Chapter Nine

IN THE STEPPE

Michael and Nadia had regained their freedom, much like during their earlier trek from Perm to the Irtych riverbanks. Yet their current circumstances differed from before. Their previous journey was comfortable, they'd traveled in a well-appointed tarantass with fresh, reliable post-horses that had carried them swiftly to their destination. Now they were forced to walk, with no possibility of finding alternative transportation. They had no money or supplies, unsure of where their next meal would come from, and still faced a daunting journey of three hundred miles. Also, Michael now relied on Nadia's eyesight to navigate their way, his own vision still clouded by the effects of his injury.

They had just lost the friend who fate had brought to them, and they worried about what might become of him. The memory of Nicholas's sacrifice weighed heavily on their hearts, adding to the burden of their arduous journey. The late summer sun beat down mercilessly as Michael lay on the ground, concealed beneath the roadside thickets, his clothes dusty and worn from their travels. At his side stood Nadia, silent and ready, her keen eyes scanning the horizon for any sign of danger or pursuit. Her hand rested near Michael's shoulder as she awaited his signal to resume their journey, knowing each step forward would test their resilience and determination.

The time was ten o'clock, and a chill had settled over the land. Over three hours had passed since the sun had set, leaving only starlight to pierce the oppressive darkness. Not a single dwelling could be seen in any direction across the desolate landscape. The final Tartar rider had vanished into the distance, his horse's hoofbeats long since faded into silence. Michael and Nadia found themselves isolated in the vast emptiness.

"What's going to happen to him?" the girl cried out, her voice trembling with emotion. "Dear Nicholas! Meeting us must have sealed his fate!" Michael remained quiet, his shoulders tense with unspoken concern.

"Michael," Nadia persisted, clutching at his sleeve, "have you forgotten how he stood up for you when the Tartars were tormenting you? How he put his life on the line for my sake? For both our sakes?"

Michael kept his silence, the weight of their situation clear in his rigid posture. He sat motionless with his face covered by his hands, as if trying to shut out the world. Was he lost in thought? Though he offered no response, perhaps he was listening to Nadia's words, letting them sink into his troubled conscience.

Indeed, he was hearing her, because when the young girl asked, her voice softening with concern, "Which way should I guide you, Michael?"

"To Irkutsk!" came his answer, resolute despite everything they'd endured.

"Along the main road?"

"Yes, Nadia," he replied, his determination clear in those simple words.

Unwavering in his determination, Michael remained steadfast in his commitment to reach his goal, regardless of circumstances. Taking the main road seemed the most direct route, though it carried obvious risks. They could always veer off into the countryside if Feofar-Khan's advance forces were seen, using the dense forests and rolling terrain for cover.

With their hands clasped together, fingers interlocked for support and guidance, Nadia and Michael began their journey, their footsteps falling into a synchronized rhythm on the well-worn path.

They rested at Joulounov-skoë village the following day, September 13th, after covering twenty miles through difficult terrain. The village lay in ruins, abandoned, with only hollow-eyed windows and scorched walls bearing witness to the recent violence. Throughout the night, Nadia had searched for Nicholas's remains along their path, examining the rubble and the fallen with trembling hands, but her efforts proved futile. Each unidentified body made her heart race until closer inspection revealed it wasn't him. With dread, she wondered if they had taken him to Irkutsk for brutal punishment, a fate perhaps worse than death.

Weak from hunger, their stomachs cramping from two days of minimal sustenance, Nadia discovered a cache of preserved food in one of the abandoned houses, dried meat wrapped in cloth and "soukharis," a type of dehydrated bread that maintains its nutritional value indefinitely because of the drying process. The discovery felt like a minor miracle in their otherwise bleak circumstances.

Together with Michael, she gathered as much as they could physically transport, stuffing their pockets and makeshift sacks with the precious dried provisions. This would sustain them for many days ahead, and water would pose no concern in this region, which was well-irrigated by the various small tributaries flowing into the Angara River, their surfaces glinting like ribbons of silver in the harsh light.

The pair pressed onward, with Michael maintaining a steady, purposeful stride that he tempered only out of consideration for Nadia. Though exhaustion weighed heavily upon her, she forced herself to keep pace, her legs trembling with each step, taking comfort because his blindness concealed her deteriorating condition. Her breath came in ragged gasps she tried to silence.

Yet Michael sensed her struggle, his acute hearing picking up the subtle changes in her breathing and gait. "You're exhausted, dear one.

"I'm fine," came her steadfast reply, though her voice wavered slightly.

"If your strength fails, I'll carry you myself," he insisted, his powerful shoulders squaring with determination.

"Very well, Michael," she conceded, knowing his was no idle offer.

The travelers encountered the small Oka river that day, but found it shallow enough to wade across without trouble. The frigid water numbed their feet as they picked their way between slick stones. Though the sky remained overcast, the weather stayed mild, the dense clouds hanging low over the landscape like a gray wool blanket. While they worried about potential rain making their journey more difficult, only brief showers passed over them, leaving behind the fresh scent of wet earth.

They maintained their previous pace, walking together with joined hands and minimal conversation, each lost in their own thoughts. Nadia remained vigilant, scanning their surroundings, her eyes darting to investigate every rustle in the grass and distant movement. They stopped twice daily to rest, dedicating six hours each night to sleep, though their slumber was often fitful and light. In the occasional hut they passed, Nadia found small portions of mutton, trading what few valuables they could spare. However, contrary to Michael's expectations, the region was devoid of pack animals, all horses and camels had been slaughtered or stolen, leaving behind only empty corrals and abandoned stables. With no choice but to continue on foot, they pressed forward across the vast, tiresome steppe, where the wind whispered through endless waves of golden grass.

Along their path, the third Tartar column had left unmistakable evidence of their march toward Irkutsk. Scattered remains dotted the landscape: lifeless horses, discarded wagons with broken wheels and splintered axles, and most tragically, the bodies of Siberian victims strewn near village entrances, their frozen faces bearing witness to their last moments. Despite her revulsion, Nadia forced herself to witness these grim scenes, knowing they carried valuable lessons about their enemy's movements.

The greatest threat wasn't what lay ahead, but what followed behind them. Ivan Ogareff, leading the Emir's army's advance guard, could appear at any moment, his ruthless reputation preceding him like a dark shadow. By now, the invaders would have seized the boats sent downstream on the lower Yenisei at Krasnoiarsk, commandeering them for their own crossing. With no Russian forces stationed between Krasnoiarsk and Lake Baikal to resist them, the path lay wide open for the invaders to sweep across the defenseless territory. Michael knew it was only a matter of time before Tartar scouts would emerge from the endless grasslands.

During each stop, Nadia would ascend a nearby hill and scan the Western horizon with concern, her hand shielding her eyes from the harsh sun as she searched in vain for any dust clouds that might show approaching horsemen. The ritual had become almost compulsive, performed three or four times during each rest period, though the empty horizon brought both relief and growing dread.

They would then continue their journey, with Michael slowing his pace whenever he noticed Nadia struggling to keep up, her boots dragging in the dusty earth. Their conversation was sparse, focusing on Nicholas, each word measured against the rhythmic crunch of their footsteps. Nadia would reminisce about all the ways their brief companion had helped them during their short time together, from his clever insights to his minor acts of kindness that had made their desperate flight more bearable.

Michael, in his responses, tried to reassure Nadia about Nicholas's fate, despite knowing in his heart that their friend was doomed to die. The weight of this knowledge sat in his chest, making each comforting phrase feel like a betrayal. He couldn't bring himself to share his true beliefs about Nicholas's inevitable death, choosing instead to protect her with gentle lies.

Michael turned to the girl one day and whispered, "Nadia, you never tell me anything about my mother." His voice carried an unusual vulnerability, breaking their unspoken agreement to avoid such tender subjects.

His mother! The subject had always given Nadia pause, making her throat tighten with unspoken grief. Why stir up painful memories that were better left buried in the past? Wasn't his mother, that brave Siberian woman, already gone? Hadn't Michael already bid his last farewell to her lifeless form on the vast Tomsk plains, where the wind had carried away his quiet sobs?

"Please, Nadia," Michael urged, his fingers fidgeting with the hem of his coat. "Tell me about her. It would mean a lot to me."

Finally, Nadia broke her silence on the matter. She revealed everything about her interactions with Marfa, starting from their chance encounter in Omsk. She described how she had felt drawn to the elderly prisoner, not knowing her identity and how warmly Marfa had responded to her. Back then, she knew Michael only as Nicholas Korpanoff, a stranger traveling under an assumed name.

"The man I should have been all along," Michael said, his expression growing darker, shadows deepening around his eyes.

A moment later, he continued, his voice thick with self-reproach, "I've failed to keep my oath, Nadia. I swore I wouldn't see my mother!"

"But you didn't seek her out, Michael," Nadia countered, leaning forward. "It was pure chance that brought you together."

"I swore no matter what happened, I wouldn't reveal myself." His hands clenched into fists at his sides.

"Michael, Michael! How could you not react when they raised the whip against Marfa?" Nadia's voice rose with emotion. "No oath should stop a son from protecting his mother!"

"I broke my oath, Nadia," Michael said, bowing his head in shame. "May God and the Father forgive me!"

"Michael," the girl said, her dark eyes filled with concern, "I need to ask you something. Don't answer if you feel you shouldn't. I won't be upset by anything you say!"

"Go ahead, Nadia." His voice was gentle despite the tension in his shoulders.

"Now that they've taken the Czar's letter from you, why are you still so determined to reach Irkutsk? Most men would have given up by now, after everything we've been through."

Michael squeezed her hand but remained silent, his face a careful mask that revealed nothing of his thoughts.

"Did you know what was in that letter before leaving Moscow?" she pressed, watching his expression intently.

"No, I didn't." The words came out clipped and decisive.

"Are you expecting me to think your only purpose in traveling to Irkutsk is to reunite me with my father, Michael?" Her voice softened with a mix of gratitude and suspicion. "After all these dangers and hardships, there must be more to it than that."

"I won't lie to you, Nadia," Michael responded with solemnity. "It would be dishonest to let you believe that. I'm following where my duties lead me. But think about it, aren't you the one guiding me to Irkutsk now? You've become my eyes, and your hand steers my path. The help I once offered you has been returned many times over. I can't predict if our misfortunes will end, but when the time comes for you to express gratitude for bringing you back to your father, I'll be thanking you in return for helping me reach Irkutsk." His voice carried a weight of unspoken burdens, yet held steady with determination.

"My poor Michael!" Nadia's voice trembled with feeling, her fingers tightening around his. "Please don't talk like that. You haven't answered my question. Tell me, why this desperate rush to reach Irkutsk now?" Her eyes searched his face, hoping to glimpse some revelation in his stoic features.

"I must arrive before Ivan Ogareff does," Michael burst out, his composure cracking. The name seemed to taste bitter on his tongue.

"Even in your condition?" she asked, unable to hide her concern.

"Yes, even now, and I swear I'll make it there!" His jaw clenched with fierce resolve, his entire bearing radiating an iron determination that brooked no argument.

There was something deeper behind Michael's fierce declaration than mere hatred for the traitor. Nadia sensed her companion was holding back, either unable or unwilling to reveal his full motives. His every word seemed measured, as if speaking freely might betray some vital secret.

On the fifteenth of September, after three days of travel, they arrived at Kouitounskoe village. The young woman was in terrible pain. Though her feet were so sore she could barely walk, blisters forming and breaking with each determined step, she persevered through her exhaustion with a single thought driving her forward: "Since he cannot see my suffering, I must continue until I can go no further." She bit her lip to keep from crying out when sharp stones pierced through her worn boots.

This stretch of their journey was free from obstacles and dangers, now that the Tartars had moved on, though it remained grueling. They pressed on like this for three days, sleeping in abandoned barns and subsisting on what meager provisions they could find. Evidence of the third invasion column's swift eastward advance was clear in their wake, the scattered cold ashes and decaying bodies they left behind. Burned-out homesteads dotted the landscape, their blackened timbers reaching toward the sky like accusing fingers, while carrion birds wheeled overhead in ever-watchful circles.

Looking westward, there was no sign of activity; the Emir's vanguard remained absent. Michael pondered the potential causes for this unexpected delay. Could Russian forces be posing a serious threat to Tomsk or Krasnoiarsk? Was there a possibility that the third column had become separated and vulnerable to isolation from the primary force? Such circumstances would benefit the Grand Duke's defense of Irkutsk, any postponement of the invasion improved their chances of resistance. Though Michael entertained these optimistic possibilities, he recognized them as a dream. The Grand Duke's survival rested on his shoulders, and each passing hour brought both opportunity and danger.

Nadia continued her arduous journey, her feet dragging through the dust and debris of the ravaged countryside. Though her spirit remained unbroken, her body was reaching its limits, betrayed by trembling muscles and labored breath. Michael understood this reality all too well. Had he not lost his sight, Nadia would have pleaded with him: "Michael, go on without me! Leave me in a shelter somewhere! Complete your mission to Irkutsk! Find my father and tell him my location! Let him know I'm waiting! You must go now! Don't worry about me, I'll stay hidden from the Tartars! I'll keep myself safe until you both return! Please, Michael, continue on! I cannot take another step!" Her imagined words echoed in his mind with the desperation of exhaustion, though she remained silent beside him.

Nadia had to pause frequently to rest, her legs trembling with each stop. During these breaks, Michael would lift her into his powerful arms without hesitation, cradling her against his chest. Free from worrying about her weariness, he could then press forward at his tireless pace, his feet finding sure purchase on the rough terrain.

They reached Kimilteiskoe on September 18th at ten o'clock at night, the air heavy with autumn's chill. Standing atop a hill, Nadia glimpsed a long luminous streak on the horizon, the Dinka River, its waters reflecting what little moonlight filtered through the clouds. Silent flashes of heat lightning danced across its surface, unaccompanied by thunder, creating an eerily beautiful display. Nadia guided Michael through what remained of the village, their footsteps crunching through layers of destruction. The ashes they found were cold, scattered by recent winds, suggesting the Tartar forces had moved through at least five or six days earlier.

Exhausted, Nadia lowered herself onto a stone bench just outside the village, her muscles aching in protest. "Should we stop here for a while?" Michael suggested, his face turned toward her with concern.

"Night has fallen, Michael," Nadia said, unable to mask the weariness in her voice. "Wouldn't you like to rest for a few hours?"

"I'd prefer to get across the Dinka first," Michael responded, his jaw set with determination. "I want that river between us and the Emir's scouts. But you're exhausted, my dear Nadia! I can hear it in every breath you take."

"Let's go, Michael," Nadia insisted, grabbing his hand and pulling him onward with renewed determination despite her fatigue.

The Dinka river cut across the Irkutsk road about two or three miles ahead, its waters invisible in the darkness but audible as a distant murmur. Encouraged by her companion, the young girl was determined to make this final push forward. The lightning flashes illuminated their path in brief, stark bursts, casting eerie shadows across the terrain. They traversed an endless desert plain, through which the small river meandered like a silver ribbon. The landscape was flat, without a single tree or hill to break its monotony, leaving them exposed under the vast night sky. The air was still, almost unnaturally so, allowing even the faintest noise to carry across vast distances like a whisper in an empty hall.

Michael and Nadia froze, as if rooted to the spot, their breathing shallow and controlled. A dog's bark echoed across the steppe, sharp and clear in the stillness. "Did you hear that?" Nadia whispered, her fingers tightening around Michael's sleeve.

A heart-wrenching cry, the desperate last plea of someone facing death followed the bark. The sound sent chills down their spines, hanging in the air like a ghost's lament.

"Nicholas! Nicholas!" the girl called out, her voice filled with dread, scanning the darkness for any sign of movement. Michael listened, his body tense and alert, and shook his head in response, his expression grim in the intermittent flashes of lightning.

"Hurry, Michael, we must go," Nadia urged, her breath coming in short gasps. Though she had been struggling to walk moments before, a sudden surge of energy now coursed through her veins, driving her forward with desperate determination.

"We've strayed from the path," Michael observed, noticing the change from dusty ground to grass beneath his feet. His boots sank into the softer earth with each step, making their progress more difficult.

"We had to!" Nadia insisted, her voice sharp with urgency. "The sound came from over there, to the right!" She gestured into the darkness, her hand trembling in the air.

Within minutes, they had covered half a mile from the river, their legs burning from the effort. Another bark echoed through the air, fainter this time, but closer. Nadia halted in her tracks, her body going rigid with anticipation.

"Yes!" Michael exclaimed, hope lighting up his features. "That's Serko barking!... He must have followed his master!" His words carried both relief and worry, knowing the loyal dog would never leave Nicholas's side willingly.

"Nicholas!" the girl shouted out, her voice cracking with emotion. No response came, only the whisper of wind through the grass.

Michael strained to hear, cupping his hands behind his ears and turning slowly in place. Nadia scanned the landscape, which lit up with flashes of electric light, but saw nothing beyond the endless waves of prairie grass. Then another sound reached them, a weak voice calling out, "Michael!" The cry was barely more than a whisper on the wind, but it was enough to send their hearts racing.

Suddenly, a blood-covered dog rushed up to Nadia, its fur matted and dark with crimson stains, panting from exertion.

It was Serko! Nicholas had to be nearby! Only he would have whispered Michael's name like that, with such desperate familiarity! But where was he? Nadia found herself too weak to call out again, her throat constricting with fear and exhaustion. Michael, down on the ground, began feeling his way around with his hands, fingers searching through the tall grass and loose soil.

Serko let out another bark, fierce and protective, and rushed at an enormous vulture that had descended from above, its wingspan casting an ominous shadow in the dim light. When Serko charged at it, the bird took flight but then swooped back down to attack the dog, talons extended. Serko jumped up to meet it with unwavering loyalty, but the vulture's mighty beak struck his head with devastating force, sending him crashing to the ground, lifeless, his last act one of protection.

In that moment, Nadia let out a horrified scream that pierced the prairie night. "Look... over there!" she cried out, her trembling finger pointing into the darkness.

A human head protruded from the earth, pale and ghostly in the intermittent flashes of electric light! She had stumbled upon it in the darkness, nearly losing her footing.

Nadia collapsed to her knees beside the buried figure, her hands shaking uncontrollably. It was Nicholas, buried up to his neck in the ground, a cruel Tartar punishment that left victims to perish slowly from thirst or fall prey to wolves and scavenging birds, a fate worse than a quick death.

The victim lay entombed in the earth, enduring unimaginable agony. The soil was packed he couldn't shift an inch, his arms pinned against his sides like a body prepared for burial. Trapped in this earthen prison, this living grave, the poor soul could do nothing but yearn for death's merciful release. His parched throat burned with each labored breath, and the weight of the earth pressed against his chest like an iron vise.

Three days earlier, the Tartars had buried their captive in this cruel fashion. For three endless days, Nicholas had waited for rescue that arrived too late. Vultures had discovered his exposed head at ground level, and his faithful dog had spent hours fighting off these savage scavengers, protecting his master. The ground around him bore evidence of the brutal battle, scattered feathers and deep claw marks in the soil where the loyal animal had stood its ground.

Frantically, Michael carved into the earth with his blade, desperate to free his companion. The frozen soil crumbled beneath his frenzied strikes, each second feeling like an eternity. Nicholas's eyes, which had been shut until that moment, fluttered open, glazed with exhaustion and pain.

Upon seeing Michael and Nadia, a faint smile crossed his lips. "Goodbye, dear friends," he whispered. "I'm thankful to have seen you one last time. Remember me in your prayers." His voice was barely audible, each word a tremendous effort against his depleted strength.

Despite the ground being packed as solid as rock, Michael persisted in his digging, finally managing to extract his friend's body. His hands were raw and bleeding from the effort, but he could not feel the pain. With trembling hands, he checked for a heartbeat... There was one! Faint and irregular, but present beneath his fingers.

Determined to give him a proper resting place rather than leaving him exposed, Michael widened the cruel pit where Nicholas had been buried alive. Now it would serve as his last resting place, though this time with the dignity and respect his friend deserved. Beside him lay the loyal Serko, master and faithful companion united in death, their shared fate a testament to unshakeable loyalty.

A distant sound echoed from the road, half a mile away. Michael Strogoff strained his ears, every muscle tensing as he listened. The unmistakable rhythm of hoofbeats grew clearer, a cavalry unit was approaching the Dinka, their cadence too precise to be ordinary travelers. "Nadia, Nadia!" he whispered, his voice tight with warning.

Nadia rose from her prayers at his call, her face still wet with tears. "Look!" he urged, gesturing toward the road.

"The Tartars," she breathed, her voice quavering with fear.

Indeed, it was the Emir's vanguard, galloping along the Irkutsk road, their weapons glinting in the harsh light.

"They won't stop me from giving him a proper burial," Michael declared, his jaw set with determination as he resumed his solemn task. The approaching danger only made his movements more purposeful, more urgent.

Michael and Nadia knelt beside the freshly dug grave, offering their last prayers for Nicholas. They had just laid his body to rest, his hands folded across his chest, a small wooden cross fashioned from broken branches marking the site. Their hearts were heavy with grief for their loyal companion, whose only crime had been his unwavering dedication to them, a devotion that cost him his life at the hands of their pursuers.

"At least here," Michael murmured as he scattered earth over the grave, his calloused hands trembling, "he'll be safe from the steppe wolves."

His expression hardened as he watched a group of horsemen passing in the distance, their silhouettes dark against the pale sky. With contained anger, he raised his fist toward them, his knuckles white with fury. Turning to his companion, he said, "Come, Nadia. We must move on before they spot us."

Michael was forced to avoid the main road, which had fallen under Tartar control, its dusty length now patrolled by enemy riders. Instead, he had to traverse the steppe and find an alternate route to Irkutsk, picking his way through the wild grass and rocky outcrops. While crossing the Dinka River was no longer necessary, he faced a new challenge, Nadia was immobile but could still use her sight to guide him through the treacherous terrain. Carrying her in his arms, her slight form wrapped in his worn coat, he pressed southwest through the province, always keeping watch for the telltale dust clouds of approaching patrols.

They still had to cover one hundred and forty miles of difficult terrain. Questions plagued them: How would they manage such a distance? Could their bodies withstand the extreme exhaustion? What would sustain them along the journey? How could they scale the formidable Sayansk Mountains? Neither Michael nor Nadia had answers to these daunting questions, but they shared an unspoken determination that drove them forward, one painful step after another.

Yet somehow, through sheer force of will and despite the biting autumn winds that tore at their clothes and the nights spent huddled in whatever shelter they could find, twelve days later, on October 2nd at six in the evening, Michael Strogoff stood before the vast expanse of Lake Baikal. The ancient sea, as the locals called it, stretched out before him like a sheet of hammered steel beneath the darkening sky, its waters disappearing into the misty horizon.

Chapter Ten

BAIKAL AND ANGARA

Lake Baikal sits at an elevation of 1,700 feet above sea level. This massive body of water stretches approximately 600 miles and spans seventy miles across. Its true depth remains a mystery, though some estimates suggest it plunges more than a mile into Earth's crust. According to Madame de Bourboulon's account, local boatmen insist the lake prefers to be addressed as "Madam Sea", they claim it becomes turbulent if referred to as "Sir Lake," with waves rising as if in protest. A curious local belief persists among Siberians that Russians never drown in its waters, though they offer no explanation for this supposed immunity.

The vast freshwater lake, which receives water from over three hundred rivers and countless mountain streams, lies encircled by majestic volcanic peaks that pierce the clouds like ancient sentinels. Its waters find their sole exit through the Angara River, which flows past Irkutsk before joining the Yenisei River just upstream from Yeniseisk, carving a path through the rugged Siberian landscape. The surrounding mountain range, part of the Toungouzes chain, extends from the greater Altai mountain system, creating a natural amphitheater that cradles the sacred waters.

This region experiences unusual weather patterns, with autumn merging into an early winter, pausing for the traditional transition of seasons. By early October, darkness falls by five in the evening, and nighttime temperatures plummet to freezing point, creating ghostly wisps of steam above the lake's surface. The first snowfall, destined to remain until summer, already covers the peaks of the surrounding mountains, transforming them into white-capped guardians. During the harsh Siberian winter, the lake's surface freezes several feet thick, becoming a solid pathway for caravan sleighs to traverse, their runners creating intricate patterns across the crystalline expanse.

Lake Baikal experiences fierce storms, whether because of the discourteous habit of some people referring to it as "Sir Lake," or perhaps because of natural weather patterns. Like all inland seas, it produces short, choppy waves that pose a serious threat to the various vessels, rafts, prahms, flat bottom boats, and steamboats, that traverse its waters during the summer months. The wind howls across the surface, whipping up whitecaps and sending spray high into the air, while dark clouds gather over the distant shores.

Michael had reached the lake's southwestern shore, bearing Nadia, whose entire being seemed focused through her gaze alone. Yet their situation appeared hopeless in this desolate area, what fate awaited them but death from hunger and exhaustion? And yet, considering the massive four-thousand-mile journey the Czar's courier had undertaken, what remained was modest: forty miles along the lakeshore to reach the Angara River's mouth, then another sixty miles from there to Irkutsk. The total distance of one hundred miles might take a robust individual three days to cover on foot, assuming favorable conditions and sufficient strength to maintain a steady pace.

Was Michael Strogoff destined to face another challenge? The question hung heavy in the crisp air, as ominous as the gathering storm clouds above.

Providence seemed to show mercy, sparing him from further hardship. The area near Lake Baikal's edge, a barren wasteland, teemed with life. Where desolation reigned, roughly fifty people had gathered at the lake's corner, their presence bringing an unexpected vitality to the otherwise stark landscape. Their movements and voices carried across the water, breaking the usual silence of this remote location.

As Michael emerged from the mountain pass carrying Nadia, she spotted the assembled crowd. For one terrifying moment, she feared they'd encountered a Tartar patrol searching the Baikal shoreline, an encounter that would have left them with no escape route. Her anxiety, however, subsided as she made out the familiar shapes of Russian clothing and heard snippets of her native tongue carried on the wind.

With a very weak voice, she said "Russians!" before her strength gave out completely, her eyes falling shut as she slumped against Michael's chest, the exhaustion of their journey overwhelming her.

Their presence hadn't gone unnoticed, several Russians spotted them and came to their aid, guiding the sightless man and young woman to a nearby raft that was anchored at a small inlet. Strong hands helped steady Michael as he made his way across the uneven shoreline, still cradling Nadia.

The vessel was moments away from departure, its wooden planks creaking against their moorings. Its passengers were refugees from various walks of life, brought together by shared circumstance at Lake Baikal, merchants, farmers, and craftsmen alike, their social distinctions erased by common adversity. Having been forced back by Tartar scouts who patrolled the surrounding territories with increasing frequency, they sought sanctuary in Irkutsk. With the invaders controlling both shores of the Angara River, making the journey by land was impossible, too many eyes watched the paths and roads. Their only hope lay in traveling downriver through the heart of the city itself, using the waterway as their path to safety.

The thought of their scheme made Michael's spirits soar, though he masked his excitement, determined to maintain his disguise more carefully than ever. Years of practiced deception had taught him the value of restraining visible emotion, even as his heart raced with anticipation.

The escapees had devised an uncomplicated strategy. They would take advantage of a lake current that flowed along the upper shore toward where the Angara River began. By riding this current, they aimed to reach Lake Baikal's outlet. From there, the Angara's swift waters would carry them toward Irkutsk at eight miles per hour. With luck, they could expect to catch sight of the city in just a day and a half, assuming the weather held and they encountered no unexpected obstacles along the way.

They were forced to build their own watercraft since none could be found. What they created was a basic raft, constructed in the style used for timber transport on Siberian waterways. Using trees from a nearby fir forest on the riverbank, they fashioned a sturdy platform by binding the logs together with flexible willow branches. The resulting craft was spacious enough to carry a hundred passengers, its broad deck reinforced with cross-beams and sealed with pitch gathered from the forest. The craft might have been simple, but it represented their best hope for salvation.

Michael and Nadia were brought aboard the makeshift vessel, helped by several fellow refugees who had witnessed their arrival. The young woman had regained consciousness by then, though she still appeared weak from her ordeal. After they were both given something to eat, a simple meal of dried fish and bread, she made herself comfortable on a cushion of leaves gathered from the surrounding forest and drifted into a profound slumber.

In the bustling town, Michael Strogoff maintained strict silence about the events at Tomsk when questioned by the curious passengers and crew. He presented himself as a resident of Krasnoiarsk, claiming he hadn't reached Irkutsk before Tartar forces occupied the Dinka's left bank. His story, delivered with quiet conviction, seemed to satisfy most inquiries. He suggested that most likely, the main Tartar army had established their position outside the Siberian capital, though he was careful not to provide too many details that might expose his true identity.

Time was of the essence, as the temperature continued to plummet with each passing day. The mercury dipped below freezing during the nighttime hours, creating a crystalline frost that coated the raft's logs each morning, and ice crystals had formed across Lake Baikal's vast surface. While the raft could still navigate the lake without difficulty, cutting through the thin sheets of ice with its sturdy hull, the Angara River posed a potential challenge, as larger ice fragments could obstruct their passage between its shores and damage their vessel.

The raft was released from its moorings at eight o'clock and began drifting with the current near the shoreline. Several strong moujiks guided it using long poles, their muscles straining against the water's pull, while a seasoned Baikal boatman of sixty-five years served as commander. The sun and lake winds had weathered his complexion into deep leather-like creases, and a thick white beard cascaded down his chest like a frozen waterfall. A fur cap worn smooth with age topped his stern countenance, and he wore a long great-coat cinched at the waist that reached his feet, its hem dark with spray. This quiet elder maintained his post at the stern, directing operations through hand signals, his weathered hands moving with practiced precision. The crew's primary task was keeping the vessel within the shore current, fighting against crosswinds and eddies while avoiding any drift toward treacherous open water.

The raft accommodated Russians from every walk of life, their bodies pressed together in uneasy fellowship. Alongside destitute moujiks, women clutching shawls tight against the cold, the elderly with rheumy eyes, and wide-eyed children were several pilgrims caught unaware by the invasion, as well as a handful of monks in rough-spun robes and a priest whose silver cross glinted in the morning light. The pilgrims, each carrying a well-worn staff and a gourd fastened to their belts with fraying rope, sang psalms in mournful tones that echoed across the water. They came from diverse regions: one from Ukraine with his melodious accent, another from the Yellow Sea area with weather-beaten features, and a third from

Finland with ice-blue eyes. The Finnish pilgrim, an elderly man with joints stiffened by countless miles, wore a locked collection box at his waist, much like those found at church entrances, its metal dulled by years of faithful service. He maintained strict devotion to his cause, everything gathered during his hard journeys were meant for others, not himself, a fact clear in his tattered clothing and calloused feet. Such was his commitment that he didn't even possess the key to the box, which would remain sealed until his journey's end, whenever and wherever that might be.

A group of religious men, Monks, journeyed southward from the Empire's northern reaches. Their pilgrimage had begun in Archangel three months earlier, when the first snows had dusted the northern coastline. Along their route, they had made stops at many holy sites: the hallowed isles off Carelia's shoreline, where ancient wooden crosses stood against the wind, the monasteries of Solovetsk and Troitsa with their golden domes gleaming in the sun, the Kiev sanctuaries of Saints Antony and Theodosia, their walls heavy with centuries of prayers, the Kazan monastery, and the Old Believers' shrine, where incense still lingered in the air. Now, dressed in their traditional garments, robes, cowls, and serge clothing worn smooth by constant wear, they were making their way toward Irkutsk, their boots marking the dusty path before them.

The village priest was a simple man, one among the six hundred thousand ordinary clerics scattered throughout the Russian Empire, each serving their communities with quiet dedication. His attire was as humble as the peasants', reflecting his equal social standing with the moujiks, a worn cassock patched at the elbows and mud-spattered boots that had seen many seasons. He tended his own plot of land like any farmer while performing his religious duties, conducting baptisms in the old stone font, joining young couples' hands in marriage beneath tarnished icons, and offering final blessings at graveside funerals. When danger approached, he had sent his wife and children to safety in the Northern provinces, though the parting had torn at his heart. Devoted to his parish, he remained until the last possible moment, continuing to offer comfort and guidance to those who stayed behind, only fleeing when necessary. With the Irkutsk road blocked by the advancing threat, he had made his way to Lake Baikal, following the ancient paths of traders and pilgrims before him.

On the front section of the raft, the priests huddled together, their black robes rustling in the breeze as they offered prayers at steady intervals that pierced the quiet night. After each prayer verse, their voices rang out with "Slava Bogu", Glory to God!, the sacred words carrying across the dark waters like a shield against unseen dangers.

The night passed without incident, though the cold air bit into their bones. Nadia remained in a daze while Michael kept vigil beside her, adjusting the blankets around her shoulders and only drifting into brief, restless sleep. As dawn broke, strong headwinds had slowed their progress, the raft's wooden planks creaking against the current, leaving them still forty miles from where the Angara River emptied into Lake Baikal. They estimated reaching their destination between three and four in the afternoon, but this delay didn't worry them. If anything, they preferred it, knowing that traveling downriver after nightfall would provide better cover for their entry into Irkutsk, when the shadows would help conceal their movements from unfriendly eyes.

The elderly boatman's sole concern centered on ice forming across the water's surface, his weathered face creasing with worry as he studied the river ahead. After a frosty night, ice fragments could be spotted floating westward, their crystalline surfaces catching the early morning light. These particular pieces posed no threat, as they had already moved past the river mouth and couldn't enter the Angara. However, ice chunks from the lake's eastern section might get pulled by currents between the river's banks, creating problems. Such an occurrence could slow their progress or, worse still, form an impassable barrier that would halt the raft, leaving them stranded in dangerous waters.

For this reason, Michael watched the lake's conditions with keen attention, monitoring for any significant accumulation of ice. He turned to Nadia, who had now awakened and sat huddled in her thick wool coat, for updates on the situation, and she reported her observations to him, her breath forming small clouds in the frosty morning air.

The Baikal's surface was witness to remarkable events as the ice blocks drifted. From deep within the lake bed, where nature had created natural artesian wells, spectacular fountains of boiling water burst forth. These powerful streams soared skyward, transforming into clouds of vapor that caught and reflected the sun's rays before condensing in the frigid air, creating halos of crystalline mist that danced above the water's surface. Such an extraordinary display would have captivated any traveler fortunate enough to visit this Siberian lake during more peaceful times, though now it served as both a beautiful distraction and a potential warning sign of changing conditions beneath the surface.

The boatman's keen eyes spotted the Angara's mouth at four o'clock, nestled between towering granite cliffs that cast long shadows across the churning waters. The right bank revealed Livenitchnaia's modest port, with its white-washed church and scattered wooden dwellings perched along the waterfront, their weathered facades telling stories of harsh winters past. More concerning was the sight of ice blocks floating downstream from the East, making their way between the Angara's banks toward Irkutsk, their crystalline surfaces glinting in the wan light. Yet their numbers remained manageable, not enough to impede the raft's progress, and the temperature hadn't dropped to speed up their formation.

With a gentle thud, the vessel reached the small dock and came to a halt against the worn wooden pilings. To conduct needed repairs, the aging ferryman, required an hour's stop. Because: With the raft's logs loosening and their bindings frayed by the constant motion and spray, tighter binding was crucial to withstand the swift Angara River waters which could destroy even the strongest vessel.

Though the weathered boatman hadn't expected picking up any more refugees at Livenitchnaia, two figures emerged from an abandoned dwelling, their desperate movements visible even at a distance, and sprinted toward the shoreline just as the raft contacted the bank, their boots kicking up loose gravel in their haste.

Sitting on the raft, Nadia stared at the coastline. She cried out, but caught herself, grabbing Michael's hand just as he lifted his head, her fingers trembling with urgency against his weathered palm.

"What's wrong, Nadia?" he asked, alert to her distress.

"Look, it's them," she said, her voice barely above a whisper. "The two who traveled with us."

"You mean the French and English travelers we encountered in the Ural mountain passes?" Michael's shoulders tensed as he spoke.

"Yes, that's them," she confirmed, tightening her grip on his hand.

The sudden realization hit Michael, his maintained disguise was in danger of unraveling. When Jolivet and Blount would see him now, they'd recognize him not as Nicholas Korpanoff but as his true identity: Michael Strogoff, the Czar's trusted messenger. The journalists had crossed paths with him twice after parting ways at the Ichim station, first witnessing him publicly whip Ivan Ogareff at Zabediero camp, then present at his sentencing by the Emir in Tomsk. They knew who he was and understood the gravity of his mission, and their presence here threatened to expose everything he'd fought so desperately to protect. His jaw clenched as he considered the implications, knowing that even the slightest recognition could put not just him, but everyone aboard the raft in danger.

Making a swift decision, Michael turned to his companion. "Nadia," he instructed, "when they come aboard, please direct them to me. I must handle this myself."

Having found their way to the port of Livenitchnaia, Blount and Jolivet arrived by the same turn of events that had guided Michael Strogoff there. After witnessing the Tartars' entrance into Tomsk, they had left before seeing the brutal conclusion of the festival, their journalistic duties compelling them to press onward. Thus, they didn't know the Emir had spared their former companion from death, though he had ordered him blinded, a fate they would have considered devastating.

After their successful acquisition of horses, they departed Tomsk that very evening, resolute in their plan to send future correspondence from the Russian military encampment in Eastern Siberia. They pushed forward at a relentless pace toward Irkutsk, determined to outrun Feofar-Khan's forces, stopping only when necessary to rest their mounts. Their strategy would have succeeded if not for the sudden emergence of a third military column advancing northward through the Yenisei valley, its banners marking it as another Tartar contingent. Like Michael before them, they found themselves blocked before reaching the Dinka, forcing them to retreat toward Lake Baikal, their original plans in shambles but their determination undiminished.

After spending three uncertain days at the location, huddled in makeshift shelters and rationing their dwindling supplies, they were relieved when the makeshift vessel showed up through the morning mist. The escapees shared their strategy with the others, outlining each detail of their proposed crossing. There was a real possibility they could slip through under the cover of darkness and make their way into Irkutsk, using the river's natural flow to mask their approach. They determined this was their best option to pursue, despite the considerable dangers that lay ahead.

Without delay, Alcide approached the elderly ferryman and requested passage for himself and his traveling companion, stating he would provide whatever payment was asked for, regardless of the amount. His fingers played with the purse of coins at his belt as he spoke.

"Payment isn't accepted here," the weathered boatman responded, his deep-set eyes reflecting years of hardship on these waters. "The only currency is the risk to one's own life!"

The pair of reporters boarded the vessel, with Nadia observing them settle into positions at the front of the raft, their bodies tense with anticipation. Harry Blount maintained his characteristic English reserve, having spoken a word to her throughout their journey across the Urals, his stern face set like granite against the approaching darkness. Alcide Jolivet appeared more somber than was his custom, his usual wit and charm subdued by the gravity of their situation, and given the current situation, his serious demeanor was quite understandable. His hands gripped the rough wooden railings as he stared ahead into the gathering gloom.

As Jolivet took his position on the raft, he felt someone grasp his arm with urgent fingers. Upon turning, he found himself face-to-face with Nadia, sister to the man who had shed his identity as Nicholas Korpanoff to reveal himself as Michael Strogoff, the Czar's messenger. Just as he was about to cry out in astonishment, he noticed her finger pressed against her lips, signaling for silence, her eyes conveying the gravity of discretion.

"Join us," Nadia called out, her voice controlled to sound casual. Alcide stood up with feigned nonchalance and followed her, gesturing for Blount to come along, his practiced journalist's instincts telling him something momentous was about to unfold.

The correspondents had been startled to find Nadia on the raft, but their astonishment turned to utter shock when they spotted Michael Strogoff, a man they'd believed dead, sitting quietly in the shadows of the raft. Their faces paled at the sight of him, as though seeing a ghost materialize before their eyes.

Michael remained motionless as they approached, his head tilted toward the sound of their footsteps. When Jolivet turned to question Nadia, she explained, her voice thick with emotion, "He cannot see you. The Tartars burned his eyes. My poor brother is blind now." Her hands trembled as she spoke the devastating truth.

Deep sympathy washed over the faces of Blount and his companion as the horror of Michael's fate sank in. They settled beside Michael, clasping his hand in solidarity and waiting for him to speak, the gentle lapping of water against the raft's sides filling the heavy silence between them.

"Gentlemen," Michael whispered, his fingers tightening around their clasped hands, "you must not know my true identity or my mission in Siberia. I need you to keep my secret. Can I trust you with this?"

"I give you my word," Jolivet declared without hesitation, his French accent thick with sincerity.

"I swear on my honor as a gentleman," Blount added, his British resolve clear in every syllable.

"Very well, then." Michael's shoulders relaxed at their pledges.

"Is there any way we can assist you?" Harry Blount inquired, leaning forward. "Perhaps we could help you complete your mission?"

"I must do this alone," Michael responded, his jaw set with determination.

"But those scoundrels have taken your vision," Alcide protested, his voice rising with indignation. "Surely you cannot."

"I have Nadia with me, and her eyes are all I need!" Michael's voice carried an edge of steel that brooked no argument.

Thirty minutes later, the raft departed from Livenitchnaia's small harbor and entered the flowing waters, the wooden planks creaking beneath them as they pushed off from shore. Evening was settling in at five o'clock, with darkness approaching like a heavy curtain drawn across the sky. The night ahead promised to be pitch black and bitter cold, as the temperature had already dropped below freezing, sending shivers through the small group huddled on the craft. A cutting wind swept across the water, carrying with it the first hints of winter's cruel embrace.

Despite their promise to keep Michael's secret, Alcide and Blount remained by his side, speaking in hushed, urgent tones. The blind man pieced together their whispered information with his existing knowledge, forming a clear picture of the situation like assembling fragments of a shattered mirror. The evidence was undeniable, the Tartars had surrounded Irkutsk, with all three military columns now united into an iron ring around the city. Without question, both the Emir and Ivan Ogareff were positioned outside the capital, their forces poised like predators waiting to strike.

Yet a mystery remained, why was the Czar's messenger so desperate to reach the city? The Imperial letter he carried could no longer be delivered to the Grand Duke, and he remained unaware of its contents, the words forever sealed away from his sightless eyes. Like Nadia before them, Alcide Jolivet and Blount found themselves puzzled by this inexplicable urgency that drove the blind man forward despite all odds.

The group maintained silence about earlier events, the only sounds the creaking of the raft and the splash of water against wood, until Jolivet felt compelled to address Michael, his voice carrying a note of genuine remorse. "We should apologize for refusing to shake your hand when we parted ways at Ichim."

"Your reaction was justified, you believed me to be cowardly," Michael responded, his voice carrying no trace of bitterness. "Anyone would have thought the same in those circumstances."

The Frenchman added with satisfaction, rubbing his hands together, "Well, you gave that scoundrel a proper thrashing with the knout. He'll bear those marks for quite some time! I've never seen someone wield that weapon with such precision."

"Not for long," Michael replied, a shadow passing across his face as he turned away.

Within thirty minutes of departing Livenitchnaia, Blount and his fellow traveler learned of the harrowing ordeals that Michael and his companion had endured, the brutal imprisonment, the desperate escapes, and the relentless pursuit across the harsh terrain. They found themselves impressed by his remarkable fortitude, matched only by the young woman's unwavering loyalty through every trial and tribulation. Their assessment of

Michael echoed the Czar's words in Moscow with profound understanding: "Here is a Man!"

The raft navigated between massive ice chunks swept along by the Angara's powerful current, its wooden planks creaking with each impact. The shoreline created an enchanting illusion, though the raft moved swiftly, it seemed to hover motionless while a series of dramatic landscapes paraded past like scenes from a living painting. Towering granite cliffs gave way to untamed gorges where torrents of water thundered down in pristine white cascades. Occasional clearings revealed smoldering villages, their blackened timbers still releasing thin wisps of smoke into the crisp air, followed by dense pine forests aflame, their burning canopies casting an eerie orange glow across the water's surface. While evidence of the Tartars' destruction marked every vista, from scorched earth to abandoned settlements, the warriors themselves remained unseen, having concentrated their forces near Irkutsk.

Throughout the journey, pilgrims' prayers echoed across the water, their murmured supplications mixing with the rush of the river and the crack of shifting ice. The seasoned boatman maintained their course, his weathered hands steady on the steering oar. With practiced skill honed by years on these treacherous waters, he fended off encroaching ice blocks, keeping the raft centered in the Angara's swift current, his eyes scanning ahead for the safest passage through the frozen obstacles.

QuantumDigitalPublishing.io

Chapter Eleven

BETWEEN TWO BANKS

The absolute darkness of night had descended by eight o'clock, just as the earlier sky had predicted. With the moon in its new phase, no lunar light penetrated the blackness, leaving only the faintest glimmer of starlight struggling through gaps in the cloud cover. The riverbanks vanished into invisibility when viewed from the water's center, their familiar contours reduced to formless shadows against an even darker backdrop. Towering cliffs merged with the thick, low clouds above, creating an oppressive ceiling that seemed to press down upon the water's surface. Every so often, an eastern breeze would stir, only to fade away within the confined walls of the Angara valley, leaving behind an eerie stillness broken only by the gentle lapping of the water.

The night's shroud worked to the advantage of those attempting to escape, concealing any movement upon the river's surface from prying eyes. Even with Tartar sentries positioned along both riverbanks, their torches mere pinpricks in the darkness, the raft stood a good chance of slipping by unnoticed in the inky blackness. The attackers had likely left the river unobstructed upstream of Irkutsk, knowing full well no reinforcements would come to the Russians from the province's southern regions, where the rebellion had already severed all lines of communication. Winter itself would soon create an impassable barrier, as frost would bind the ice fragments scattered between the shores, transforming the flowing water into an immobile sheet of white.

The raft drifted in complete stillness, with the pilgrims' once-loud voices now reduced to audible whispers of prayer, too faint to reach the shoreline. The escapees pressed themselves flat against the platform, leaving the raft riding so low it broke the water's surface, the weathered planks creaking beneath their weight. Up front, the aged boatman huddled with his crew, their gnarled hands gripping long poles, focused on fending off the drifting chunks of ice that threatened their passage.

The ice flows proved helpful, provided they didn't block the raft's path. Although a single boat might have been visible even in the dark, the raft's appearance blended with the various sizes of drifting ice chunks, looking like just another shadow among the river's natural obstacles. The loud collisions between ice blocks masked any telling sounds that might have given them away, from the occasional splash of the poles to the suppressed coughs of the freezing passengers.

Frost coated every surface, and delicate crystalline patterns formed along the raft's edges as the bitter cold cut deep. The group of refugees had nothing but flimsy birch branches for protection as they huddled close, sharing what little warmth they could muster, their breath forming small clouds that dissipated in the night air. The temperature had plunged to ten degrees below freezing, and even the gentle breeze, having swept across the snow-covered eastern peaks, seemed to slice through their very bones, numbing fingers and toes despite their desperate attempts to keep moving and maintain circulation.

In the raft's rear, Michael and Nadia endured their mounting misery in silence, their bodies pressed together for whatever meager warmth they could find. Nearby, Jolivet and Blount weathered the harsh embrace of the Siberian winter as best they could, their faces buried deep within the collars of their frost-covered coats. Not a whisper passed between them now. Their dire circumstances consumed their every thought, each person lost in private contemplation of their mortality. They knew that at any moment, their precarious situation could turn deadly.

For a man on the verge of completing his vital task, Michael exhibited remarkable composure, his features set in stone despite the biting cold that threatened to overwhelm them all. His resolute spirit had never wavered, even during the most critical moments, drawing strength from some deep internal well that seemed bottomless. He could almost grasp that precious instant when he would be free to turn his thoughts to his mother, to Nadia, and to his own concerns, like a runner glimpsing the finish line through the fog. Only one last fear now plagued his mind: the possibility that ice might block the raft's passage before reaching Irkutsk. This single worry consumed his thoughts, gnawing at his concentration like a relentless beast, and he stood ready to attempt a daring maneuver if circumstances demanded it, his muscles tense beneath his frozen garments.

Exhausted but revitalized by a brief respite, Nadia's physical strength had returned. Though her hardships had tested her body, they had never once weakened her iron resolve. Her determination, forged in the crucible of their harrowing journey, remained as unshakeable as ever. She felt compelled to stay by Michael's side, knowing he might need her guidance for whatever challenges lay ahead. As they drew closer to Irkutsk, thoughts of her father grew vivid in her mind, each passing moment bringing fresh waves of anticipation and longing. She pictured him within the besieged city, separated from his loved ones, yet fighting the invaders with unwavering patriotic spirit, organizing defenses and rallying the citizens to resist. Just hours separated her from falling into his embrace, where she would deliver her mother's last message, and they would never face separation again. If Wassili Fedor's exile proved permanent, she would share his fate, making a new life in this harsh but beautiful land. Her thoughts then drifted to her loyal companion, her "brother," who had made this reunion possible through countless sacrifices and unwavering dedication. Once the Tartar threat was eliminated, he would journey back to Moscow, and she feared their paths might never cross again, leaving an emptiness in her heart that no future friendship could fill.

Alcide Jolivet and Harry Blount shared an identical thought, this was the stuff of gripping journalism. Both men recognized the raw dramatic power of the scene before them, each crafting how they would shape it into a compelling story. Blount's mind turned to his faithful readers at the Daily Telegraph, while Jolivet pictured his beloved Cousin Madeleine poring over his words, perhaps sharing them with her literary circle in Paris.

Despite their professional detachment, neither could suppress their emotional response to the unfolding events. The weight of history pressed upon them, demanding they serve as more than mere observers but as chroniclers of this pivotal moment.

"All the better!" Jolivet mused to himself, adjusting his worn leather notebook. "One must feel to make others feel! There's a famous line about that somewhere, though it escapes me now." Straining his experienced eye, he tried to penetrate the darkness shrouding the river below, his pencil hovering over the blank page. The night air carried whispers of danger, and his journalistic instincts told him the actual story was yet to unfold.

Brilliant flashes pierced the darkness, transforming the riverbanks into surreal landscapes, sometimes a blazing forest, sometimes the smoldering remains of a village. The Angara River was lit up from shore to shore, the light so intense it seemed to turn night into an unnatural day. Countless ice blocks drifted by like mirrors, each one catching and reflecting the dancing flames in a rainbow of colors as the river's whims carried along them. Among these drifting ice fragments, the raft moved and unnoticed, its occupants crouching low to maintain their shadowy sanctuary.

Yet these illuminated stretches weren't where the real peril lay, for light could reveal as much as it could conceal.

The fugitives faced an unexpected threat, one they couldn't have expected or evaded, lurking beneath the very waters that carried them to safety. Alcide Jolivet discovered it by chance when he dangled his hand into the water from the raft's edge, his journalist's curiosity getting the better of his caution. The current felt thick against his fingers, with an unusual, oily texture that made him recoil. Using both touch and smell, his nostrils flaring at the distinct petroleum scent, Alcide realized with certainty that a layer of liquid naphtha was flowing on the river's surface, creating an invisible but deadly companion to their journey.

This revelation raised alarming questions. Their raft was now gliding across this flammable substance, but where had it come from? They wondered whether this was a natural occurrence on the Angara River or if the Tartars had released it. Could this be part of a sinister plan to set Irkutsk ablaze? The mere thought of a spark igniting this invisible menace made their precarious situation even more treacherous.

Alcide pondered these thoughts, deciding to share this information only with Harry Blount. Together, they kept quiet about this additional threat, not wanting to worry the rest of their group. Their fellow travelers already carried enough burden without the knowledge that they were floating atop a potential inferno.

The terrain of Central Asia is well-documented to be saturated with hydrogen, much like a liquid-filled sponge. Throughout the region, from Bakou's harbor along the Persian border by the Caspian Sea, across Asia Minor, into China along the Yuen-Kiang, and throughout Burma, countless natural oil springs bubble up from beneath the earth's surface. This region mirrors the famous "oil country" found in North America. The phenomenon was so common that local inhabitants had for centuries used these natural seepages for light and heat, treating them as gifts from the earth itself.

A fascinating ritual unfolds at the port of Bakou during certain religious ceremonies, where local fire-worshipers create an extraordinary spectacle.

They pour liquid naphtha onto the Caspian Sea's surface, and because the oil is less dense than water, it floats and spreads across the waves. As darkness falls, they ignite this floating layer of mineral oil, transforming the sea into a breathtaking display of undulating flames that dance and ripple with the evening winds, creating what appears to be an ocean of living fire. The ceremony dates back centuries, and travelers from distant lands often journey to witness this mesmerizing demonstration of nature's raw power harnessed by human hands.

What might be a cause for celebration in Bakou could turn into a catastrophic disaster on the Angara River. A fire, whether started or by accident, could spread across Irkutsk in mere seconds. While there was no risk of careless accidents on the raft itself, the real danger came from fires burning along both sides of the Angara. If even a single burning straw or spark were to land on the water, it could ignite the entire naphtha-filled current, creating an unstoppable inferno that would race downstream with devastating consequences.

Jolivet and Blount's fears were palpable. Their years of journalistic experience had taught them to recognize dangerous situations, and this one made their skin crawl. The situation begged the question: wouldn't it be wiser to seek refuge on the riverbank until the threat passed? "Well," Alcide remarked with certainty, his voice carrying a mix of determination and concealed anxiety, "I can tell you one person who won't be abandoning ship!"

The speaker directed his words of Michael Strogoff, who maintained his characteristic stoic expression despite the implied challenge.

The raft continued drifting between ice floes that were converging around them, the wooden beams creaking with each collision. They had not yet encountered any Tartar scouts, showing they hadn't reached the enemy outposts. Around ten o'clock, Harry Blount spotted several dark shapes moving across the ice, leaping from block to block and drawing nearer, their fluid movements casting eerie shadows in the dim light.

"Tartars!" he thought to himself, his heart racing. He crept over to the elderly boatman and pointed out the mysterious figures, his finger trembling in the cold.

The old man studied them, squinting through the darkness before declaring, "Just wolves! I'd rather face them than Tartars. Still, we'll need to defend ourselves, and be quiet!" His weathered face betrayed both relief and concern.

The group would need to protect themselves from the vicious creatures that prowled the province, driven by their desperate hunger and the bitter cold that had descended upon the region like a merciless blanket. The wolves had detected smelling the raft and would launch their attack, their yellow eyes gleaming with predatory intent from the shoreline. With Tartar outposts likely nearby, the group couldn't risk using their guns. The sound would carry for miles across the frozen landscape. They positioned the women and children in the raft's center, huddled together for warmth and safety, while the men formed a defensive ring around them, clutching poles and knives with white-knuckled grips, ready to fend off the approaching threat. Though the defenders remained silent, the night air resonated with the wolves' haunting howls, a chorus of hunger that echoed across the icy expanse.

Unwilling to stay passive, Michael positioned himself where the ferocious pack was attacking. Armed with his knife, he struck at any wolf that came within range, driving his blade deep into their necks and throats. Jolivet and Blount were active, fighting the creatures with desperate strength. Their fellow travelers fought alongside them with equal valor, jabbing with poles and slashing with whatever weapons they possessed. Despite the eerie silence of the battle, broken only by snarls and the sound of tearing flesh, many of those fleeing suffered serious wounds from the wolves' razor-sharp teeth and powerful jaws.

The conflict showed no signs of ending soon. More wolves kept arriving from the Angara's right shore to join the attack, their bodies slinking across the ice like dark shadows. "This is endless!" exclaimed Alcide as he wielded his blood-covered dagger, his breath coming in ragged gasps in the frigid air.

The ravenous wolves showed no signs of retreat, with fresh packs still pouring across the frozen expanse even thirty minutes into the brutal assault. Fatigue had taken its toll on the desperate survivors, whose resistance was crumbling under the relentless onslaught. Muscles trembled from exhaustion, and movements grew slower with each passing minute. Just as their situation seemed dire, ten massive wolves, their crimson eyes blazing with feral hunger in the blackness, launched themselves onto the raft with bone-jarring force. Jolivet and his companion plunged headlong into combat with the savage creatures, their blades flashing in the dim light, and Michael was moving to join the fray when something unexpected occurred.

The wolves abandoned both the raft, and the frozen river's surface, their claws scrabbling against ice as they fled. Their dark shapes scattered in all directions like leaves in a storm as they retreated to the riverbank, whimpering in clear terror. These predators hunt in darkness with supreme confidence, but now an intense light flooded the entire waterway, turning night into an eerie twilight.

It was: A massive conflagration was the source. The massive bonfire engulfed the small settlement of Poshkavsk, transforming its buildings into towering infernos that reached toward the starless sky. The Tartars had arrived and were completing their destructive mission with methodical efficiency, the orange glow of their torches visible as they moved between structures. From this position, their forces controlled both sides of the river beyond Irkutsk, their campfires dotting the shoreline like malevolent stars. The escapees had now entered the most perilous stretch of their journey, with twenty miles still separating them from the capital city, each one promising new dangers.

Through the darkness, the raft drifted among scattered ice floes, catching glints of distant light that reflected off the frozen surfaces like mirror shards. The escapees lay still on the wooden platform, daring to breathe, knowing that even the slightest movement could reveal their presence to the watchful eyes that lined the shores. Their bodies pressed against the cold planks. They could feel every subtle shift and crack of the ice against their craft.

Behind them, a fast inferno was consuming the town. The wooden buildings, constructed of fir, burned like massive torches, over a hundred and fifty structures ablaze. The air filled with the terrible mixture of crackling flames, collapsing timber, and the fierce cries of the Tartars. Taking advantage of a nearby ice chunk, the elderly boatman guided the raft toward the right bank, putting three to four hundred feet between them and the burning remnants of Poshkavsk, its orange glow casting long shadows across the frozen river.

Terror gripped Jolivet and Blount at the thought of their raft floating on flammable liquid; their knuckles whitened as they gripped the wooden planks below. The burning buildings, transformed into massive furnaces, shot millions of sparks skyward, reaching heights of five to six hundred feet. The flames' reflection made the trees and cliffs along the right bank appear to be ablaze as well, creating an otherworldly scene of double destruction. Just one spark landing on the Angara's surface could ignite the entire river, spreading devastation from shore to shore like wildfire across a summer meadow. Within moments, such an event would spell doom for the raft and everyone aboard, leaving them with no escape from the liquid inferno.

The wind, fortunately, was not blowing in their direction. Coming from the east, it pushed the inferno toward the left side, carrying the deadly shower of sparks away from their vulnerable craft. This gave the escapees a precious chance to avoid the deadly threat, though they remained tense and vigilant. They made it past the burning settlement, their hearts pounding with each yard gained. The fiery glow diminished, the sound of crackling wood subsided to a distant roar, and the flames vanished behind the steep cliffs that emerged at a sharp bend in the river.

Midnight was approaching, bringing with it a bone-chilling cold. Darkness once again provided its protective cover over the raft, wrapping them in its concealing embrace. Though invisible in the blackness, the Tartars moved about near the riverbank, their voices carrying across the water. Their guard posts were marked by blazing fires, creating orange beacons that the raft's crew avoided.

The blocks of ice made navigation treacherous, forcing the crew to maneuver with greater precision through the floating maze. The elderly helmsman rose to his feet, joints creaking in protest, while the moujiks took up their poles again, muscles straining against the current. Their task grew more challenging by the minute as ice continued to clog the waterway, scraping against the raft's wooden planks with ominous groans.

Michael inched forward with Jolivet close behind, both men crawling on their bellies to maintain their balance, straining to catch the urgent exchanges between the old boatman and his crew. Every whispered command could mean the difference between safe passage and disaster.

"Watch the starboard side! She's listing heavy!"

"Ice floes approaching from port, three gigantic masses!"

"Push them away with the hooks! Put your backs into it, brothers!"

“The closing channel will trap us within the hour!”

"If that be the Lord's will," the old man responded, crossing himself with gnarled fingers. "We cannot fight His decisions. We can only accept them with grace."

"Did you catch that?" Alcide whispered.

"Indeed," Michael answered with quiet determination. "But the Lord stands with us! We must keep faith."

Conditions grew dire as the temperature continued to plummet. A halt to the raft's progress would spell disaster. Not only could they not reach Irkutsk, but the ice would soon tear apart their makeshift vessel, forcing them to abandon it. The willow bindings would snap under the relentless pressure, the pine logs would splinter and vanish beneath the frozen crust like matchsticks in a storm, leaving the desperate travelers with nowhere to go but atop the treacherous ice blocks. Come daybreak, the first golden rays would expose their position, and patrolling Tartars would spot them, showing no mercy as they slaughtered them.

Michael made his way back to where Nadia waited, his boots crunching on the frozen deck. Drawing near, he took her hand, feeling its familiar strength despite the biting cold, and asked the same question he always did: "Nadia, are you ready?" And as always, she answered, her breath visible in the frigid air, "I am ready!"

The ice floes continued to impede the raft's progress for several more miles, their jagged edges scraping against the wooden hull. If they reached a narrower section of the river, the ice would create an impassable blockade, crushing them between its merciless jaws. Their speed was already diminishing, each minute bringing fresh anxiety. They faced constant challenges, violent collisions with ice blocks that shuddered through the entire vessel and necessary diversions, sometimes to prevent dangerous impacts that could splinter their craft, other times to navigate through channels that seemed to close as quickly as they appeared. As time passed, the obstacles grew concerning, looming larger and more threatening in the darkness. Time was running out, and their survival hung in the balance.

At 1:30, the raft hit a dense ice barrier, becoming stuck. The drifting ice from behind continued to push against the raft with relentless force, wedging it in place as if it had run aground on some frozen shoal, the creaking of timber growing more ominous with each passing moment.

This section of the Angara River was only half its regular width, causing ice to accumulate and freeze together under increased compression and frigid temperatures. About 500 feet downstream, the river expanded again, where ice chunks broke free from the frozen mass and resumed their journey toward Irkutsk. The ice barrier wouldn't have formed if the riverbanks hadn't constricted the flow, creating a natural bottleneck that trapped both water and ice. However, there was no way to undo what had happened, and those fleeing had to abandon their hopes of reaching their destination, watching as their last chance slipped away.

The stranded group needed whaling tools to cut paths through the frozen expanse, equipment that could have led them to the wider river section, and possible salvation. But without even basic implements to crack the frost-hardened ice, which had become as impenetrable as stone in the bitter cold, they found themselves trapped, their frozen prison growing stronger with each passing minute.

Their dire situation worsened as gunfire erupted from the right riverbank, sending bullets raining down on their makeshift raft. The enemy had spotted them, their muzzle flashes piercing the darkness like angry fireflies. Almost immediately, more shots rang out from the left bank, catching them in a deadly crossfire that echoed across the frozen river. The helpless group now served as targets for Tartar marksmen on both sides, pinned down with nowhere to take cover. Despite the darkness making precise aim difficult, the random barrage struck and wound several members of their party, their cries of pain mixing with the sharp crack of rifles and the dull thud of bullets striking wood and ice.

"Nadia," Michael whispered close to her ear, his breath forming small clouds in the frigid air.

Without a word and prepared for anything, Nadia grasped Michael's hand, her fingers trembling but her grip firm.

"We need to get past their line," he murmured, his lips moving. "Lead the way, but be careful. No one can spot us leaving the raft. One flash of movement could give us away."

Nadia complied. Together they slipped across the ice in the darkness, broken only by brief flashes from gunfire that cast eerie, momentary shadows. Nadia crawled ahead of Michael as bullets rained around them like hailstones, striking the frozen surface with sharp, crystalline cracks. Their hands soon bled from the jagged ice as they scrambled over, leaving faint crimson trails that disappeared into the darkness, but they pressed onward without pause, driven by desperate necessity.

The barrier's far side came into view after ten minutes of grueling travel. The Angara waters resumed their unimpeded flow, creating a constant, muffled rushing sound beneath the ice. Several ice fragments, breaking free from the main floe, drifted downstream toward the town, their edges scraping against the larger ice sheet. Michael's intentions became apparent to Nadia as she observed a particular ice block connected to the floe by just a thin strip rocking with the current.

"Let's go," Nadia urged, her voice barely above a breath. Together, they positioned themselves on the ice chunk, distributing their weight as their combined mass caused it to break free with a soft crack.

The ice block began its journey downstream, rocking with each ripple and swell. As the river expanded before them into a dark ribbon under starlight, their escape route emerged through the frozen landscape. The sounds of gunfire reached their ears in sharp staccato bursts, along with desperate screams and Tartar battle cries that echoed across the ice. These mixed sounds of suffering and savage triumph grew fainter as distance separated them, until only the whisper of water against ice remained.

"Those poor souls!" Nadia whispered, her words forming small clouds in the frigid air.

For thirty minutes, Michael and Nadia drifted on their ice floe, carried by the river's relentless flow. Each crack and groan of the ice beneath them brought fresh fear it might splinter, sending them plunging into the deadly cold waters. The powerful current kept them centered in the river's path like a practiced helmsman, making any diagonal movement unnecessary until they approached Irkutsk's stone quays, their dark shapes looming larger with each passing minute. Michael remained silent, his jaw clenched tight enough to make his temples ache, every sense alert for danger in the surrounding darkness. Never had his goal been close, within reach.

He could feel it in every fiber of his being. Success was within his grasp, separated only by a diminishing stretch of icy water!

The darkened horizon shimmered with twin rows of lights near midnight, where the Angara's shores melded into darkness. Irkutsk's illumination beckoned from the right bank, a constellation of lanterns and torches marking civilization's edge, while the Tartar encampment's fires blazed on the left, their savage orange glow reflecting off the low-hanging clouds.

"Finally," Michael Strogoff whispered, standing half a mile from the city walls.

Nadia's sudden scream cut his relief short, piercing the night like a blade through silk.

The sound made Michael leap to his feet on the unstable ice, sending hairline cracks spider-webbing beneath his boots. He thrust his arm toward the river's course, his face taking on an eerie cast in the strange blue glow that now bathed the waters. As if comprehending the brilliant flames spreading across the water's surface, their otherworldly radiance growing brighter with each passing moment, he cried out in despair, "No! Even the heavens conspire against us!"

QuantumDigitalPublishing.io

Chapter Twelve

IRKUTSK

Serving as Eastern Siberia's capital, Irkutsk boasts a substantial population of thirty thousand residents during peacetime. The city features a prominent hill on the Angara River's right bank, adorned with various churches, an imposing cathedral, and residential buildings scattered in a charming, unplanned fashion. The wooden houses, painted in cheerful colors, stand shoulder to shoulder with more austere stone structures, their weathered facades telling tales of countless Siberian winters.

When viewed from the Siberian highway's vantage point, twenty miles away atop a mountain, the cityscape creates an almost Eastern appearance with its distinctive features: cupolas piercing the sky, bell-towers standing proud, spires as delicate as minarets, and domes resembling rotund Chinese vessels. However, this oriental illusion dissolves once visitors enter the city itself. The broad, European-style streets and familiar Russian architecture reveal Irkutsk's true character as a frontier outpost of western civilization, though one cannot help but notice subtle Asian influences in the decorative details of buildings and the occasional temple rising above the rooftops.

This vibrant city blends Eastern influences, with elements of both Byzantine and Chinese heritage, yet transforms into a European landscape through its modern features. Well-paved streets with proper sidewalks crisscross the city, while a network of canals weaves throughout, their waters reflecting the bustling life above. Towering birch trees line the thoroughfares, their silver-white bark catching the sunlight, and buildings constructed of brick and wood, some reaching multiple stories, dot the cityscape. The streets bustle with various vehicles, from traditional tarantasses to elegant broughams and coaches, their wheels clattering against the cobblestones as they navigate the busy thoroughfares. The sophisticated residents keep up with contemporary culture, even following the latest fashion trends from Paris, their attire a testament to the city's cosmopolitan character.

Irkutsk served as a haven for all Siberians in the province, causing the city to be populated, its neighborhoods teeming with life from dawn until dusk. The city was well-stocked with many provisions, from necessities to exotic luxuries. As a major trading hub connecting China, Central Asia, and Europe, Irkutsk handled countless varieties of goods, its warehouses and markets overflowing with silks, tea, furs, spices, and precious metals. Given these resources, the authorities felt confident in welcoming the peasants from the Angara valley, even though this meant leaving empty land between the city and the advancing invaders, a strategic decision that would test the city's resilience.

The city housed the governor-general of Eastern Siberia, who led the regional administration from an imposing three-story mansion overlooking the central square. Under his authority worked several officials: a civil governor who managed provincial affairs and supervised tax collection, a police chief whose responsibilities were considerable because of the large exile population and frequent disturbances, and a mayor who headed the merchant class and regulated trade matters. The mayor wielded significant influence over the citizenry and possessed considerable wealth, evidenced by his ownership of several prominent businesses and his lavish entertainment of foreign dignitaries.

The military force stationed in Irkutsk comprised two primary units: a 2,000-strong Cossack infantry regiment, known for their fierce loyalty and exceptional horsemanship, and a police contingent distinguished by their silver-trimmed blue uniforms and helmets that gleamed in the winter sun. Because of the unfolding crisis, the Czar's brother had taken refuge within the city walls since the enemy first advanced into the territory, occupying an entire wing of the governor's residence with his personal staff and guard detail.

The Grand Duke embarked on a significant journey through the remote provinces of Central Asia, inspecting military outposts and meeting with local administrators. He traveled through major Siberian cities without royal fanfare, choosing a military style over princely pomp, often sleeping in garrison quarters rather than governors' mansions. With his officers and a battle-hardened Cossack regiment escort, he made his way across the Trans-Baikalcine provinces, enduring bitter winds and treacherous mountain passes. He stopped to visit Nikolaevsk, the easternmost Russian town on the Sea of Okhotsk's shore, where he reviewed the Pacific naval installations and conferred with regional commanders.

As the Grand Duke began his return journey toward Irkutsk from the empire's edges, planning to continue to Moscow, news of the invasion struck like lightning through the telegraph offices. He rushed to reach the capital, pushing his convoy to exhaustion through day and night, arriving mere moments before all contact with Russia was severed. In those final precious minutes, he exchanged a handful of urgent telegrams with St. Petersburg and Moscow, sending his responses before the lines went dead with an ominous silence. With the wires cut and the postal routes blocked, Irkutsk now stood cut off from the outside world, a fortress of Russian authority marooned in a sea of uncertainty.

As news reached Irkutsk of Ichim, Omsk, and Tomsk falling to enemy forces, the Grand Duke resolved to mount a stalwart defense of Siberia's capital city. He approached this grave task with the same remarkable composure and resolve he had showed in previous crises. With reinforcements far off and the scattered Siberian troops too few to halt the advancing Tartar armies, the Duke recognized that an assault on Irkutsk was inevitable. His priority became fortifying the city to withstand an extended siege, as this appeared to be their best hope for survival.

Preparations began when Tomsk was captured by the Tartars. Along with this devastating news, the Grand Duke received word that the Emir of Bokhara and his allied Khans were leading the invasion. However, he remained unaware that their lieutenant was Ivan Ogareff, a Russian officer whom the Grand Duke had demoted, though he had never met the man in person. The Duke ordered strengthening the city's defensive walls, the stockpiling of provisions, and the organization of the civilian population into work brigades. Every able-bodied man was asked to assist in the fortification efforts, while warehouses were filled with grain, salted meats, and other essential supplies that would sustain the population through a prolonged encirclement. Despite the gravity of their situation, the Grand Duke's calm leadership helped maintain order and purpose among the anxious citizens of Irkutsk.

The people living in Irkutsk province had no choice but to flee their communities, abandoning generations-old homesteads and farms in the face of the advancing threat. Those unable to seek shelter in the provincial capital were forced to evacuate to the region beyond Lake Baikal, where they would be looked after from the invaders' destruction, though many faced arduous journeys through difficult terrain. All grain crops and animal feed were gathered and stored within Irkutsk city, which, serving as the last stronghold of Russian authority in the Far East, was reinforced to withstand an extended siege by hostile forces.

In 1611, its founders established Irkutsk where the Irkut and Angara rivers meet, along the Angara's right bank, recognizing the strategic value of this natural confluence. Two wooden drawbridges supported by sturdy piles driven deep into the riverbed, each span engineered to withstand both the region's harsh winters and spring floods linked the city to its suburbs across the water. The left bank offered strong defensive advantages, with its elevated position and obvious lines of sight. When danger threatened, the suburbs were driven out and the bridges demolished, leaving only blackened stumps of the support pillars visible above the water's surface. The Angara's considerable width, combined with its swift current and exposed approaches, made any crossing attempt under the defenders' fire impossible, creating a natural moat that had protected the city through many conflicts.

However, the river could be crossed both upstream and downstream from the city, leaving Irkutsk vulnerable to attack from the east, where no defensive walls had been built up. This oversight had long worried military strategists, who recognized that an determined enemy force might ford the Angara at shallower points and outflank the city's primary defenses.

The citizens threw themselves into strengthening the city's defenses, working around the clock. The Grand Duke watched with pride as his people showed remarkable dedication to the task, knowing their determination would serve them well in the coming battle. Everyone, from military personnel and traders to outcasts and farmers, united in protecting their shared home. Women and children carried stones while craftsmen applied their skills to reinforce weak points. They completed impressive earthen barriers a week ahead of the Tartar forces reaching the Angara River, the fresh-packed soil rising fifteen feet high in places. A water-filled trench was dug between the inner and outer walls, its muddy depths studded with sharpened stakes. Now: Too well-fortified for a swift capture, the city's constructed yet formidable defenses showed the inhabitants' resolve. Surrounding and besieging the city would be the enemy's only option, a prospect testing both sides' endurance in the harsh Siberian climate.

Near Irkutsk, the Tartar force from the Yenisei valley appeared on September 24th. They took control of the abandoned outskirts, where all structures had been flattened to provide clear lines of fire for the Grand Duke's artillery, though these guns were few and modest in size. The Tartars established their encampment along the Angara's banks, their tents and campfires stretching for a mile along the shoreline, awaiting reinforcements from two additional columns under the Emir and his confederates.

On September 25th, these separate forces merged at the Angara camp, their combined numbers darkening the landscape like a vast shadow. Under Feofar-Khan's unified command, the invasion force was now complete, save for the troops left to hold their conquered territories, their garrisons spread thin across the vast Siberian expanse.

The Tartar army, led by Ogareff, found a way around what seemed an impossible crossing of the Angara River near Irkutsk. Several miles upstream, they constructed makeshift bridges using boats requisitioned from nearby fishing villages, lashing the vessels together with heavy ropes and covering them with wooden planks. This ingenious solution allowed a substantial force to cross. The Grand Duke, lacking any field artillery to reach such distances, could do little to stop this maneuver and was required to remain within Irkutsk's walls, watching as enemy forces accumulated on both sides of the river.

After establishing themselves on the river's right bank, the Tartar forces advanced toward the city with methodical precision. Along their approach, they set fire to the governor-general's summer residence, sending plumes of black smoke into the winter sky as an obvious message of their intentions. They surrounded Irkutsk and prepared their positions to begin the siege, establishing a series of fortified camps at strategic points around the city's perimeter.

The frustrated military engineer Ivan Ogareff found his plans thwarted at every turn, his initial confidence eroding with each passing day. Though skilled in conventional siege warfare, he lacked the equipment for swift action, the heavy artillery and siege engines that might have made a decisive difference. His primary goal, to catch Irkutsk off guard, had slipped through his fingers like melting snow. The battle of Tomsk had slowed the Tartar forces' advance, costing them precious time and resources, while Irkutsk's defenders had fortified their positions with surprising speed, transforming the city into a formidable stronghold. These setbacks forced Ogareff to abandon his hopes for a quick victory and instead commit to a lengthy, formal siege of the city, a prospect that pleased neither him nor his restless troops.

The Emir, acting on his counsel, launched two separate attacks to seize the stronghold, though these attempts resulted in heavy casualties. His forces targeted vulnerable sections of the fortifications, but the defenders showed remarkable bravery in beating back both assaults. Leading the defense, the Grand Duke and his commanders displayed exceptional leadership, joining the fight and rallying townspeople and rural folk to defend the walls. Showing admirable dedication, the city and countryside populations fought, forming bucket brigades to fight fires and tending to the wounded under heavy fire.

During their second assault, the Tartars breached one gate, flooding through the opening like a wave of steel and horsehair. A fierce battle erupted along Bolchaia Street, which stretched for two miles beside the Angara River, with fighting that raged from doorway to doorway and rooftop to rooftop. However, the combined forces of Cossacks, police, and local citizens mounted such a formidable defense, using overturned carts as barricades and raining projectiles from upper windows, that they repelled the Tartar invaders, forcing them to retreat in disarray back through the shattered gate.

Unable to take the city by force, Ivan Ogareff devised a cunning strategy. His scheme involved infiltrating the town, gaining the Grand Duke's trust, and then, at the opportune moment, betraying the city by opening its gates to the besieging army. This would also allow him to exact his revenge against the Czar's brother. His companion, the Tsigane woman Sangarre who had followed him to the Angara, encouraged him to proceed with this treacherous plan, whispering dark promises of glory and retribution in his ear during their clandestine meetings beneath the city walls.

Time was of the essence. The Russian forces stationed in Yakutsk were marching toward Irkutsk, gathering their strength along the Lena River's upper reaches. They would reach the city within six days, which meant Ogareff had to ensure Irkutsk's betrayal before then. He could not afford to wait any longer. The winter winds were growing fiercer, and each passing hour brought the possibility that the vigilant defenders who scrutinized every newcomer with increasing suspicion might discover his true identity.

On the evening of October 2nd, military leaders convened for a strategic meeting in the governor-general's palace's grand salon. Overlooking: Overlooking the river below, the palace stood at the end of Bolchaia Street. From the palace windows: The Tartar encampment was visible, and longer-range artillery could have made the palace impossible for the attackers to occupy. Thousands of enemy campfires flickered across the darkening landscape, like malevolent fireflies.

In the meeting chamber, several dignitaries had assembled: the Grand Duke, General Voranzoff, the city governor, the merchant guild leader, and various military officers. They gathered to discuss and evaluate different strategic options. Maps and dispatches littered the massive oak table, and servants moved around the room's perimeter, keeping the oil lamps burning bright against the encroaching night.

"Ladies and gentlemen," the Grand Duke addressed the group, his stern face illuminated by lamplight, "you're all aware of our current predicament. I remain confident that we can maintain our position until reinforcements arrive from Yakutsk. Once they join us, we'll be capable of repelling these savage invaders, and I assure you, they'll pay a heavy price for daring to encroach upon Muscovite soil." His words carried the weight of imperial authority, though the shadows under his eyes betrayed nights of restless planning and concern.

"Your Grace," General Voranzoff responded, his weathered hand resting on the hilt of his saber, "I can guarantee that every citizen of Irkutsk stands ready to support our cause."

"Correct, general," the Grand Duke responded, adjusting the gold-braided collar of his uniform, "and I respect their patriotic spirit. Thankfully, they've been spared from the ravages of disease and starvation so far, and I'm hopeful they'll continue to avoid such hardships. But what impresses me is their remarkable bravery defending the walls. Their dedication has not gone unnoticed. Note my words, honored merchant, and please convey this message to them."

"On behalf of our town, I express our gratitude, Your Highness," the merchant leader replied, bowing as he spoke. His silk robes rustled in the lamplight. "If I may inquire, what is the latest we can expect the relief forces to arrive?"

"Only six days, your Highness," the Grand Duke responded with renewed vigor. "A courageous and resourceful courier entered the city this morning, having braved the enemy lines under cover of darkness. He informed me that General Kisselef is leading fifty thousand Russian troops, advancing across the frozen landscape. They reached Kirensk along the Lena River two days ago, and neither ice nor snow will slow their progress. These fifty thousand capable soldiers, well-armed and determined, will strike the Tartars from the side, bringing us swift liberation."

"We stand prepared to follow your commands whenever your Highness orders an attack."

"Excellent," the Grand Duke answered, a glimmer of satisfaction crossing his features. "Once we spot the relief forces' vanguard on the ridges, we'll destroy these trespassers who dare besiege our city."

The Grand Duke turned to General Voranzoff, his military bearing clear in every movement. "Tomorrow we shall inspect the fortifications on the right bank," he declared. "The Angara is carrying ice floes now, and once it freezes, the Tartars might attempt a crossing. We must ensure every defensive position is secure."

"Your Highness, if I may observe?" ventured the merchant leader, stepping forward with assuring one who knew the region's waters.

"Please proceed."

"I have witnessed the Angara during temperatures of thirty and even forty degrees below zero," the merchant explained, gesturing toward the sound of rushing water beyond the walls. "Even then, ice continues to flow without the river freezing solid. This occurs because of the river's powerful current, which never sleeps, even in winter's harshest grip. Therefore, I can assure Your Highness that if the Tartars have no alternative means of crossing, they will never enter Irkutsk by the frozen river. Nature herself stands as our guardian."

The governor-general nodded in agreement, his weathered features reflecting years of frontier service.

"That's indeed fortunate," the Grand Duke replied, stroking his chin. "Still, we must remain prepared for anything that might happen. The Tartars are known for their resourcefulness."

Turning to face the police chief, who stood at rigid attention near the chamber door, he inquired, "Do you have anything to report?"

"Yes, Your Highness," the police chief responded, stepping forward and producing a folded document from his uniform pocket. "I've received a petition that was sent to you through my office."

"Who sent it?"

"It comes from the Siberian exiles, there are five hundred of them in town, as Your Highness is aware. They've been most eager to make their voices heard."

The political exiles scattered across the province had gathered in Irkutsk as soon as the invasion began. Following orders, they left their villages where they had worked in various roles, as doctors, professors at the Gymnasium, instructors at the Japanese School, and teachers at the School of Navigation, to assemble in the town. Many had brought valuable skills and knowledge with them, despite their status as exiles. Both the Czar and the Grand Duke had faith in their patriotism, providing them with weapons and equipment, and these exiles had proven their valor beyond doubt, fighting with determining men seeking redemption.

"What request do the exiles make?" the Grand Duke inquired, leaning forward in his ornate chair.

"Your Highness," the head of police responded, bowing, "they wish to form their own special unit and be located at the forefront of the first offensive. They're eager to prove themselves."

"Indeed," the Grand Duke replied, his voice thick with unconcealed emotion, rising to his feet as he spoke, "these exiles are Russians, and they have every right to defend their homeland! They've suffered enough for their past deeds."

"I can assure Your Highness with confidence," the governor-general stated, straightening his military jacket, "these men will prove to be among your finest troops. Their dedication is unmatched."

"They'll need someone to lead them," the Grand Duke responded, pacing across the polished floor. "Who do you have in mind?"

"The men would like to propose," the police chief interjected, exchanging glances with the governor-general, "one of their own who has proven himself in battle. He's shown exceptional courage under fire."

"Russian, is he?" the Grand Duke's eyes narrowed with interest.

"Indeed, from our Baltic territories. A man of considerable military experience."

"Tell me his name."

"Wassili Fedor, Your Highness. He's earned the respect of every man in the unit."

In the harsh city of Irkutsk, Dr. Wassili Fedor, Nadia's father, served both as a physician and a patriot. Beyond his medical duties, he channeled his energy into strengthening the city's defenses, often working late into the frigid Siberian nights to organize patrols and fortifications. His influence extended to fellow exiles, whom he united for their common survival, creating an informal network of support that stretched throughout the city's snow-laden streets. These displaced citizens had caught the Grand Duke's attention through their remarkable dedication, sacrificing their lives in various battles for their beloved Russia, from street skirmishes to full-scale defensive operations against rebel forces.

Though Wassili Fedor's courage earned him recognition multiple times, during the brutal winter siege, he remained humble, never seeking rewards or special treatment, preferring instead to tend to his patients and maintain his modest practice. When the exiles formed their own military unit, they selected him as their leader, a decision made without his knowledge while he was away treating wounded soldiers at the eastern garrison.

Upon hearing this name from the police chief, the Grand Duke showed his familiarity with it, a slight smile of recognition crossing his weathered face.

"Yes," General Voranzoff confirmed, adjusting his medal-laden uniform, "Wassili Fedor has proven himself both worthy and brave. He's always commanded considerable respect among his fellow men. Even the most hardened veterans seek his counsel."

"How much time has he spent in Irkutsk?" the Duke inquired, drumming his fingers on the polished surface of his desk.

"Two years now, Your Excellency, without incident," the chief responded with certainty.

"And his behavior?"

"His behavior," the police chief replied, straightening his posture, "shows complete adherence to the special regulations that bind him. He has never once given us cause for concern."

"General," the Grand Duke declared with sudden decisiveness, "I want you to bring him before me at once. This matter requires my personal attention."

The Grand Duke's commands were carried out, and within thirty minutes, Fedor stood before him in the ornate chamber. A towering figure in his forties, the Duke possessed a solemn, melancholic expression that seemed etched into his features. His life story could be captured in one word, struggle, as he had battled and endured hardships throughout his years, from military campaigns to political upheavals and personal losses. Looking at his face, one could see where his daughter Nadia Fedor had inherited her looks, as their features were similar, from the sharp eyes to the proud set of their jaw.

The Tartar offensive had dealt him a devastating emotional blow and crushed a father's dreams while he remained stranded eight thousand miles away from his hometown. The distance felt like an insurmountable chasm, made worse by the cruelty of timing. He had received word through correspondence about his wife's passing, the letters bearing tear-stained edges and words of consolation that brought little comfort. Along with this heartbreaking news came word his daughter had secured governmental permission to reunite with him in Irkutsk. Nadia was set to depart from Riga on July 10th, carrying with her his last hopes for family connection. With the invasion beginning on July 15th, and if Nadia had crossed the border by then, her fate among the invading forces remained unknown. One can only imagine the distressed father's torment, having received no word about his daughter since that time, each passing day adding additional weights to his already heavy heart.

Wassili Fedor stepped into the Grand Duke's chamber, made his obeisance with the practiced grace of a man who understood ceremony, and stood awaiting the Duke's words, his weathered face betraying none of his inner turmoil.

"Wassili Fedor," the Grand Duke began, his voice carrying the gravity of command that filled the ornate chamber, "your fellow exiles have requested permission to create an elite fighting unit. They understand that joining this corps means they must be prepared to fight until none remain standing? This is not a decision to be made, nor a commitment that allows for half-measures."

"They understand this, your Grace," Fedor answered, his voice steady despite the weight of what he represented.

"They have chosen you to lead them," the Grand Duke stated, studying Fedor's weathered features with keen interest.

"Me, your Highness?" Fedor's composure wavered for just a moment, betraying his surprise.

"Will you accept command of these men?" The question hung in the air between them, heavy with significance.

"If it serves Russia, then yes." The words came without hesitation, born of years of unwavering loyalty.

The Grand Duke addressed Captain Fedor, his voice carrying the full authority of his station. "You are no longer an exile."

"I am grateful, your Highness," Fedor replied, choosing his words. "But may I lead those who still bear that burden?"

"None bear it any longer!" declared the Czar's brother, rising from his seat with sudden vigor. In that moment, he had pardoned all of Fedor's fellow exiles, transforming them from outcasts to fellow soldiers with a single proclamation that echoed off the chamber's gilded walls.

Overwhelmed with emotion he could no longer conceal, Wassili Fedor clasped the Grand Duke's extended hand before taking his leave, his steps lighter than they had been in years as he withdrew from the chamber.

After Fedor's departure, the Grand Duke turned to his officers with a knowing smile, his gold-trimmed uniform catching the lamplight. "The Czar will approve these pardons. After all, we require heroes to protect Siberia's capital, and I have just created some. Men fight harder when they have something to prove, and to preserve."

This merciful act of pardoning the Irkutsk exiles proved both just and wise, transforming condemned men into loyal defenders when the city needed them most.

The darkness had fallen, wrapping the city in its winter shroud. The flames from the Tartar encampment glowed through the palace windows like malevolent eyes, visible across the Angara River where they cast dancing reflections on the water. Ice chunks floated downstream with hollow scraping sounds, with some becoming trapped against the old bridge supports while others rushed past in the current, their edges gleaming in the firelight. As the trader had noted, The Angara would struggle to freeze. This meant Irkutsk's defenders needn't worry about an assault from that direction, though the open water provided little comfort given their other vulnerabilities. As the clock struck ten with deep, resonant tones, the Grand Duke prepared to send his officers away and head to his chambers, when a commotion erupted outside the palace, shouting voices and hurried footsteps.

The door burst open moments later with a bang that echoed through the chamber, and an aide-de-camp hurried in, his boots leaving wet tracks on the polished floor as he made his way to the Grand Duke.

"Your Highness," he announced, out of breath, "a messenger has arrived from the Czar!"

Chapter Thirteen

THE CZAR'S COURIER

The council members all lurched forward at once, their chairs scraping against the wooden floor. A messenger had arrived from the Czar in Irkutsk! The very notion sent ripples of excitement through the chamber. Had the officers considered how unlikely this was, given the Tartar blockades and treacherous conditions, they would have doubted the news.

"This messenger!" the Grand Duke cried, rushing toward his aide-de-camp with such haste that his ceremonial sword clattered against his hip.

Into the room stumbled a man who looked spent, his breathing labored and irregular. He wore a Siberian peasant's garments, now in tatters and pierced with bullet holes that told silent stories of narrow escapes. A traditional Muscovite cap sat atop his head, dusted with the grime of long travel, and his face bore the mark of a fresh scar healed, pink and raw against his weathered skin. His exhausted appearance and ruined shoes, held together by crude repairs, suggested he had traveled far by foot across the harsh terrain.

"Are you His Highness the Grand Duke?" he inquired, his voice hoarse but steady.

The Grand Duke approached him, studying the mysterious arrival with keen interest. "Are you serving as the Czar's courier?" he questioned.

"Indeed, your Highness,".

"From where do you come?"

"Moscow, your Highness,".

"When did you depart Moscow?"

"The fifteenth of July,".

"What shall I call you?"

"Michael Strogoff," the man declared, yet something in his bearing suggested there was nothing simple about him at all.

This was, in truth, Ivan Ogareff, who had assumed the identity of the man he believed he had rendered helpless. Not a soul in Irkutsk, including the Grand Duke himself, could recognize him, and he saw no need to disguise his appearance. Having the means to verify his false identity, he knew his claim would go unchallenged. He had come, driven by an unwavering determination, to expedite the invasion's goal through acts of betrayal and murder. His lips curved into the faintest of smiles, knowing how perfectly his deception had already taken root.

The Grand Duke dismissed his officers after Ogareff's response, leaving just himself and the impersonator of Michael Strogoff in the chamber. The heavy oak doors closed with a resonant thud, the sound echoing off the stone walls.

For several moments, the Grand Duke studied Ivan Ogareff before asking, "Were you present in Moscow on July 15th?" His piercing gaze sought any sign of deception, any crack in the courier's composure.

"Indeed, your Highness. The previous evening, on the 14th, I had observed His Majesty the Czar at the New Palace." Ogareff's voice remained steady, each word measured and delivered with practiced confidence.

"Do you carry correspondence from the Czar?"

"I do. Here it is," Ogareff replied, reaching into his weather-worn coat with deliberate movements.

Ivan Ogareff presented the Imperial message to the Grand Duke. Ivan Ogareff had compressed the paper until it was tiny, folding and refolding it countless times into a tight square no larger than a copper coin.

"Was it delivered to you in this condition?"

"No, your Highness. I had to destroy the outer envelope to conceal it from the Emir's men.

"Did the Tartars capture you?"

"Indeed, your Highness. The rebels held me captive for quite some time," Ogareff explained, his face showing measured distress. "That's why my journey took seventy-nine days, departing Moscow on July 15th, as stated in the letter, I didn't reach Irkutsk until October 2nd.

With deliberate movements, the Grand Duke examined the letter, unfolding it. With each crease releasing its secret, the paper crackled. There was his brother's handwriting, the Czar's signature preceded by the official imperial formula, the ink still dark against the weathered paper. The letter's authenticity was beyond question, as was the courier's identity. Though the Grand Duke had harbored some suspicions about Ogareff's face, noting something familiar yet disconcerting in his features, he maintained a neutral expression, and his doubts soon melted away like morning frost under the sun.

After a long moment of silence, the Grand Duke studied the letter with careful deliberation, absorbing every word, his fingers tracing the lines of text. "Tell me, Michael Strogoff, are you familiar with what this letter contains?" he inquired, his voice measured and controlled.

"Indeed, your Highness," Michael replied, standing at rigid attention. "I memorized it in case I needed to destroy the physical letter to keep it from the Tartars. That way, I could still deliver its message to you without fail, even under the most dire circumstances."

"And you understand this letter commands us to fight to the death rather than surrender the town?" The Grand Duke's eyes narrowed as he spoke.

"I do, your Highness," Michael confirmed, his jaw set with determination.

"Are you aware it tells me about the troop movements organized to halt the invasion?" The Grand Duke's fingers drummed on the paper.

"Indeed, your Highness, but their efforts have proven futile." Michael's voice carried a hint of regret.

"Explain yourself."

"Feofar-Khan's soldiers now control Ichim, Omsk, Tomsk, and many other major Siberian cities."

"But there was resistance? Did our Cossacks not engage the Tartars?" The Grand Duke leaned forward, his expression intense.

"Frequently, your Highness," Michael responded.

"And they suffered a defeat?"

"Their numbers were too few to stand against the enemy. Our brave soldiers fought valiantly, but they were overwhelmed."

"Where did these battles occur?" The Grand Duke's fingers tightened on the letter's edge.

"At Kolyvan and at Tomsk." Though Ogareff had spoken until this point, he now added, hoping to demoralize Irkutsk's defenders by magnifying the defeats, "And a third time near Krasnoiarsk." His voice carried just the right note of regret and military professionalism.

The Grand Duke pressed his lips together so tightly that no words escaped, his knuckles white against the paper he held. "Tell me about this recent clash."

"With respect, your Highness," Ogareff replied, bowing his head in deference, "it was more than a clash, it was a full-scale battle."

"A battle?" The Duke's voice carried both disbelief and dread.

"Our forces numbered twenty thousand Russians, drawn from the frontier regions and Tobolsk province. We faced an army of one hundred and fifty thousand Tartars. Despite fighting, we were overwhelmed." Ogareff's hands moved in subtle gestures as he painted the scene. "The field ran red that day."

"You dare lie to me!" the Grand Duke burst out, his fury contained. He half-rose from his chair, trembling with rage.

Ivan Ogareff maintained his cool demeanor, not flinching from the Duke's outburst. "Every word is accurate, your Highness. I witnessed the battle of Krasnoiarsk myself, it's where I was taken." His eyes met the Duke's, the perfect picture of a devoted officer delivering painful news.

The Grand Duke regained his composure, sinking back into his chair with measured control, and with a subtle gesture of his hand, showed that he accepted Ogareff's account. "When did this battle of Krasnoiarsk occur?" he inquired, his voice now steady and deliberate.

"September second, Your Highness, just as the sun was rising," Ogareff replied without hesitation.

"Have all the Tartar forces gathered in this location?" The Duke's fingers drummed on the arm of his chair.

"Yes, every one of them. They've merged their position along the river-bank."

"What's your assessment of their numbers?"

"I'd say around four hundred thousand soldiers, well-armed and ready for battle," Ogareff stated with calculated precision.

Once again, Ogareff inflated the size of the Tartar forces, continuing his pattern of deception. His practiced eyes observed any sign that the Duke doubted his words.

"Should I expect any reinforcements from the western provinces?" the Grand Duke inquired, leaning forward in his seat.

"Not until winter ends, Your Highness. The passes are already becoming treacherous with early snow."

"Listen, Michael Strogoff." The Grand Duke's voice took on a steely edge of determination. "Even if these savages numbered six hundred thousand, and even without support from either eastern or western regions, I shall never surrender Irkutsk! This city will stand against any force they dare bring against us!"

Ogareff's sinister gaze narrowed, a shadow of malice flickering across his features. He mused that the Czar's brother did not know the true consequences of betrayal, nor how close that betrayal lurked.

The Grand Duke, being strung, struggled to maintain his composure upon hearing such catastrophic intelligence. His fingers drummed against his thigh as he paced around the chamber while Ogareff watched him, like a predator eyeing its marked prey. Pausing at the frost-rimmed windows, the Duke observed the flickering fires of the Tartar encampment dotting the darkness like malevolent stars and listened to the sound of ice chunks breaking apart in the Angara River with thunderous cracks.

Fifteen minutes passed in tense silence before he spoke again, the only sounds heard were the crackle of the hearth and his boots against the wooden floor. Picking up the letter once more, its paper now crumpled from his repeated handling, he studied a particular section and said, "You know this letter warns me about a traitor I should guard against?"

"Yes, your Highness," Ogareff replied, his voice measured.

"He intends to infiltrate Irkutsk disguised, win my trust, and then hand the town over to the Tartars." The Duke's voice carried a mixture of disgust and disbelief.

"I am aware of this, your Highness. I also know that Ivan Ogareff has made a personal vow of vengeance against the Czar's brother." Ogareff's words carried just the right note of concerned loyalty.

"For what reason?" The Duke's brow furrowed.

"From what I understand, the Grand Duke had sentenced the officer to a degrading punishment that left him forever marked with shame," Ogareff responded, his own face a masterpiece of sympathetic concern.

"Indeed, I recall that. It only proves that this scoundrel, who later turned against his homeland and led these savage invaders, deserved such punishment. Such men have no honor, only self-interest."

"His Majesty the Czar," Ogareff stated, his voice carrying the weight of imperial authority, "was especially concerned that you be warned of Ivan Ogareff's murderous schemes against you. He feared for your safety above all else."

"Yes, the letter mentions this," the Duke replied, touching the document on his desk.

"His Majesty spoke to me about it, instructing me to be watchful of this traitor. He emphasized the gravity of the situation."

"Have you encountered him?" The Duke leaned forward.

"Yes, your Highness, following the battle at Krasnoiarsk. Had he realized I carried a letter for your Highness exposing his plans, I wouldn't have escaped unharmed. The fighting was fierce that day."

"Not at all, you would have perished!" the Grand Duke declared, pounding his fist on the desk. "Tell me, how did you manage your escape?"

"I plunged into the Irtych River," came the response, delivered with just the right mix of modesty and pride. "The current carried me far from danger."

"And your entry into Irkutsk?"

"During an evening raid against a Tartar force. I joined the town's defenders, revealed my identity, and was escorted to your Highness. The soldiers recognized the urgency of my mission."

"Well done, Michael Strogoff," the Grand Duke commended, his weathered face brightening with relief. "You've showed great courage and dedication in your perilous mission. Such loyalty to the Czar and Empire won't go unrewarded. I won't forget this. Is there anything you wish to request?"

"Only to fight by your Highness's side," Ogareff answered with calculated humility.

"Granted, Strogoff. From this day forward, you'll serve on my personal staff and live in the palace. Your rooms will be prepared at once."

"And if Ivan Ogareff should appear before your Highness using a false name, as he intends?" he pressed, feigning concern.

"With your help, we shall expose him, for you know his face. He will die under the knout, (a **harsh, heavy whip**) like the traitor he is. You may go!"

Ogareff offered a precise military salute, mindful of his supposed position as a captain of the Czar's couriers, and withdrew with measured steps through the ornate palace doors.

Ogareff's treacherous scheme had unfolded, exceeding even his own expectations. Having earned complete trust from the Grand Duke through his masterful performance, he now stood poised to betray that confidence at the moment of his choosing. His position within the palace itself gave him intimate access to the town's defensive strategies, fortification plans, and troop movements. With such privileged information at his disposal, he controlled Irkutsk's fate. That not a soul in the city could recognize him or expose his true identity made his deception complete, a perfect disguise that would ensure his victory. With everything aligned to his advantage and the pieces of his plot falling into place, he determined to begin his plan, while fortune still favored his deception.

The situation grew more dire by the hour. They had to seize the town before Russian forces could arrive from the North and East, an event that would occur within days. If the Tartars captured Irkutsk, dislodging them would prove difficult. Even if they were forced to retreat, they would ensure the city's complete destruction first, and would not leave before the Grand Duke had been killed at Feofar-Khan's command.

At the break of dawn, Ivan Ogareff made his rounds of the fortifications, where soldiers, officers, and townspeople greeted him with enthusiasm. They saw this supposed messenger from the Czar as their vital connection to the empire they served. His presence alone seemed to lift their spirits, though each warm welcome only fueled his contempt for their blind trust.

With unwavering confidence, Ogareff spun elaborate tales about his fictional journey. True to his calculating nature, he steered conversations toward the dire military situation, embellishing both the Tartar victories and their army's size, just as he had done when deceiving the Grand Duke.

He insisted that any reinforcements, if they arrived at all, would prove inadequate. He planted seeds of doubt, suggesting that any battle near Irkutsk's walls would end in disaster, much like the devastating defeats at Kolyvan, Tomsk, and Krasnoiarsk. With each retelling, he added subtle details that made his fabrications more convincing, watching with satisfaction as worry lines deepened on the faces of his listeners. His words spread through the garrison like poison, weakening the resolve of even the most stalwart defenders.

Ogareff measured his suggestive remarks, allowing them to penetrate the thoughts of Irkutsk's defenders. He maintained an air of reluctance when responding to questions, emphasizing that they must battle until their last breath and destroy the town before surrendering. His voice would drop to near whispers during these conversations, as if sharing painful truths that weighed heavily upon his conscience.

These deceptive claims would have caused greater damage if possible, but both the military forces and citizens of Irkutsk possessed too strong a sense of national pride to be swayed. Among all those confined within this isolated city at the edge of Asia, whether soldier or civilian, merchant or laborer, nobleman or peasant, not one considered the possibility of surrender. The Russians held nothing but absolute disdain for these invading barbarians, their contempt clear in every stern face and resolute gesture. Even the children played at defending imaginary walls, mimicking their parents' unwavering determination to protect their homeland at any cost.

At first, no one suspected Ivan Ogareff's villainous role; everyone believed he was the Czar's courier rather than a traitor. After reaching Irkutsk, Ogareff developed a close relationship with Wassili Fedor, one of the city's most valiant defenders. Worry about his daughter Nadia consumed Wassili Fedor. According to her last letter from Riga, she had planned to leave Russia, but her fate remained unknown. Had she traversed the provinces now overrun by invaders, or had she been captured? Wassili found his only solace in fighting the Tartars, though such opportunities were too rare for his liking. The evening of the false courier's arrival, Wassili visited the governor-general's palace. There, he confided in Ogareff about Nadia's departure from European Russia and expressed his deep concerns for her safety. Though Ogareff had encountered Nadia in Ichim when she was with Michael Strogoff, he had paid her no more attention than the two reporters also present at the post-house. Thus, he could offer Wassili no information about his daughter.

His face a masterpiece of practiced sympathy, Ogareff listened to the worried father's words. Behind his concerned expression, however, his calculating mind was already searching for ways to use this information to his advantage. He leaned forward in his chair, maintaining the perfect image of an attentive friend and loyal servant of the Czar.

"When did your daughter depart from Russian soil?" Ogareff inquired.

"Around the same period you did," Fedor responded, his weathered hands clutching the edge of the table.

"I departed from Moscow on July 15th," Ogareff stated with careful precision.

"That's when Nadia must have left Moscow too. Her letter stated this," Wassili said, pulling a crumpled piece of paper from his pocket as if to verify the date once more.

"She was still in Moscow on July 15th?" Ogareff's voice carried a note of calculated curiosity.

"Indeed, she was there on that specific date," Wassili confirmed, his eyes clouding with worry as he remembered.

"Then it would have been impossible for her, No, wait, I'm getting my dates confused." Ogareff furrowed his brow in an feigned display of mental calculation. "it seems quite that your daughter crossed the border, and your only remaining hope is that she might have halted her journey upon hearing about the Tartar invasion!" His voice carried just the right mixture of concern and encouragement to appear genuine.

The father dropped his head in despair, his weathered hands trembling at his sides! He was well aware of Nadia's determined nature, that unwavering spirit she'd inherited from her mother, and knew without doubt she would have embarked on her journey regardless of circumstances. Ivan Ogareff's cruel act was needless, a calculated twist of the knife. A single word from him could have put Fedor's mind at ease, could have lifted the crushing weight from the old man's shoulders. Even though Nadia had crossed the border under the conditions we know about, Fedor could have calculated that she was looked after by comparing two crucial dates: when his daughter would have reached Nijni-Novgorod, and when the travel ban was announced. This simple math would have shown him that Nadia had avoided the invasion's dangers and remained, albeit, within the Empire's European territory, protected by the very restrictions meant to contain the populace.

Ogareff, true to his cruel nature and indifferent to others' pain, could have uttered that crushing word, could have granted this small mercy to a suffering father. Yet he held his tongue, savoring the anguish he had cultivated. Fedor walked away with shattered hopes, his shoulders slumped and steps unsteady, this final meeting having extinguished his last glimmer of optimism like a candle snuffed out in a dark room.

Over October 3rd and 4th, the Grand Duke questioned the man claiming to be Michael Strogoff, pressing him to recount everything he'd learned in the New Palace's Imperial Cabinet. Ogareff, having prepared for such interrogation, answered without a moment's pause. He emphasized how the Czar's government had been caught entirely off-guard by the invasion, explaining that the rebels had planned their uprising in absolute secrecy. Before Moscow even received word of the attack, he detailed how the Tartars had seized control of the Obi line. The Russian provinces, he stressed, were unprepared, lacking the troops and resources for effective resistance against the Siberian invaders.

In the shadows of Irkutsk, Ivan Ogareff moved through the city, examining its defenses. His treacherous eyes focused on the Bolchaia Gate, which he intended to betray to the enemy. He scrutinized every detail of the fortifications, noting their vulnerabilities with calculated precision. Under the guise of strengthening the city's protection, he walked the ramparts daily, mapping each weakness and identifying the optimal points where the Tartar forces could breach the walls. The guards, believing him to be their savior, shared additional information about patrol schedules and ammunition stores, aiding in their own destruction.

As evening fell, he visited the glacis of the gate, (the **gentle, sloping embankment fortified** in front of the gate) pacing along its length, his footsteps echoing against the stone fortifications. He felt secure in his observations, knowing the nearest enemy positions were at least a mile from the city walls, hidden behind the rolling terrain. Yet his solitude was not complete, while he believed himself unobserved, a shadow detached itself from the darkness beyond the earthworks, moving with feline grace. It was Sangarre, who had risked death to contact Ogareff, her dark cloak making her invisible against the twilight sky.

For 48 hours, those under siege experienced a calmness that was unusual, given how the Tartars had behaved since beginning their blockade, with their previous relentless assaults and provocations. These orders came from Ogareff, who orchestrated every detail of the deception. As Feofar-Khan's second-in-command, he wanted to pause all forceful attempts to capture the city, knowing that patience would serve his treachery better than brute force. His strategy was to wait for the defenders' vigilance to weaken, counting on human nature's tendency to relax when danger appears to recede. Meanwhile, thousands of Tartar soldiers remained stationed at strategic positions, prepared to storm the gate, their weapons ready and their horses saddled. Ogareff expected the defenders would abandon their posts, lulled into complacency by the false peace, allowing his forces to launch their attack when he gave the signal, a signal already arranged and awaiting only his command.

He knew he had to act without delay. Everything needed to be finished before the Russian forces arrived at Irkutsk. Ogareff had made his preparations, and as night fell, he arranged for a message to be dropped from the fortifications into Sangarre's waiting hands. The parchment, weighted with a small stone and sealed with wax, contained his last instructions for coordinating the assault.

The time was set. In the dead of night, between October 5th and 6th, at precisely two in the morning, Ivan Ogareff would execute his plan to surrender Irkutsk to the enemy. The darkness would mask his treachery, and the late hour would ensure most of the city's defenders were drowsy at their posts, their reactions dulled by exhaustion and the false sense of security that had settled over the fortifications.

Chapter Fourteen

THE NIGHT OF THE FIFTH OF OCTOBER

The strategy devised by Ivan Ogareff was carefully planned, and barring any unexpected complications, he was sure of its success. The crucial element was ensuring the Bolchaia Gate remained either unprotected or defended when he surrendered it. To achieve this, the defenders' attention needed to be diverted elsewhere in the city. He had coordinated this diversionary tactic with the Emir, spending countless hours refining every detail until it was flawless.

The diversion would unfold upstream and downstream along the Irkutsk riverbank. While mounting serious assaults at these locations, they would also stage a mock attempt to cross the Angara from the opposite shore. This multi-pronged approach would leave the Bolchaia Gate vulnerable, especially since the Tartar forces on that side had withdrawn, giving impressing a retreat. The defenders would have no choice but to spread their forces thin, as Ogareff had calculated.

The autumn day of October 5th marked a critical turning point. Within just twenty-four hours, the Emir would seize control of Eastern Siberia's capital, while Ivan Ogareff would capture the Grand Duke himself. Anticipation hung heavy in the air as the conspirators completed their preparations, knowing Irkutsk's fate would be decided by tomorrow.

The Angara camp buzzed with unusual activity throughout the day. Those watching from the palace windows could observe significant military preparations across the river. Tartar forces streamed toward the camp, bolstering the Emir's army with each passing hour. This military display, staged to intimidate those under siege, unfolded before their watchful eyes, with the glint of weapons and armor visible even at a distance.

The menacing warning came from Ogareff, who alerted the Grand Duke about an imminent assault. According to his intelligence, enemy forces planned to strike from positions above and below the town. Based on this information, he advised the Duke to bolster defenses at these vulnerable points, emphasizing the gravity of the threat with chosen words and grave expressions. Following a strategic meeting in the palace war room, military commanders issued directives to focus their defensive efforts along the Angara's banks and at the town's extremities, where earthen fortifications guarded the river. Redeploying troops began, with soldiers hurrying through the streets to their new positions as the afternoon shadows lengthened across Irkutsk.

Ogareff's plan aligned with his intentions. While he expected some defenders would remain at the Bolchaia Gate, he counted on their numbers being minimal. His strategy was twofold: create such a significant diversion that the Grand Duke would have no choice but to commit all his forces to counter it, and unleash a catastrophe so terrible that it would shatter the morale of those under siege. A cruel smile played across his face as he contemplated the chaos that would soon unfold.

The people and soldiers of Irkutsk remained vigilant throughout the day, their nerves taut with anticipation. They had implemented defensive measures to guard against attacks on unthreatened areas, fortifying walls and establishing new observation posts at strategic points. The Grand Duke and General Voranzoff made their rounds, reinforcing positions through their directives and offering words of encouragement to boost troop morale. Under Wassili Fedor's command, forces held the northern section of the town, ready to respond wherever the threat was most severe, with scouts positioned at regular intervals to relay signals at the first sign of enemy movement. They positioned their limited artillery to defend the Angara's right bank, rationing their precious ammunition for maximum effect. These preparations, executed in good time following Ivan Ogareff's timely warning, offered reasonable hope of withstanding the impending assault. Should they repel the Tartars, the discouraged attackers would postpone further attempts on the town for some days. Meanwhile, reinforcements dispatched to aid the Grand Duke could arrive at any moment, their approach watched for by lookouts stationed in the highest towers. Irkutsk's fate hung in the balance, with the lives of thousands resting on the outcome of the coming battle.

The sun had risen at 5:40 AM and set at 5:40 PM, spending eleven hours traversing the sky. As dusk settled in, it would wage a two-hour battle with nightfall before complete darkness enveloped the landscape. With cloudy skies and no moon in sight, the intense darkness would work to Ivan Ogareff's advantage, providing ideal cover for his forces to maneuver undetected.

The bitter cold of recent days had heralded the onset of Siberia's harsh winter, and tonight's frost was biting, with temperatures plummeting well below freezing. Along the Angara's banks, Russian soldiers maintained their concealed positions without fires for warmth, enduring the brutal temperature while their breath formed frozen clouds in the air. In the river below them, massive ice chunks drifted with the current, a steady procession that had continued throughout the day between the shorelines, their grinding and cracking creating an eerie symphony in the growing darkness.

The Grand Duke and his commanders viewed this development as helpful, studying the river's conditions from their elevated position in the town. If the Angara's channel remained blocked, crossing would be impossible. The Tartars could not deploy either rafts or boats through the treacherous maze of ice. Even crossing on ice was out of the question, as the thin, newly-formed ice sheet couldn't support the weight of an attacking force without shattering into deadly fragments that would plunge soldiers into the freezing waters below.

While this situation seemed to benefit Irkutsk's defenders, Ogareff showed no signs of concern. Being a traitor, he knew the Tartars did not intend to cross the Angara, and their activities there were a diversionary tactic, designed to draw attention away from their true objectives.

As evening approached ten o'clock, the river's condition underwent an unexpected transformation, much to the amazement and misfortune of those under siege. The impassable waterway became navigable, as if nature itself had conspired against the city's defense. The Angara's channel had cleared; where countless ice blocks had been drifting by for days, now only five or six remained between the shores, bobbing in the dark waters. Upon noticing this striking change, Russian officers informed the Grand Duke, theorizing that the ice had likely accumulated at a narrow section of the Angara upstream, creating a natural dam that trapped the deadly flow of ice fragments.

The Russians knew they were exposed. With the Angara crossing now accessible to the enemy forces, they had every reason to maintain heightened vigilance. Guards doubled their patrols along the riverbank, torches were lit to better monitor the water's surface, and soldiers stood ready at their posts, knowing that each passing moment could bring an assault from across the cleared channel.

Midnight struck without incident. Silence reigned beyond the Bolchaia Gate on the Eastern front. Low-hanging clouds and dense forest merged, making an impenetrable darkness. Meanwhile, flickering lights dotted the Angara encampment, showing significant troop movements. For about a mile upstream and downstream from where the fortification met the riverbank, a low rumble suggested Tartar forces were mobilizing, awaiting their orders. Another hour crept by without incident, marked only by the occasional howl of winter winds through the trees.

The massive cathedral bell in Irkutsk was moments away from tolling 2 AM, yet the enemy forces showed no signs of launching their attack. Growing uncertainty crept through the ranks of the Grand Duke and his commanders, their breath visible in the frigid night air as they consulted in hushed tones. Had they misread the Tartars' intentions of a surprise assault on the city? Combat noise, the crack of rifles from forward positions and the screech of artillery shells overhead filled previous nights. But now, an eerie silence prevailed, broken only by the crunch of snow beneath patrolling soldiers' boots and the distant crack of river ice. The officers maintained their vigilance, prepared to issue commands as the situation developed, their hands never far from their weapons as they scanned the darkness beyond the fortifications.

Ogareff's quarters comprised a spacious ground-floor chamber within the palace, with tall windows that opened onto a side terrace. A short walk along this frost-covered terrace offered sweeping views of the flowing river below, its dark waters churning against ice-crusted banks.

The room lay shrouded in complete darkness as Ogareff stood vigil by the window, his breath disturbing the stillness as he waited for the precise moment to execute his plan. He alone held the power to give the crucial signal. His strategy was clear: once the signal drew most of Irkutsk's defenders to the assaulted areas, he would slip away from the palace like a shadow and make his way to the Bolchaia Gate. Should he find it unprotected, he would throw it open to the waiting forces; if not, he would guide the overwhelming force of attackers against its meager defense, ensuring swift victory.

He lurked in the darkness like a predator poised to attack, muscles tense with anticipation. before two o'clock, the Grand Duke requested Michael Strogoff, the only name by which they knew Ivan Ogareff. An aide-de-camp arrived at the closed door and called out, his voice echoing through the empty corridor.

Ogareff, standing motionless by the window and concealed in the shadows, remained silent, a cruel smile playing at the corners of his mouth. Palace staff were unconcerned by the Czar's missing courier, a fact duly reported to the Grand Duke.

At two o'clock, deep chimes resonated through the palace halls from the clock. It was time to start the planned diversion with the Tartars awaiting the signal to attack. Ivan Ogareff threw open the window with practiced stealth and positioned himself at the northern corner of the side terrace, his movements deliberate and controlled.

From high above, Ogareff watched the churning waters of the Angara River below, its dark surface reflecting the scattered moonlight like shards of broken glass. He retrieved a match from his coat pocket, struck it against the rough stone balustrade, (a **stone railing or protective barrier**) and used its flickering flame to ignite a small bundle of tow that had been bathed in priming powder. With calculated precision born of meticulous planning, he cast it into the rushing current, tracking its descent with cold satisfaction.

Ogareff, in his cruelty, had the river's surface slicked with oil, the rainbow sheen a testament to his merciless act. The region above Irkutsk was rich with naphtha springs, along the right bank between Poshkavsk suburb and the main town, a natural resource that would now serve as an instrument of destruction. Ogareff had seized control of the massive storage tanks containing the flammable liquid, positioning his men to guard them days before. A simple breach in the reservoir walls, executed under cover of darkness, was all it took to release torrents of oil into the river, his chosen weapon to set Irkutsk ablaze and bring chaos to its streets.

They executed the operation earlier that night, explaining why the raft bearing the genuine Imperial Messenger, Nadia, and the escapees now drifted upon a stream of petroleum. The precious fuel gushed from massive storage tanks through their ruptured walls, cascading downhill until it reached the river. There it formed a floating layer, buoyed by its natural buoyancy, spreading an iridescent sheen across the water's surface. Such were the ruthless tactics of Ivan Ogareff, a traitor who, in league with the Tartars, employed their savage methods against his own people with calculated precision!

Flaming oil spread across the Angara River's surface, igniting with the speed of lightning as if the water itself were pure alcohol. Blue fire raced between the riverbanks, sending spirals of vapor skyward, the heat so intense it scorched the air itself. The few remaining ice chunks, caught in the burning liquid, dissolved like wax over intense heat, releasing sharp hisses of steam that mixed with the acrid smoke billowing above.

artillery fire erupted from both the northern and southern edges of the town. Enemy guns blazed, their thunderous reports echoing across the water, while thousands of Tartar soldiers charged toward the fortifications with savage war cries. Wooden buildings along the riverbank burst into flames everywhere, their ancient timbers crackling and splintering in the inferno, and the night's darkness vanished in the brilliant conflagration that painted the sky an apocalyptic orange.

"Victory at last!" Ivan Ogareff exclaimed, his voice carrying the weight of weeks of careful manipulation and deceit.

His satisfaction was well-earned. The diversionary tactic he had orchestrated was devastating. Irkutsk's defenders now faced an impossible choice between repelling the Tartar assault and battling the raging inferno. Church bells pealed through the chaos as every able citizen rushed either to defend against the attackers or to fight the spreading flames that threatened to consume the entire city. The screams of panic and shouted orders merged into a cacophony of terror.

The Bolchaia Gate stood unprotected. Following Ogareff's cunning proposal, crafted to deflect suspicion by making it appear motivated, only a skeleton crew of guards remained, selected from among the exiles' small contingent. He had convinced the military command these men would fight with particular zeal to prove their loyalty, knowing full well they would be defeated within minutes.

Ogareff stepped back into his chamber, which was now bathed in an eerie glow from the burning Angara River. The dancing orange light cast grotesque shadows across the walls, reflecting his own twisted triumph. As he prepared to depart, the door burst open, revealing a woman with soaked garments and disheveled hair, her silhouette stark against the hallway's darkness.

"Sangarre!" he blurted out, assuming only the gypsy woman would dare enter his quarters . His hand moved toward the weapon at his belt, a habit born of years of treachery.

But he was mistaken, it was Nadia who stood before him, her face flushed with urgency and determination!

Earlier, when the flames had raced across the river's surface like a demonic serpent, Nadia had cried out in terror. In that moment, Michael had wrapped his powerful arms around her and plunged them both into the frigid depths of the river, seeking shelter from the encroaching fire. An ice floe carried them, drifting and spinning through the current to within thirty fathoms of Irkutsk's nearest quay, the flames reflecting off the black water around them.

After diving under the water one last time to avoid a burning patch of oil, Michael guided Nadia to safety on the quay, both of them gasping and shivering in their drenched clothes. At last, Michael Strogoff had completed his mission, he had made it to Irkutsk, though not in the manner he had ever expected!

"We must get to the governor's palace!" he told Nadia, helping her to her feet with trembling hands.

They rushed through the chaos-filled streets, dodging panicked citizens and falling debris, reaching the palace entrance within ten minutes. Though flames from the Angara River leapt against the palace walls like hungry crimson fingers, the sturdy stone structure remained unscathed. However, the wooden buildings along the riverbank were not so fortunate, they had erupted into an inferno, their structures crackling and groaning as they surrendered to the relentless fire.

The grand palace stood with its doors wide open, allowing Michael and Nadia to slip inside unnoticed. Their wet clothes attracted no attention amid the chaos within, droplets pooling beneath their feet on the polished marble floors. The vast ground floor hall teemed with activity, officers rushing to receive commands and soldiers hurrying to carry them out, their boots echoing against the high ceiling. In the swirling crowd of uniforms and stressed faces, Michael and Nadia found themselves pulled apart by the surging mass of bodies.

Frantic, Nadia raced through the corridors, calling out for Michael while trying to find her way to the Grand Duke. Her heart pounded against her ribs as she navigated the maze-like passages. Suddenly, a lit doorway appeared before her, golden light spilling onto the hallway floor. She rushed inside, only to freeze in horror, her blood turning to ice, there stood the very man she had encountered at Ichim and glimpsed again in Tomsk. The traitor whose treacherous actions would soon deliver the town to its enemies now stood mere feet away, face to face with her, his cold eyes widening in recognition.

"Ivan Ogareff!" Her voice pierced the air like a blade.

The man froze at the sound of his name, his shoulders tensing beneath his uniform. With his true identity exposed, everything he had plotted would crumble into dust. Only one option remained: silence the one who spoke it. He lunged at Nadia with the speed of a striking snake, but she pressed herself against the wall, brandishing a knife with unwavering determination, its blade catching the lamplight.

"Ivan Ogareff!" Nadia shouted again, her voice stronger this time, knowing the despised name would bring someone to her aid. The words echoed down the corridor like a death knell.

"Silence!" the traitor snarled through gritted teeth, spittle flying from his lips in his fury.

"Ivan Ogareff!" For the third time, she called out, her voice strengthened tenfold by pure hatred, each syllable ringing with years of accumulated loathing.

Blind with rage, Ogareff yanked a jeweled dagger from his belt and charged at her with murderous intent, forcing her to back into a corner. The cold stone walls pressed against her spine as death approached. Just as hope seemed lost, an unstoppable force seized the villain and slammed him to the floor with bone-jarring force.

"Michael!" Nadia cried out, relief flooding her voice.

Michael Strogoff burst into the room, having followed Nadia's desperate cry through the winding corridors. He had located Ivan Ogareff's quarters by tracking her voice, his keen hearing compensating for his blindness as he arrived through the doorway that stood ajar, his breath coming in controlled bursts.

"Stay calm, Nadia," he said, positioning himself as a shield between her and Ogareff, his stance betraying years of military training.

"Brother, watch out!" Nadia exclaimed in alarm, her heart pounding. "He has a weapon, and unlike you, he can see!"

Ogareff rose to his feet, brushing dust from his uniform as a smirk crossed his face. He sized up his blind opponent with predatory satisfaction. Confident in his advantage, he lunged at Michael with lethal precision. But in one swift motion, the blind man caught Ogareff's armed hand with uncanny accuracy, wrenched away his weapon with crushing force, and sent him crashing to the floor with a thunderous impact.

Ogareff's face flushed with fury and humiliation as he recalled the weapon at his side. Drawing his sword with a metallic hiss, he lunged forward again. His opponent was sightless, this would be an easy victory over a mere blind man! The thought of being bested by someone so handicapped made his blood boil with rage.

Nadia, watching in horror as her companion faced this deadly threat, rushed toward the door, crying out for help. Her fingers fumbled with the heavy latch as panic threatened to overwhelm her.

"Keep the door shut, Nadia!" Michael commanded, his voice cutting through the tension like steel. "Stay silent, I need no help! This scoundrel poses no danger to the Czar's courier today! If he has the courage, let him attack, I stand ready!" His words carried an authority that seemed to freeze the very air in the room.

Ogareff coiled himself like a tiger preparing to attack, moving in complete silence. He masked even his breathing, determined that the blind man would not detect his presence. His boots ghosted across the wooden floor as he circled his prey. His goal was to deliver a fatal strike before his opponent could sense him approaching, his sword gleaming in the dim light.

Nadia observed the dramatic scene with a mix of horror and awe, finding herself confident despite her fear. Michael's composure seemed to flow into her like a calming wave. Though armed with only his Siberian knife and unable to see his adversary's sword, Michael appeared to have divine protection on his side. Remarkably, how he stayed aligned with the sword's point while moving, his head cocked as if listening to some invisible guide.

Ogareff observed his peculiar opponent with unmistakable unease, his fingers tightening around the sword's hilt. The blind man's extraordinary composure unsettled him, defying all logic and expectation. Though his rational mind insisted that he held every advantage in this mismatched duel, his adversary's stillness left him chilled to the marrow. He had already chosen his target, decided where to strike, mapping out the killing blow in his mind. Yet something held him back from dispatching this sightless challenger, an inexplicable hesitation that gnawed at his confidence.

Finally, he lunged forward with practiced precision, thrusting his blade straight at Michael's heart in what should have been an unstoppable attack. With the slightest motion of his knife, more than a twitch, the blind man deflected the attack as if swatting away an annoying insect. Michael remained untouched, his stance unwavering, waiting for Ogareff's next strike like a statue carved from living stone.

Beads of cold sweat dotted Ogareff's forehead as he stumbled backward, his boots scraping against the floor, only to surge forward again with renewed desperation. But just like his first strike, this second assault proved futile against his opponent's supernatural defense. The knife had deflected the blow from his ineffective blade, the metallic ring of their weapons echoing through the space between them.

Consumed by a mixture of fury and dread before this immobile figure, he found himself transfixed by the blind man's wide-open eyes, unable to look away from their milky depths. Though these eyes couldn't see him, were incapable of sight, they seemed to bore into the depths of his soul with terrifying accuracy, holding him in their terrible, mesmerizing grip. It was as if those sightless orbs could perceive something far beyond mere physical presence, reading the very essence of his being.

Suddenly, Ogareff let out a piercing shriek that echoed off the stone walls. Understanding struck him like lightning, freezing his blood. "He can see!" he screamed, his voice cracking with hysteria, "He can see!" Like a cornered predator seeking escape, he retreated step by step toward the room's far end, gripped by overwhelming terror, his boots scraping against the floor.

The statue sprang to life as the blind man strode toward Ivan Ogareff, each footfall deliberate and menacing. Standing before him, mere inches from his face, he declared with cold precision, "I can see! I see the scar from the knout (a **harsh, heavy whip**) I struck you with, you treacherous coward! The mark of your shame is plain as day! And I see where I shall strike you now! Draw your weapon! I grant you the honor of a duel! Your sword against my knife!"

"He can see!" Nadia gasped, clutching her hands to her chest. "Could it be possible?" Her words hung in the tension-filled air.

Ogareff, realizing his doom was at hand, summoned every ounce of courage and lunged at his unflinching opponent with a desperate snarl. Their blades met in a shower of sparks, but with one precise movement of Michael's knife, guided by the skilled hand of the Siberian hunter, the sword shattered into glittering pieces. In the next instant, Ogareff crumpled to the ground with a dull thud, his heart pierced, his life extinguished, his face forever frozen in an expression of disbelief.

The door burst open with a resounding crash. The Grand Duke strode in with his officers behind him, their boots clicking on the wooden floor as they halted at the entrance. As he moved forward with measured steps, his eyes fell upon the lifeless form on the floor, the very man he had believed to be the Czar's messenger, now lying in a widening pool of crimson.

"Who handles this death?" he demanded, his voice sharp with anger, his hand gripping the hilt of his ceremonial sword.

"I am," Michael stated, standing tall and unwavering.

One officer pressed a pistol against Michael's temple, the cold steel contacting a metallic click.

"Tell me your name," the Grand Duke commanded, his face flushed with fury, moments away from ordering the man's execution.

"Your Highness," Michael replied, meeting the Duke's gaze without flinching, "perhaps you should instead ask about the identity of the man lying dead before you."

"I already know that man! He serves my brother! He carries messages for the Czar!" the Duke thundered, his voice filling the chamber.

"Your Highness, you are mistaken. This man is no royal courier. This is Ivan Ogareff!"

"Ivan Ogareff!" The Grand Duke's voice echoed with shock, his face draining of color as the implications dawned on him.

"Yes, Ivan the Traitor!"

"Then who in heaven's name are you?" the Duke whispered, taking an unconscious step backward.

"I am Michael Strogoff!" The declaration rang through the room with unmistakable authority.

Chapter Fifteen

CONCLUSION Modern English

Michael Strogoff's eyes had never been burned. A remarkable occurrence, involving both mental and physical aspects, had prevented the searing blade wielded by Feofar's executioner from harming his vision. An extraordinary twist of fate had rendered the white-hot sword that should have destroyed his sight powerless.

During the execution, his mother Marfa Strogoff had been present, reaching out toward her son. Michael had looked at her with the intense love of a son believing he was seeing his mother for the last time. Her anguished face, etched with terror and despair, had stirred emotions so profound within him they manifested. Though his pride fought against it, tears welled up from his heart and gathered beneath his eyelids. As these tears evaporated across his corneas, they created a protective barrier. The vapor from his tears, forming between the glowing sword and his eyes, neutralized the blade's burning effect. This phenomenon mirrors what happens when metalworkers dip their hands in water vapor before handling molten iron, a principle known as the Leidenfrost effect that had saved his sight.

Realizing the peril he faced if his secret was revealed, Michael grasped that his safety depended on absolute silence. The Tartars would execute him immediately if they learned their punishment had failed. Yet he also recognized an opportunity, his apparent sightlessness could serve as the perfect cover for his mission. Since others believed him blind, they would grant him freedom of movement, considering him harmless and defeated. This meant he had to maintain the deception, fooling everyone including Nadia, and never letting his guard down for even a moment. Having weighed his options, he committed to risking everything to convince all who crossed his path that he could not see. The masterful way he carried out this deception proved his remarkable dedication, as he learned to rely on his other senses and move as though sightless, all while observing everything around him.

Only one person knew the reality of his situation, his mother, to whom he had confessed the truth during their reunion in Tomsk, as he embraced her in the darkness and covered her face with tender kisses. In that intimate moment, he had allowed himself this one breach of his careful deception, unable to maintain the pretense before the woman who had given him life.

Michael had read the Imperial letter when Ogareff displayed it before his eyes, the same eyes Ogareff wrongly believed he had destroyed. The letter revealed the traitor's vile schemes, explaining Michael's extraordinary determination throughout the latter half of his journey. It was the reason he felt such an overwhelming need to reach Irkutsk and deliver his message in person. He had learned the devastating truth: the town would be betrayed, and the Grand Duke's life was in grave danger. The fate of both the Czar's brother and all of Siberia now rested in his hands. Every step, every moment of pretended blindness had led to this crucial revelation.

Michael related the tale to the Grand Duke, his voice trembling with emotion as he described Nadia's crucial role in their journey. He spoke of her unwavering loyalty and courage, qualities that had proven invaluable throughout their perilous adventure.

"Tell me of this young woman," the Grand Duke inquired, intrigued by the remarkable companion who had aided the Czar's courier.

"She is Wassili Fedor's daughter, the exile," Michael explained, his voice filled with respect and admiration for his faithful traveling companion.

"Captain Fedor's daughter," the Grand Duke corrected him, "is no exile's child any longer. Irkutsk has no more exiles within its walls." His words carried the weight of authority and the promise of redemption for those who had served the city in its time of need.

Overwhelmed by joy after enduring so much sorrow, Nadia sank to her knees before the Grand Duke, her eyes brimming with grateful tears. He helped her rise with one hand while extending his other to Michael, a gesture that symbolized the integrity of their shared triumph over adversity.

Within the hour, Nadia was embracing her father at last, their tears mingling as they held each other close. Reuniting Michael Strogoff, Nadia, and Wassili Fedor marked the pinnacle of happiness for them all, their long journey complete after countless trials and tribulations that had tested their very souls.

The Tartars' two-pronged assault on the town had failed, their military strategy proving no match for the defenders' determination. At the Bolchaia Gate, Wassili Fedor and his small but resolute contingent repelled the initial wave of attackers, fighting with the fierce dedication of those protecting their homeland. Fedor had stayed and defend this position through sound military intuition, which proved to be the right decision as the battle unfolded.

Meanwhile, the townspeople got the fire under control through their coordinated efforts and unwavering resolve. The naphtha fuel burned across the water's surface, creating an eerily beautiful but dangerous spectacle, and the citizens' quick response contained the flames to the waterfront buildings, sparing the rest of the town from damage. Before dawn broke, Feofar-Khan's forces retreated to their encampment in disarray, leaving many casualties strewn across and beneath the town's defensive walls, a grim testament to the cost of their failed siege.

Sangarre, the gypsy who had tried to reach Ivan Ogareff, was among those who perished, her body discovered near the water's edge where she had fallen during the chaos of battle.

The attackers halted their assaults for two days, their morale shattered by Ogareff's death. He had been the driving force behind the invasion, the only one whose laid schemes could unite and motivate the khans and their warriors to attempt conquering Asiatic Russia. Without his strategic mind and manipulative influence, the various tribal factions began showing signs of discord and uncertainty.

Though Irkutsk's defenders remained vigilant and the siege persisted, dawn on October 7th brought the thunderous sound of cannon fire from the surrounding heights. This was General Kisselef's relief force announcing its arrival to the Grand Duke, their artillery echoing across the valley in a welcome symphony of salvation.

The Tartars chose not to await an assault. Unwilling to risk engaging in combat near Irkutsk's fortifications, they dismantled their encampment along the Angara, leaving behind supplies and equipment in their haste to avoid being caught between the city's defenders and the approaching relief force. At last, Irkutsk found itself free from siege, its citizens emerging to survey the abandoned battlefield.

Among the first Russian troops to enter the city were two of Michael's companions, the ever-united Blount and Jolivet. They had managed their escape by crossing the Angara's frozen surface before flames could engulf their makeshift raft, crawling and sliding across the treacherous ice while dodging burning debris. Alcide Jolivet later recorded this close call in his journal with characteristic wit: "ended up like a lemon in a bowl of punch!" His British colleague noted it as "a rather sporting adventure."

The group was overjoyed to discover that Nadia and Michael had survived unharmed, and especially relieved to learn that their courageous friend had not lost his sight. Harry Blount made a notable observation in his records: "Even red-hot iron sometimes cannot destroy the function of the optic nerve." Jolivet, not to be outdone, added his own flourish: "The eyes of a true Russian patriot cannot be dimmed."

After settling in Irkutsk, the two journalists focused on organizing their travel notes and experiences. They spent long evenings by candlelight, comparing observations and cross-referencing details. They sent detailed articles to London and Paris about the Tartar invasion, and, their accounts aligned, with no contradictions even in the smallest details. Their editors, long accustomed to their fierce competition, were shocked by this unprecedented collaboration.

The Emir and his allies suffered a string of defeats in the remaining days of the campaign. Like all who dared challenge the mighty Russian Empire, their invasion proved disastrous. The Czar's forces encircled them and reclaimed each captured town, pushing the invaders back across the steppes they had traversed months before. Nature itself turned against the invaders as a brutal winter descended, with temperatures plummeting far below zero. The bitter cold claimed countless lives, leaving only a handful of survivors to make the long journey back to their Tartar homeland, their dreams of conquest shattered like ice beneath the winter sun.

With the Ural Mountain passage to Irkutsk now cleared, the Grand Duke prepared to return to Moscow. However, he postponed his departure to attend a moving ceremony scheduled after Russian forces had retaken the city, one that would mark the beginning of a new chapter for two of the journey's most valiant survivors.

Michael Strogoff approached Nadia and, with her father present, asked her: "Sister Nadia, when you departed from Riga for Irkutsk, did you leave behind any regrets besides missing your mother?" His voice was gentle but carried an undercurrent of nervous anticipation.

"None whatsoever," Nadia replied, her clear eyes meeting his without hesitation.

"So your heart holds no attachments there?"

"None, brother," she answered, a slight tremor in her voice betraying her growing awareness of his meaning.

"Then, Nadia," Michael continued, his weathered face softening with emotion, "I believe God brought us together and guided us through these trials because He intended us to share our lives forever." His words hung in the crisp air between them, weighted with promise.

"Oh!" exclaimed Nadia, embracing Michael with the same fearless devotion she had shown throughout their perilous journey. She turned to Wassili Fedor, blushing, and said, "Father..." Her voice trailed off, filled with hope and seeking blessing.

"Nadia," Captain Fedor responded, clasping both their hands in his, "nothing would bring me greater happiness than to call you both my children!"

They held their wedding ceremony in the grand cathedral of Irkutsk, its golden domes gleaming in the winter sunlight. The same bells that had once warned of danger now rang out in celebration, their joyous peals echoing through the streets.

Jolivet and Blount attended the ceremony, intending to report on it for their respective readers, though for once their competitive spirits were subdued by the solemnity of the occasion.

"Doesn't this make you want to follow their example?" Alcide asked his companion, elbowing him as they watched the newlyweds emerge from the cathedral.

"Bah!" Blount responded, adjusting his collar with affected indifference. "Now, if I had a cousin like yours..."

"My cousin isn't available for marriage!" Alcide interrupted with a laugh, his eyes twinkling with mischief at their old joke.

"Ah, that's even better," said Blount, pulling out his notebook with sudden interest. "Word is there's tension brewing between London and Peking. Wouldn't you like to see the situation firsthand?"

"By heaven!" Alcide Jolivet burst out, already reaching for his own well-worn notebook, "I was about to suggest the same thing!"

And so these two inseparable companions, their competitive friendship as strong as ever, embarked on their journey to China, eager for their next grand adventure in the vast Asian continent.

Several days after the festivities, Michael and Nadia Strogoff, with Wassili Fedor by their side, began their journey back to Europe. The path that had brought such hardship on their outward journey now brought only joy on their return. They moved in a sleigh that glided like a speeding train across Siberia's ice-covered steppes, the frozen landscape sparkling beneath bright winter sunlight.

The group paused their journey at the Dinka's edge, just short of Birskoe. There, Michael located the burial site of their dear friend Nicholas. They placed a cross to mark his last resting place, and Nadia offered a solemn prayer for their loyal companion whose memory would forever live in their hearts. As they stood in reverent silence, snowflakes fell around them, as if nature itself were paying tribute to the brave man who had sacrificed everything to help them complete their mission. Before departing, Michael placed his hand on the wooden cross and whispered a quiet promise to honor Nicholas's courage by living the life of peace they had all fought so hard to secure.

In Omsk, they found Michael's mother Marfa waiting at the Strogoff family home, her weathered face beaming with joy through tears of relief. She embraced Nadia with overwhelming affection, having long considered her a daughter in her heart, and pulled both young people close as if afraid they might disappear again. On this momentous day, the resilient Siberian woman could acknowledge her son and declare her pride in all he had achieved, no longer forced to hide their connection from prying eyes.

Several days after their stay in Omsk, Michael and Nadia crossed into Europe, leaving behind the vast steppes that had witnessed their extraordinary journey. When Wassili Fedor made his home in St. Petersburg, his children remained close by, establishing themselves in a comfortable residence within walking distance, venturing out only to visit their elderly mother in her cozy Siberian cottage.

The Czar welcomed the brave courier into his service with grand ceremony, appointing him as a personal attendant and giving to him the Cross of St. George in recognition of his unwavering loyalty. As years passed, Michael Strogoff climbed to prominent positions within the Empire, his wisdom and courage serving Russia. Yet it is not his tale of achievement that merits telling, but the story of his hardships and ordeals, a testament to the strength of the human spirit in the face of insurmountable odds.

Epilogue

Michael Strogoff Books I & II

The Horizon of Duty

Irkutsk, Siberia, Twenty Years Later

The frost-laden winds of Siberia still whispered Michael Strogoff's name. To the villagers, he remained the "Courier of Iron," the man who had defied betrayal, blindness, and Tartar savagery to deliver the Czar's warning and save a nation. Yet in the quiet of his stone-hewn home overlooking the Angara River, Michael was simply a husband, a father, and a keeper of stories. Beside him, Nadia Fedor, now Nadia Strogoff, traced the lines of a map unfurled on their oak table, a gift from the Czar himself, its edges gilt with imperial insignia. Their children, dark-haired and sharp-eyed, played by the hearth, their laughter a testament to a peace hard-won.

The Czar's gratitude had been lavish: lands, titles, and a medal struck in Michael's honor. But the courier had asked only for a quiet post in Irkutsk, where he might serve as steward of the frontier he had bled to protect. Siberia, once a jagged tapestry of peril, now hummed with telegraph lines and nascent railways, threads of progress stitched by a regime eager to solidify its grasp. The Emir's rebellion had been crushed, his ambitions buried in the ashes of his own fortresses, but the memory of those flames lingered in Michael's dreams.

Historians would later write of this era as a fulcrum: the moment Russia's eastward march turned inexorable. Scholars marveled at how a single man's resolve had safeguarded Irkutsk, the linchpin of the empire's defenses. Yet in their monographs, they often overlooked the woman who had guided him through darkness. Nadia's diaries, discovered decades later, told a quieter truth, of fear dispelled not by valor alone, but by the unyielding grip of two hands clasped in trust.

On the outskirts of Moscow, a marble monument now stood, engraved with names of those who had perished in the Tartar revolt. Among them, Ivan Ogareff's was etched in smaller script, a cipher of infamy. The Czar, it was said, visited it once, his face unreadable as snow. His reign had grown heavier, tempered by the knowledge that loyalty was as fragile as it was vital.

As twilight draped Irkutsk in gold, Michael walked the riverbank, his steps sure, his gaze, restored by surgeons years prior, fixed on the horizon. Nadia joined him, her arm threaded through his. "Do you ever wonder," she asked, "what might have become of us if we'd faltered?" He smiled, the scar on his brow softening. "We did not falter. And so, the world turned."

In St. Petersburg, engineers drafted plans for a railroad that would one day span the continent, binding east to west. They called it the Trans-Siberian, a steel artery through the wilderness Michael had once crossed on horseback. Progress, he mused, was its own kind of courier.

**** From the journals of Pyotr Vassiliev, Imperial Historian, 1891**

Also by...

Juan José Piedra

The Dreamscape 2032 Steampunk Stillness Project

<u>Pre-Orders Coming Soon</u> Where You Can Witness the Birth of Legends!

In the Age of Steam, the first dreamers dared to defy the earthbound chains of fate.

From coal and gear, spring and fire, they carved a path into the unknown, igniting an unstoppable journey that would stretch beyond the stars. Now, in a sweeping eight-book saga, **Juan José Piedra** unveils the epic chronicle of a civilization's ascent from humble beginnings to celestial destiny.

Across these novellas, heroes are forged in the fires of invention, secret protector races awaken from the ashes of forgotten wars, and the vast, hidden architecture of the cosmos reveals itself to those brave enough to seek it.

In this legendary series, you will find:

- **Worlds Reborn**: Steam-powered cities, lost technologies, and celestial frontiers.

- **Champions of Destiny**: Inventors, rebels, explorers, and guardians who defy the odds.
- **A Tapestry of Wonders**: From the tick of the first clockwork heart to the hum of quantum drives.
- **The Eternal Struggle**: Between freedom and control, vision and destruction, hope and despair.

The spark of invention becomes the flame of destiny. The flame becomes a beacon across the void.

Be part of the Legendary Epic Saga! Pre-Orders Coming Soon!

Coming soon to all major bookstores & digital platforms including Book.io on the Cardano Blockchain!

Juan José Piedra

Forging Legends in the Age of Steam and Stars

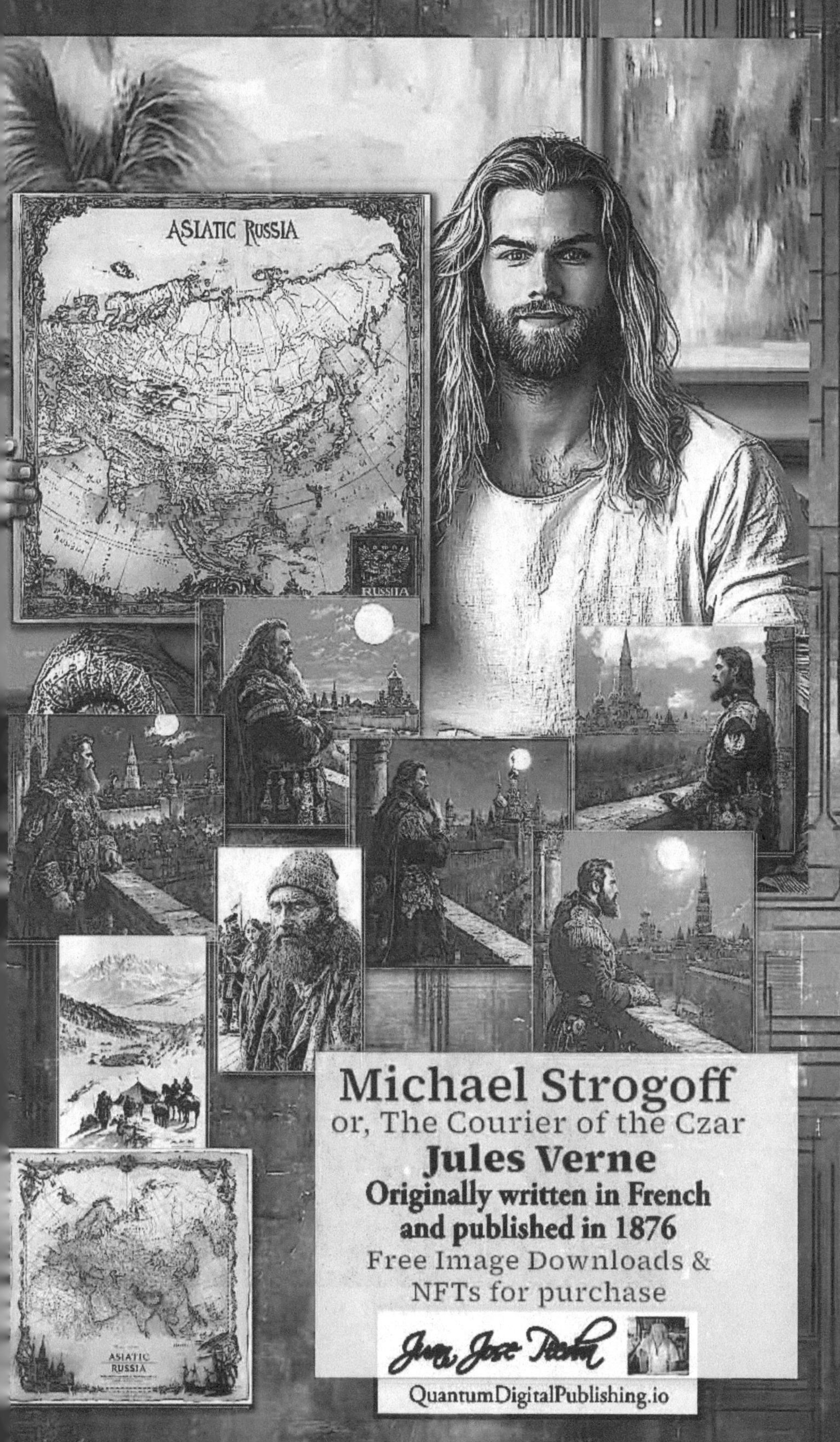
ASIATIC RUSSIA
RUSSIA
Michael Strogoff
or, The Courier of the Czar
Jules Verne
Originally written in French
and published in 1876
Free Image Downloads &
NFTs for purchase
QuantumDigitalPublishing.io
ASIATIC
RUSSIA

About Jules Verne

Michael Strogoff I & II

Jules Verne

Jules Verne, one of the "fathers of science fiction," is renowned for his imaginative and scientifically plausible stories that have captivated readers for generations. Michael Strogoff, or the Courier of the Czar is a prime example of his mastery in blending historical accuracy with thrilling adventure.

Set in the late 19th century during the reign of Tsar Alexander II, the novel takes place in a Russia on the brink of turmoil. The political landscape is fraught with tension, particularly in the Siberian provinces, where a rebellion led by the traitor Ivan Ogareff threatens the stability of the empire.

The story follows Michael Strogoff, a dedicated courier summoned by the Czar to deliver a crucial message to his brother, the Grand Duke, in Irkutsk. Strogoff's journey is fraught with danger, as he must navigate through a war-torn landscape filled with physical and emotional challenges. The narrative explores themes of loyalty, sacrifice, and the resilience of the human spirit, making it a compelling read for fans of historical fiction and adventure.

Verne's writing style is characterized by vivid descriptions and a sense of urgency that keeps readers engaged. Michael Strogoff is a testament to his ability to create a rich and immersive world that resonates with contemporary readers. The book's enduring appeal lies in its timeless themes and the universal human experiences it portrays.

As you embark on this journey with Michael Strogoff, prepare to be transported to a world of intrigue, danger, and heroism. May this classic tale of courage and loyalty inspire and entertain you as it has countless readers before you.

Enjoy your adventure through the pages of Michael Strogoff, or the Courier of the Czar.

Michael Strogoff (Originally written in French in 1876) is an adventure novel set in the vast expanse of the Russian Empire during a fictionalized Tartar rebellion. Though often published as a single volume, some editions split the story into two parts. Below is a consolidated summary of the two-book structure brilliantly written by **Jules Verne**:

Book ONE: The Mission

The story begins in Moscow, where **Michael Strogoff**, a fearless Siberian-born courier for Tsar Alexander II, is entrusted with a critical mission: to warn the governor of Irkutsk, the Tsar's brother, of an impending invasion by Tartar forces led by the ruthless **Feofar Khan** and his traitorous ally, **Ivan Ogareff** (a disgraced Russian officer). The rebellion threatens to sever Siberia from Moscow and overthrow imperial rule.

Michael departs immediately, traveling across Siberia via the Ural Mountains and the vast steppes. Along the way, he meets **Nadia Fedor**, a young Lithuanian woman journeying to join her exiled father in Irkutsk. The two form a bond, and Nadia becomes his steadfast companion.

Their journey grows perilous as Tartar forces, aided by Ogareff's spies, close in. Michael faces natural disasters, betrayals, and ambushes. A pivotal moment occurs when he is captured and tortured by the Tartars. To protect his mission, Michael endures a searing-hot blade that blinds him (or so it seems). Despite this, he escapes with Nadia's help, continuing toward Irkutsk under the guise of a helpless beggar.

Book TWO: The Siege and Resolution

In the second half, the Tartar army besieges Irkutsk. Unbeknownst to the defenders, Ivan Ogareff infiltrates the city disguised as a fisherman, plotting to open the gates to Feofar Khan. Meanwhile, Michael and Nadia, now reliant on her guidance due to his supposed blindness, arrive at the city's outskirts.

Michael reveals his true identity to Russian soldiers and delivers the Tsar's warning, foiling Ogareff's plans. In a climactic confrontation, Michael's "blindness" is exposed as a ruse (his eyes were saved by tears evoked during the torture). He duels Ogareff, kills him, and ensures Irkutsk's defense holds.

The rebellion collapses, and Michael is hailed as a hero. Nadia reunites with her father, and Michael returns to Moscow, honored by the Tsar. The story closes with themes of loyalty, sacrifice, and the triumph of duty over personal suffering.

Key Themes

- **Loyalty and Duty**: Michael's unwavering commitment to the Tsar and Russia.
- **Resilience**: Endurance against physical and psychological trials.
- **Deception and Betrayal**: Ogareff's treachery contrasts with Michael's integrity.
- **Imperialism**: Reflects 19th-century Russian geopolitics and colonial tensions.

Legacy

While less fantastical than Verne's other works (*20,000 Leagues*, *Around the World*), *Michael Strogoff* is celebrated for its intense pacing, historical flavor, and vivid portrayal of Siberia. It remains a classic of adventure literature, blending political intrigue with a personal odyssey of courage.

Acknowledgements

Michael Strogoff I & II

I wish to acknowledge my wife and lifelong creative partner, Jessie Keener, N.D. A remarkable woman whose wisdom, heart, and intellect have shaped every step of this journey. A Naturopathic Doctor with over 40 years of experience, Jessie brings the world into every conversation. Raised by the sea and seasoned by her early years in Brazil, she is as well-traveled as she is well-read, with thousands of books under her belt and a passion for knowledge that's truly inspiring.

A gifted communicator, Jessie hosted her own public access television show for many years, always championing truth, health, and the human spirit. She's currently working on her own powerful book: Who Will Save Our Doctors? A timely exploration of how today's medical professionals are being compromised by outdated protocols and the overwhelming influence of Big Pharma.

Her brilliance, integrity, and creative fire continue to light the way for thousands.

Glossary Of Terms

Michael Strogoff I & II

- **Hasseurs:** Likely refers to a type of mounted irregular cavalry or horsemen, possibly of Central Asian or Tartar origin, known for their skill in scouting, raiding, and engaging in guerrilla-style warfare. These riders would have been lightly armed and highly mobile, adept at navigating the vast steppes and rugged terrain of Siberia. Their role in the novel aligns with the depiction of Tartar forces, who rely on fast-moving, opportunistic cavalry units to disrupt Russian defenses and terrorize local populations.

Verne's use of such terms reflects the historical reality of Central Asian warfare, where nomadic horsemen played a crucial role in military campaigns, relying on their superior horsemanship and knowledge of the land to conduct swift attacks and strategic retreats. In the novel, such forces would have contributed to the challenges faced by Michael Strogoff on his perilous journey across Siberia.

- **Chef d'oeuvre:** Is a French expression meaning "masterpiece" or "masterwork." It is used to describe something that represents the pinnacle of skill, craftsmanship, or artistry.

In the novel, Verne may use this term either literally, referring to an exceptional work of art or craftsmanship, or figuratively, to highlight a particularly remarkable event, strategy, or achievement, perhaps in the context of military tactics, deception, or a daring feat by Michael Strogoff or his adversaries. The phrase conveys a sense of excellence and perfection in whatever it is applied to.

- **Sang Froid:** Is a French term that translates to "cold blood" in English, but it is used figuratively to mean composure, self-control, or unshakable calmness in the face of danger or crisis.

In the novel, characters like Michael Strogoff exhibit sang-froid by maintaining a steady, fearless demeanor even in life-threatening situations, such as when he faces the Tartars, endures torture, or executes his mission under extreme pressure. His ability to think clearly and act decisively, without letting emotions overwhelm him, is a defining trait of his heroism.

- **Imperturbable:** describes a person who remains calm, composed, and unshaken, even in the most difficult or dangerous situations. It refers to an unyielding steadiness of mind and an inability to be disturbed or flustered by external pressures.

Michael Strogoff himself embodies imperturbability, as he endures extreme hardships, braving the vast Siberian landscape, outmaneuvering enemies, and even facing torture, without losing his resolve. His imperturbable nature allows him to complete his mission with unwavering focus, making him a true model of resilience and self-discipline.

- **Provençals:** Refers to people from Provence, a region in southeastern France known for its distinct culture, language, and traditions. The term typically evokes imagery of lively, warm-hearted individuals, often associated with Mediterranean influences, music, and storytelling.

In the novel, Provençals might be referenced to describe a particular character's background, temperament, or expressive nature. Given Jules Verne's attention to regional characteristics, a Provençal character would likely exhibit traits such as vivid storytelling, warmth, enthusiasm, or a strong sense of identity linked to their homeland.

- **Corps Diplomatique:** Refers to the collective body of diplomats representing various nations within a foreign country or at a government's court. This term encompasses ambassadors, envoys, ministers, and other diplomatic officials responsible for managing international relations and negotiations.

Jules Verne often uses such terms to highlight the presence of high-ranking foreign representatives or to emphasize the political and strategic elements within the novel's setting. In Michael Strogoff, the "Corps Diplomatique" would likely refer to the gathering of officials, correspondents, and representatives who observe and report on events unfolding in Russia, particularly regarding the Tartar invasion and the Czar's response. Their role in the narrative underscores the political weight and international implications of the conflict.

- **Physiognomists:** Refers to individuals who study and interpret facial features and expressions to determine a person's character, emotions, or intentions.

Physiognomy was a widely accepted pseudo-science in the 19th century, based on the belief that a person's physical appearance, particularly their facial structure and expressions, could reveal their inner nature or even predict their fate. In Michael Strogoff, Verne may use this term to describe characters who observe and assess others based on their facial traits, especially in tense or strategic moments when someone's true identity, trustworthiness, or intentions are in question. This aligns with the novel's themes of deception, disguise, and the ability to read people accurately in high-stakes situations.

- **Chasseurs:** Wore the simple uniform of an officer of chasseurs of the guard - "Chasseurs" refers to a type of light cavalry or infantry soldier in the Russian or French military, known for their speed, agility, and reconnaissance abilities.

The term "chasseur" (French for "hunter") was used in European armies to denote elite troops specialized in skirmishing, scouting, and rapid movements. In the Russian context, Chasseurs were often associated with Cossacks or other mobile forces that played crucial roles in frontier defense and rapid deployment during military campaigns.

- **Facade:** Refers to the front or outward appearance of a building, often designed to be impressive or decorative.

The term can also metaphorically signify a deceptive outward appearance, where something or someone presents a false or misleading exterior to conceal true intentions or feelings. However, in the novel, it is most commonly used in its architectural sense, describing the exterior of structures in Russian cities such as Irkutsk or Moscow, which are depicted with detailed attention to their grand and imposing designs.

- **Polonaise:** Refers to a traditional Polish dance of a stately and processional nature, characterized by a moderate triple meter and elegant, flowing movements.

It can also refer to a type of music composed in the style of this dance, often used to evoke a sense of grandeur and national pride. Given

Verne's detailed descriptions of cultural elements throughout the novel, the term might appear in reference to a formal event, a piece of music played in a Russian or Polish setting, or even as an allusion to the refined customs of the aristocracy.

- **Imperial Fête:** Refers to a grand celebration or festivity organized by or in honor of the Russian Emperor (Czar) and the imperial court.

Such events were often elaborate and lavish, featuring ceremonial banquets, music, dancing, and military displays, reflecting the wealth, power, and grandeur of the Russian Empire. These fêtes could be held on various occasions, such as official visits, victories, coronations, or national holidays, showcasing the splendor and dominance of the ruling monarchy.

- **Steppes:** Refers to vast, treeless plains that stretch across Siberia and Central Asia. These landscapes are characterized by their flat or gently rolling terrain, covered mainly with grasses and sparse vegetation, and are subject to extreme weather conditions, including harsh winters and scorching summers.

In the novel, the steppes of Siberia serve as a significant setting for Michael Strogoff's journey. These vast, open expanses emphasize the great distances he must travel, the dangers he faces from both natural elements and enemy forces, and the isolation of the Russian frontier. The steppes are both a physical and symbolic obstacle, representing the endurance and resilience required to complete his mission.

- **Iemschik:** (or Yamshik), refers to a Russian postilion or coachman who drives a horse-drawn vehicle, such as a tarantass, along the czarist empire's postal roads.

The Iemschiks were an essential part of the imperial postal and transport system, responsible for ferrying travelers, couriers, and government officials across vast distances, particularly in remote regions like Siberia. They often worked at relay stations, known as "yam" stations, where fresh horses could be quickly harnessed to allow for continuous travel. These drivers were known for their hardiness, familiarity with the rugged terrain, and ability to handle their horses skillfully.

- **Versts:** Killometers or versts, Refers to a Russian unit of distance measurement, approximately equal to 1.066 kilometers (0.662 versts).

The verst was commonly used in the Russian Empire to measure long distances, particularly in the vast and rugged expanses of Siberia, where Michael Strogoff's journey takes place. Given the immense scale of Russia, travel distances were often measured in versts rather than versts or kilometers.

- **Tarantass:** Is a traditional Russian carriage or traveling vehicle, designed for long-distance journeys across the vast and rugged terrain of Siberia.

Description:

The tarantass is a large, four-wheeled carriage, typically constructed with a suspension system made of leather straps or wooden springs, allowing it to absorb shocks on rough roads.

- **Cravat:** A neckcloth; a piece of muslin, silk, or other material worn about the neck, generally outside a linen collar, by men, and less frequently by women.

"cravat" refers to a piece of cloth worn around the neck, typically tied in a knot or bow, serving as a decorative and functional accessory.

- **Kibick or Telga:** The term "kibick" is likely borrowed from Russian кибитка (kibítka) and is an obsolete synonym for kibitka, a type of vehicle. "Telga" refers to a type of four-wheel horse-drawn vehicle used primarily for carrying loads in Russia and other countries. The telga is nothing but an open four-wheeled cart, made entirely of wood, the pieces fastened together by means of strong rope.

"kibick" (also spelled kibitka) and "telga" refer to types of Russian horse-drawn vehicles commonly used for travel across Siberia and the vast Russian Empire.

- **Overawe:** Means to intimidate, subdue, or control someone through fear, authority, or an imposing presence.

Explanation in Context:
The term "overawe" is often used to describe how powerful figures, military forces, or intense situations instill fear or submission in others.

- **Khanat:** Khanates were typically nomadic Turkic peoples, Tatar and Mongol societies located on the Eurasian Steppe.

"Khanat" refers to a territory or political entity ruled by a Khan, a sovereign leader of a Mongol, Tartar, or Central Asian tribal state.

- **Damascus Blade:** Refers to a sword or dagger made from Damascus steel, a highly prized metal known for its exceptional strength, sharpness, and distinctive wavy pattern.

Explanation in Context:
Damascus steel was historically renowned for its superior quality, capable of cutting through lesser weapons and maintaining a sharp edge.

- **Sesame par excellence:** Is a figurative phrase derived from the famous magical command "Open, Sesame!" from Ali Baba and the Forty Thieves in One Thousand and One Nights.

Definition in Context:
"Sesame" symbolizes a powerful key, something that grants access or opens doors effortlessly.

- **Podorojna Papers:** Refers to an official travel permit or passport issued by the Russian government, granting the bearer the right to travel freely and requisition transportation along their journey.

Definition in Context:
"Podorojna" (or Podorozhnaya Gramota in Russian) was an official document in Imperial Russia, primarily used for government couriers, military personnel, or officials traveling on state business.

- **Kwass:** A jug of kwass, the ordinary Russian beer.

"Kwass" (also spelled Kvass) refers to a traditional Russian fermented beverage made from black or rye bread, which is mildly alcoholic and widely consumed by people of all social classes in Russia.

- **Zingaris or Tsiganes:** Refers to Gypsies, or the Romani people, a nomadic ethnic group known for their distinct culture, traditions, and lifestyle.

Definition in Context:

The terms "Zingaris" (from Italian) and "Tsiganes" (from French and Russian) both refer to the Romani people, a traditionally itinerant group spread across Europe and Russia.

- **Copecks and Roubles:** Refers to the units of currency used in the Russian Empire during the 19th century.

Definition in Context:
Rouble (₽ or рубль): The primary unit of Russian currency.

- **Eccentric Curvette:** An eccentric curvette refers to an unusual or irregular version of a curvette, which is a light leap performed by a horse where both hind legs leave the ground just before the forelegs are set down. In the context provided, the horses in question galloped continuously but also executed many unconventional curvettes as they moved along.

"Eccentric Curvette" refers to a sudden, exaggerated movement made by a horse, particularly a spirited or well-trained one, while galloping or changing direction.

- **Na Pravo: To the right, Na Levo:** Are Russian directional commands used primarily to guide horses or riders.

Definition in Context:
"Na Pravo" (На Право) – Russian for "To the right" or "Turn right."

- **En Règle:** Is a French phrase that means "in order" or "according to the rules."

Definition in Context:

"En Règle" is used to indicate that something is legitimate, proper, or compliant with official regulations, laws, or procedures.

- **Moujik:** (also spelled "Muzhik") is a Russian term referring to a peasant or laborer in Imperial Russia.

Definition in Context:

A Moujik is a common Russian peasant, typically a serf or free farmer, belonging to the lower class of society.

- **Postilion:** Refers to a horse-mounted guide or driver who rides one of the lead horses to steer and direct a carriage, tarantass, or postal relay coach.

Definition in Context:

A Postilion is a rider who controls a team of horses pulling a carriage or relay post vehicle, often without reins, relying on voice commands, a whip, and their own riding skills.

- **Confrere:** Is a French term meaning "colleague" or "fellow member of the same profession."

Definition in Context:

In the novel, "confrère" is used primarily by the French journalist Alcide Jolivet to refer to his British counterpart, Harry Blount.

- **Na Vodkou:** Is a Russian phrase meaning "with vodka" or "to vodka."

Definition in Context:

It is typically associated with Russian drinking customs, where vodka is a central part of social gatherings, toasts, and celebrations.

- **Tsigane:** Refers to a member of the Romani people, also commonly known as Gypsies.

Definition in Context:
The term "Tsigane" (or "Tzigane") is derived from the Russian and French words for Roma people, who have historically been nomadic communities spread across Europe and Asia.

- **Pour-Boire:** Refers to a small gratuity or tip given as a token of appreciation for a service rendered.

Definition in Context:
"Pour-boire" is a French term that literally translates to "for drink", implying a sum of money given to someone, traditionally to buy a drink but more commonly as a tip.

- **Postmaster:** Refers to the official in charge of a postal station, responsible for managing horses, carriages, and relay services for travelers, particularly couriers and government officials.

Definition in Context:
In Imperial Russia, especially along the vast and rugged roads of Siberia, post stations were crucial for long-distance travel.

- **Discomfiture:** Refers to a state of frustration, defeat, embarrassment, or distress caused by an unexpected failure or setback.

Definition in Context:
The term is often used to describe the feeling of being thwarted in one's plans, whether in battle, strategy, or personal ambitions.

- **Incendiarism:** Refers to the deliberate act of setting fire to property, buildings, or other structures, often as a method of warfare or destruction.

Definition in Context:

In the novel, incendiarism is used as a strategic tool by the Tartars and their allies to cause chaos and destruction, particularly during their invasion of Siberia.

- **Saryn na kitchou!:** Is a Tartar battle cry that can be roughly translated to "Down on your knees!" or "On your faces!" in English.

Definition in Context:

This phrase is shouted by the Tartar invaders as a command to those they are attacking, demanding immediate submission.

- **Kreml:** The term "kreml," Often spelled as "Kremlin," refers to a major fortified central complex found in historic Russian cities.

"Kreml" refers to the Kremlin, which is a fortified central complex found in many Russian cities, most famously in Moscow.

- **Bivouacked:** A site where people on holiday can pitch a tent temporary living quarters specially built by the army for soldiers.

"bivouacked" refers to the act of setting up a temporary encampment in an open area, usually without tents or permanent shelter, often for the purpose of resting or preparing for further travel or battle.

- **Dipterals:** Refers to large swarms of insects, specifically two-winged flies or mosquitoes, which are commonly found in the Siberian wilderness.

Definition in Context:
The word "Dipterals" derives from the biological classification Diptera, which is the scientific order for insects with two wings, such as flies, gnats, and mosquitoes.

- **Deh-Baschi:** Is a Tartar military title referring to an officer or commander, likely in charge of a group of ten soldiers.

Definition in Context:
The term "Deh-Baschi" is derived from Turkic and Persian origins, where:

- **Pendja-Baschi:** Is a Tartar military title, referring to an officer in charge of a group of fifty soldiers.

Definition in Context:
The term "Pendja-Baschi" is derived from Turkic and Persian origins, where:

- **Beng:** Is a Tartar term meaning "prince" or "chieftain."

Definition in Context:
"Beng" is a title used to denote a high-ranking leader or noble among the Tartars.

- **Il est un petit homme, Tout habille de gris, Dans Paris!:** Is a French nursery rhyme that appears in the novel.

Definition in Context:

This lighthearted French song is sung by the French journalist Alcide Jolivet, one of the two European correspondents in the novel.

To Those Who Ride Into the Storm

A Poem for Michael Strogoff

Through winds that howl and rivers wide,
Where frozen specters stalk and hide,
Beyond the reach of hearth and home,
The lone courier dares to roam.

His steed is swift, his course unknown,
A shadow cast where few have flown.
The road is cruel, the night is deep,
Yet duty wakes where others sleep.

The sky is torn with icy breath,
The path ahead is laced with death,
Yet forward still, his fate is sworn,
For he who rides must face the storm.

No banners raised, no songs resound,
No gilded halls, no laurel crowned,
Yet kingdoms rise and wars are stayed
By those who ride and are not swayed.

So let the tempest rail and roar,
Let lightning lash the barren shore,
For empires stand, as they have sworn,
On those who ride into the storm.

www.ingramcontent.com/pod-product-compliance
Lightning Source LLC
LaVergne TN
LVHW030907080826
845145LV00010B/2791

* 9 7 8 1 9 6 7 4 0 5 2 3 7 *